Maggie bristled. "My sister didn't take her life."

Nate glanced down at his notes. "Let's go back to the beginning. What happened after you entered the house?"

She explained how she had searched the rooms and, finding nothing, had made her way to the attic. "The upstairs was pitch-black. I couldn't see anything and waved my hand in the air to find the pull cord for the overhead light bulb. The moon shone through the window and—" She struggled to find her words.

His voice softened. "That's when you saw your sister?"

She nodded. Tears pooled in her blue-green eyes and slowly trickled down her cheeks. Nate pulled his handkerchief from his pocket and shoved it into her hand, his fingers touching hers for longer than necessary.

Maggie seemed oblivious to the way his hand burned where it touched hers. What was happening to his ability to remain neutral? No one had ever affected him like the woman sitting close to him.

SOLDIER PROTECTOR

USA TODAY BESTSELLING AUTHOR

DEBBY GIUSTI

2 Thrilling Stories

The Officer's Secret and *The Soldier's Sister*

LOVE INSPIRED
INSPIRATIONAL ROMANCE

LOVE INSPIRED®

INSPIRATIONAL ROMANCE

ISBN-13: 978-1-335-43058-8

Soldier Protector

Copyright © 2022 by Harlequin Enterprises ULC

The Officer's Secret
First published in 2011. This edition published in 2022.
Copyright © 2011 by Deborah W. Giusti

The Soldier's Sister
First published in 2013. This edition published in 2022.
Copyright © 2013 by Deborah W. Giusti

Recycling programs
for this product may
not exist in your area.

Love Inspired
22 Adelaide St. West, 41st Floor
Toronto, Ontario M5H 4E3, Canada
www.LoveInspired.com

Printed in U.S.A.

CONTENTS

Debby Giusti is an award-winning Christian author who met and married her military husband at Fort Knox, Kentucky. Together they traveled the world, raised three wonderful children and have now settled in Atlanta, Georgia, where Debby spins tales of mystery and suspense that touch the heart and soul. Visit Debby online at debbygiusti.com, blog with her at seekerville.blogspot.com and craftieladiesofromance.blogspot.com, and email her at Debby@DebbyGiusti.com.

Books by Debby Giusti

Love Inspired Suspense

Her Forgotten Amish Past
Dangerous Amish Inheritance
Amish Christmas Search
Hidden Amish Secrets
Smugglers in Amish Country

Amish Witness Protection

Amish Safe House

Amish Protectors

Amish Refuge
Undercover Amish
Amish Rescue
Amish Christmas Secrets

Visit the Author Profile page at LoveInspired.com for more titles.

THE OFFICER'S SECRET

If you remain in my word, you will truly be my disciples,
and you will know the truth,
and the truth will set you free.
—*John* 8:31–32

Prologue

The night lay cold and dark outside the car just like the layer of regret that hung around Maggie Bennett's heart. She had left Fort Rickman as a young teen, vowing never to return. Too many painful memories were associated with the army post, memories Maggie had secreted away in the deepest recesses of her heart. Tonight, she prayed those memories would remain hidden forever.

Squinting through the rain-spattered windshield, she approached Fort Rickman's main gate and parked in front of the Visitor's Center. The clock on the dashboard read 2:15 a.m., a chilling reminder of the urgency of the middle-of-the-night plea that brought her here.

If not for her sister's phone call, Maggie would still be sound asleep at home in Alabama instead of seeking entry to the Georgia army post she had left sixteen years ago. Dani's attempt at reconciliation last week when the two sisters had met for lunch had been as unexpected after their years of separation as tonight's phone call. Maggie had been surprised that Dani would reach out to her so soon after opening up communication again, but she wasn't going to let her sister down. Not this time.

With a heavy sigh, she pulled her key from the ignition and stepped from her car, shivering, not so much from the cold February night air but in anticipation of what awaited her. Perhaps Dani's outreach would move them beyond the pain of their estrangement.

How had the years passed without either of them making an effort to reconnect? After more than a decade of silence, her sister's invitation to meet for lunch had been a welcome first step. Both of them had been guarded at the onset. Then slowly, recalling their childhood days, the sibling bond had semisurfaced and opened them to share at least a bit more deeply.

Maggie had known intuitively that Dani had changed, even before she had mentioned her time in Afghanistan. The deployment had provided an opportunity for her sister to reflect on the purpose of her life and, as she had told Maggie, she'd eventually realized her marriage to Graham had been a huge mistake. As soon as Dani had returned to the States, she had tried to explain to her husband the way she felt, but he hadn't wanted to listen. Evidently Dani had been more insistent tonight.

Over lunch, Dani had also alluded to a possible illegal operation she had uncovered during her deployment, something that could put her in danger if the wrong people found out. She hadn't divulged any of the details to Maggie, although she had voiced her own hesitation about telling Graham. He traveled to the Middle East with the civilian contracting job he had on post, and for a reason her sister never divulged, Dani felt she couldn't confide in him—nor could she confide in the military police on post, who Dani believed could in some way be connected to the Afghani operation. All of which made

Maggie wonder whether her sister thought Graham was involved, as well.

The old Dani never worried about the future, but Maggie had heard concern in her sister's voice a week ago and had seen the glint of fear in her eyes, no matter how hard Dani had tried to cover her anxiety with a nervous laugh.

Neither sibling had mentioned their father's death or leaving Fort Rickman years earlier, yet the topic had hovered like a dark cloud over their time together until, in parting, Dani had opened her arms and the two women had embraced, both with some hesitation and neither making the most of the moment. Yet the outreach on Dani's part had been significant enough to, if not knit the tear, at least bandage the wound she doubted would ever completely heal.

Pushing aside the guilt that had claimed her heart for too long, Maggie tugged her coat closed against the wind and hurried inside where the glare of fluorescent lights greeted her along with the brisk "Welcome to Fort Rickman" of the military policeman on duty.

With a perfunctory nod, she pulled her driver's license and registration form from her purse. After giving him the documents, she raked her free hand through her chestnut-colored hair, painfully aware of her disheveled appearance.

If only she had changed into something more presentable than faded jeans and a baggy orange sweater prior to starting out on her journey. As distraught as Dani had sounded over the phone, Maggie's focus had been on packing a suitcase and heading for the highway. She'd made the trip in a little over two hours.

"Ma'am, your reason for entering post?"

The MP's question brought to mind a number of answers. "I'm here to see my sister, Major Danielle Bennett. She lives at Quarters 1448 Hunter Road."

Referencing Maggie's license and registration form, he typed information into a computer database before he handed them back to her along with the visitor's pass. After a hasty word of thanks, Maggie scurried to her car, threw the pass onto the dashboard and climbed behind the wheel. A sense of déjà vu, mixed with sadness, slipped around her shoulders as she drove through the main gate and entered post.

Maggie passed the Post Exchange and Commissary and caught sight of the old movie theater in the distance. All too vividly, she remembered sitting by herself, while a few rows over, Dani watched the movie surrounded by friends—mainly boys taken with her raven hair and rounded curves. As a young teen, Maggie had been bashful, gawky and underdeveloped.

Uncomfortable dwelling on the reality of her childhood, she refocused her eyes on the road ahead. Speed limit thirty miles per hour, a road sign warned. Maggie checked her speedometer. Easing up on the accelerator, she made the first of a series of turns that eventually led to the old housing area where brick homes sat guarded by stately oaks. She entered the subdivision painfully aware of even more memories that bubbled up from her youth. Despite the years that had passed, the streets were still familiar. Maggie turned right at the first intersection and pulled to a stop in front of Quarters 1448 where her sister now lived.

For a long moment, she stared at the Federalist-style structure built in the early 1900s, knowing farther down the road and on the opposite side of the street sat another two-story house with the identical floor plan where Dani and Maggie and their parents had lived when the girls were teens. Their dad's assignment had been cut short by his death—a tragedy that haunted her still. Dani carried the guilt on her shoulders, while Maggie carried it in her heart.

Pulling in a calming breath and forcing her mind back to the problem at hand, she yanked the keys from the ignition, grabbed her purse and overnight bag and stepped onto the sidewalk. This wasn't the time to revisit the past.

Maggie needed to focus on her sister's problems. Dani's voice had been stretched thin over the phone when she'd called, and the nervous laughter Maggie had heard at lunch last week had been replaced with labored pulls of air brimming with tension. The fact that Dani had even called made Maggie realize how desperate her sister was for help.

Graham had moved out a week ago, but he kept coming back, insisting their marriage could be saved. Finally, Dani had told him point-blank she wanted a divorce. Never one to be pushed around, Graham had balked at first until he finally realized Dani wouldn't change her mind.

The Graham Hughes Maggie remembered usually got what he wanted. And from what Dani had said, it sounded as if Graham wanted his marriage intact, which was why Maggie had packed a suitcase and driven two hours to arrive at Fort Rickman in the middle of the night. Not that Maggie could provide protection, but she could offer her sister much-needed support.

Before closing the driver's door, she dug into her handbag for the house key Dani had insisted she take when they'd finished their lunch last week and were ready to part company again.

"Just in case," she'd said, giving no other information as she had shoved the key into Maggie's hand. Now glad of her sister's forethought, Maggie climbed the steps to the front porch and knocked repeatedly on the door. When no one answered, she slid the key into the lock and stepped inside, feeling an immediate sense of coming home.

Her gaze swept Dani's living room, taking in the two Queen Anne chairs, the couch and love seat and then the marble-topped coffee table decorated with memorabilia her sister had kept that honored their military dad. His medals and the flag that had draped his coffin were both displayed in glass cases, reminders of the man he once had been.

Leaving her suitcase and purse in the foyer, Maggie shrugged out of her coat and followed a lone light into the kitchen. Neat, uncluttered, every item in its place and, just as with the living room, so like their house of old. Their mother had been a meticulous housekeeper, and from the looks of Dani's quarters, she kept her own house as tidy as their mother had up until her own death years ago.

Circling through the dining area, Maggie stopped at the foot of the stairs. She glanced up and listened, hearing nothing except the wind buffeting the house.

"Dani?" On the phone her sister had mentioned being tired. Had she gone to bed?

Maggie flipped on the upper hall light and climbed the wooden stairway that wound to the second story. A small bathroom sat at the top of the landing, flanked by two bedrooms. Searching for her sister, she glanced into each room—one of which had been turned into an office—before she headed for the master suite and tapped on the door.

Stepping into the darkened interior, Maggie switched on the lamp, noting the neatly made bed and undisturbed accent pillows. The bath and dressing area beyond sat vacant, as well. Backtracking to the head of the stairs, she peered over the banister, debating her options, then refocused her gaze on the closed door at the end of the hallway.

Her pulse quickened, pounding against the tendons in her neck, filling her ears with the thump of her own heartbeat. Visions from the past returned to taunt her as they often did in the stillness of the night.

Her father's body shrouded in death.

Her mother's screams of disbelief.

Maggie shook her head ever so slightly, scattering the memories that clouded her consciousness.

"Let the dead bury the dead," came the words from scripture. Maggie had moved on with her life and didn't need reminders to draw her back in time.

What about Dani?

Over lunch and again on the phone tonight, she had sidestepped mention of their father's death. The realization that Dani could still be caught in the past unnerved Maggie. With purposeful steps, she walked to the end of the hallway. The stairs to the attic sat behind the closed door. Maggie grabbed the knob and tugged it open.

Light from the hall spilled across the bottom steps. Pulling in a fortifying breath, she climbed the stairs, one foot after the other. At the top, she peered into the darkness and swatted the air, hoping to make contact with a pull string for the overhead light just as she had done years ago in her childhood quarters.

A sound below punctuated the stillness. Footsteps or the creaks of an aged house? Perhaps Dani was home after all. Maggie turned to descend the stairs she had just climbed.

A moonbeam broke through the dormer window, cascading light into the corner of the attic where an overturned ladder-back chair lay on the floor.

The hair on the back of her neck rose in protest.

"No!" Maggie screamed as she raised her eyes and focused on her sister's body, hanging from the rafters.

Chapter One

Chief Warrant Officer Nathaniel Patterson, U.S. Army Criminal Investigation Division, got the call at 0315. *Possible suicide at Quarters 1448 Hunter Road.*

Arriving fifteen minutes later, he parked behind two MP sedans and stepped from his car, adjusting his weapon on his hip. Although Nate hadn't known Major Bennett, the death of an officer was significant, and tonight, the combined resources of the military police and the army's major crime unit, the CID, had been called in to investigate the case.

Headlights signaled an approaching vehicle. Nate waited as his friend and fellow agent, Jamison Steele, crawled from his late-model sports car. Dressed in a tweed sports coat and gray trousers, he looked like a fashionable young executive in contrast to Nate's run-of-the-mill navy blazer and khaki slacks.

With a hasty nod, Jamison fell into step beside Nate and followed him up the front steps in silence. Before either man could knock, Corporal Robert Mills opened the door. The young MP had the makings of a future CID special agent if he learned to keep his somewhat self-centered ego in check. Nate chalked it up to youth. Hopefully over time, his impetuous nature would mellow.

Raising his right hand to his forehead, Mills saluted the two warrant officers. "Evening, Mr. Patterson. Mr. Steele."

The agents returned the salute and stepped into the brightly lit foyer. Nate glanced into the living room where a woman sat huddled in a high-backed chair. Blue-green eyes looked up with the hollow stare of shock he'd seen too many times at crime scenes. The raw emotion written so clearly on her face brought home the tragic reality of what had happened tonight.

Their eyes met and held for an instant, causing an unexpected warmth to curl through Nate's gut. Then, tugging on a strand of her auburn hair, she dropped her gaze, breaking their momentary connection and leaving Nate with an emptiness he couldn't explain. Probably the middle-of-the-night phone call and his attempt to respond as quickly as possible that had thrown him slightly out of sync.

Or maybe it was the woman—a family member, perhaps.

Putting a human face on the tragedy—a very pretty face—intensified his desire to learn the truth about what had happened tonight. Nate was good at what he did. Tonight he wanted to be even better. The woman deserved as much. So did the victim waiting for him upstairs.

Bottom line, the army took care of its own in life and especially so in death. He motioned Corporal Mills into the kitchen as Jamison headed upstairs. Nate pulled out a small notebook and ballpoint pen from his breast pocket then, lowering his voice, he nodded toward the living room. "So who's the woman?"

"She's the sister of the deceased, sir. Name's Margaret Bennett, but she goes by Maggie. She found the major's body in the attic."

Nate knew how tough it was to lose a sibling. He thought of his own brother. Although eight years had separated them in age, they'd always been close.

He scribbled Maggie's name on a blank page of his notebook. "Apparent suicide?"

"Roger that, sir. Major Bennett hung herself from a rafter. Sergeant Thorndike's upstairs. He wanted me to check for prints."

A half-empty bottle of cabernet sat on the counter. Nate pointed to a wineglass, stained with residue. "Be sure to send off a toxicology sample on whatever's in the bottom of that glass."

"Yes, sir."

Opening the dishwasher, Nate used a latex glove he pulled from his pocket and lifted a second wineglass onto the counter. "Check the bottle and both glasses for prints. Let me know what you find."

"Will do, sir."

Nate nodded his thanks to Mills, returned the notebook to his pocket and grabbed a water glass from the cabinet, which he filled from the tap. Leaving the kitchen, he approached the woman in the living room.

"Excuse me, ma'am. I thought you might be thirsty."

Maggie Bennett glanced up with tear-filled eyes and a drawn face that expressed the heartbreak of a deeply personal loss. The two sisters must have been close. His heart went out to her, understanding all too well the pain she must be feeling.

"I'm Special Agent Nate Patterson, U.S. Army Criminal Investigation Division." With his free hand, he pulled out his CID identification, although he doubted Ms. Bennett would question his credentials. At the moment, she looked like a frightened stray caught in a trap. A beautiful stray, he decided, noting her high cheekbones, arched brows and full lips. But her strikingly good looks were overshadowed by a blanket of grief that lay like a black veil over her alabaster skin.

"I'm the lead investigator on this case, ma'am. Please accept my condolences as well as the heartfelt sympathy of the CID and the Military Police Corps here at Fort Rickman."

She bit her lip, then mumbled a broken, "Thank… thank you."

"I'll be upstairs for a few minutes. When I return I'd like to talk to you about your sister." He placed the water on the end table.

She gave a brief, pained smile of thanks at the offered glass and then looked back at him. "Yes, of course. Whatever you need to know."

Nate climbed the stairs to the second floor, feeling the weight of Maggie's grief resting on his shoulders. He'd give her a few minutes to gather strength before he saddled her with the endless questions that any death investigation required.

Reaching the second landing, Nate glanced into the home office on the right where Corporal Raynard Otis attempted to access the victim's laptop computer files. The soldier looked up, a full smile spreading across his honey-brown face. "Hey, sir. How's it going?"

"You tell me, Ray."

"Should have something for you shortly."

"That's what I like to hear."

Nate continued on to the open attic door. Rapid

flashes of light confirmed the military photographer was already on the job. Within the hour, photos would appear on Nate's computer, systematically capturing every detail of the attic scene.

On the opposite side of the hallway, Jamison questioned a military policewoman and jotted down pertinent information she shared, information the CID team would review over and over again until all the facts were in and a determination could be made about the actual cause of death. Foul play needed to be ruled out. Hopefully, the case would be open and shut.

Climbing the stairs to the attic, Nate eyed the rafter and the thick hemp rope wrapped around the sturdy crossbeam. Without forethought, he touched his breast pocket where he had tucked the notebook, containing Maggie's name, as if to shield her from the grim reality of her sister's death. Lowering his gaze, he took in the victim's black hair and swollen face.

God rest her soul. The prayer surfaced from his past. His mother's influence, no doubt. She had raised him to be a believer, although his faith had never been strong, and for the past eight months, he had tuned God out of his life completely.

Once again, his hand sought the notebook as his eyes refocused on the body.

Death by strangulation was never pretty, yet despite the victim's contorted features, he recognized the same classic beauty that the very much alive sister sitting downstairs possessed. The deceased, with her low-cut silk blouse and snug-fitting leggings, appeared to be the more flamboyant sibling in contrast to Maggie's modest jeans and sweater, but appearances could lie, and more than anything else, Nate needed the truth.

A chair lay at Major Bennett's feet. Classic suicide scenario. In all probability, the victim had stood on the chair to secure the rope around the crossbeam and the noose around her neck. Kicking over the chair would leave her hanging and preclude the major from saving herself, should she have second thoughts about taking her own life.

Staff Sergeant Larry Thorndike stepped forward. The military policeman was mid-fifties with a receding hairline and an extra twenty pounds of weight around his middle.

"The victim worked in Headquarters Company of the 2nd Transportation Battalion," Staff Sergeant Thorndike offered as Nate glanced his way. "The major redeployed home from Afghanistan fourteen days ago as part of the advance party."

"Same unit that had two casualties in Afghanistan this week?" Nate asked.

"That's right, sir. Captain York—the company commander—and his driver hit an improvised explosive device. Now this. It's hard on the unit. Hard on everyone."

Nate knew all too well the tragic consequences an IED could cause. Was that what had led to the major's suicide? Had she felt in any way responsible for the captain's death? "How long before the medical examiner gets here?"

"The ME should be here any minute."

"Did you talk to the sister?"

The sergeant nodded. "But only briefly. She's pretty shook up."

An understatement from what Nate had seen.

"Ms. Bennett had enough sense to call for help," Sergeant Thorndike continued. "When I arrived she was white as a sheet and hyperventilating. Said she lives in Independence, Alabama. Received a phone call at approximately 2330 hours from the deceased. The victim sounded anxious, according to the sister. Major Bennett had fought with her estranged husband, Graham Hughes, shortly before the phone call."

"The major used her maiden name?"

"Roger that, sir."

"Has the husband been notified?"

"Negative. We're trying to track him down. Evidently he moved out a few days after Major Bennett arrived stateside."

"Alert the post chaplain to a possible notification of next of kin. I'll want to talk to the husband. Let me know when you find out where he's staying."

"Will do, sir." The sergeant unclipped his cell phone from his belt and stepped to the corner of the attic to call the chaplain.

Nate neared the body. He examined the knots that formed the noose and then the victim's neck and hands, noting her intact skin. No signs of struggle. Blood had pooled in her extremities, consistent with death by hanging and the beginnings of rigor mortis. It all looked like a textbook suicide, and yet… Something about it bothered him, and it took a minute to put his finger on it.

The sergeant closed his cell. "Chaplain Grant will be here shortly, sir."

Nate pointed to the victim's bare feet. "Where are her shoes?"

"Main floor, sir. Under a table by the door."

"It's a cold night. Why would Major Bennett walk around her house without shoes?"

The sergeant shrugged. "You got me there, sir."

Footsteps sounded on the stairs. Nate turned as Major Brett Hansen, the pathologist and medical examiner on post stepped into the attic. "Good to see you, Nate."

"Sir."

The major nodded to the sergeant and photographer. "What do we have here, gentlemen?"

Nate filled him in on the somewhat limited information accumulated so far. Wasting no time, the doc slipped on latex gloves and began his visual exam of the victim's body. Once complete, Sergeant Thorndike would lower her to the floor so additional forensic evidence could be gathered.

Knowing the procedure would take time, Nate descended the stairs to the first floor where the bereaved sister sat, legs crossed and head resting in her hands.

Peering into the kitchen, he saw Mills bent over the wine bottle. "Find anything yet?"

The MP looked up. "The glass you pulled from the dishwasher had been wiped clean, sir. We might get lucky on the bottle."

"Good man."

Entering the living room, Nate glanced, once again, at the grief-stricken woman. She appeared fragile as a butterfly and, no doubt, was devastated by what she'd discovered tonight. As much as he hated to disturb her, Nate needed information.

Moving closer, he touched her shoulder. The knit of her sweater was soft to his fingertips. "Ms. Bennett? Maggie?"

She looked up, startled. The pain in her eyes cut through him like a well-aimed laser beam.

"If I could have a few minutes of your time, ma'am."

Fatigue lined her oval face, but her ashen coloring

concerned him more. She had found her sister's body and was surrounded by law enforcement personnel trying to make sense of a tragic death. No one had time to offer her more than a perfunctory word of compassion or support.

He glanced at the empty glass on the end table. "Would you like more water?"

She shook her head and rubbed her hands over her arms. "Thank you, no."

"If you're cold, I could raise the thermostat?"

"I...I'm just tired."

"Of course." He pulled up a chair. "Could you tell me what happened tonight?"

When she didn't answer, he scooted closer. "I know it's difficult."

She nodded. "Dani called me. She was upset...almost hysterical. She had told her husband she wanted a divorce."

Nate removed the notebook and pen from his pocket. He needed to put aside the fact that this woman ignited a spark of interest deep within him and focus instead on the questions he had to ask and she, hopefully, would be able to answer.

"Graham..." Maggie hesitated. "My sister's husband wanted them to reconcile."

"Go on." Painfully aware of the heat that continued to warm his gut, Nate swallowed hard and concentrated on the information Maggie began to recount.

"They...they had argued. Graham was upset. But then so was my sister. Dani told him to leave. Obviously, he... he came back later and—"

When she failed to complete the statement, Nate asked, "When did your sister and Mr. Hughes marry?"

"Dani ran into him shortly after she transferred here to Rickman. That was two years ago. They dated a few months. She sent me a wedding announcement after they were married."

"You attended the ceremony?"

"I wasn't invited."

Could Maggie's dislike of her brother-in-law stem from being excluded from their wedding? Nate drew a question mark on his tablet before asking, "Did you know Graham?"

"Yes."

"Had infidelity been an issue?"

She wiped her hand over her cheek and sniffed. "Not that Dani mentioned. But when we met for lunch last week, she told me that their marriage was over."

Nate nodded as he continued writing. "When you entered the house, did anything indicate Graham *had* been here?"

"A bottle of wine on the kitchen counter. Dani never drank red wine."

"What about her husband?"

"I...I don't know. When I was upstairs, I heard footsteps on the first floor." Maggie bit her lip and shook her head ever so slightly, her eyes widening with realization. "Graham must have been in the house the whole time I was searching for my sister."

"Did you *see* Graham Hughes?"

"No, but it had to be him."

Had to was supposition. Maggie seemed eager to place blame on her brother-in-law's shoulders. Too eager? No matter how unlikely, if Major Bennett's death were ruled a homicide, the beautiful woman sitting next to Nate could end up being a person of interest, as well.

"Was the front door locked when you arrived?"

Maggie nodded. "I knocked. Dani had mentioned being tired. I thought she might be sleeping. When she didn't answer the door, I used the key she had given me when we met for lunch."

"Did your sister say why she wanted you to have a key to her house when you lived so far apart?"

"No, and I didn't ask for an explanation. Dani and I had been estranged for a few years. I was relieved that we were trying to patch up our differences."

"What type of differences?"

She lowered her gaze and uncrossed her legs. Nate watched her body language. Her refusal to make eye contact was telling.

Finally she shrugged and tried to smile. "Two women going their separate ways. Dani went into the military. I pursued a career in family counseling."

Nate was sure there had been more to the *differences* than Maggie was willing to admit. "Did Major Bennett invite you to visit this weekend?"

With a quick shake of her head, she said, "Dani was independent. She had a hard time accepting help."

"Yet—" Nate glanced at the small suitcase in the foyer "—you packed a bag and drove here to be with her."

"I told Dani she shouldn't be alone, that I was worried Graham might come back."

"And Major Bennett shared your concern about her husband?"

"She was more upset about something that had happened in Afghanistan. But she didn't go into the problem. Only that it was serious."

Nate raised his brow. "Serious enough to cause her to take her own life?"

Maggie bristled. "My sister didn't take her life."

Nate wouldn't state the obvious, which was that, at this early stage in the investigation, nothing indicated foul play.

"How long ago did you and your sister reconnect?"

"Dani called last week and asked if we could meet for lunch, which we did, in Alabama."

"Not here on post?"

"That's right. We met just over the state line in a little town called Hope. There's a ladies' tearoom on the square."

Nate would have someone check out the tearoom. Not that he thought Maggie was lying, but he wanted to ensure the information was accurate before he passed it up the chain of command.

"How did your sister seem? Happy? Sad?"

"She was concerned about her marriage, but she wasn't depressed, if that's what you're asking."

"What did you talk about?"

Maggie shrugged. "Her deployment. Being back in the States."

"Her marriage?"

"Yes, of course. She said marrying Graham had been a mistake."

"Did she give a reason?"

Maggie shook her head.

"What about growing up? Did you reminisce about the good times?"

"Sure. We were always close as kids."

"But that changed?" he asked.

"We…we grew apart, as I mentioned."

"Looking back to your childhood, what thoughts come to mind?"

A hint of a smile tugged at Maggie's lips. "Running barefoot in the backyard."

"Sounds as if you and your sister didn't like shoes."

"Only when we were little. Dani had a closet full when we were teens."

"But she went barefoot in the house?"

Maggie wrinkled her brow. "Not that I recall."

Nate glanced down at his notes. "Let's go back to the beginning. What happened after you entered the house?"

She explained how she had searched the rooms and, finding nothing, had made her way to the attic. "The upstairs was pitch-black. I couldn't see anything and waved my hand in the air to find the pull cord for the overhead lightbulb."

"If you hadn't been here before, how did you know about the pull cord?"

Angling her head, she paused, as if weighing her words. "My dad was military," she said at last. "We lived in similar quarters sixteen years ago."

"At Fort Rickman?"

"That's right. In this same housing area."

"A three-year assignment for your dad?"

"Yes, but—"

Maggie clasped her hands then worried her fingers. "My father…" Deep breath. "His tour of duty was cut short." She looked down as if gathering courage to go on. "Regrettably, my father committed suicide."

Not what he had expected to hear. Nate fought to keep his expression neutral as she glanced up at him with troubled eyes.

"He hanged himself in the attic of our house." She

leaned closer to Nate. "The similarity in the two deaths proves Dani would never have taken her own life."

"Because—?"

Her eyes widened as if the conclusion she had drawn was obvious. "Because Dani did everything to overcome the stigma of his death. That's why she went into the military. She idolized him. Dani tried to be the son he always wanted. Problem was she tried to prove herself to him, even after his death." She leaned closer. "Don't you see, for Dani, suicide wouldn't have been an option?"

Unless Major Bennett wanted to prove how much she loved her father by following him into death. Nate kept that thought to himself.

"You brought up depression earlier. Is there a history of depression or anxiety disorders in your family?"

"None that I know of."

"Tell me about when you were in the attic. You said the light was off?"

"That's correct. The moon shone through the window and—" She struggled to find her words.

His voice softened. "That's when you saw your sister?"

She nodded. Tears pooled in her blue-green eyes and slowly trickled down her cheeks. Nate tried to remain detached despite his desire to wipe away her pain. He pulled his handkerchief from his pocket and shoved it into her hand, his fingers touching hers for longer than necessary, as if attempting to pass on support.

Maggie seemed oblivious to the way his hand burned where it touched hers. What was happening to his ability to remain neutral? He had been around other attractive women…had dated a few along the way…but no one had ever affected him like the woman sitting close to him.

Nate turned to look over his shoulder as Jamison scurried down the stairs and motioned him into the foyer, providing the reprieve Nate needed. Time to regroup and focus on the internal warning signal that was telling him something unexpected and downright powerful was happening to his status quo.

"Excuse me for a minute." He rose from the chair and met the agent in the kitchen.

"You okay?" Jamison stared at him with narrowed eyes.

Nate straightened his shoulders. "Yeah, why?"

"You look troubled."

"An officer died tonight. That is troubling."

"Of course, it is. The ME is getting ready to release the body. They'll bring Major Bennett downstairs soon. Might not be good for her sister to watch."

Jamison was right. Maggie shouldn't be around when the body was removed.

"What did the doc say?" Nate asked.

"Only that he'll order a toxicology screen. Drugs and alcohol. As backed up as the lab is at Fort Gillem, I don't know when we'll get the results back, though."

"See what you can find out about Major Bennett's father," Nate said. "He was stationed at Rickman sixteen years ago and evidently committed suicide."

Jamison let out a low whistle. "Quite a coincidence."

Before Nate could respond, the front door opened and CID agent Kelly McQueen scurried inside and joined the men in the kitchen. She was blond-haired and blue-eyed and the best marksman in the unit.

"What do you need me to do?" she asked after Nate filled her in on what they had learned so far.

"Help me decide where Major Bennett's sister can

stay tonight," Nate said. "The downtown area has had problems with all the rain. The basement of the Freemont Hotel is flooded, and they've shut down tem-porarily."

A number of small motels were located immediately off post, but most of them were fleabag rentals that catered to a transient troop population. At this difficult time, Maggie deserved something more accommodating.

"I've got an extra room," Kelly volunteered. "She's welcome to stay at my place."

Nate nodded. "That works."

Kelly was good at her job and had compassion to embrace someone reeling with grief. Her apartment was directly across from Nate's in the bachelor officer quarters on post so he would be able to keep an eye on Maggie and offer his support.

"I'll have Mills follow us to the BOQ," said Nate. "He can bring me back here once I get Maggie settled."

The corporal responded with a thumbs-up. "Can do, sir. By the way, Ms. Bennett's driving a silver Saturn. I checked the car and her personal effects. She's clean."

"You need authorization."

Mill's face darkened.

"We'll talk about it tomorrow."

"Yes, sir."

"What about the wine bottle? Did you find prints?"

"Negative."

Nate turned back to Jamison. "Pull the major's medical records and see if there's any history of psychological problems. Also, check with the main gate and find out what time the sister, and any other guests the major may have had this evening, entered post. Question the neighbors in case the major and her husband aired their dirty laundry and find out if any strange cars or visitors stopped by this evening."

"Will do," Jamison said.

"Lieutenant Colonel Foglio lives across the street," Kelly volunteered. "That teenage son of his is staying with his dad again."

"The one with the tattoos?" Jamison asked. "What's his name? Carl, Kurt…?"

"It's Kyle," Kelly said. "After the trouble he got into last summer, I didn't think Lieutenant Colonel Foglio's current wife would allow the kid back in her house."

"Be sure to ask Foglio where his son has been this evening," Nate said to Jamison.

"You got it."

"Have we located Graham Hughes yet?" Nate asked.

Jamison pulled a notebook from his pocket. "I called his boss. Graham's a civilian contractor who works for AmeriWorks. After splitting with his wife, he moved in temporarily with a guy who has the desk next to him in the contracting office. The guy's name is—" Jamison referred to his notes "Arnold Zart. Travels between Fort Rickman and various forward operating bases in Afghanistan. He's got an apartment off post."

Nate nodded. "Once we get the sister settled in at Kelly's place, the chaplain and I will pay Mr. Zart a visit."

Jamison removed a sheet of paper from his notepad and offered the handwritten note to Nate. "Here's Zart's address."

"Thanks." Nate stepped back into the living room and motioned Kelly forward. "Maggie, this is Special Agent Kelly McQueen." Kelly offered a few words of compassion along with a warm smile.

"Agent McQueen has a spare room at her place," Nate

continued. "You'll be able to get some rest there tonight, and we can talk more in the morning."

"But I…" Maggie looked around seemingly momentarily confused.

"I'm going home shortly," Kelly said. "You and Nate can take your time and come over when you're ready."

With a final smile, Kelly headed into the foyer just as the front door opened once again. Chaplain Grant, a tall lieutenant colonel with a sincere face, stepped inside.

Nate excused himself from Maggie and approached the chaplain. "Thanks for being here, sir."

"Terrible shame."

"Yes, sir." Nate lowered his voice. "Major Bennett and her husband had separated about a week ago. He's currently staying with a guy who works with him in the AmeriWorks contracting office on post."

"Over the phone, Sergeant Thorndike mentioned a sister from Alabama."

Nate nodded. "She's had a rough night. The sister's the one who found the major's body." Nate ushered the chaplain toward the living room, introduced him to Maggie and then stepped back, giving the two of them a bit of privacy while the lieutenant colonel offered words of comfort, which Maggie seemed to appreciate.

"Have you talked to your brother-in-law?" the chaplain eventually asked her. When she shook her head, Chaplain Grant turned serious eyes toward Nate. "Might be beneficial to have Maggie with us when we notify Mr. Hughes."

"Ah, sir—?" Before Nate could register an objection to the idea, the chaplain had refocused his gaze on Maggie.

"I'm sure you and Mr. Hughes have things you'd like

to discuss, concerning your sister's internment, if you feel up to seeing him at this late hour."

Maggie nodded. "You're right, Chaplain. I...I need to talk to Graham."

Nate wasn't sure whether her current interest in her brother-in-law had to do with discussing the major's burial or establishing his guilt. Either way, the chaplain had made the offer, and Nate wouldn't withdraw it now. Besides, seeing the dynamic play out between the victim's sister and husband might reveal more information than Maggie had been willing to share.

Touching her elbow, Nate encouraged Maggie to stand. Corporal Mills approached, carrying her coat and handbag, which Nate took from him.

Nate handed Maggie her purse and helped her with her coat. "If you give me the keys, I'll have Mills drive your car to the BOQ and leave it there, while you and the chaplain and I talk to Mr. Hughes."

"What about Dani?" she asked as she placed the keys in Nate's outstretched hand.

"She'll be taken to the morgue. An autopsy will be performed sometime later today. Once you and Mr. Hughes determine how your sister should be buried, her body will be released to the funeral home. If you'd like, I can help you with the arrangements."

Nate was relieved to see her face soften. She attempted to smile. "Thank you."

Warmed by her response, he asked, "Is there anyone you'd like to call? A family member? Your mom? Maybe a boyfriend?"

Her eyes clouded as she shook her head. "My mother died a number of years ago. There's no one else."

Her loneliness in the midst of her grief cut him deeply.

Upstairs the sound of footsteps indicated the body was being prepared for transport. It was time to get Maggie out of the house.

"My car's outside." Nate put his hand on the small of Maggie's back and urged her toward the door Corporal Mills held open. The chaplain grabbed her suitcase and followed them into the damp night air. Maggie wrapped her arms around her waist and accepted Nate's steadying hand on her elbow as she walked down the steps and settled into the front seat of his car, while the chaplain slid into the rear.

A light went on in the front bedroom of Lieutenant Colonel Foglio's quarters across the street. The curtain moved ever so slightly.

Looking back at Quarters 1448, Nate's eyes focused on the attic dormer window. The copycat suicide was unusual, and often little things made a difference in an investigation. The fact that Major Bennett had been barefoot when she died bothered him. But something else troubled Nate more.

The victim would have needed light to loop the rope over the crossbeam. Why would Major Bennett then turn off the light and take her own life in the dark?

Chapter Two

Sitting next to Nate in the passenger seat, Maggie watched the headlights cut through the darkness, knowing she had kept information from the CID agent. She needed time to put some semblance of order to the confusion of her life before she made the decision to tell him.

Dani had implied some military law enforcement personnel couldn't be trusted. Maggie wasn't sure if that included the CID. Graham worked in the AmeriWorks contracting office and her sister hadn't mentioned the problem to him. Could the contractors be involved, as well?

It was hard to believe her sister was dead. Right when they were beginning to reconnect.

Oh, God, why? Maggie had been working on improving her relationship with the Lord. Hopefully He would provide the strength she needed.

Her parents, now Dani—

"Graham's staying at an apartment complex not far from post."

Nate's comment pulled her from a path to the past

where memories cut like shards of glass. Tonight another tragedy left her riddled with grief and filled with questions.

From the backseat, the chaplain once again offered words of sympathy that Maggie appreciated but wasn't able to fully comprehend. The fact that Dani was dead seemed surreal. Maggie still refused to believe it could have been suicide.

Her sister had worked too hard to get where she was in the military to take her own life. Plus, if she had wanted to end it all, she wouldn't have chosen a noose.

The chaplain finished his discourse and settled back in his seat, giving Maggie an opportunity to glance at the agent sitting behind the wheel. Despite the civilian coat and tie he wore, Nate had military written all over him with his short haircut and intense gaze. He was probably a workaholic, who put the job first. Her father had fit that bill. Although so did she, if truth be told.

Just as Dani had turned to the military for fulfillment, Maggie had allowed counseling to take over her own life. They'd both learned from their dad, no doubt.

Riding across post in silence, Maggie concentrated on seeing Graham again. The last time they were together, Maggie had been in high school. Back then, he'd been the bad boy all the girls ran after. But people changed and maybe Graham had, as well.

Would she even recognize him after all these years? No matter what, she needed to be in control of her emotions and display strength instead of weakness. Dani deserved as much.

Nate drove through the main gate and turned onto a stretch of road lined with seedy bars, pawnshops and fast-food restaurants, all low-rent businesses that preyed on young soldiers far from home. Alabama had its fair share of ticky-tacky, but nothing compared with those hawking wares to the nation's youthful warriors.

"Shouldn't be much farther." Nate checked the address written on a sheet of paper. Eventually, he pulled into an apartment complex and braked to a stop in front of a row of two-story town houses.

"Wait in the car, Maggie. Once we've established Graham is in the house, I'll come back and get you."

Trying to appeal to his common sense, she opened the passenger door. "That will delay you. There's no reason why I can't go with you now."

"She's right." The chaplain stepped from the car and glanced at Nate.

"Whatever you say, sir."

Maggie heard a hint of frustration in Nate's reply. No telling how Graham would react to this dead-of-the-night encounter. The CID agent probably wondered if having her underfoot would complicate an already difficult situation. The look on his face sent a clear message he would rather leave her in the car.

Nate hadn't known her long enough to realize she could handle adversity. She'd had enough in her lifetime, although tonight wasn't the norm. She was acting on instinct rather than reason.

Falling into step between the two officers, Maggie was struck with the irony of the moment and the army's attention to detail. The powers that be had provided a chaplain to comfort the grieving husband and a CID agent to decide whether to haul him in for questioning. If Maggie had anything to say about what would unfold, she'd demand Graham be interrogated for hours until he divulged the truth about her sister's death.

Nate flicked his gaze around the apartment complex, making her realize that, if her brother-in-law was a killer, the three of them could be in danger. The hair on the back of her neck tingled as she took in the deep shadows and hidden recesses where someone—anyone— could be hiding.

Nate stepped protectively in front of her and knocked on the door. The three of them waited in silence.

"Yeah?" A deep voice sounded through the closed door.

"I'm Special Agent Patterson, of the U.S. Army CID, and I'm here with Chaplain Grant. We're looking for Graham Hughes."

The door opened, and a tall, beefy guy, wearing a T-shirt and flannel pajama bottoms, stood in the threshold. A scruffy beard and disheveled hair completed his attire.

Resting his hand on the doorjamb, he stared at them with confused eyes. "Something wrong?"

Nate pulled out his identification and held it open. "We need to speak to Graham Hughes."

"He's not here."

Glancing around Nate and into the apartment, Maggie saw a leather couch and a coffee table covered with newspapers and a pizza delivery box.

"Are you Arnold Zart?" Nate asked.

"Yeah." The guy stifled a yawn. "Who's the woman?"

"I'm Maggie Bennett," she said, in a voice that sounded more self-assured than she currently felt. "I'm Graham's sister-in-law."

"Any suggestions where we can find him?" Nate asked, deflecting the guy's attention away from Maggie.

"No clue."

"When was the last time you saw Mr. Hughes?" Nate continued.

"We work together. I saw him at the office yesterday, that would be Friday, and only briefly after work."

"Has he been living here with you?"

"Graham and his wife are having problems. I've got a spare bedroom and told him that he could bunk here until they patched things up."

"Did he mention reconciling with his wife?"

Zart dropped his arm. "Look, I'm not comfortable talking about Graham's personal life behind his back."

Nate squared his shoulders and leaned in closer. "I could take you to the CID office if you'd feel more comfortable there."

The guy held up his hands. "Give me a break, okay?" He hesitated and then sighed. "Graham said he was going over to the Freemont Bar and Grill on Johnson Street about nine o'clock last night. A woman works there. She's been interested in him for some time. Graham needed to talk."

"A woman?" Maggie blurted out unable to remain silent. "What's her name?"

The contractor shrugged. "Graham never said."

Nate gave him his card. "If Mr. Hughes comes back, have him call me."

"Will do." The guy shut the door, leaving them standing on the front steps.

"But—?" Maggie wanted more information.

Nate took her arm and turned her toward the street. "We'll talk in the car."

She pulled her arm from his hold and huffed as she hurriedly walked along the sidewalk. "You could have searched the house."

"We don't have the authority—not at this point. But we'll track down the woman who works at the bar and grill. She might be able to lead us to Graham."

Maggie wrapped her arms around her waist, feeling tired as well as angry. "He's probably out of the country by now."

"More likely, he's with his new girlfriend."

"Well, that makes me feel better. He kills Dani and then finds another woman." She glared at Nate.

"His indiscretion may be reprehensible, but it doesn't prove he killed your sister."

"What does it prove?"

"That he's not the type of guy I'd want my sister to marry."

The sudden softness in his tone made her drop her defenses. Tears flooded her eyes. She missed her step and stumbled on the rough sidewalk.

Nate steadied her with his hand on her elbow. "It's late, Maggie. You need some sleep."

A lump settled in her throat and prevented her from speaking. Maybe the CID agent understood a bit more than she had realized. If only she could make him understand that her sister hadn't taken her own life. Maggie would do anything to convince him of the truth.

Once Maggie and the chaplain climbed into the car and buckled their seat belts, Nate pulled out of the apartment complex and onto the main road, leading back to Fort Rickman. He dug his cell phone out of his pocket, called Jamison and relayed what had happened.

"Have someone locate the owner of the bar and grill. See if he knows Graham Hughes or the woman who has taken an interest in him. We might get lucky. Otherwise, we'll have to wait until he eventually returns to Zart's apartment. I'll see you when I get back to post."

Nate disconnected and flicked a glance over his shoulder to the chaplain. "Sorry to take up your time, sir."

"You think the husband was involved in Major Bennett's death?"

"He killed her," Maggie said with conviction. "Dani fought with him earlier and kicked him out. Easy enough for Graham to return later."

"We need evidence, Maggie, to prove a crime has been committed at all," Nate explained.

"Check his alibi with the woman he's supposed to be seeing. Threaten to involve her if she doesn't tell the truth." Nate almost smiled at Maggie's attempt to tell him how to handle the investigation.

"Search his car and the apartment where he's staying," she added. "You'll uncover something."

"And if we don't find any evidence that points to his guilt?"

"Then—"

The amateur sleuth seemed to have run out of options.

"Then throw him in jail until he talks," she finally said.

"You know we can't do that. But we will find him and determine where he was tonight."

"Focus on determining why he killed my sister." With another huff, Maggie turned toward the passenger window and stared into the night.

Nate glanced at the rearview mirror, catching the chaplain's eye. "At this point, sir, we don't know much. Hopefully the autopsy and toxicology results will shed more light on the situation."

"The 2nd Transportation Battalion has had a rough few days," the chaplain commented. "I'm sure you heard about the IED explosion that took two men in Afghanistan."

"Yes, sir. Were you involved in the notification?"

"The driver was unmarried. His parents live in New Jersey. An officer from Fort Dix visited them. But the company commander lived on post and left a wife and kids."

Nate heard struggle in Chaplain Grant's voice. Most days, Nate didn't think about God or the difficulty a man of faith might have in comforting the grieving. As a CID agent, his job was to ensure the family was notified, if a crime had been committed. He left the spiritual consolation to the chaplains. Still, he found himself searching for a way to reach out to Maggie, to ease the pain and frustration she was feeling and bring her comfort.

Nate glanced at Maggie again. If the tables were turned, he'd be lashing out, as well. Fact was, when his brother died, Nate had been filled with pain and anger. Some of which he still hadn't resolved.

"Might seem strange," the chaplain said from the rear, his voice melancholy. "But the commander's wife ended up comforting me. The woman has great faith in the Almighty. She's grieving, but she knows God didn't cause the IED explosion that took her husband's life."

Once upon a time, Nate had believed God protected the faithful. Now, the memory of what had happened to Michael was never far from his mind. Truth be told, he blamed God as well as himself.

Glancing at Maggie, Nate said, "Seems impossible to trust a so-called loving God when your world falls apart."

She nodded slowly but kept her eyes trained on the passing darkness. Raindrops splattered against the windshield, adding to the oppressive gloom that had settled over all of them.

The chaplain sighed. "I don't have the answer, but I know we can't turn our backs on the Creator. He made us because He loves us, and His love is unconditional. I keep coming back to that. God knows all. How can I, as a finite creature, hope to understand why things happen? Maybe someday I'll see more clearly. Right now, I'm looking with human eyes that don't see the entire picture. I have to trust in Him. That's not always easy."

Trust in God wasn't high on Nate's priority list. Would he ever be able to soften his heart and turn to the Lord again?

What about Maggie? Would her sister's death have a long-term impact on her life, too? Maybe they'd talk about it sometime if he got to know her better.

Warmth spread through him again and his neck tingled. As much as Nate hated to admit it, even to himself, the woman's pain affected him deeply. Usually, he could trust his feelings. Tonight he wasn't sure of anything, especially when it involved Maggie Bennett.

She was alone and grieving. Nate thought of the other cases he had investigated. One death often led to another.

If he were a praying man, he'd ask that no one else—especially Maggie—would be hurt in any way by what had happened tonight.

Chapter Three

❧

Maggie scheduled an appointment to plan her sister's funeral with the chaplain for the following day before Nate dropped him off at his car. Once back on the main road, the CID agent turned warm eyes her way.

"Cold?" The light from the dash played over his lips that parted into an encouraging smile.

She shook her head. "I'm okay."

"The weatherman has predicted rain for another week. Hard to believe after the years of drought we've had in the Southeast. Now the rivers are threatening to overflow their banks, streams are swollen and…"

He was making small talk, probably to keep her mind off the tragedy. She looked back at the road, unable to think of anything *except* what had happened.

"I'm sorry about your sister," he finally offered.

"She didn't take her own life." Maggie might be driving home a point he didn't want to hear, but she had to convince this man with the genuine smile that suicide wasn't an option.

"Let me assure you, every effort will be made to learn the truth."

She sighed at the pat answer that didn't satisfy her. "It's ironic that my sister survived a war zone only to be killed once she got home."

Glancing out the passenger window, Maggie stared into the darkness before asking, "Were you ever stationed in Afghanistan?"

"Twice."

"And you made it back okay?" She turned to face him.

His eyes narrowed, and he gazed at the road ahead as if seeing something more than pavement. A muscle in his neck twitched. "Yeah, but my brother didn't."

"I'm…I'm sorry." She picked at the sleeve of her sweater. "So then you understand?"

"What you're going through?" He nodded. "A death in the family is always hard, but especially so when it's unexpected."

He pulled in a lungful of air and glanced at her. "The shock makes everything hurt even more."

She saw his own struggle reflected back at her from crystal-blue eyes visible in the half light from the dash. The counselor in her wanted him to go deeper, but the set of his jaw told her that, as far as Nate was concerned, the subject was closed.

He pointed to a cluster of apartments that appeared in the distance. "Kelly lives in the first set of BOQs."

Maggie unbuckled her seat belt and grabbed her purse once he parked the car. Nate carried her suitcase and escorted her to the second apartment on the right where Kelly opened the door and motioned her inside.

"I know it's been a hard night," the female agent said to Maggie in greeting as she took the bag from Nate's hand.

Hot tears burned her eyes. Suddenly, she wanted to get away from Nate Patterson and his sympathetic friend. To his credit, he didn't come in, but said goodbye at the door.

Kelly led the way to the guest room where a pink gingham comforter, trimmed with eyelet, covered a twin bed with a white wicker headboard. A matching nightstand and rocker sat nearby. Kelly placed Maggie's suitcase on a blanket chest at the foot of the bed.

"You'll find towels in the bathroom just across the hall. May I get you a cup of tea? Maybe something to eat?"

"I just need some sleep."

"Of course you do. If you get up before I do, the coffeepot will be ready to turn on. There's cream in the fridge. Sugar's on the counter. Help yourself to cereal or eggs, whatever you want for breakfast."

"Thank you, Kelly."

"Not a problem. See you in the morning."

Once the other woman left the bedroom and closed the door behind her, Maggie collapsed onto the bed and put her head in her hands. Tears streamed down her cheeks.

She tried to bring stability and peace to the families she counseled, but right now, she needed help herself. The harsh reality was she felt totally alone.

Maggie woke with a start, hearing the phone ring in the living room of Kelly's quarters. Visions of Dani had circled through her dreams for the few hours she'd been asleep and now returned to haunt her when her eyes were wide open.

Still wearing her jeans and orange sweater, Maggie

pulled herself from the bed and glanced at the items she had packed in her suitcase. Something seemed out of place, giving her an uneasy feeling. She shrugged it off, realizing that it was probably because she had been in such a hurry last night.

She grabbed a fresh outfit and stepped into the bathroom across the hall to change, surprised by the woman staring back at her from the mirror. She hadn't expected to see dark circles under her eyes.

Death takes a heavy toll on those left behind. Her mother's words flowed from the past.

Returning to the hallway, Maggie followed the smell of coffee to the kitchen where Kelly stood at the counter, holding half of a bagel slathered with cream cheese and jelly. "Morning. Did the phone wake you?"

"No, I was up." Not quite the truth, but Maggie didn't want to discuss her restless night.

Kelly pointed to a clean mug, sitting next to the coffeepot. "Help yourself."

"Thanks." Maggie poured a cup and drank it black.

"The phone call was from Chief Agent-in-Charge Wilson. He's the head of our CID unit at Rickman. There's a problem involving a soldier in North Georgia that I have to check into, which might take a couple of days. The guy was part of the 2nd Transportation Battalion."

"My sister's unit."

Kelly nodded. "This guy came home early because he needed surgery and had been on convalescent leave ever since."

She didn't provide any additional information. Probably more bad news. "I'll get my things if you can suggest a motel in town," Maggie said.

"Nonsense. No reason you can't stay here while I'm gone. Nate lives in an apartment across the open stairwell if you need anything."

Maggie thought of the warmth of his gaze in the car last night. "Are you sure you don't mind?"

"I insist. Speaking of Nate, he's been working all night, but he's headed over here now. He wants to talk to you."

Hopefully, he had located Graham.

"Help yourself to anything in the refrigerator." Opening a cabinet drawer, Kelly pulled out a small phone directory. "We've got delivery pizza and Chinese carryout on post. The numbers are highlighted in the book. Better yet, have Nate grill a couple steaks. Tell him Kelly said to make his special garlic mashed potatoes and Caesar salad."

"I'm sure I won't go hungry." Maggie was surprised to learn Nate cooked. Her father had never lifted his hand in the kitchen. For some reason, she'd thought all military guys would be the same.

A car door slammed outside. "Bet that's him now." Kelly crammed the last bite of bagel into her mouth. Chewing, she washed her hands and looked out the window before she headed for the door.

"How about some breakfast?" Kelly motioned Nate inside.

"Thanks, but I'll take a rain check."

Maggie raked her fingers though her hair and fluffed the bangs off her forehead. Not that she cared about the way she looked, but last night Nate had been—

"Morning, Maggie." He stepped into the kitchen, bringing a hint of the wet outdoors with him. Despite his all-night work marathon, he was clean-shaven and alert. Even his white shirt had maintained its starch.

"Coffee?" Kelly opened a cabinet and reached for a mug.

"I don't have time." He pulled a black-and-white photo printout from a folder and dropped it onto the table. "Maggie, one of our men pulled this off your sister's laptop. Does it mean anything to you?"

She stared at the picture of a potbellied earthenware figurine.

"The original is housed in the Kabul Museum," Nate continued. "Probably from the third or fourth century when the silk routes wove through what is Afghanistan today." He glanced down at the photo, then back at her. "Growing up, did your sister have an interest in ancient artifacts?"

"Not that I recall. Maybe she visited the museum while she was in Afghanistan?"

He shook his head. "It's doubtful. Her unit wasn't in that area. She downloaded the photos the day before she redeployed home. When you met with her, did she mention anything about researching artifacts?"

Not artifacts, necessarily, but over lunch, Dani *had* mentioned mailing an item stateside that would provide evidence she could take to the provost marshal on post, though she hadn't shared only details with Maggie.

Nate was staring at her. "Did you think of something?"

"No." She shook her head a little too quickly. The way he continued to stare, she wondered if he could read her mind.

Finally, she said, "Dani liked to immerse herself in the culture of the countries she visited. My hunch would be she had heard about the figurine and wanted to learn more."

Kelly glanced at the photo still lying on the table. "Sure is a strange-looking little man."

"Did you find anything else on her computer?" Maggie asked.

"Not on her hard drive." Nate pulled another paper from the folder. "But your sister had a list of names and addresses tucked inside a book on her nightstand." He looked at Maggie. "Do any of these people sound familiar?"

Nate read from the list. "Reginald Samuel. Lance Davis. Kendra Adams."

"Kendra Adams?"

"You know her?"

"I…" Maggie hesitated. "A girl by that name attended Freemont High School when we lived here. She and Dani were friends."

"Did your sister keep in touch with her after you left Fort Rickman?"

"Not that I'm aware of, but I told you, Dani and I hadn't seen each other in a number of years."

Nate appeared to accept her answer, then read the remainder of the list aloud before he raised his brow. "Do you recognize anyone else?"

Maggie shook her head. "Only Kendra. What address do you have for her?"

"A post office box in Mansell, Georgia, about fifteen miles east of here."

"She used to live in downtown Freemont," Maggie said. "What are the other addresses?"

Nate held the paper out so she could read the listings. "They're all post office boxes in neighboring towns."

Kelly arched her brows. "Strange, huh?"

Nate tried to brush it off with a shrug, but Maggie knew the names and addresses were important or he wouldn't have mentioned them. "Has anything else come to light?"

He shook his head. "The autopsy won't be done until this afternoon. We might have more answers then."

"Did you talk to Graham?"

Nate hesitated for a long moment. "We haven't been able to locate him."

Maggie let out a sigh of frustration. "As I mentioned last night, he probably hightailed it to Atlanta and booked a flight out of the country. Aren't the first forty-eight hours the most critical in a murder investigation?"

"Is it a murder case?" Kelly glanced from Maggie to Nate.

"As I said, we'll have more information after the autopsy." Nate's voice was firm. "There were no signs of struggle. The door was locked when you entered the house."

"Graham could have easily locked the door behind him. And what about the footsteps I heard?"

"The wind was strong last night. Old houses settle. The creaks can be deceptive."

Thinking back, she wasn't sure what she had heard. Maybe Nate was right about the footsteps, but he was wrong if he still thought Dani's death was suicide. He needed to find Graham and haul him in for questioning.

"Did you know your sister was taking antianxiety medication?" Nate asked.

The question caught her off guard. "Are you sure?"

"We found a half-empty bottle of Xanax in her

kitchen cabinet prescribed by an off-post physician and filled at a civilian pharmacy."

"Which doesn't prove she killed herself."

"I never said it did."

Anger bubbled up within her. "But that was the direction you were headed, wasn't it? *Mentally unbalanced major takes her own life.* I can see the headlines in the local paper."

Before Nate could respond, his cell rang. He pulled it to his ear, checking caller ID en route. "Hey, Jamison."

Nate looked down at the table. "Roger that. I'll head there now."

Returning the phone to his pocket, he turned to Kelly. "I've got to go to headquarters."

"Something turn up?"

"They located Graham."

Nate shoved the papers back into his folder then glanced at Maggie. "I'll talk to your brother-in-law about the arrangements for internment and drive you to the funeral home this afternoon, say about 1300 hours. One o'clock."

The CID agent with the deep-set eyes was building a case against Dani. Maggie's first impression of Nate had been good, and in a strange way, she felt attracted to him, but if he believed her sister had taken her own life then—

A door slammed as Nate left.

Maggie walked to the window and watched him drive away. A mixture of sadness and resolve rolled over her. If Nate believed Dani had taken her own life, Maggie would do just about anything to prove him wrong.

Even confront Graham.

Initially, she had thought he had killed her sister because of the divorce, but if Graham was involved in the illegal activity Dani had uncovered, he would have had even more motive to take her life.

Another thought came to mind that sent a chill down Maggie's spine. If Graham hadn't killed her, some other conspirator could have realized Dani was getting too close and decided she needed to be silenced. The person who killed her sister had struck once. What would stop him from killing again?

Chapter Four

Nate's first impression of Graham Hughes wasn't good. He smelled like day-old sweat and stale beer, and from the looks of his bloodshot eyes, he had evidently tied one on last night.

The husband of the deceased stood at least six-two and appeared to know his way around a weight room. All that muscle could easily overpower a woman, yet any use of force would leave telltale marks on the victim.

While Major Bennett's exposed limbs had been free of bruises, the autopsy might reveal something hidden by her clothing. Nate would know soon enough.

"You went to the bar at 2300 hours?"

"Eleven o'clock? That's right." Graham nodded to Nate from across the table. "Wanda and I were together from then on. The bartender can tell you. We stayed at the bar and grill until it closed at 2:00 a.m. Then we went back to her apartment. I was still there when Mr. Steele knocked on her door this morning."

Wanda had confirmed Graham's alibi, which had been corroborated by the apartment security guard. He said Graham's red Mustang convertible had remained parked next to Wanda's Highlander from 2:00 a.m. on. Unless Graham had snuck out of the bar, gone to post and gotten back before heading to Wanda's apartment, his alibi seemed tight.

Nate threw out a number of questions in rapid succession, but Graham's answers never varied from the initial responses he had given Jamison. Eventually, Nate mentioned burial arrangements.

"Whatever Maggie wants is fine with me."

One less problem for Maggie to worry about, for which Nate was grateful.

"How is she?" Graham asked. His eyes were soulful as he stared at Nate. "Maggie's a good person. She doesn't need more pain in her life."

"No one does, Mr. Hughes."

"You got that right."

Graham glanced down at his clasped hands resting on the tabletop and shook his head. "I should have known it wouldn't work out for Dani and me."

"How's that?"

"It might sound strange, but I sometimes wondered if Dani married me just to qualify for quarters on post. She lived in the Hunter Housing Area as a kid. The nice brick homes are usually reserved for lieutenant colonels, but a number of units were vacant when we started dating and it was common knowledge the post housing office planned to open the quarters to married majors just to get the vacancies filled."

"So she got the house. What did you gain from the marriage?"

"Validation. I've made a lot of mistakes. Dani made me feel like I'd finally turned my life around."

Nate understood about making mistakes, but what

mistakes did Graham have in his past? Had they caused his marriage to fall apart—or was that the result of other mistakes, ones he was making now? "When did you and Wanda start seeing each other?"

"I kept my distance until last night after my wife made it clear our marriage was over."

Nate scooted his chair away from the table. "I'm sorry for your loss, Mr. Hughes. Don't leave the area in case we need to get in touch with you."

He met up with Jamison in the hallway. The fashionably dressed agent held up a manila folder. "I've got an address for Kendra Adams. A street of older row houses located in an area of town known for crime."

"Let's go."

"No can do. The boss wants an update. I contacted the local authorities and filled them in."

"That's a help. Thanks." Nate glanced at his watch. He had told Maggie he would drive her to the funeral home at 1300. One o'clock. That gave him more than an hour to talk to Kendra.

As he drove across town, Nate tried to keep his mind on the case instead of the struggle he'd seen play over Maggie's pretty face and troubled eyes this morning. Last night, she'd pointed a finger at Graham, yet the man's alibi was tight as an ammo canister. No matter how fetching Maggie seemed, she was undeniably fragile, as well. Was the stress of the situation making her irrational? It seemed so obvious that the major had committed suicide. Why did Maggie refuse to see it?

Approaching the street Jamison had mentioned, Nate signaled before he turned left. Halfway down the block, he spied a woman with mocha skin, wearing a colorful caftan and a matching scarf around her head. She stepped away from a second woman whose back was to the street. The wind teased auburn hair around the second woman's slender shoulders as she waved her hands in the air.

Maggie?

Nate pulled to the curb and threw open the door. Slamming it closed behind him, he double-timed across the street.

The woman in the caftan raised her voice. "Get outta here. Leave me alone." She turned on her heel.

Maggie caught her arm. "You can't walk away from this, Kendra."

The anger written across the face of the woman Maggie had called Kendra was evident even to Nate. He had to do something before the discussion got out of hand.

"Maggie," he called.

She let go of Kendra's arm and turned. "What are you doing here, Nate?"

"I could ask you the same thing."

Maggie glanced back at the other woman. "I was talking to Kendra Adams."

The woman put her hands on her hips and stared at Nate. "Who are you?"

He held out his identification. "U.S. Army CID. I need to talk to you, Ms. Adams." Nate glanced at the row of homes on the street. "Might be a good idea to move our conversation inside."

Narrowing her eyes, Kendra looked over her shoulder. An elderly woman pulled back an upstairs curtain in the next-door dwelling and stared down at where Nate and the two women stood on the cracked sidewalk.

Expelling a deep sigh, Kendra turned and stomped up her steps. "You two had best come inside then."

The house was modestly furnished, but clean and neat. Kendra pointed Nate and Maggie toward a flowered couch and sat across from them on an overstuffed chair decorated in the same floral print.

"Like I told you outside, I don't know anything about Dani anymore." Kendra looked first at Maggie and then switched her gaze to Nate. "If she's in trouble, it has nothing to do with me."

"Your name along with an address for a post office box in Manning, Georgia, were uncovered in her quarters," Nate said. "Do you have any idea why?"

"Maybe she planned to write to me." Kendra's voice was spiked with attitude.

"For what reason?"

The woman pointed a finger back at her own chest. "Like I should know? Ask Dani."

Nate ignored Kendra's sarcastic reply. "Have you and Major Bennett kept in touch since high school?"

"She moved away in our junior year. That was the last I saw her."

"What about when she came back to post?"

She shrugged. "I ran into Dani downtown once about two years ago. We said hello, talked for a few minutes. That was it."

"You're sure that's the only time you've talked?" he pressed.

Kendra lifted her brow. "I'm very sure. You can ask Dani."

"Unfortunately, I can't. Major Bennett died last night."

Kendra's eyes widened. "She's dead?"

Maggie nodded. "Murdered."

Nate didn't confirm or deny the comment. He'd let the

mention of murder add to the anxiety pulling at Kendra's face. He still believed the major's death was suicide, but if she and Kendra had gotten mixed up in something dangerous—maybe something involving shipments into the U.S.—it might explain why she'd taken her own life.

Kendra rolled her eyes upward, and then covered her cheeks with her hands and moaned. "Oh, my God in heaven."

Nate softened his tone. "Tell us what you and Dani were doing with that Manning P.O. box."

Kendra dropped her hands and straightened her shoulders. Fear flashed in her eyes, but her jaw steeled with determination. "I don't know anything about a P.O. box."

At that moment, a rustle sounded from the hallway. Glancing over his shoulder, Nate saw a small child, probably four or five years old, peering into the living room.

"Mama?"

"Baby cakes, you scoot on into the kitchen. Mama left a sandwich for you on the table. Be a good girl now and eat your lunch."

Wide-eyed, the child raced through a swinging door at the end of the dining area and disappeared from sight.

Nate turned his focus back to Kendra. "Let me repeat my earlier question. What do you know about a post office box in Manning, Georgia?"

"Absolutely nothing." She stared back at him for a long moment and then dropped her gaze.

Reaching into his pocket, Nate pulled out his cell phone. "I'm sworn to defend and protect the Constitution, ma'am. Part of my responsibilities involves protecting children who might be in danger. Excuse me while I contact Child Services. They'll want to talk to you about any illegal activities with which you might be associated."

He tapped in a series of digits, his eyes on the phone. From the tension in the room, Nate knew Kendra was weighing her options. If she were the dutiful mother she appeared to be, he expected the woman's memory to improve within the next few seconds.

As he entered the seventh digit and placed the phone to his ear, Kendra held up her hand. "Wait."

He glanced up.

"I'll tell you what I know." She sighed and slumped back in the chair.

He hit the disconnect button and lowered the phone. "I'm listening."

"A man contacted me one night. I was in a bad way, struggling to make ends meet." She shrugged. "He said I could earn a little extra. Buy some nice things for my child. So I asked the man what I had to do. He told me to rent a box at the post office in Manning. He said his friend would call me when a special package arrived addressed to me."

"Did he tell you what the package would contain?"

"No. And I didn't ask. About three weeks later, I got a phone call, telling me a box had arrived."

"What else?"

"That's all he said. I drove to Manning and picked up the package. The caller said I was to deliver it to Wally's Pawn."

"On Military Drive?" Nate asked.

"That's it. A man by the name of LeShawn took the package and paid me for my trouble."

"Did he open the box while you were there?"

"No. He put it in a back room. Then he gave me seventy-five dollars and told me someone would call if they needed me again."

"How many packages have you received?"

"Hmm?" She looked at the ceiling. "At least five. No, six boxes in the last year."

"Do you remember the return address or the name of the sender?"

"They were all different names from different military APOs. I can't remember anything specific."

"Who contacted you, Kendra?"

"He never told me his name."

"And you have no idea what the boxes contained?"

She shook her head.

Maggie scooted forward on the couch. "What if they're smuggling something illegal into the United States? If Dani was looking into it then maybe she was killed because of what she had learned."

A low, guttural sound crept up from deep within Kendra. She glanced furtively toward the kitchen. The look on her face revealed the gravity of the mistake she had made.

"I never would have gotten involved, except my daughter has medical problems, which means specialists and medication. Money's always tight."

"Did you recognize the voice of the men who called you?" Maggie asked.

Kendra shook her head.

"Could one of them have been Graham?"

"Graham Hughes?" She thought for a moment. "I'm not sure. Maybe. I heard he and Dani were together again." Kendra's eyes widened. "You think he's involved?"

"We're not sure of anything at this point," Nate said.

"But should this turn into a criminal investigation, Ms. Adams, the authorities will look more leniently on you if you continue to provide information." He gave her his card. "I don't have to tell you, you may be in danger. Feel free to call me at any time."

Maggie dug in her purse and pulled out her own business card. She hastily wrote down Kelly's landline phone number, too. Handing it to Kendra, she said, "Call me if you need to talk. My cell is listed on the front of the card. The number of where I'm staying is on the back."

Leaving the house, Nate sensed Maggie's concern about Kendra's safety. "I'll alert the local police to increase surveillance in this area. The FBI and Postal Inspectors need to be brought onboard, as well."

"Do you think it is a smuggling operation?"

"More than likely, based on her description. It's a classic setup. When we get to the other people on your sister's list, I'm sure we'll hear a lot of similar stories."

Maggie glanced back at Kendra's house. "She must have been desperate."

"Which is when people often make mistakes. I want you to drive back to post while I stop at the pawnshop. I'll let you know if I learn anything new."

Maggie shook her head. "If this involves Dani, I'm going with you. Besides…" She gave him a quick once-over. "Dressed in that coat and tie, you hardly look like the typical pawnshop clientele."

"You don't fit the bill, either, Ms. Bennett."

"No, but together we might be able to pull it off. We'll say I'm interested in pawned jewelry."

"What am I, your jewelry consultant? I don't like it, Maggie."

"Do you have another option?"

"I'll change clothes and come back undercover."

"Which will waste time."

"Go back to post, Maggie. I want to keep you safe."

Her brow raised. "Then you can play the role of my protective boyfriend." She turned and headed to her silver Saturn, leaving him to stare after her.

Protective boyfriend?

As Maggie slipped behind the wheel, Nate opened the door to his own car and then turned to look over his shoulder. A dark-colored sedan sat parked at the end of the block. Although the windows were tinted, someone appeared to be hunkered down behind the wheel.

The person could have pulled off the road to talk on his cell phone or he could be waiting for someone. Neither option seemed to fit. Was the driver there because of them, because of the talk they'd had with Kendra?

Nate's gut tightened as he thought of Kendra's adorable daughter, knowing what could happen because her mother had gotten involved with people working outside the law.

Then he thought of Major Bennett's body hanging from a noose. If she had been involved with a smuggling operation and didn't know how to untangle herself, suicide could have provided a way out. But if she hadn't been involved and instead had stumbled onto something illegal, that knowledge may have led to her murder.

Nate glanced at Maggie, who was adjusting the rearview mirror in her car. In jest, she had mentioned a protective boyfriend. If her sister had been murdered, Maggie would need more than a boyfriend to protect her. She would need a special agent to keep her alive.

Chapter Five

Maggie turned her Saturn into the pawnshop parking lot and braked to a stop next to Nate just before a sedan drove past. She had spied the car in her rearview mirror shortly after leaving Kendra's neighborhood. Now, seeing the vehicle zip out of sight, her uneasiness grew. Why would anyone have tailed her to the pawnshop?

"Follow my lead," Nate said, as she stepped onto the pavement. "Don't give anything away. And don't mention Kendra or the list of names."

Did the man think she had no sense? She let out an exasperated sigh. "I may not be involved with law enforcement, but I do know how to keep a secret."

He raised his brow.

"What?" she asked, nonplussed by his expression.

He continued to stare at her, causing a nervous tingle along the side of her neck.

"I'm not saying that I have any secrets, if that's the reason for that silly expression on your face. Besides, we were talking about *not* tipping our hands to the pawnshop owner. You're becoming paranoid. Probably too much focus on your job. Aren't all military guys over-achievers?"

His lips formed a smile. "That's debatable. Besides, you're the one who keeps mentioning secrets. I'm trying to learn what's being mailed to the people on the list we found in your sister's quarters."

"Then we're working toward the same goal."

His smile faded. "Are we, Maggie?"

"Why the verbal cat-and-mouse game, Nate? Do you think I'm not interested in the truth?"

"I'm just wondering what's making you uptight."

Her mouth dropped open. "Uptight?"

Maggie straightened her shoulders and tried to still the sporadic pounding of her heart, which—no matter what he thought—was not brought on by any lack of truthfulness on her part.

Rather, that dizzying feeling came from the way his eyes seemed to see beneath her skin to the very essence of who she really was, as if Nate had the ability to strip away the layers she wrapped protectively around her heart. She'd always been the shy wallflower next to her outgoing sister. It was disconcerting to have someone look that closely at her.

Needing to set him straight without delay, she widened her eyes and pursed her lips for emphasis. "The last thing I am is uptight or nervous."

Nate reached for a strand of hair that had blown across her cheek. His finger skimmed her flesh, causing a streak of lightning to zip along her spine. Goose-flesh rose on her arms, which she rubbed, hoping to halt her body's unexpected reaction to his touch.

In an attempt to cover her own confusion, Maggie returned the look Nate had given her with a levelheaded stare punctuated with a firm set of her jaw and narrowed eyes. "Let's get this done. Remember you're helping me find jewelry."

"And we're dating, right?"

Another jolt to her midsection. She needed to get her emotions under control lest Nate read more into the relationship than two people working to uncover the truth.

Truth? There it was again.

"Do you have any idea what the packages Kendra intercepted could contain?" Maggie needed to redirect the conversation.

"Drugs would be my guess. Afghanistan produces more than ninety percent of the world's heroin supply. A kilo of the pure stuff in country—in Afghanistan— runs about $5,000. By the time it hits the streets in the U.S., it can bring in up to $300,000. That's a profit some men can't resist."

"So we're looking for white powder?"

"The purer the heroin, the whiter the color. It can also be dirty brown, though. There's a black heroine that comes in from Mexico known as black tar. But we need to be on the lookout for *anything* that could be shipped from the Middle East to the U.S. illegally."

"Such as?" she pressed.

"Precious gems, even artifacts."

Like the earthenware figurine pictured in the computer photo pulled from her sister's laptop. Dani may have had problems when she was young, but no matter what Nate might think, her sister would never have gotten involved with an illegal operation. Maggie wasn't as sure about Graham.

She rolled her eyes. "So we're looking for precious

stones, ancient artifacts, powder in an assortment of colors or all of the above?"

"Basically, yes."

"Humph." She put her hands on her hips and paused for effect. "That certainly narrows down our search."

Without waiting for a response, she walked toward the pawnshop. As attractive as Nate might be, his efficient cop demeanor could be annoying at times. Especially his recent insinuations that she was holding something back, something he seemed to feel would point to Dani's culpability in a smuggling ring. As far as Maggie was concerned, she had a right to keep certain information under wraps. She owed that to her sister's memory. She also owed it to herself.

Pushing on the glass door, she stepped into the dimly lit interior. Nate followed her inside. Both of them stood, taking in the eclectic assortment of items people pawned for money—everything from electric knife sharpeners and mixing bowls to camcorders and cameras. Rows of shelves were jammed with computers, DVD recorders and other electronic items.

The merchandise seemed positioned to catch the eye of the soldiers, who frequented the pawnshops. If they were anything like the down-on-their-luck folks in Alabama, the troops stopped in close to payday when their bank accounts were empty and their families needed to be fed.

Not that she was passing judgment. She glanced at Nate who was doing a one-eighty, probably making a mental log of everything he saw.

According to what Maggie could determine, he was a take-charge guy who never saw a problem he couldn't fix. But was there something more below the surface?

Something he kept hidden from the world? He'd tensed when mentioning his brother's death. Undoubtedly, Mr. Special Agent had his own cross to carry.

A noise caused her to turn as a young man, mid-twenties, sporting facial hair and glasses, stepped through a fading, burnt sienna curtain that separated the front of the store from a room in the rear. Maggie tried to catch sight of what lay behind the divider but all she could see was a pile of corrugated boxes and more clutter.

The rumpled T-shirt and baggy jeans the clerk wore seemed in keeping with the lack of cleanliness everywhere Maggie looked. Focusing her attention back on him, she realized the pawned items would require time for her and Nate to examine them and perhaps provide an opportunity for the clerk to reveal something he shouldn't, such as a bit of information that might have bearing on her sister's death.

Digging deep within, Maggie pulled out a sunny disposition to go along with the smile she didn't feel but plastered across her lips. She forced a buoyancy into her step as she picked her way toward the clerk who had taken up residence behind one of the display cases.

"I'm interested in jewelry," Maggie said. "Pearls, silver, gold, precious stones."

The kid's expression lightened up a bit. "Don't see much gold these days. Most folks sell it for cash. The jeweler down the street gets most of that business." He pointed to the north, never realizing he might be encouraging an interested shopper to go elsewhere.

"Are you the owner?" Maggie asked, trying to pump up the guy's ego, even though there was no way Mr.

Goatee with the pudgy, baby cheeks could manage a business, even one in such disarray as Wally's Pawn.

The kid shook his head. "Wally owns the place. I work part-time."

"And you are...?"

"Ronald Jones. Most folks call me Bubba."

"Nice to meet you, Bubba." She glanced around the store. "Can you point out some of your better jewelry items for sale?"

"There are a few silver bracelets in the showcase by the window." Maggie followed his gaze and spied an assortment of thin bangles and silver-plated charm bracelets.

"Anything foreign?" She tried to hold Bubba's attention as Nate meandered around the store, feigning boredom. More than likely, he was casing the place, searching for anything that seemed suspicious.

"There's a set of stacking dolls from Russia." Bubba pointed over his shoulder to the top shelf. "They're hand painted. 'Course, one's broken."

"Could I see them?"

"Yes, ma'am." As he turned to retrieve the children's toy, Maggie shot Nate a questioning glance.

He shrugged. Evidently unable to find anything that looked significant, he nodded toward the orange curtain.

"Here you are." Bubba placed the stacking dolls on the glass-topped counter, looking proud of his offering.

Glancing at the now-empty spot on the shelf where the dolls had once been, Maggie spied a ceramic statue of a rather stout figure, which could have been a distant cousin to the one in the photo pulled from Dani's computer.

At least that's what Maggie thought until Bubba

placed the figurine in her outstretched hand. Instead of a piece of antiquity, she saw a hand-glazed Friar Tuck of Robin Hood fame.

Maggie motioned to Nate. "Come here, and see the cutest little dolls Bubba found for me. Plus there's an unusual statue you might like."

Stepping to her side, Nate almost laughed at the comical friar, then fighting back his mirth, he turned to gaze playfully into her eyes. "But I thought you were interested in jewelry, my love."

His exaggeration should have caused her to at least smile. Instead, she felt overpowered by his nearness and tried in vain to quiet her rapid pulse and pounding heart. Their boyfriend-girlfriend charade was proving dangerous to her health. Undoubtedly, she had underestimated Nate's ability to get into character.

"You folks from around here?" Bubba asked.

"Alabama." Noting the clerk's confused frown, Maggie wrapped her arm around Nate's elbow and snuggled close. "My honey's stationed at Fort Rickman. I drove over this afternoon."

Bubba's frown turned upward. "We get lots of military folks in here."

"I bet you do." Maggie stood poised to pull back her arm as soon as the clerk turned away. However, Bubba continued to stare at them with a smug look on his face that could mean anything.

Nate disentangled himself from her grasp and then proceeded to drape his arm around her shoulder and lower his cheek to smell her hair. An explosive warning went off in her brain that ricocheted through her body. *Too close for comfort,* the warning kept playing through her head.

"Now, sweetie." Nate's voice was mellow like chocolate. "I told you I'd buy you something pretty today."

"Promise?"

"Cross my heart." Nate shifted his gaze from her to the curtain. "Do you have anything in the back, Bubba? Maybe a big-ticket item?"

The clerk pursed his lips but didn't move.

Nate rubbed his fingers along Maggie's arm, causing an assortment of erratic sensations to tangle through her anatomy.

"Something wrong, sweetie? You seem a bit stand-offish." Nate's eyes twinkled, causing her heart rate to increase even more. If she wasn't careful, she'd be in danger of cardiac arrest. She pulled in a steadying breath determined he wouldn't get the best of her. Besides, two could play this game.

Maggie wrapped both arms around Nate's neck and batted her lashes, pleased to see a pulse spot pound on his forehead. Keeping her eyes on the special agent, she said, "Bubba, you wanna check in the back room in case you've got any jewelry I might be interested in buying?"

The kid hopped from one foot to the other, then flicked his gaze to the orange curtain, looking ill at ease by their obvious display of affection. Or was there something in the rear room he didn't want to reveal?

His cheeks reddened. "I'll be back in a flash."

Bubba hustled through the curtain, leaving Maggie with her arms wrapped around Nate and her heart doing somersaults. His breath came in shallow pulls. A purely masculine lime scent teased her nose. Her neck warmed, and she no longer thought of Bubba or the back room. Instead she was totally focused on the tiny scar on Nate's chin, his parted lips and the lazy way his eyes were taking her in as if he were a giant magnet, drawing her close.

Time stopped and all she knew was the strength of Nate's embrace and a sense of security that wrapped around her like a warm blanket on a cold night.

"I found something you might like." Bubba stepped through the curtain.

The sound of his voice brought Maggie back to reality. No matter how good Nate felt, she didn't belong in his arms. She stepped away, but her skin continued to tingle where their flesh had touched. For an instant, her equilibrium faltered.

Nate grabbed her arm. "You okay, honey?"

The sincerity of his voice caused another bubble of warmth to boil within her. Pulling in a short breath, she smiled, slipping back into character. "I'm fine, sweetie. Let's see what Bubba found."

The clerk placed a small cigar box on the counter and opened the lid with a flourish. "Look at this," he said unable to mask the enthusiasm in his voice. The box contained a rhinestone brooch, probably circa 1940s, with matching screw-back earrings.

"They're very nice, Bubba, but not exactly what I'm looking for." She glanced at Nate. "What do you think?"

"Honey, whatever you like is fine with me."

Maggie checked her watch. "It's almost noon. Why don't we think about it over lunch?"

Bubba's face dropped somewhat. "You sure you folks don't want to buy the pin and earrings now?"

Nate pointed to the showcase by the wall. "I'd like to take a closer look at the .45 caliber you've got for sale."

"While you guys talk guns, I need to freshen up before we go to the restaurant," Maggie said. "Bubba, could you point me to your restroom?"

"In the back."

"Through the curtain?"

"That's right. On the left."

Nate's eyes held a glint of appreciation for what she'd accomplished.

As the men headed for the distant display case, Maggie slid between the panels of the curtain. The back room was small and even more cluttered than the main showroom.

Knowing she had to make every minute count, she looked in the stack of boxes and did a quick inventory of the piles of items on the floor. A desk sat in the corner. Holding her breath, she slid open the drawers and rifled through a number of manila files, none of which provided any information that seemed pertinent to the boxes being shipped into the U.S.

Stepping into the restroom, Maggie ran the water in the sink to cover any noise she might make as she opened an assortment of cardboard cartons piled on the concrete floor. Most were empty. A few contained garden tools and other yard equipment, but she found nothing of value nor anything that might be smuggled illegally into the United States.

The bell on the outside door tingled. "How's it going, Bubba?" A deep voice filtered through the curtain.

"Hey, LeShawn. You workin' this afternoon?"

"Wally wants me to do inventory." The voice and accompanying footsteps drew closer.

Her heart thumped a warning. A man named LeShawn had paid Kendra for delivering the mailed package.

Maggie closed the carton she was examining and then realized she had left the water running in the restroom. Racing for the sink, she placed her hand on the faucet just as a tall guy, probably six-three, pulled back the drape.

"Morning." She smiled, ignoring the startled look on his long face. Too late, she spied the desk drawer she'd inadvertently left open. There was nothing she could do at this point except exit stage right.

Halfway to the curtain, LeShawn grabbed her arm. "What's going on, lady?"

Despite her runaway pulse, Maggie narrowed her eyes and glared up at him. Her voice was low when she spoke. "You probably noticed my boyfriend out front. He's packing heat and doesn't like anything to upset me."

LeShawn stared at her for a long moment while her mouth dried to cotton and her heart hammered in her ear.

Finally, he released his hold.

A wave of relief washed over Maggie. She turned on her heel, stepped through the curtain and slipped back into girlfriend mode.

Motioning to Nate, Maggie trained her eyes on the young clerk. "Thanks, Bubba, for letting me use your restroom. We'll be back later if we decide to buy the rhinestone pin."

She started for the door, arm-in-arm with Nate, but stopped short when a thought hit. Turning, she smiled once again at Bubba and then at LeShawn, who had pulled back the curtain and was staring at her.

"Have you seen any small earthenware potbellied figurines in your shop, Bubba?" she asked.

Nate glanced at the clerk, while his fingers tightened on Maggie's arm.

Bubba failed to hide the surprise that washed over his baby face. His neck flushed and he tried to speak. "Ah...ah..."

"That's not something we ever see around here, lady." LeShawn quickly helped him out.

Bubba's hesitation and LeShawn's attempt to fill in the blanks were telling. At least one of them, if not both, *had* seen earthenware potbellied figurines.

Maggie had learned something significant, but there was another question she needed to have answered. What role did the ancient artifact play in her sister's death?

Chapter Six

Driving back to post from the pawnshop, Nate glanced in his rearview mirror at Maggie, who was following him in her own car. Using his side mirrors, he searched for the dark sedan he'd seen earlier. The car had trailed him and Maggie all the way from Kendra's house to Wally's Pawn. Nate had alerted the police, who promised to increase surveillance in that neighborhood, but he continued to be concerned about Maggie's safety.

She had done an amazing job with Bubba at the pawnshop. The woman had the instincts of a cop. Nate almost chuckled. Then he thought of the way she'd felt in his arms. When she'd snuggled close, his world had gone into aftershock. Talk about vertigo. Everything had swirled around him, except Maggie. He hadn't been able to take his eyes off her.

Pulling into the BOQ area, he waited as she parked and climbed into his car. A light mist started to fall and the sky darkened, but Maggie's floral perfume brought a sense of springtime to the dismal day.

He touched her hand. "Thanks for checking the backroom at Wally's."

"As cautiously as Bubba was guarding that room, I thought for sure he was trying to hide something."

"You didn't see anything unusual?"

"Nothing except a lot of clutter."

"No potbellied earthenware figures like the photo downloaded to your sister's computer?"

"Bubba can't keep a secret, can he?"

Maggie had acted heroically and her initiative had caused the pawnshop clerk to reveal his hand. LeShawn's attempt to deflect attention away from Bubba had been telling, as well. Without doubt, the earthenware figurine played into whatever was being shipped from Afghanistan, and both of the men were involved. But who else?

Leaving post through the main gate, Nate turned onto the road leading back to Freemont. The rain intensified, and he clicked on the windshield wipers.

Maggie glanced out the window. "God evidently listened to the prayers of the good people in Georgia."

He raised a brow. "How's that?"

She pointed to the standing water and overflowing sewers they passed. "How many people begged the Lord to end the years of drought? God evidently responded."

"I don't think they prayed for floods."

"But they prayed for rain, and God always gives us more than we ask for."

"Do I notice a bit of skepticism in your voice?"

She shook her head. "Not really. Things began to make sense a few months ago when I started going back to church."

"The world's still messed up, Maggie. Lots of folks have problems."

"You're right, but I feel better knowing God's in control. That realization makes me want to be part of the solution when I reach out to others."

"Which you do in your counseling practice."

She turned thoughtful eyes to gaze at him. "I used to do it with my head. Now I'm trying to do it with my heart."

Nate's hands tightened on the wheel. A faint thread of understanding wove through him along with her words. Other investigations had been matters of intellect. He'd been doing his job. Putting the pieces together. Head knowledge. Common sense. This time, with Maggie, something deeper was involved.

He was attracted to her physically, but it was more than that. Maybe for once, he'd gone beyond the intellect to the heart of the matter and had seen a glimmer of hope, which was something he needed to ponder in the future.

Right now the funeral director waited and a tough job had to be tackled. Nate planned to stay with Maggie and help her with any decisions she needed to make.

Heart or intellect? He needed to guard both, especially when he was around Maggie.

The funeral director was sympathetic and Maggie remained strong throughout the process of arranging for her sister's burial. She chose a fitting resting spot near a grove of pecan trees as well as a marble headstone and concluded the arrangements in time to make the meeting she had scheduled with Chaplain Grant.

Nate drove her to the chaplain's office in the Main Post Chapel complex and waited in the lobby, giving Maggie time alone with the clergyman.

Jamison met Nate there.

"I thought it might be easier to talk privately here." Jamison pointed to a small room across the hall from the Chaplain's office. The area was usually reserved for counseling.

As soon as the two agents sat down, Jamison asked, "How's Maggie doing?"

"Amazingly well, really. She's got an internal strength that seems to be supporting her."

"It's got to be tough, but then you can relate."

Nate thought of Michael's funeral. "Yeah. Maybe."

After mentioning the dark-colored sedan and then recounting what had happened at Wally's Pawn, Nate said, "The local police are keeping an eye on Kendra's neighborhood, but I want you to contact the Postal Inspectors and the FBI. The pawnshop needs to be kept under constant surveillance as well as the post offices on the list uncovered in Major Bennett's quarters."

Jamison nodded. "Looks like Wally's serves as the collection point for all the shipped goods."

"My thoughts exactly." Nate rubbed his hand over his chin. "Kendra said she gave the packages to a guy named LeShawn. He was at the shop today, a tall African-American, mid-thirties. See what you can find out about him. Also Ronald Jones. He goes by Bubba."

Jamison jotted down the names before Nate continued. "I have a feeling Wally's dealing in stolen weapons on the side." He gave Jamison the serial number off the .45 caliber Bubba had shown him. "Run a trace and see whether the firearm's stolen. If it is, civilian law enforcement will have a reason to haul all of them in for questioning."

"Will do."

"Did you learn anything about Maggie's father or his suicide?" Nate asked.

"The archived report was brief. Lieutenant Colonel Bennett took his own life. The funeral was held at the Main Post Chapel, and he was buried in his family's plot in Wisconsin where he'd grown up."

"Any indication as to why he had committed suicide?"

"Nothing was in the record."

"What about Graham Hughes?" Nate asked.

"I contacted the cab company. No pickups anywhere near where Graham was staying last night. Nor is there a record of any cabs gaining entry to post within an hour each way of the time of death."

"That still doesn't rule out the estranged husband."

"We talked to a second contractor who works with AmeriWorks. He said Graham keeps his nose clean and his eyes off the women."

"But he could have been hiding his philandering. After all, he was at Wanda's all night."

Jamison tapped his pencil against his notepad. "Seems to me someone would be talking if he was a womanizer."

"What about Arnold Zart?"

"I spoke with him at length. He's not real quick on the uptake, but he said last night was the first time Graham had shown any interest in another woman."

"Which doesn't prove anything." Nate couldn't hide the frustration in his voice.

"What's eating you?" Jamison followed his gaze across the hall to the closed door of the chaplain's office. "It's her, isn't it? I can see it, man. You're involved?"

"Involved?"

"Totally over the top. She gets to you." Jamison

spread his hands. "Although I can't blame you. She's beautiful. Plus the pain she's going through gives her a certain vulnerability. Guys like that."

"I'm not any guy."

"No, you're not. You're a dedicated special agent who usually has great vision and believes in the Uniform Code of Military Justice." Jamison shook his head. "But nothing points to foul play in this case."

"Unless the connection between Major Bennett and whatever's being brought into the U.S. via the mail led someone to set up a murder to look like suicide."

"Guilt over her involvement in criminal activity could be what *caused* her suicide," Jamison suggested.

"What if she could have stumbled onto the operation and was killed to keep quiet?"

"The house was clean, Nate. No prints. No forced entry. No signs of a struggle."

"Have the alcohol and toxicology screens come back yet?"

"Blood alcohol was consistent with having consumed one to two glasses of wine. Still awaiting tox results."

Nate thought of the bottle of cabernet on the kitchen counter. "There were two wineglasses. Mills said the one in the dishwasher had been wiped clean of prints. Tell me, why would Major Bennett wipe down a glass she was going to wash?"

When Jamison failed to reply, Nate supplied the answer. "Because someone else wiped it down. Someone who drank wine with her that night. The same person wiped his prints off the bottle, as well. And who would Major Bennett let into her home? Who would know enough about her family history to set the stage for the suicide in just that way?"

"You think it has to be Graham Hughes?"

Nate leaned back into the chair. He glanced, once again, at the chaplain's office. "I don't know what to think."

Maggie was convinced Graham had killed her sister. Was she influencing Nate? Jamison was right. The evidence didn't seem to point to murder. But all the evidence wasn't in yet.

"What about her shoes?" Nate asked. "Did they dust them for prints?"

Jamison glanced through the file he'd pulled from his briefcase. "Not that I can see."

"I'm driving Maggie to Major Bennett's quarters as soon as she finishes talking to the chaplain. She needs to pick out the major's uniform for burial. I'll bag the shoes and bring them back to headquarters."

"I could notify Mills and have him stop by the house."

Nate shook his head. "Not a problem. I'll handle it."

Jamison hesitated, his lips pursed. "I hate to tell you, but Chief Wilson is ready to get this investigation wrapped up."

"It's been less than twenty-four hours."

"I know, but Sergeant Thorndike overheard a conversation the provost marshal had with the commanding general."

"The old man was putting pressure to bear?"

"Evidently."

"Thorndike talks too much."

"I'm just telling you what he told me." Jamison checked his watch and then grabbed his briefcase. "I need to get back to headquarters and make those calls you requested."

A few minutes after Jamison left, the chaplain's door

opened. A sense of relief washed over Nate. Maggie appeared calm and seemingly at peace, despite her puffy eyes. Evidently, she'd shed tears with Chaplain Grant. Hopefully they were cathartic.

Returning to her sister's home would be difficult. Nate was glad he could be with her to offer support, but when he pulled to a stop in front of Quarters 1448, his cell phone rang.

He glanced down at the caller ID before he raised the cell to his ear. "Kelly, give me a second." He turned to Maggie. "I'm sorry, but this won't take long."

"You go ahead and talk, Nate. I'll go inside."

"Are you sure?"

She nodded. Her eyes were clear, and the look of resolve on her face reassured him. "When you're through talking to Kelly, you can help me with Dani's uniform."

"You've still got the key to her quarters?"

Maggie nodded as she climbed from the car.

He watched her walk toward the house. Arranging for her sister's burial seemed to have given Maggie a feeling of usefulness despite her grief.

Nate returned the phone to his ear. "Sorry to keep you waiting, Kel."

"I'm driving through Atlanta and thought you might want me to stop by Fort Gillem."

He smiled. "To hustle our forensic lab along? Yeah, thanks. The blood alcohol came back, but I need the tox report. There's a rumor that Chief Wilson wants the case wrapped up ASAP, but I want to make sure we have all the facts in first."

"Sounds pretty straightforward from what I've heard," Kelly said before she disconnected. Like everyone else, she had an opinion about the case. Suicide was the option of choice, except Maggie was convinced her sister had been murdered. And now she had Nate starting to wonder.

Had Graham Hughes returned to the quarters and killed the major, as Maggie believed? If the major hadn't taken her own life and if Graham hadn't killed her, then who else would want the major dead?

Was there something else happening here that Nate hadn't yet figured out? Something that had put Major Bennett in harm's way and had led to her death?

Something that now placed others in danger?

Chapter Seven

Maggie stepped into the cool interior of Quarters 1448, all too aware she had found her sister's body the last time she'd come through that very same door. For a moment, she wished she had remained in the car with Nate, but he was busy with a phone call, and she didn't need to be a burden. He'd already done so much to support her throughout the day.

A momentary sense of calm filled her when she thought of his crystal-blue eyes and the compassion she read in his gaze. The man had a heart. Something she hadn't expected from a military officer, especially someone involved in law enforcement.

Moving into the living room, she noticed the curtains had been drawn, casting the interior of the home in shadow. Just as it had last night—actually early this morning—her gaze locked on her father's medals. The Bronze Star, the Meritorious Service Medal—others she couldn't name which he had worn with pride. As a child, she had thought he had placed more emphasis on the medals than he had his daughters.

Maggie, being more of an introvert, hadn't sought

the attention Dani demanded. With black hair, expressive eyes and an energetic personality, Dani had made her presence known at every opportunity. In contrast, Maggie preferred to huddle in the corner with a book, living vicariously through the stories she read.

Not that either girl had been able to pull their less-than-demonstrative father from his job. Long workdays left little time to interact with his children. A fact of life Maggie accepted.

If anything, their father's aloofness coupled with their mother's illness forced the two sisters to depend on one another. Until—

Once again, tears swamped her eyes, like a cresting river ready to overflow its banks. Maggie counseled the grieving but was at a loss as to how to ease her own pain now. Time would help, she knew that much.

Life would get better if she lived in the moment and didn't try to anticipate the future. She'd done that today with Nate's help. Preparing for Dani's funeral had given her a sense of purpose for which she was grateful.

Pulling a tissue from her purse, she wiped the tears from her cheeks and inhaled deeply, fighting to gain control of her frayed emotions. She had a uniform to retrieve, which needed to be delivered to the funeral director.

With renewed determination, she grasped the banister and climbed the steps, wishing she and Dani could have had more time together. Here in her sister's home, Maggie could almost hear her laughter. Not that she could recall Dani laughing on the phone last night. Her voice had been tense and filled with apprehension.

Stepping onto the upper landing, Maggie tried to focus on the bedroom. Instead her gaze strayed to the attic door, hanging open like a giant cavern of pain and darkness. A lump lodged in Maggie's throat and brought more stinging tears to burn like salt water in her eyes.

Grabbing the knob to the master suite, she pushed into the room and away from the terrible memories of last night that played with her mind. A shuffle came from the built-in closet. She turned toward the sound and startled when a man stepped forward.

"Graham!"

He stared at her with that same cocky attitude that had girls flocking around him in high school. Including her. Although taller and broader, his appeal hadn't diminished. "Good to see you, Maggie."

"How dare you come back here." A fire ignited in the pit of her stomach, stoked by the smirk he plastered on his square face. "How can you have the gall to come back to the place where you killed my sister?"

His face twisted. "I didn't kill her. I loved her."

"You killed Dani and then spent the night with another woman. I don't call that love. I call it sick, disgusting."

"You have to let me explain." He stepped closer. "You've *never* allowed me to explain—not any of it."

She held up her hands, palms out, willing him to stop. The air thickened, and she suddenly couldn't breathe. A vision of her sister's body, hanging from the rafters, swirled through her mind.

"Maggie, you've got to understand—"

"Understand what? That you lied to every woman who ever cared for you? That you can't be trusted? That you only think of yourself and never of anyone else?"

"I've thought about you."

For half a heartbeat, she was once again that teenage girl enamored with her sister's boyfriend. Then he took another step.

"Stay away from me, Graham."

His voice softened. "That's not what you said years ago."

She remembered all too well the things she had told him—foolish words that should never have been spoken.

"Don't, Graham." Her breath came in ragged gulps. She backed into the corner of the room, before realizing she could go no farther.

"There was a reason for everything that happened, Maggie."

She steeled herself to the velvet tone of his voice and fisted her hands. "You mean there's a reason why you killed Dani?"

"I did no such thing." His tone was emphatic.

"You killed her and made her death look like a suicide. I found her, just the way my mother found my father. You planned it that way, didn't you? You wanted to get back at me."

"Are you feeling guilty, Maggie?"

"Why would I feel guilty when you killed her?"

"I'm not talking about Dani." He reached for her hand. "Why didn't you tell anyone the truth about that night?"

Maggie jerked away. "What would I tell them? That I'd made a terrible mistake? Right after that the dominos started to fall. Dani got in trouble and then my father's death."

"You weren't to blame, baby."

"Don't call me that."

The bedroom door burst open. Nate stormed into the

room, gun drawn and aimed at Graham. "Back away from her."

Graham turned. "What the—"

"Now," Nate demanded.

Letting out a frustrated groan, Graham backed up toward the closet.

Nate glanced at Maggie, his face washed with concern. "Did he hurt you?"

She shook her head. "I...I'm okay."

He flicked his gaze back to Graham. "What are you doing here, Mr. Hughes?"

"Getting some of my things. You can talk to Jamison Steele. He told me that I could retrieve my personal items. Besides, I've got an alibi for last night."

"Yeah," Maggie spit out. "Another woman."

"Grab what you need, Mr. Hughes, and then leave the quarters immediately."

Graham stared first at Maggie and then at Nate as if deciding whether to comply. Finally, he pulled a few items from the dresser and stomped out of the room. His footfalls were heavy on the steps as he retreated downstairs and left through the back door. The sound of a car engine could be heard from the rear alley.

Maggie had felt confusion before, but now she was even more twisted inside. Tears streamed down her cheeks, clouding her eyes and making it impossible for her to see Nate. His strong arms wrapped around her. Folding into his embrace, she found his shoulder, soaking in the strength of him.

She needed him, needed his stability and levelheadedness, all the things that made him so opposite Graham. Nate stood for reason and righteousness. He was a good and honorable man.

What did he see when he looked at her? Did he see the mixed-up woman who had made bad choices with lasting repercussions? She had to keep the truth about who she was from Nate, no matter how much she wanted to bare her soul and tell him about the teenage girl who had fallen in love with her sister's boyfriend. All Maggie had wanted was someone to love. She'd never considered how her actions would change her family forever.

Nate felt Maggie's heart pounding against his chest. Her tears dampened his shirt, and her breath fanned his neck between her gut-wrenching sobs. He rubbed his fingers over her back, drawing her closer.

The very fiber of his being was tuned to Maggie's need, and at this moment, nothing else mattered except keeping her safe. His cheeks caressed her hair, like strands of gold mixed with spun silk. He inhaled, smelling her flowery perfume and the clean scent of shampoo.

A sense of his own manliness swelled within him, a sensation filled with so many emotions—righteousness coupled with mercy, virtue armored with strength. For the first time, he had a glimpse into his soul and was surprised by the goodness he found amassed there.

With Maggie in his arms, he felt invincible. Not in a worldly puffed-up way, but as a just warrior who battled evil and turned wrong to right. The power of those thoughts made him heady and mystified by the effect Maggie had on him.

"It's okay, honey," he soothed.

His fingers caressed her neck and tangled in her thick hair. "I'm here. No one's going to hurt you."

"Oh, Nate," she whispered.

What was happening to his ordered world? Right now,

it was swirling out of control, but instead of crashing into destruction, he was being raised to something wonderful and larger than himself—larger than both of them.

Slowly, Maggie's sobs subsided. She pulled back slightly and stared into his eyes, searching his face. All rational thought left him, and he was aware of only the sweetness of her lips and how much he wanted to caress them with his own.

He lowered his mouth to meet hers.

The trill of his cell phone filled the breath of space between them. Maggie broke away from his embrace, sending his world toppling into confusion. For a matter of seconds, he couldn't move.

Her eyes, big as the universe just a moment ago had once again clouded. "Better answer that call." Her voice was husky with emotion.

Nate groped for his cell.

"Jamison, your timing couldn't be worse," Nate wanted to shout into the phone when he recognized the caller ID. Instead he listened as the agent talked about the surveillance that law enforcement had established around Wally's Pawn.

When they disconnected, Nate jammed his phone back in his pocket. Maggie stood with her arms around her waist, looking vulnerable and exposed. They'd gotten too close. She had to have felt it as much as he had.

Turning away from him, she opened one of the drawers, sifting through her sister's things. "I don't know where anything is." She changed the focus from what had just happened to the task of gathering clothing for her sister's burial.

Nate walked to the closet and pulled out the major's dress blue uniform, which he laid on the bed next to the small tote bag Maggie was quickly filling. Whether the funeral director needed all she packed was debatable, but Maggie felt useful and that was important.

She rummaged once again in the chest of drawers and found a small leather-bound book, which she pulled out and then flipped through.

"Something special?" he asked.

"A Bible." Her voice signaled surprise. Turning the pages, she eventually stopped and silently read a passage. Tears filled her eyes once again.

She pulled in a ragged breath and shook her head as if deeply moved by what she had read. "Over lunch, my sister talked about trying to get her life together. She mentioned her search for God. I...I had told her to turn to scripture."

Maggie looked at him as if seeking approval. If it relieved some of the sorrow he currently saw written so plainly on her face, he'd do anything to help, even agree with her that a passage in scripture had influenced her sister. He'd also escort Maggie to Sunday services in the morning, if that's what she wanted. He would do anything for her, except pull her back into his arms again, no matter how much he longed to do just that.

His recent show of affection had taken advantage of her vulnerability. He couldn't prey on her loneliness and pain. What had happened between them was colored by the situation and not from any real interest on her part.

Following the funeral, Maggie would leave Fort Rickman, which he knew held memories the beautiful counselor would probably want to shut out of her life. When she shut out the memories, she'd shut him out, as well.

"I think we have everything," he said. "Why don't you keep the Bible if it brings you comfort."

She clutched it to her chest and nodded. He grabbed the uniform and the tote bag and held the bedroom door open for her. With her back ramrod straight and the Bible clutched in her hands, Maggie walked rapidly to the top of the stairwell, never glancing at the attic door that still hung open.

Nate closed it as he passed, then followed Maggie down the stairs. He hadn't questioned her about the run-in with Graham. There would be time for that later when her emotions weren't so raw.

Right now he wanted to get her back to Kelly's BOQ. Maggie looked exhausted. Dark lines circled her eyes and her cheeks were splotched from the tears she had cried. She probably had not slept much last night and stress had, no doubt, drained whatever reserve she had.

At the bottom of the stairs, Nate stopped and searched for the major's shoes, but couldn't find them. Evidently Corporal Mills had picked them up after all. He would check with Jamison when he got back to headquarters, after he dropped Maggie off at the BOQ and delivered the major's uniform to the funeral director.

On the way outside, Maggie opened the metal mailbox that hung next to the front door.

"Anything?" he asked.

"Just some junk mail." Her voice was flat and devoid of emotion as she pulled out the flyers.

The sooner he could get her away from the house, the better. He'd made a mistake bringing her here. He should have picked up the uniform without Maggie, but she had insisted on doing everything for her sister. He understood that need and remembered his desire to feel useful when Michael had died. Although he hadn't been able to do anything to wipe away his own guilt. That was the harsh reality of what had happened eight months ago. Something Nate would live with for the rest of his life.

He looked at Maggie standing on the porch and sorting through the advertisements, and a wave of regret washed over him. If only they had met under different circumstances, he and Maggie might have had a chance to build a relationship of trust. As it was now, he would always be the special agent who had let her down when it came to investigating her sister's death.

Chapter Eight

Placing the major's uniform on the backseat, Nate rounded his car to the passenger side and opened the door for Maggie, who was still sorting through the mail. He glanced down, then stooped lower to examine the two-inch gash in his rear tire.

The sound of a car engine distracted his attention. He stood as a military police sedan pulled to a stop. Sergeant Thorndike rolled down his window and scratched his graying hair.

"Looks like you've got a problem, sir."

An understatement for sure.

"Need some help?" the sergeant asked.

"Thanks, but I can handle it. Did you see anyone who looked suspicious when you entered the housing area?"

"I passed Mills on my way here. He mentioned seeing the Foglio kid." Thorndike pointed to the brick quarters across the street. "I thought I saw him hanging out down the block. Decided I'd talk to his dad and see if he was behaving himself."

Maggie shoved the mail into her purse and approached the car. Thorndike glanced her way, then at

Nate. "I'd be happy to drive Ms. Bennett back to her motel, sir."

"She's staying at Agent McQueen's BOQ. I'll take her there after I change the tire, which won't take long. You pay the Foglios a visit, and see if anyone remembers anything more about last night, or if anyone was hanging around my car just now."

"The boy's dad claimed he was asleep when Major Bennett was killed. At least that's what he told Mills. I'll let you know if the story changes."

Nate made short work of the tire and had settled Maggie into the front of his car when Sergeant Thorndike exited the quarters across the street.

Approaching Nate, he said, "Mrs. Foglio's at home. She said Kyle has been helping her inside with chores."

"But you saw him on the corner?"

"Sure thought it was him, sir. The boy's the spitting image of his real mom, and that gal was trouble. She kept complaining her husband was up to no good, but she was the one with the problem."

"You know the other Mrs. Foglio?"

"Only by reputation. I was stationed with Foglio a long time ago when he was a general's aide and married to the first Mrs. Foglio. She was a gossip and always talked behind her husband's back. Said he was vindictive and mean. Not that anyone believed her. Glad to see the lieutenant colonel's done better the second time around. The current Mrs. Foglio seems nice enough, although I had the feeling she was covering up for her stepson today."

Or maybe Thorndike saw what he wanted to see. The teen had given the sergeant a hard time last summer. Thorndike could hold a grudge. Of course, there always was the possibility that the kid truly was trouble. Kelly had been suspicious of the boy, as well.

The teen had gone to stay with his mom after leaving last summer, but he had returned to Fort Rickman just a few days ago. Nate didn't believe in coincidences, yet he could see no connection between the major's death and Kyle Foglio being on post. In this case, the two seemingly random events were probably just that.

As Thorndike drove away, Nate's eyes settled on Maggie, waiting in the front seat of his car. She had dropped her head into her hands, and the pitiful spectacle of her continuing grief cut into him like a razor blade.

Why didn't you tell anyone the truth about that night? The accusation Graham had hurled at Maggie circled through Nate's memory.

What was she holding back? If it had a bearing on the major's death, Nate needed to know. No matter what, he wanted to help her.

Nate let out a long sigh, realizing he wanted to do more than help. He wanted to hold her close as he had done upstairs. Only this time, he would never let her go.

Maggie remained silent as Nate drove her back to Kelly's BOQ. He promised to drop off Dani's things at the funeral home before he returned to CID Headquarters for another briefing. Once inside the apartment, Maggie headed straight to bed. After what seemed like hours of tossing and turning, she finally dozed off but woke with a start later that evening when the phone rang.

She hurried into the living area and picked up the receiver. "Hello?"

Silence and then a dial tone.

She hung up.

Her stomach growled and propelled her to the kitchen. Her options included a lunch meat sandwich or the pizza Kelly said she could order by phone and have delivered.

Outside a car door slammed. Maggie edged back the kitchen curtain and peered through the window into the darkening night. Nate's car sat parked under a streetlight. As she watched, he stepped onto the pavement and headed toward the BOQ complex.

Her pulse quickened. Needing Nate's support, she had thrown herself into his arms at Dani's quarters. Actually Maggie had needed him to protect her from the memories that had surfaced after seeing Graham. If Nate hadn't been there—

She shook her head. No reason to look back.

The door to Nate's BOQ closed, and she peered outside once again. This time she saw only the empty walkway.

The phone in the living room rang, and her heart rate picked up a notch. She grabbed the receiver and tried to control the enthusiasm bubbling up within her.

"Hi, Nate." A smile circled her lips but quickly disappeared in response to the silence that greeted her.

"Hello?"

Someone pulled in a deep breath.

"Who is this?"

When no one answered, she slammed the receiver back on the cradle and punched in *-6-9 to retrieve the caller's phone number. Either the post phone service didn't provide the service or the call had come from an untraceable number.

Maggie's frustration subsided, replaced with an eerie sense of foreboding. Silly, she knew, but she was in a strange apartment and so much had happened. She lowered the blinds in the living area and debated calling her special agent neighbor. As much as she should stay away from Nate, she also needed to focus on something other than her sister's death and the memories of the past, which included Graham Hughes.

Nate had to be tired. He didn't need her underfoot, and he probably had a girlfriend. Then she thought of what had happened this afternoon. His breath had been as ragged as hers, and the electricity that had passed between them gave no evidence of anyone else in his life.

Of course, the moment had been an accidental encounter when he had sensed her need for comfort. Nothing more, she told herself as she combed her hair and refreshed her makeup. Looking into the guest room mirror, she laughed. Who was she trying to kid? The guy got to her, in a good way. If she spent a little time in his company tonight, she'd be able to get her thoughts off her problems.

Her stomach growled again. Plus, she was hungry.

Maybe Nate would like to share a pizza. With that in mind, she hurried to his door and knocked. When he answered, with his tie undone and shirt partially unbuttoned, she struggled to breathe.

"Maggie?"

His surprise took her aback. Had he been expecting someone else?

She glanced into the neatly furnished BOQ. "Am I disturbing anything?"

"I was thinking of throwing a couple steaks on the grill and was about to call you. I thought you might be hungry."

So he *was* thinking of her.

Maggie smiled as she stepped into his apartment,

feeling a sense of rightness. The soothing notes of a solo sax filled the room. A couch and matching chair in earth tones surrounded a square coffee table on which sat a stack of books and a framed five-by-seven photograph. As Maggie neared, she gazed at the picture of Nate in the camouflaged army combat uniform with his arm slung over the shoulder of a younger version of himself dressed in similar military attire.

Large grins were plastered on both faces as if the two men shared a joke no one else understood. Perhaps, she reasoned, their levity had to do not only with a familial brotherhood, which would explain their similar features, but also their shared love of the military.

She pointed to the photo. "Your brother?"

"Michael." The single-word response held both pride and pain.

She waited for Nate to provide more information. When he didn't, she took in the rest of the room with a quick glance. A bookcase filled with military texts hugged the far wall opposite the state-of-the-art sound system and a flat-screen TV. A high-tech computer sat perched on a desk in the corner.

"You like technology." She hoped her statement would turn the focus away from the photograph.

"Just a geek at heart." He smiled, sending a flutter to her midsection and relief that he'd moved beyond the seemingly raw emotion he still carried concerning his brother's death.

She and Dani had only started to reunite after years of being estranged. As significant and good as that coming together had been, Maggie had survived for years without having Dani in her life. Nate, on the other hand, appeared to have had a strong attachment to his little brother. He had mentioned eight months having passed since the young man's death. Maggie thought back to her father's death. Sixteen years and the wound still gaped open at times.

Nate motioned her toward the kitchen. "I was going to make a salad. There's French bread plus fresh strawberries for dessert."

Maggie licked her lips, causing Nate to laugh.

"Join me," he said, placing his hand on her arm and walking her into the small, cozy kitchen where the smell of sautéed garlic and onions teased her senses.

She inhaled deeply. "Makes me think I'm on a cooking show." She raised her brow, teasing. "Cooking with Nate?"

"A bachelor has to eat. Plus, I like mushrooms with my steak." He tossed fresh Portobellos into the garlic-onion mix.

"May I help with something?"

"Lettuce is in the fridge. If you're so inclined, I'll leave the salad to you."

She opened the refrigerator and reached for the plastic bag filled with washed greens, noting the milk and orange juice, an egg carton, deli lunch meat and an assortment of cheese and condiments. On a lower shelf, two steaks marinated. A refrigerator told a lot about a man. This one screamed neat and organized. No excess. No waste.

"Tomatoes and cucumbers are in the bottom crisper drawer," he said.

She placed both on the counter where he had laid a carving board and knife next to a wooden salad bowl. A small wrought-iron table with two chairs sat in the corner nook set for two.

Maybe she *had* interrupted his Saturday night plans. "Looks like you were expecting company."

"I told you, I planned to see if you were hungry."

"That's very thoughtful of you, Nate. Thank you."

With one hand on the open refrigerator door and the other reaching for the steaks, he glanced back at her and winked. "I'm a nice guy, Maggie."

His smile was disarming, and her cheeks flushed with warmth. As always, she regretted her fair skin that revealed so much about what she was feeling.

Right now she was feeling at home with the handsome warrant officer. Although the longer he continued to stare at her, the more she struggled to keep her expression neutral. Inside, she felt like Match Light charcoal ready to burst into flame.

Nate turned back to the meat he had pulled from the fridge. "Fire's ready. My jacket's in the living room. Slip it on, if you feel like joining me outside."

Maggie reached for the navy blazer and draped the lightweight wool over her shoulders. The smell of Nate's aftershave swirled around her, filling her with a sense of comfort and security. Nate proved to be accomplished with the grill and before long the steaks were on the table, and she was sitting in the chair he held for her.

"Everything looks and smells delicious. I haven't had a decent meal in…" She tried to think back but got stuck on what had happened to her sister.

Nate seemed to pick up on her struggle and directed her down a different path. "It's nice to have someone to eat with for a change."

"You and Kelly don't get together for potlucks?"

"Occasionally. Although we often work different

shifts. Kel is a great investigator, but our relationship is purely professional, if that's what you were asking."

Maggie hadn't intended to ask anything about their relationship and had only thought about two single people finding friendship after a long day at work. Although she felt a glow of pleasure, learning the two special agents weren't involved. Not that she should be interested in Nate in any way except as an officer of the law, looking into her sister's death. But the man did something to her equilibrium, especially when his blue eyes stared at her as they were doing now, upping her internal thermostat and making her skin pink even more.

She dropped the napkin onto her lap and lowered her head, saying her own private blessing, hoping to calm her flushed skin with a thankful word to the Lord. When she glanced up, Nate was still staring at her, sending more sparks coursing through her veins. At this rate, she'd be charbroiled before the meal was over.

"So you and God are tight?" He reached for his fork, evidently aware of the prayer she'd offered for both herself and Nate.

Recalling the ambiguous comments regarding faith he had made the night before, Maggie weighed whether she should step through the door he seemed to have cracked open. Her counselor side couldn't resist the opportunity to find out more about his psychological as well as spiritual wounds and won the toss.

"Did your brother's death derail your relationship with God?" She stabbed a bite of salad to diffuse the impact of her question.

"There wasn't much to ruin."

"When we were with Chaplain Grant last night, you said it was hard to trust a loving God when your world fell apart. Michael's death must have affected you deeply."

He broke off a hunk of French bread and slathered it with butter. "His death affected a number of things in my life, including the way I look at God."

"God doesn't want you to be in pain, Nate. You know that, don't you?"

He raised his brow and smiled, a hint of embarrassment evident in the curl of his lips. "For some reason, I feel like I'm undergoing counseling."

"Sorry. Force of habit." She smiled back, realizing Nate had sidestepped the issue at hand. Then, trying to cover the awkwardness, she changed the subject to the saxophone player whose music filtered softly into the kitchen. The steak smelled delicious, and she dug into the meat, feeling ravenous, which was a good sign.

Their conversation moved from music to bestselling books and eventually movies they'd both seen. They kept the tone light so nothing could bring them back to either Dani's or Nate's brother's deaths. Later, as they sipped coffee and ate the plump strawberries Nate served with a dollop of yogurt on top, they ran out of safe topics.

Nate fiddled with the napkin he had tossed on the table. His body language screamed he had something on his mind.

"Church services at the Main Post Chapel are at 11:00 a.m.," he finally said. "If you'd like to attend tomorrow, I could drive you."

"And pick me up afterward, as well?"

"I'll attend the service *with* you, Maggie."

"Despite your feelings?"

"Yes, despite my feelings." He held up his hand, palm

out. "And no more questions. I'll handle my relationship with God. You let me know if you'd like to go to church."

"I would. Thank you."

He took a sip of coffee and eyed her over the rim of his mug as if something else needed to be said. Finally, he sighed. "You heard the chaplain mention two men who were killed in Afghanistan a few days ago?"

How could Maggie have forgotten? "The men in Dani's unit?"

"That's right. One of the men was from New Jersey, as the chaplain said. The other man was a company commander in your sister's unit. His body is being flown back to Fort Rickman tomorrow. The unit will be there to pay him honor as his remains are taken off the aircraft and transported to the funeral home we visited today."

She waited for him to continue.

"After church, I'll drive you back to Kelly's BOQ. But I wanted you to know where I'd be in the afternoon."

"If the public is invited, Nate, I'd like to honor the fallen commander, as well. The least I can do is to pay my respects." She rubbed her finger over the lip of her mug. "And represent my sister. I...I think she'd want that."

Nate nodded as if he understood. "I hoped you would feel up to it. The ceremony is as heartwarming as it is heart wrenching. The honor paid to the remains, the support of the men, standing in formation...well, it makes you realize the cost of war."

"I never underestimate the price some people have to pay in service to our country." She paused for a moment and then added, "Your brother, for instance. It must have been hard on your parents."

Nate looked down at the table and brushed crumbs

into his hand. When he spoke his voice was raw with emotion. "They never talk about him when we're together, which I must admit, isn't often."

Maggie stared at him, knowing full well she was looking through a counselor's eye, but also that she was beginning to care about this military man with the wounded heart.

"Are they more concerned, perhaps, about the son who survived?" she asked.

His eyes captured hers, surprise written on his face. "Meaning?"

"Meaning your mom and dad might fear talking about Michael is too troubling for *you* to handle."

He shook his head. "That's ridiculous. I deal with death cases as a CID agent on a regular basis. I was in Afghanistan for more than a year, Maggie. Death was a way of life there."

"But the other men weren't family."

"Not family, but there's a camaraderie in the military that civilians don't understand. We're united in our common purpose and our allegiance to the flag and to this nation. That bond is like a brotherhood."

"But no matter how strong the military bond is, Michael was your flesh-and-blood brother. From the looks of the picture you keep on your coffee table, your relationship was close. My guess is Michael idolized his big brother and considered you his hero."

Nate scooted his chair back and stood. "I'm not a hero."

"Of course you are. You served in a war zone. You've dedicated yourself to serving your country. That makes you a hero by default."

"I told you." She hadn't expected the intensity in his voice. "I'm not a hero. I've made mistakes. Big ones."

"Everyone makes mistakes, Nate. No one is perfect."

"Yeah, but some mistakes cost more dearly than others."

Maybe it was her years of helping people expose their internal wounds, but she could see beneath the anger. If only Nate would allow her to lead him into the pain he tried to cover over, maybe she could help him begin to heal. She wondered if he gave himself permission to reflect on what had happened and the role he had played.

Too often painful events were pushed aside or buried in the past, where they festered like an abscess hidden deep within the body. Eventually the infection would surface.

Had Nate buried the memory of his brother's death so deep that he ignored the pain it was causing? If only she could expose it to the light of day and find the truth about what had happened eight months ago. If he was at fault, he needed to ask God's forgiveness and then forgive himself. Only then would he be healed.

Whether he realized it or not, Nate displayed classic symptoms of guilt. He felt responsible for his brother, more than likely, because the younger sibling had followed him into the military. That alone could weigh heavily on anyone's shoulders. But there was something else that cut deeper than failing to live up to a brother's adulation.

"What happened, Nate, that makes you feel responsible for your brother's death?"

He stared at her, his jaw firm.

"It's more than Michael wanting to follow in your

footsteps, isn't it?" She continued to push. "There's a deeper issue you haven't been able to tell anyone."

The pulse point on his temple thumped. His hands fisted, and his lips clamped shut. He looked at her, but she knew he didn't see her. He was seeing what had happened in Afghanistan.

She lowered her voice. "Were you there when he died?"

He shook his head.

"But you think there's something you could have done to have prevented it." She said it as a statement and the narrowing of his gaze proved she'd zeroed in on exactly how he felt.

"I…I shouldn't have believed him."

Maggie didn't understand the last comment, but if she let Nate talk, the truth would come out.

"Michael was young and too naive for his own good."

She nodded, hoping Nate would continue.

Instead, he placed his cup in the sink and stood for a long moment before he asked, "Would you care for more coffee?"

The change of subject caught her off guard. "You've got to face the problem one of these days, Nate, in order to heal."

"I'm fine, Maggie."

"No you're not. You're carrying the guilt of your brother's death all alone."

"And who can I share it with? You? You recognize my sin because you've got your own, don't you, Maggie?"

She tensed. "I don't know what you mean."

"I mean there's something you're keeping from me. Graham said as much today, but for some reason you can't trust me enough to tell me the truth."

"I...I trust you."

"Do you, Maggie? Then level with me. What's the secret?"

"I don't know what you're talking about."

"Yes, you do. It's written all over your face. Or maybe I can recognize it because I know about taking responsibility when a loved one dies."

"I didn't kill Dani. Her husband did."

"Graham's alibi holds up, Maggie."

"You believe the woman who spent the night with him? She's lying, Nate. Graham killed Dani when he returned to their quarters late last night. Then he hung her body from the rafter to make her death look just like my father's suicide."

"But why would he do that, Maggie?"

"It has to do with what Dani uncovered in Afghanistan. She got too close to something and Graham had to find a way to stop her without making anyone suspicious." She trembled as the memory of Dani's death and her father's returned to haunt her. "The war, the deployment, fatigue and jet lag on the long flight back to the States added fuel to the fire so everyone would believe Dani had taken her own life."

Maggie pushed back her chair and stood. "You believe it was suicide. So does Jamison. Kelly probably does, as well. No one's looking deeper. No one's trying to uncover pieces of the puzzle that don't fit."

Nate stepped closer and reached out to capture a wayward strand of hair to tuck behind her ear. "What pieces of the puzzle do you hold, Maggie?"

She pulled back as if he'd burned her, knowing she had to get away from his piercing blue eyes that seemed to bore through her.

"Thanks for dinner, Nate. I'm suddenly very tired."

Without another comment, she hurried through the living room and out of his BOQ, wanting to distance herself from the special agent.

Entering Kelly's apartment, Maggie locked the door behind her. Tears rolled down her cheeks. Why couldn't she be stronger, like Dani had been? Why did she always have to be the quiet one who hid in the corner and never stood up for herself?

That's why her dad never seemed to notice her. Dani had said as much. Those hateful words about how their father didn't have time for Maggie because she was timid and unassuming.

Sixteen years and Dani's words still stung. Her sister hadn't been thinking when she'd hurled the comments at Maggie and attacked her with what Dani knew would hurt most. She had been reacting to her own pain. Rumors had circulated through school that day implying Graham was interested in someone else. Dani's fear of abandonment had sent her into a rage. Although she hadn't known who the other girl was, Dani had taken out her frustration on Maggie.

Her sister's actions had been bad enough, but then, Maggie had struck back. She had wanted to prove herself to her sister, prove that she had a backbone and could stand up for herself. But she'd gone too far, never realizing the terrible consequences for her actions that eventually led to their dad's suicide.

Nate wanted to know her secret. She couldn't tell him. She couldn't tell anyone.

He had mentioned that Maggie didn't trust him. The truth was she couldn't trust herself.

Besides, Nate should be focusing on Dani's murder

instead of digging up painful memories that needed to remain buried in the past.

Wiping the tears from her cheeks she started toward the bedroom when the phone rang.

Nate?

Did she even want to talk to him? With another swipe at the tears, she lifted the receiver to her ear.

Silence. Then a pull of air and a low, maniacal chuckle. Someone was making fun of her.

"Who is this?"

"Spike."

The hair rose on her neck. She slammed the receiver back on the cradle, and her stomach roiled in protest. Why had she forgotten to mention the earlier hang-up call to Nate?

The phone rang again, sending a shiver up Maggie's spine. She raised the receiver to her ear.

"Graham, I know it's you. Don't call me again." She disconnected the phone from the wall and headed to bed.

Hopefully, she'd sleep.

But when she laid down, she wasn't surprised when sleep didn't come.

Chapter Nine

The next day Nate polished the brass insignia on his uniform, shined his shoes until he should see himself in the reflective leather and dressed for both the Sunday church service and the honor ceremony following.

On the way out of his quarters, he glanced at his reflection in the mirror, hoping he looked better than he felt. He'd been up for hours, thinking of everything that had happened with Maggie last night.

She had forced him to look back eight months. Even after all this time, the bottom line remained the same. He had been the one who had made the mistake, and that mistake had cost his brother's life. As long as he lived, Nate would always carry the heavy weight of responsibility on his own shoulders. He couldn't talk to his parents and was inclined to keep his distance. Whenever he went home, all he could see was Michael's face.

Checking that his medals were lined up perfectly on his chest, Nate grabbed his hat and walked across the stairwell to Kelly's door. He hadn't expected to have the wind knocked out of him when Maggie opened it, looking beautiful beyond words.

"Let me get my purse." Nate stepped inside, inhaling the sweet perfume that lingered after she moved down the hallway. The smell of freshly perked coffee mixed with the scent of shampoo and perfumed soap, filling the apartment with an uplifting bit of hope that spring would come despite the overcast February day.

Maggie's footfalls sounded from the hallway as she returned to join him. Nate readied himself for another jolt of adrenaline when she rounded the corner and stepped close. Her eyes were tired, but her smile lit up the room and warmed him despite the cool temperature outside.

She wore a navy dress with a matching jacket made of a soft, pliable material and had tied a gold paisley scarf around her neck that brought out the highlights in her hair.

He held the door for her and touched her back as he escorted her along the walkway toward his car. The sun tried to peer out from behind the clouds. For the family of the fallen soldier's sake, Nate hoped the rain would stay at bay so the honor guard ceremony could be performed without a glitch.

Once they were headed for the Main Post Chapel, Maggie turned to him. "You look very dashing in your uniform."

He hadn't expected the pinpricks that caused his neck to warm. "The CID routinely wears civilian clothes while covering an investigation. Today everyone wanted to look their best. Besides..." He smiled. "I wanted to keep up with you. Nice dress."

Her lips turned upward for a moment while her fingers played over the sleeve of her jacket. "When Dani called the other night, sounding so upset, I threw a few things in a suitcase, intending to spend the weekend. I packed this outfit to wear to church. You'll see me in it tomorrow for my sister's funeral."

"You look lovely."

She glanced down as if gathering her thoughts. "When I was talking to the Chaplain yesterday, he said he was able to get an eight-by-ten of Dani in uniform from her unit, but he suggested having an earlier picture from her childhood that would include my parents and me."

"Is that going to be a problem?"

She shook her head. "I don't think so. I called my neighbor while I was in the chaplain's office. She has a key to my place and promised to mail a photo I have of all of us. Dani was a sophomore and I had just started high school. The picture was taken..."

Maggie hesitated for a long moment. "It was taken when we first moved to Fort Rickman and before my father's death. I...I thought it might be good to include a memory of better times in the service."

"Is your neighbor bringing the photograph to the funeral?"

"She has to work, but she promised to mail it overnight express with a Sunday delivery. I wasn't sure about Kelly's address so I told my friend to send it to Dani's quarters."

"We can check later to see if the package arrived."

"Thanks, Nate."

They rode in silence for a few minutes, until Maggie asked, "Has the toxicology screen come back yet?"

He shook his head. "Unfortunately, no. Our forensic lab is located near Atlanta. Kelly stopped by yesterday on her way through the city, hoping to speed up the process. Might take a few more days before we get the results."

"I thought about it all last night. Graham must have drugged her."

Evidently Maggie hadn't been able to sleep, either.

"If Dani did have some wine, he could have slipped a sedative into her glass," Maggie continued. "Once she passed out, he carried her upstairs to the attic."

"But you said your sister didn't like wine."

"She'd never buy it herself—especially not red wine—but if Graham brought over the bottle, she wouldn't go so far as to refuse to have a glass with him. Graham knew that."

"Why wouldn't he just kill her downstairs? A man as strong as Graham could have strangled her or used his fists to incapacitate her. Why go to all the trouble to fake a suicide?"

"Because he didn't want to make her death draw any suspicion. Our dad's suicide would just make people think 'Like father, like daughter.' Plus Graham knew how important our father was to Dani. I told you that she idolized him and always tried to gain his attention. Anyone who didn't know her well enough to know how hurt she was by his actions might believe she'd choose to imitate him in that way."

Nate and Maggie seemed to go over the same threads of information each time they were together, yet they never wove the pieces together. Throughout the Sunday church service, Nate kept thinking about the threads that led nowhere instead of listening to Chaplain Grant's sermon. Maybe it was Nate's unease being in church, but the chaplain seemed less than exuberant in his praise for the Lord, probably because of what awaited him after the service.

The entire post was feeling the pain of the deaths. Counting the death of the soldier killed in the hunting accident that Kelly was investigating, the 2nd Transportation Battalion had lost four of its own in less than two weeks. That high of a casualty rate would place a pall on anyone, even a man of the cloth.

After the service, Nate drove with Maggie to the airfield on post. They passed a number of hangars and three helicopters parked on the nearby tarmac before he pulled into a parking spot and held the passenger door open as she stepped from the car. Taking her arm, he ushered her through the crowd of somber people to where a row of chairs reserved for the dignitaries had been placed near a podium, backdropped with the American flag. Across from the VIP area, the 2nd Transportation Battalion's rear detachment and various personnel who had been in the advance party stood in formation.

The sun peeked through the clouds, sending rays of light into the doleful day. Not even the sporadic brightness could lighten the tension in the crowd of onlookers who had gathered to pay their respects to the fallen company commander.

Nate checked his watch. "The plane is scheduled to land in ten minutes. The dignitaries should be taking their seats soon."

As if on cue, the side door to the nearest hangar opened and the post commanding general, chief of staff and command sergeant major stepped into the muted sunlight. Chaplain Grant followed, escorting a woman, probably mid-thirties, with two young children in tow. She was dressed in a navy skirt, white blouse and red jacket. The children wore the same colors in patriotic matching plaids. The youngest child, an adorable tow-headed boy with big eyes, carried a small American flag that he waved as he walked across the tarmac beside his mother.

Nate tightened his jaw, steeling himself to the poignant reminder of the high cost of war. Maggie moaned under her breath, and he knew she had been affected by the widow and children, also.

"A yellow ribbon," Maggie whispered. The corsage and bow pinned to the woman's lapel were visible as she turned and hurried her children along.

Nate nodded, remembering all too well when he and his brother had left for Afghanistan. Their mother had tied a yellow ribbon around the oak tree in their front yard—the same tree the brothers had climbed as boys. Although faded, the ribbon was still in place the last time Nate had been home.

As if in unison, the crowd emitted a sigh of anticipation when a plane appeared in the distant sky. Nate glanced at Maggie to ensure she was okay, needing something to look at instead of the small family that watched the aircraft's approach for landing.

Maggie leaned into Nate. Her tired eyes held tears she blinked to keep at bay. Without forethought, he reached for her hand and their fingers entwined.

A state representative, the mayor of Freemont and the city manager took their places beside the fatherless family, followed by the chief of police, fire chief and a handful of city council members.

From the other side of the tarmac, the military band began to play a patriotic march that sounded almost too spirited for the soulful occasion. After the plane landed and taxied to a stop, the cargo hatch opened, and the honor guard marched up the ramp and into the belly of the craft.

A hush fell over the crowd, leaving only the cadenced footfalls of the soldiers to echo in the stillness of the day. With stoic faces, they carried the flag-draped casket onto the soil of the country the captain had loved so much. Passing in front of the wife and children, who stood with the other dignitaries, the honor guard placed the casket on the metal bier that had been prepared. In slow motion, they saluted the casket, paying tribute to their comrade in arms. Nate and the others in uniform followed suit.

The commanding general moved to the podium and addressed the crowd, highlighting Captain York's heroism and valor and the great loss his death was to his family, his unit and his country.

The chaplain replaced the general at the microphone for prayer. Maggie bowed her head and folded her hands. Nate lowered his gaze as the chaplain's words floated around them.

"Dear Father in Heaven, provide support for this strong woman and her two children in the days ahead. Comfort them as they mourn and allow them to know that her husband and their father was, indeed, one of America's finest heroes—a soldier, a leader, a commander, who put You, Lord, and this country first. Let peace reign not only in our hearts today but throughout the world because of the dedication to duty of our brave military and those special patriots who have made the ultimate sacrifice. Draw them into Your heavenly home and surround them with Your love. Amen."

At the conclusion of his prayer, the chaplain walked to the widow's side and encircled her with a supportive embrace, no doubt intoning his own private words of consolation before the state representative added his remarks about the fine man who had lost his life, protecting freedom.

Once the scheduled speakers had taken turns at the podium, the chaplain again returned to the microphone. "Mrs. York has asked to address you this morning." He turned and motioned her forward.

In a clear, strong voice, the attractive widow leaned into the microphone. "Mark would have been pleased to see so many people here. He also would have been humbled. As Chaplain Grant mentioned, my husband was a man who knew the Lord and loved Him above all things. He also loved his country and the men and women with whom he served. You honor him today, and in doing so, you honor our country, as well. Thank you, and God bless you all."

Tears rolled down Maggie's cheeks as the honor guard lifted the casket into the hearse. Nate and the other military in uniform saluted just before the chaplain escorted the family to the waiting limousine.

Nate pulled a handkerchief from his pocket and offered it to Maggie. "Thanks," she murmured, her voice husky with emotion. She dabbed at the moisture on her cheeks and allowed him to take her arm as they hastened back to his car.

The motorcade stretched for blocks. A police escort led the way with their lights flashing. Behind the family and dignities, a stream of military personnel and townspeople caravanned through the front gate of post and onto the main thoroughfare that headed toward the funeral home. All along the road, people stood with their hands over their hearts, watching in silence, their faces grief-stricken, as the sky darkened overhead.

"I had no idea of the outpouring of support the family would receive." Maggie stared at the throng of people, who stood motionless even as a light drizzle of rain began to fall.

Nate followed her gaze. "The good folks in this area of the country understand the sacrifice some are called to make."

"But surely Captain York isn't the first person from Fort Rickman to have lost his life?"

"Unfortunately there have been others, but the townspeople pay honor to every fallen soldier whose body is returned home. It's always poignant, and their support is heartfelt. The chaplain says the families find great comfort in the expression of sympathy."

"Did you…did you experience the same thing when your brother died?"

A lump jammed Nate's throat and prevented him from speaking, but his mind was sharp as he recalled how the people in his hometown had given Michael a hero's welcome just as Freemont had done for Captain York. They had also reached out to Nate and talked about his valor in combat. He hadn't wanted the kind words or the focus on himself. As he had told Maggie last night, Michael was the hero, not him.

Maggie touched his arm. "Are you okay, Nate?"

He nodded. That's all he could do. No matter how much he wanted to tell her about what had happened in Afghanistan, he couldn't. She was right. He carried the guilt of his brother's death because he had made a terrible mistake.

Nate could never forgive himself. Even harder to realize was that God couldn't forgive him, and if God couldn't forgive him, no one else could, either.

Not his parents.

Not Michael's girlfriend, Angela.

Not even Maggie, despite what she had said last night about the Lord not wanting to cause him pain.

Maggie sensed Nate's internal struggle. He had cracked open the door to his past last night. She needed to do the same. But nothing came easily these days, especially since her sister's death. Maggie had lived with the past sealed in the locked vault of her heart. If she could, she would have thrown away the key.

Seeing the confusion that shadowed Nate's eyes forced Maggie to break open the lock on her past. "For so long, I harbored resentment for the military because of everything that had happened after my father's death. In addition, my mother had been diagnosed with cancer a year earlier, and my family was still trying to adjust."

"That's got to be hard on a kid."

The empathy she heard in Nate's voice comforted Maggie and gave her the courage to continue. "My mother had participated in an experimental and expensive new treatment at a special cancer center in Texas for three months. She returned home, seemingly cured. At least that's what my father had told us."

As painful as the memories were, Maggie needed to tell Nate what she had faced. "After Dad died, we had to leave our home on post and move to Alabama. In what seemed like a swirl of grief and turmoil, we packed up our belongings and headed to a rural town, where we didn't know anyone. Dani was outgoing and made new friends easily. She joined the ROTC program at the high school and got involved. I remember my mother telling her that she'd made good choices."

Nate turned to gaze at her. "What about you, Maggie?"

"I was shy. Making friends was difficult. Looking back, I realize I should have gone to counseling, but that would have placed more of a stigma on our family. Or at least that's what my mother thought at the time."

"So you decided to become a therapist to help others just as you had needed help yourself?"

"And to dispel some of the misperceptions people have. Folks are more open now, but at that time in rural Alabama, I would have been seen as even more of an anomaly had I sought help."

"Could you talk to your mom about what you were feeling?"

Maggie shook her head. "Regrettably, we did everything as a family to mask our pain and tiptoed around the truth. Besides, my mother's cancer returned, no doubt brought on by the stress of losing her husband, so I never told her how isolated I truly felt."

Nate reached out and took Maggie's hand. She appreciated the warmth of his touch and the encouragement he offered in that small action.

When she spoke, her voice was a whisper. "I've always wanted to right all the wrongs that happened."

"Just like your sister."

Maggie nodded. "Maybe we weren't that different after all."

"My brother was eight years younger, but we were close." Biting his upper lip, Nate shook his head ever so slightly. "I thought about leaving town before his funeral and heading back to my unit. The wound of his death was still too raw, and I didn't think I could survive the comments made by so many."

"I know the feeling. Part of me wants to run away."

He turned to stare into her eyes. "But you can't, Maggie."

"That doesn't stop me from wishing I could."

"I guess not." He let out a ragged breath and refocused his gaze on the road. "Michael's girlfriend, Angela, was standing outside the church when my parents and I pulled into the parking lot the day of my brother's funeral. The soft swell to her belly was evident. I did the math from the two weeks when my brother had come home for R&R."

"Oh, Nate."

"Close as I could figure, Angela was five months along. My parents hadn't mentioned her pregnancy, and I realized they probably didn't know." He shook his head. "Silly kids. They hadn't thought about the consequences of their lovemaking. Nor had they realized their child would never get to know firsthand what a great guy Michael had been."

"At least, your brother died with honor." She pulled in a deep breath and glanced once again at the crowds lining the street. "Dani's funeral will be like my father's with the unspoken stigma of suicide hovering over the service."

"Chaplain Grant will ensure she's given a proper burial, Maggie."

"Hopefully, but it will be what he doesn't say that people will remember." She glanced at Nate, waiting to see if he would respond.

He squeezed her hand and then released it to make the next turn. "The truth will come out, Maggie."

"Maybe, but it seems to me everyone is blinded by what they want to see." Maggie shoved a strand of hair behind her ear and pursed her lips. "Doesn't it stand to reason that Dani may have been killed because of that list of names and post office boxes?"

"I notified the CID in Afghanistan. They're trying to track down information on that end. The Postal Inspection Service has the post offices under surveillance and the FBI's involved, but we need a break, something concrete that will change this to a murder case."

"What about Kendra's testimony? Isn't that enough to establish wrongdoing?"

"She's not a credible witness. I had the local police do a check. She's had a series of run-ins with the law."

"So you don't believe her because she has a past?"

"I never said that." He turned weary eyes toward Maggie. "I'm attempting to get to the truth, okay? But I need evidence. Something factual that I can take to my commander. Chief Wilson is convinced your sister took her own life. Nothing, including the autopsy, indicated she struggled. We're still waiting for the toxicology screen."

"There's something I didn't tell you." Maggie hesitated. "My sister said the military police were involved in whatever had happened in Afghanistan. The night before last, when you questioned me, I...I didn't know who could be trusted." She shook her head. "So much had happened."

He glanced at her, their eyes locking. "Can you trust me now?"

She nodded, confident she could share what Dani had said. "My sister said that she had uncovered some type of an illegal operation in Afghanistan. She mailed evidence, as she called it, back to the States, to her quarters."

"Maybe one of the boxes Kendra talked about?"

"I don't know. Dani planned to take whatever it was to the provost marshal. She said he'd know what to do."

"The provost marshal is a good man."

He might be a good man, but Maggie needed him to be fair and impartial about her sister's death. Dani had tried so hard to redeem her father's memory. Now Maggie felt the need to do the same for Dani. As the lead investigator, surely Nate could influence others in the CID. Although at this point, Maggie wasn't sure what Nate actually believed.

Hopefully, something would happen to prove what she knew to be true. She thought of Kendra and her young daughter. Just so no one else would be hurt.

Chapter Ten

The police escort led the caravan to the funeral home. Nate parked and walked with Maggie to where the honor guard stood at attention. The funeral director opened the rear door of the hearse, and with the same uniform precision they had executed on the tarmac, the military detail removed the coffin and carried it inside.

With Captain York safely delivered to his destination, Nate and Maggie returned to his car, their clothing damp from the lightly falling mist.

Nate pulled onto the main road heading back to post. "I'll drop you off at Kelly's. Then I've got to stop by headquarters and contact the CID lab to find out if they've completed the toxicology screen. Plus there's a briefing with the provost marshal at 1600 hours. Four o'clock."

"Are you going to mention the evidence Dani mailed to her quarters?"

"I need to present all the information, Maggie."

"But what if it gets into the wrong hands?"

"Then we'll deal with whatever happens." Although he wouldn't voice his suspicions, Nate was concerned that Major Bennett's warning about law enforcement could have been to protect her own involvement in the mail ring. He needed to review the information the CID and MPs had accumulated thus far in case there was something he hadn't pieced together.

"Would you mind driving by Dani's quarters on the way to Kelly's?" Maggie glanced at her watch. "The photograph my neighbor sent should have arrived by now."

The tension in Maggie's face eased somewhat when Nate parked in front of Quarters 1448. Grateful for a momentary lull in the rain, they both stepped onto the sidewalk.

She pointed to the package sitting by the front door and brushed past him to retrieve the box. "Thank goodness the picture arrived in time."

Returning to the car with the package in hand, Maggie stopped short as a door opened across the street. The teenager with the piercings stepped onto his front porch. Seeing them, he turned and hurried back inside.

A military police sedan approached where Nate and Maggie stood. Sergeant Thorndike braked to a stop and leaned out the window. "Sir. Ma'am."

"Everything okay, Sergeant?"

Thorndike threw a glance at the now closed door of the quarters across the street. "Just keeping an eye on the hoodlum."

"The boy's name is Kyle Foglio, Sergeant. No matter how he looks, he's a family member living on post."

Clamping down on his jaw, the sergeant's face reddened with frustration. His brow wrinkled and crow's feet appeared at the corners of his eyes. Nate hadn't realized how the man had aged over the last few months. Thorndike was "short"—close to the twenty-year mark and ready to retire. He had told Nate on more than one occasion, he planned to buy a house on a lake in rural Florida and live the good life.

Nate had to wonder in the worsening economy if a military retirement would be adequate to sustain the sergeant and his family. Word was his wife had gotten into some credit card overspending trouble last year. Would the "little woman," as Thorndike called her, be happy living in the country far from the shopping malls she seemed to love?

"Did you get the message the provost marshal wanted to see you, sir?"

Nate nodded. "I'm scheduled to brief him at 1600 hours."

"Roger that."

The sergeant glanced once again at Lieutenant Colonel Foglio's quarters and rubbed his hand over his jaw as he turned back to Nate. "I did some investigating on my own, sir. Found out Mrs. Foglio took in the mail and watered the houseplants when Major Bennett was deployed and Graham Hughes was traveling due to his contract work."

Maggie inhaled sharply. "The family had a key to my sister's quarters?"

"That's right, ma'am."

Thorndike chewed on his lip, then narrowed his gaze as he looked first at the package Maggie still held in her hands and then at Nate. "The kid gave Agent McQueen a hard time, sir, so I'm not the only one who thinks he should be kicked off post."

The sergeant's voice was laced with attitude, which Nate chose to ignore. He'd give Thorndike the benefit of the doubt. Everyone had been working long hours and nerves were pulled thin, including his own.

"I'll see you at the briefing, Sergeant."

"Yes, sir." Thorndike touched his hand to his forehead in an informal salute and drove away.

Nate opened the passenger door for Maggie and after she was settled inside, he glanced, once again, at the quarters across the street. Kelly had brought Kyle Foglio in for questioning last summer after he had tried to buy beer on post using a false ID. The kid had gone berserk during the interrogation, shouting that she would pay for messing with a lieutenant colonel's son. Kelly had calmly instructed the father to control his child. To Lieutenant Colonel Foglio's credit, the boy had left post the following morning, supposedly because his mother wanted him back with her. No one had been sorry to see him go.

Was there a connection between Mrs. Foglio having a key to Quarters 1448 and Major Bennett's death? Seemed doubtful, yet Nate wouldn't disregard anything at this point. He wished he had more time to investigate. If only Chief Wilson, the head of Fort Rickman's CID unit, and the provost marshal on post weren't so set on classifying Major Bennett's death as a suicide.

Nate mulled over the information he had on the case as he drove in silence back to the BOQ. Before Maggie got out of the car, he reached for her hand. "Will you join me for dinner tonight?"

She nodded. "I'd like that. Can I run to the store and get anything? I saw a grocery just outside the main gate."

"You stay put at Kelly's. I'll throw something on the grill again so it'll be easy."

Nate felt a warm sense of anticipation as he drove

back to headquarters despite the rain that started to fall with a vengeance. Then he thought about Major Bennett's funeral in the morning. Realizing tonight might be the last evening he'd have with Maggie, his optimism took a nosedive.

Somehow within the last forty-eight hours, Maggie Bennett had worked her way into— He sighed, knowing he might as well admit it. Maggie had worked her way into his heart.

After she left Fort Rickman and returned to Alabama, how long would it take him to get over her? Nate shook his head and groaned. Maybe a lifetime.

Maggie glanced at the clock in Kelly's kitchen and wondered when Nate would get home. Evidently the briefing had run long. Walking into the living area, she pulled back the curtains that covered the glassed upper portion of the back door and gazed at the sky. The last rays of the winter sun hung low on the horizon, and dark clouds were rolling in from the west, signaling more rain.

Earlier, a storm had caused additional problems for Freemont and the surrounding area. The evening news had mentioned growing concern as the river neared crest level in the downtown area. A local campground south of Freemont had been evacuated, and the townspeople were cautioned to stay clear of the raging water and the strong currents that threatened to wash everything downstream. At least Fort Rickman was on higher ground.

Maggie's cell phone chirped. She walked into the entryway where she'd left her purse on a small table by the door. Retrieving the phone, she glanced down at her sister's Bible, which she'd placed on the table earlier. With her free hand, she touched the leather surface. The passage Dani had marked flashed through her mind.

Lord, how many times shall I forgive my brother when he sins against me? Dani had scratched out *brother* and inserted *sister* above the printed line.

Maggie shook her head ever so slightly. She didn't deserve forgiveness. Especially from her sister.

Knowing this wasn't the time to reflect on the meaning of the scripture or Dani's attempt to alter the text, Maggie raised the phone to her ear.

Kendra's panicked voice greeted her. "Someone broke into my house." Maggie gasped, but didn't get a chance to reply before Kendra continued. "Luckily I had taken my daughter to my mother's place to spend the night. When I returned, I saw the lock on the back door had been pried open. Whoever broke in, trashed my house. Papers were scattered everywhere."

"Did they take anything?"

"I can't find the CID agent's card. I had placed it on the windowsill above my sink in the kitchen, close to the phone. It's not there now, and it's not in the pile of rubble on the floor."

"Did you call the police?"

"I was too afraid. Someone might be watching my house. They could have seen Agent Patterson when you two talked to me yesterday." Kendra lowered her voice. "They're probably watching me still."

Maggie thought of the dark sedan that had followed her out of Kendra's neighborhood. "I'll call Nate. He'll come over to help you."

"No!" The woman's reply was sharp. "I don't want any more trouble. I called my mother and told her I was going out of town for a while. She'll take care of my baby girl."

"You can't run away."

"Isn't that what you and Dani did in high school?"

Maggie sighed. If only it had been that simple. "My father died. We were forced to move off post. My mother wanted to get away from this area. Besides, at the time you didn't seem to care much about what happened to Dani the way you literally left her holding the bag after the two of you were caught shoplifting."

"She told me that her dad would talk to the cops. That we'd both be okay. Instead she moved away, and I ended up getting caught anyway. I got a year in juvie."

"Dani didn't want to leave you or Freemont High."

"I don't know why she butted into my life in the first place." Anger replaced some of the fear Maggie had heard in Kendra's voice earlier. "For some reason, Dani wanted to be part of the gang, but she was from post. None of us had what she was used to."

"She needed a place to belong. That's what you gave her, Kendra."

"I don't know about that. I think my brother Rodney was the attraction. Someone said she used him to make Graham jealous. Then there was that rumor that he liked someone else. After you all moved, Graham changed, like he was hurt inside."

"Did he mention my sister?"

"He said someone had messed with his mind. He never mentioned anyone's name."

"That was high school, Kendra."

"Yeah, but things happen then and a person may never be able to move on. You know what I'm saying?"

Maggie did know, all too well.

"I saw Dani downtown in Freemont one day not too long after she moved back to Fort Rickman," Kendra continued. "She looked good dressed in her uniform.

I was real proud of her, going into the service, like her dad. She used to tell me how much he loved her. I kept wondering what it would be like if my dad had stayed around. Sometimes I'd dream about having a father like you and Dani had, a father who loved me and doted on me."

Dani had painted a picture for Kendra that wasn't true. No matter how much Dani had craved attention, their father had turned a blind eye to her need to be loved. He'd turned a blind eye to Maggie, as well.

Nate's face played through her mind. Warmth washed over her. He represented what she had craved as a kid. Security. Affirmation. Someone who cared.

Kendra pulled in a ragged breath. "Listen, I've got to get out of here. Give me twenty-four hours. Then you can tell Agent Patterson, but if he steps in now, he'd do more harm than good."

"I don't like it, Kendra."

"But you owe me."

"For what?"

"For not telling Dani that you were the girl with Graham that night down at the river."

A warning pounded through Maggie's head and a roar filled her ears. Would that one mistake continue to dog her for the rest of her life? "Fine," she said. "Twenty-four hours. But Kendra, after that you've got to find a way to let me know you're all right. These people are dangerous. Don't trust anyone."

"Don't worry about me. I know how to take care of myself," Kendra replied. "I'll be fine."

Maggie froze, too shocked to even say goodbye as Kendra ended the call. *I'll be fine.* Those were the last words Dani had said to her two nights ago. Maggie wanted to believe that Kendra was going to be fine, that she had the situation under control, but she couldn't help but worry that, like Dani, Kendra's certainty that she'd be "fine" would turn out to be wrong. *Dead* wrong.

Chapter Eleven

Maggie stepped back into the kitchen and wrapped her arms around her waist, trying to focus on anything except Kendra's phone call. Nate. Dinner. Dani's funeral.

If only she had gone to the store as she had suggested to Nate earlier in the day. Surely he would be tired when he got home. She could have had dinner ready, if he hadn't insisted he had everything under control, which seemed to be his mantra.

Opening the refrigerator, she pulled out a head of lettuce, feeling confident Kelly wouldn't mind if she made a salad. Maggie found a bag of frozen peas and a heat-and-serve potato casserole in the freezer. Nate could grill the meat, but she would ensure the rest of the meal was prepared.

Cooking would occupy her hands and her mind and help to push aside everything Kendra had said. For the past two days, Maggie had focused on Dani and her funeral. Tonight Kendra had added another element that had Maggie worried. The element of danger. Would Kendra get hurt for answering the questions she and Nate had asked?

"Don't go there," she said aloud, forcing her mind onto more pleasant thoughts like the way Nate had escorted her throughout the honor ceremony and how drop-dead gorgeous he looked in his uniform.

Drop-dead?

"Wrong choice of words," she mumbled as she washed the lettuce under a flow of cool water from the tap.

A sound startled her. She glanced into the living area at the glass portion of the rear door that opened onto a small back stoop.

Footsteps?

A tingle of concern played along her neck and put her nerve endings on alert.

There was no mistaking the sound. Someone was climbing the stairs to the back porch.

She turned off the water and sidled toward the refrigerator, hoping the nearby dividing wall to the rest of the apartment would block her from the view of anyone outside.

A lamp in the living area shone brightly, but the porch light was off, causing the window to reveal nothing except an expansive sea of black.

Again a shuffling sound came from outside. As Maggie watched, the doorknob turned. Her throat constricted. *Oh, no.*

The lock held, but seconds later, the sound of splintering wood filled her ears.

Where was the phone? She had to call for help.

She glanced furtively at her purse still sitting on the table in the entryway. Getting to her cell would place her in full view of the back door where the curtains hung open.

What about the landline? If only Kelly had an extension in the kitchen. Maggie flicked her eyes over the countertops then turned to gaze at the only noncellular phone she could see, which sat on an end table near the back door.

Another crack of wood sent slivers of fear ricocheting along her spine. Kendra had said someone had pried the lock off her door. Was the same person now trying to gain entry into Kelly's apartment?

Maggie glanced at the front door. Her car was in the parking lot. Would she be able to reach it in time? Or would the culprit round the apartment complex and grab her in the open lot? She needed her car keys, but they were in her purse. Could she move fast enough to escape?

Suddenly there was silence. Maggie strained to hear any noise that might indicate what would happen next. All she heard was the pounding of her heart.

She eased open the drawer where Kelly kept her silverware. Her fingers wrapped around a sturdy butcher knife, sharp enough to do damage, if she needed to defend herself.

Once again, she peered around the dividing wall.

Staring at the back door, she saw a shadowed form through the window. Lifting his arm, he hurled something at the—

A loud crash. Glass exploded.

Maggie screamed.

Run! an inner voice warned.

She dashed into the entryway. The back door creaked open, and glass crunched underfoot. Someone was inside the apartment, coming toward her.

A rush of adrenaline pushed her forward. She yanked her purse off the table and reached for the front doorknob, failing to unlatch the dead bolt. The knife dropped to the floor.

Using both hands, she flipped the bolt and turned the knob. The door flew open.

Cold, damp air swirled around her as she raced across the walkway. She spied her car, sitting in the parking area.

Movement. She glanced into the darkness, seeing someone in the shadows, barely able to sneak a glimpse as she ran as fast as she could.

Shaved head. A flash of metal. Body piercings?

Help me, Lord.

She fumbled with her purse as she ran. Where were her keys?

Footsteps sounded behind her.

She wouldn't make it to her car in time.

A hand grabbed her shoulder.

She jerked to get away.

"Maggie?"

The voice—

"Nate?" She turned, seeing his face twisted with concern. "Oh, thank God it's you."

She fell into his arms.

"What happened?" He pulled her back to stare into her eyes. "Tell me," he demanded.

She pointed to the BOQ. Her words came out in gasps. "Someone…someone tried…to break in. Glass shattered. The back door."

He grabbed her arm and encouraged her to move with him to where his car was parked. Opening the door, he handed her the keys. "Lock yourself in. If anyone approaches you, lay on the horn. I'll call for backup and check the rear of the complex."

He lifted his cell to his ear and punched in a number on speed dial. "This is Patterson. I'm at the BOQ complex. I need backup now."

After insuring she was safely locked inside his car, Nate raced toward the rear of the complex.

Maggie's heart hammered in her chest. She gasped for air. Dani was dead. Kendra was on the run.

And now Nate was heading right into the face of danger. She moaned, glancing once again to where Nate had disappeared around the corner of the large BOQ complex.

Not Nate. Please, dear Lord, keep him safe.

Chapter Twelve

Nate found nothing behind the BOQ except broken glass and Kelly's back door hanging open. From the looks of the splintered wood, the perpetrator had tried to pry off the lock. When that hadn't worked, he had broken the glass in the window portion of the door. Careful not to disrupt evidence in the crime scene, Nate entered the apartment and checked to ensure the invader wasn't still inside.

The sound of sirens greeted Nate as he headed back to the parking lot. Maggie was sitting in his car, eyes wide and arms wrapped protectively around her shoulders. Two military police cars pulled into the lot and screeched to a stop.

"Dispatch said you had a problem, sir." Sergeant Thorndike saluted as he stepped from the sedan. Corporal Mills followed suit from the second car.

"Someone broke into Agent McQueen's BOQ. Apartment 2A. Shattered the glass on the back door." Nate glanced at Maggie. "Ms. Bennett was inside and ran out the front."

Nate pointed to the rear of the complex. "You men

check out the back entrance. Dust for prints, and see what you can find while I talk to Ms. Bennett."

"Roger that, sir."

The two MPs double-timed around the corner and out of sight. Maggie released the lock and opened the car door as Nate approached.

"What did you find?" she asked.

"Shattered glass and an empty apartment."

"Did they take anything?"

"They? How many people did you see, Maggie?"

"A shadowed form at the back porch before the glass broke, but there was someone in the parking lot. He had a shaved head and was wearing jeans and a sweatshirt. I think it was the teen that lives across from Dani's house."

"You saw him?"

"Or someone who looked liked him."

"Let's get inside. Sergeant Thorndike and Corporal Mills are sweeping the back for evidence. I want you to check the apartment and ensure your things weren't disturbed."

Maggie went toward the bedrooms when they entered the apartment. Nate headed to the living area where the two MPs were working the crime scene. "Find anything?"

"Not yet, sir." Corporal Mills glanced up from dusting the door for prints. "Did Ms. Bennett get a visual?"

Nate shook his head. "Negative to the person who broke in."

"Would have made our job easier if she could ID someone," Thorndike said.

"But she did see a kid with a shaved head in the parking lot."

"Only one that comes to mind is Lieutenant Colonel

Foglio's son." The sergeant turned to Mills. "Call it in. See if one of our MPs can search the area. If the kid is still around, they'll find him."

Mills stepped outside to call as Maggie's footsteps sounded from the hallway. Approaching Nate, she said, "Nothing appears to have been disturbed in the bedrooms, but I found this on the floor." She held out a large shard of glass.

"I'll take that, ma'am." Thorndike stepped toward her and held open a plastic evidence bag into which she dropped the broken glass fragment.

"Probably stuck to the perpetrator's shoe." The sergeant looked at the bottom of his military boots. "See how they're imbedded in my soles?"

Maggie nodded then turned worried eyes to Nate. "That means he went into the guest bedroom."

"Evidently." Nate pointed around the living area. "Does anything appear to be moved around or missing?"

He followed Maggie's gaze as she looked at the photographs of Kelly and her mother, the books stacked on the coffee table, the teacup collection on a shelf in the corner.

She turned back to him and shook her head. "I don't notice anything out of place. Kelly's bedroom appeared neat and tidy, just the way she had left it."

Nate couldn't help but think of what would have happened to Maggie if he hadn't arrived home in time. He had checked his mailbox in the open-air walkway farther down the complex and was heading back to his BOQ when Kelly's door had opened and Maggie raced toward the parking lot. He'd run after her. When she'd turned to look into his eyes, he'd seen terror written across her face.

The Foglio teen had given Kelly problems last summer and had promised to make her pay. The kid needed to be brought in for questioning. If anything pointed to his involvement in the break-in, Nate would ensure he never stepped foot on Fort Rickman again.

"Sergeant Thorndike and Corporal Mills will handle everything here," Nate said to Maggie. "Let's go over to my place. I'll call Kelly and tell her what happened before I write up the report and fix you something to eat."

She shook her head. "I'm…I'm not hungry."

Her face was pale and reflected the shock she had to be feeling. Knowing she needed to get away from the scene of the crime, Nate placed his hand on the small of her back and ushered her toward the door. "I'll be back shortly," he told Thorndike.

Once inside his own apartment, Nate insisted Maggie relax while he contacted Kelly. She was relieved to know Maggie hadn't been hurt and promised to be back at Fort Rickman as soon as her investigation in North Georgia was over. After he hung up, Nate made a pot of coffee and fixed sandwiches for both of them. Nate filled out the paperwork electronically while Maggie sat on the couch and picked at her sandwich. Before he could submit the completed form, he glanced over, surprised as well as relieved to see she'd drifted to sleep.

Long lashes fanned her cheeks and a faint smile slipped over her full lips. *Please, Lord, allow her dreams to be as sweet as she is.*

Surprised by the thought, he tried to remember the last time he'd had any dialogue with the Lord. Certainly not since Michael's death. Maybe Maggie was rubbing off on him in a good way.

Nate had grown up in a strong Christian home,

although his faith in God had never been more than lukewarm. After Michael's death, too many questions haunted Nate—questions about a loving God and the tragedy of a life cut short. Somehow the concept of a merciful Lord didn't work for a grief-stricken warrant officer who carried the blame for his younger brother's premature death.

Once again, a bad taste bubbled up from Nate's gut.

Was he making another mistake now? Despite his earlier prayer and the rising crime rate, he wasn't ready to buy into God nor was he totally convinced Dani had been murdered.

Quick as lightning, a vision of Maggie's body, lying in the pile of broken glass, flashed through his mind. Silken locks streamed around her lovely face as blood seeped from wounds made by a crazed intruder.

Nate's stomach roiled and a queasy sense of foreboding made him shiver. If Dani had been murdered, the killer could have come after Maggie tonight.

Maggie woke, hearing a door open. Her gaze flicked over the couch to the coffee table and the photo of Nate with his arm draped around his younger brother. Raking her fingers through her hair, she sat up, realizing she must have fallen asleep. Footsteps caused her to turn. Nate stood in the doorway.

"You're awake," he said, his voice upbeat.

"Sorry, I dozed off."

"I doubt you've gotten much sleep these last few nights." He walked to where she sat. "They boarded up the broken window with plywood and cleaned up the glass. It's a temporary fix, but you'll be safe tonight."

"Did you learn anything new about what happened?"

"We pulled in Lieutenant Colonel Foglio's son for questioning. He admitted walking across the parking lot to get to his girlfriend's house. She lives in the next housing area. The dad confirmed the kid's story."

Maggie heard hesitation in his voice. "But?"

"But there's a more direct path so he must have planned his route to include the detour. Kelly came down hard on Kyle last summer when he first appeared on our radar. The kid claimed he'd make her pay."

"Where's Kyle now?"

"Being held overnight. I told his dad the experience might make him realize where he's headed, if he doesn't do an about-face."

"Did the dad agree?"

Nate nodded. "He knows if his son is involved in a crime, the commanding general will be notified. Foglio could be relieved of his position on post and transferred to another duty station because of his son. He used to oversee the contractors on post and had to travel a lot. Now he's got a better job he wouldn't want to lose."

Maggie shook her head, feeling a swell of anger and frustration. "That's the army way, isn't it? If there's a problem with a kid, you ship off the family to another installation." A jumble of memories played through her mind of the MPs talking to her parents, mention of the chain of command, her father being called in to see the commanding general.

Nate furrowed his brow. "You know a soldier who has kids—whether he's an officer or a noncommissioned officer or enlisted—has to be responsible for his family members' actions on post, Maggie. If a man can't control an unruly teen, how is he going to handle a company or battalion or brigade of men during combat?"

"It all comes down to the mission, doesn't it, Nate? Combat. War fighting."

"We don't focus on war, Maggie. Ask any soldier, and he or she will tell you that we're peacekeepers first. Sometimes the only way to ensure the peace is to stand up for what is right."

"And what about you, Nate? Are you keeping the peace, or trying to find my sister's killer? I told you, Graham killed her."

"How can you be so sure?"

Needing to convince Nate of Graham's guilt, she said, "Dani and Graham dated for a while during high school. When their relationship started to got bad, she tried to make him jealous by flirting with other guys. A rumor circulated that Graham was interested in someone else. Then there was a party down by the river with no adult supervision." She shrugged. "You know kids."

Nate nodded.

"Dani and Graham broke up, and a few days later, I heard our dog barking. Spike was a good watchdog, but he was chained in the backyard and couldn't defend himself. By the time I got outside, Graham had slit his throat." Remembering the dying animal's gasps for air brought tears to Maggie's eyes.

"And your dad, Maggie?"

"He died soon thereafter."

Nate let out a lungful of pent-up air.

"Last night someone called Kelly's landline." Maggie swiped at the wayward tear that escaped down her cheek. "The first time, I thought it was a prank call. The second time he whispered Spike's name." She glanced up at Nate. "It had to have been Graham."

Nate's eyes narrowed. "Why didn't you tell me earlier?"

"I...I didn't think you'd understand."

He sighed with frustration. "What else did the caller say?"

"Nothing else."

"But you think it was Graham because he mentioned your dog's name? Did you see Graham kill your dog?"

She raised her hands. "Why do you always doubt what I tell you?"

"Did anyone see Graham do it?" Nate pressed.

"No, but I heard him gloating at school over how upset Dani was about it. He all but admitted he'd done it. But you're missing the point. If the caller last night wasn't Graham, how would he know about Spike?"

Nate shook his head as if she were making up the story. Why didn't he believe her? "You don't bend, do you, Nate?"

He raised his brow. "Bend?"

"It's your way or no way. Aren't I right? Was that what happened in Afghanistan with your brother? Did you boys get into an argument so you lashed out at him? He got hot under the collar, hurled a few negative comments your way and then stomped off and got himself killed?"

The muscles in Nate's neck stiffened. She had said something that hit too close to the truth he always demanded from her.

The phone rang. In that split second, he slipped back into agent mode. He glanced at the caller ID and lifted the cell to his ear. "Patterson."

His face darkened, his eyes lowered. "Do you have a

positive ID?" He nodded in response to something the caller said. "That's right. A young daughter."

Maggie's stomach tightened.

"Have you notified the grandmother?" Nate paused, listening. "Roger that. Let me know any further developments." He slipped his cell back into his pocket before he looked at Maggie.

"It's Kendra, isn't it?" she asked.

Nate pulled in a breath before he spoke. "The Freemont police IDed a body they pulled from the river. The name they have is Kendra Adams."

"Oh, no." Maggie's hand flew to her mouth.

"The police found her car on the side of the road near a bend in the river. Evidently, she was trying to leave town. Suitcases were in the back of her car. She told her mother she would return for her daughter as soon as she could."

"Why did she park close to the river? The news reports have been warning people about the strong current."

"She'd been forced from her car, Maggie. Her arms were scraped, and there were marks around her neck. Kendra had been dragged to the river's edge and strangled to death before her body ever entered the water."

Maggie's chest constricted. She shook her head, unable to accept the senselessness of another death. "Ken... Kendra called me earlier and said someone had tried to break into her house. Whoever it was pried the lock off her back door."

"You should have told me. I could have notified the police. They would have increased surveillance."

"She said the police would cause her more trouble and

begged me to keep silent for twenty-four hours. They were watching her, weren't they, Nate?"

"More than likely. They must have known she had talked to us."

"There was a dark sedan that followed me out of Kendra's neighborhood and all the way to the pawnshop."

Nate nodded. "I saw it, too."

"But you didn't mention it?"

"I didn't want to worry you."

"The person or persons who killed Kendra could be the same people who killed Dani."

"I still don't have anything to substantiate that theory. Jamison questioned Graham again this afternoon."

"Did he make up another alibi?"

"He was with Wanda."

"And you believe him?"

"Maggie, it's not just me. The head of the CID unit here at Rickman, Chief Agent-in-Charge Wilson is convinced your sister's death was a suicide."

"What about the smuggling operation and Kendra's murder?"

"We're not even sure what Dani uncovered in Afghanistan. Show me evidence, Maggie. I need something to prove a tie-in."

"What about the list of names and post office boxes?"

"That's not enough to hold up in court."

"I thought military justice didn't need evidence." She huffed.

"Oh, come on. You're being unreasonable. Evidence is needed in a military court of law just as it is in a civilian court."

"Some of my things were out of place when I opened my suitcase at Kelly's apartment. Did you have a soldier rifle through my suitcase without a search warrant the night Dani died."

"He took the initiative on his own, Maggie, which was the wrong thing to do. I talked to him about it later, but as you recall, we were investigating a possible homicide."

"So you're admitting Dani was murdered?"

"I'm saying initially murder couldn't be ruled out."

"And now?"

"Now, I'm not sure."

"You're blinded to the truth, Nate."

"Why is it so hard for you to believe your sister took her own life just as your father did?" He stared at her for a moment. "It's you, isn't it? You feel responsible for both of their deaths."

His words stung as if he'd slapped her with his hand. Digging her fingernails into her palms, she steeled herself, unwilling to let him see the effect his accusation had on her.

Lowering her voice, she spoke slowly and distinctly. "You're the one who struggles with responsibility issues, Nate. What did you do that makes you feel the blame for your brother's death?"

Once again, he stared at her as if weighing whether to divulge the secrets he carried. "Okay." He nodded. "I'll tell you the truth. Then maybe you'll share your story with me."

Suddenly, she wasn't sure she wanted him to continue.

He lowered himself onto the couch and put his head in his hands for a long minute. When he finally looked up, his face was stretched tight. "I'd gotten word Michael's best friend had made some black market sales to the Afghanis. It's a problem over there. Cigarettes are a big ticket item. The evidence was shaky, and my brother went to bat for the guy. Said he was a good soldier and did everything by the book."

The pulse throbbed on Nate's neck. "I should have gone with my initial gut reaction, but because Michael vouched for the guy, I gave him a pass. But when new evidence came in against him, I couldn't ignore it. I had no choice but to bring him in for questioning. Michael thought I was shoving my weight around because I didn't like the guy and that I'd been out to get him from the start."

Nate ran his hands over his face. Maggie knew the next part of the story would be more difficult to tell.

"My brother had come back from patrol a few hours earlier and hadn't caught any shut-eye. Unbeknownst to me, he was tasked to pull his friend's patrol duty—the duty the guy couldn't do because I had him in custody."

A lump formed in Maggie's throat. The ending was one she didn't want to hear, but she couldn't stop Nate now.

He looked at her with somber eyes that revealed the pain he carried. "The last time I saw Michael, he was heading out of the forward operating base, lead Humvee in the convoy. The only thing he said to me was 'Thanks a lot.'"

She scooted closer and rubbed her fingers over his arm. "Oh, Nate, I'm so sorry."

"Had I hauled the guy in when I first suspected wrong doing, he might have confessed, and my brother would still be alive."

"You're not responsible."

"None of this would have happened if I had done my

job and questioned the guy until he told the truth." Nate's crystal-blue eyes turned on her.

Suddenly, the focus was on Maggie. "Do...do you still think I'm not telling the truth?"

"You didn't tell me about the prank caller last night, Maggie, or about Kendra leaving Freemont. I think you're keeping something else from me. Something about what happened long ago. It all ties together, doesn't it? Your father's death, Dani going into the military."

Maggie felt exposed. Nate knew she was to blame. She could see it in the way his brow furrowed and his gaze narrowed. No matter what, she could never tell him what had started the terrible chain reaction that led to her father's death. She'd rather turn her back on him now, than open a wound she had tried so hard to heal.

"I need to lie down, Nate. I'll keep my cell on and call you if I have a problem."

Rising from the couch, she hurried to the door. He raced after her and grabbed her arm. "Are you running away?"

She hesitated. "I...I guess I am. Just like you've been running away, Nate. You can't help me until you get over your brother's death." She searched his face. "What I don't understand is that you have a family. You could tell them what happened. They'll know you're not to blame."

Because they love you, she failed to add as she ran from his BOQ and locked herself in Kelly's apartment. Maggie needed to distance herself from Nate's penetrating gaze that went straight to her core and saw the essence of who she truly was. Did he realize she didn't deserve to be loved? She had caused too much pain, too much death.

Everything started long ago with a terrible mistake

she had made, never realizing the effect it would have on too many people's lives.

But now she was back in the place where it had all fallen apart, and the last of her family was dead. Could she bear to stay and find answers, to prove the guilt of her sister's killer, or would her own guilt drive her away again?

Chapter Thirteen

$\sim\!\!\!\!\!\!\!\sim$

As much as Nate wanted to race after Maggie, he had to let her go. She was running away from something in her past, just as Nate had tried to escape the reality of Michael's death. Maggie was right. Nate had turned his back on his family, not the other way around. Maybe they deserved to know what had led up to Michael being on patrol that fateful day, but Nate wasn't ready to expose himself to more pain.

He glanced at his watch. Mentally adjusting to the time in Afghanistan, he retrieved a number from the contact list on his cell and hit the call key, relieved when a voice answered on the other end.

"This is Mr. Patterson, CID, Fort Rickman, Georgia. I called yesterday and spoke to Special Agent Damian Jones. Is he available?"

"Yes, sir. I'll get him for you."

Nate drummed his fingers on his desk until the agent came on the line. "Unfortunately, I don't have answers for you yet," Damian said in greeting. "We brought in the dogs and searched the area, looking for earthenware figurines as well as drugs. Nothing turned up. Funny, though. After your phone call yesterday, I kept thinking about the improvised explosive device that killed Captain York and the other soldier in the 2nd Transport. It had been bothering me before, but after talking to you, I decided we needed to give it a relook. My people are combing through the wreckage yet again. No one's happy, but, I promise you, if there's anything that points to U.S. soldiers setting the IED, we'll find it."

"Something concerned you about the way the explosive had been rigged?" Nate checked the file he had opened on his computer and paused for a long moment as his words traveled halfway around the world. "Your exact words were 'the device looked too sophisticated.'"

"That's right. Not that the local terrorists don't copycat everything we do, but this was a perfect replica and screamed *Made in the USA*." Damian let out a deep sigh. "Hard enough when the enemy strikes. Having someone on our side involved decimates morale, yet we both know there are evil men who would do anything for their own gain."

"Even kill."

"Roger that. I'll contact you if anything turns up."

Nate disconnected, thinking of what Damian had said about copycats and perfect replicas. Had Dani's death been an exact copy of her father's suicide? Scrolling through the archived CID files, Nate pulled up the report on Lieutenant Colonel Bennett's death sixteen years ago. As Jamison had mentioned, the information was sketchy, either because the person who had updated the database failed to include all the details or because the actual hardcopy report had been less than complete.

Another search revealed a Colonel Glen Rogers, who had been the provost marshal at that time, command-

ing the military police on post. Hopefully he would remember the death investigation his MPs had conducted.
Knowing military personnel often retire at their last
duty station and remain in the local area, Nate flipped
through the pages of the Freemont phone directory and
quickly found a listing for Glen Rogers, Colonel Retired.
He plugged the number into his cell but was routed to
voice mail. Nate left a brief message and asked the colonel to contact him at his first convenience.

Needing to clear the cobwebs that clogged his brain
and wanting to ensure Maggie was safe, Nate pulled a
fleece jacket from his closet and left his apartment. The
bright lighting in the open walkway outside provided a
good deterrent to keep perpetrators from approaching
the front of the complex. The rear, on the other hand,
sat cloaked in darkness and backed onto a wooded area,
where Nate now headed.

Earlier while Maggie had catnapped, he'd tested the
plywood Thorndike and Mills had used to shore up Kelly's broken window. The makeshift fix secured the rear
entrance, but Nate needed to confirm no one was hanging around in the shadows. Rounding the complex, he
moved quietly into a stand of trees where he had a clear
view of the entire area.

His eyes quickly acclimated to the dark, and he
scanned the shrubbery and underbrush but saw nothing suspicious. The crickets and cicadas chirped their
night songs accompanied by an occasional tree frog
while a light mist added more moisture to the damp
and chilly night.

Lights blazed inside Kelly's BOQ, and Nate imagined
Maggie curled up on the couch, arms wrapped protectively around her waist. Although Nate wanted to pro-

vide the protection she needed, he had to give her the freedom she demanded.

When the first morning light filtered over the horizon, Nate left the woods and headed back to his BOQ for a quick shower and a pot of high-test coffee. He downed three cups while rehashing his conversation with Damian Jones. *Copycat* kept circulating through his mind.

On his way to the kitchen to pour a fourth cup, his cell rang. "Patterson."

"Corporal Otis, sir. That toxicology report you wanted arrived." Nate listened to the results then disconnected and pushed speed dial for Kelly's cell. Her voice sounded groggy when it came over the line.

"I need to bounce some ideas around, concerning Major Bennett's death. Do you mind?"

She groaned. "At this time of night?"

"The sun's up, Kel. It's morning."

"Not in North Georgia. Besides, you're entirely too energetic."

"Sorry, but it's important. I keep thinking about the attic light being off when Maggie found her sister. Seems to me if Major Bennett killed herself, she wouldn't turn off the light. Plus, her shoes were downstairs under a table."

"Hmm?" Kelly had taken the bait and now seemed interested in reviewing the case. "Maybe she had a few obsessive-compulsive tendencies and liked everything nice and neat."

"Yes, but it's winter. Those old quarters are drafty, yet she climbed the stairs to the attic without shoes."

"And you're saying what?"

Nate wasn't sure what he was trying to establish, but voicing the problem out loud sometimes helped the pieces fall into place. "Let's consider what would happen if someone had killed her and then tried to make it look like suicide. There were no visible signs of a struggle. What's that tell you?"

"That she had been incapacitated in some way. Probably drugged."

"Maybe the perpetrator slipped something into her wineglass, which he wiped clean and placed on a rack in the dishwasher."

Kelly played along. "Her shoes could have fallen off as he carried her up the stairs."

"Exactly. Later he would have wiped them, as well, and then placed them under a table."

"If prints had been removed, the person understood how cops gather evidence."

"And who would best know those procedures, Kelly?"

"Another cop?"

"Bingo."

"Ah, Nate." Kelly sighed. "You could be getting into hot water with this one."

"But the pieces fit, *if* she were murdered. The shoes, the two wineglasses. Plus, Maggie said the attic was dark when she found her sister. No reason for the major to turn off the light before she put the noose around her neck. But someone leaving the attic might pull the light switch, knowing a dark house with a lone light shining through the attic dormer window would draw suspicion."

"He—or she—never expected Maggie to show up that night," Kelly added.

"That's right. Had Major Bennett been found in the daytime, the light may not have been noticed."

"What about the tox screen?" Kelly asked.

"I just got the report. Her specimen was positive for

benzodiazepines. Specifically alprazolam. You might know it by the trade name Xanax. Interestingly, a civilian doctor prescribed Xanax for Major Bennett the week prior to her death."

"She could have popped a few pills to overcome any last-minute anxiety if she were planning to take her own life."

Kelly's comment held water, yet the major seemed like a woman who stood by her decisions. If she had decided to commit suicide, she wouldn't turn to chemical aids to get her through it.

"She kept her pills in a kitchen cabinet," Nate added. "The killer could have used her own prescription meds to drug her."

"Did you get the results for the residue left in the wineglass on the counter?" Kelly asked.

"Negative for Xanax, and the glass in the dishwasher had been wiped clean."

"Had the perpetrator planned to kill her from the get-go?"

"I'm not sure, Kel. But suppose someone in law enforcement stopped by her house to talk to her. The major told her sister that she had uncovered something unsettling in Afghanistan and suspected law enforcement could be involved."

"You're saying Major Bennett trusted the killer and invited him into her house to discuss the situation."

"That's it exactly. Only, he's in on the deal and realizes she needs to be silenced. She may have left the pills on the counter. If she stepped out of the kitchen for a minute or two, he would have had enough time to slip the drugs into her glass."

"Wouldn't she recognize the medicinal taste?"

"Maggie told me that her sister didn't like red wine—she might not have been familiar enough with the taste to suspect anything."

"Yet she drank it that night?"

Nate sighed. "Work with me, Kelly. Maybe the cop convinced her wine would help her relax."

"Only, the combination of drugs and alcohol knocked her out. He carried her upstairs and made her death look like it was self-inflicted."

"And identical to the way her father died sixteen years earlier."

"Time out, Nate. How does the guy know about the dad's death?"

"Good question." And one Nate couldn't answer. Unless…? The killer had to have known the family and understood the importance of Major Bennett following in her father's footsteps. Graham had an alibi, but things weren't always as they seemed.

Nate's neck tingled. Maybe Maggie had been right about Graham all along.

Chapter Fourteen

The next morning, Maggie woke with a dull ache in her temples and a stiff spine. She'd fallen asleep on the couch in Kelly's living area, close enough to the plywood-covered back door to hear any shuffling sounds outside should the assailant try to gain entry again. Cell phone in hand, she'd been ready to contact Nate at the first indication of anything suspicious. The last time she had checked the time, the clock in the kitchen had read 4:00 a.m.

Maggie made a pot of coffee, but the hot brew stuck in her throat, and she ended up pouring it down the drain. Once dressed, she waited for Nate who looked equally out of sorts when she opened the door to his knock. At other times, his presence had buoyed her flagging spirits, but today the memory of the way they had parted last night added to the melancholy day.

They rode in relative silence to the Main Post Chapel where the hearse sat in the driveway. Maggie steeled herself to what lay ahead before she walked into the chapel where Dani's casket waited in the narthex. The honor guard took their positions on either side of the casket as the first strains of organ music filtered through the church. A sea of mourners filled the sanctuary and turned to watch Maggie's slow procession down the center aisle behind the casket to her seat in the front pew on the left.

Graham sat across from her on the opposite side of the aisle, looking tired. Dark circles rimmed his eyes, due, no doubt, to late nights spent with the woman from the bar and grill. The thought of him racing into the arms of another woman the night Dani had died filled Maggie's stomach with bile. She wanted to walk across the aisle and slap his face. Instead, she tugged at the edge of her jacket and kept her eyes facing forward, unwilling to acknowledge his presence.

Someone had placed the photographs of her sister and family on a small table near the altar along with a bud vase containing one yellow rose. Maggie stared at the pictures, trying to find something good on which to focus. At this moment, all she could think about was the senseless waste of life.

Nate slipped into the pew next to her. As much as she appreciated his support, she felt betrayed by his inability to realize what had really happened that fateful night. Was he still so hung up on his own brother's death that he was unable to make an accurate judgment about her sister's murder?

The funeral passed in a blur. The all-male choir of uniformed soldiers sang patriotic hymns that dated back to Civil War days. After the last strains of an especially moving selection ended, an officer in Dani's unit read from scripture about the many mansions the Lord had prepared for those who died.

Similar words had been intoned at her father's funeral, but Maggie had been too young to realize the long-term consequences of that death. Once again, her throat thickened and tears streamed down her cheeks. She wiped them with a tissue and gritted her teeth, determined not to let Nate or Graham have the satisfaction of seeing her pain.

Chaplain Grant moved to the pulpit. Maggie focused on the scripture he read and the kind words he said about Dani and her career in the army. He exalted her heroism and love of country, and his praise brought a lump of pride to Maggie's throat and more tears to her eyes.

At the conclusion of the service, the pallbearers took their places beside the casket and, with uniform precision, began their return march to the hearse. Maggie walked behind the honor guard. Once the casket had been placed within the waiting vehicle, Nate took her arm and ushered her to the limousine provided by the funeral home.

She settled into the rear seat. Nate climbed in beside her, sitting close enough for Maggie to feel the heat from his body. Although aware of his nearness, she kept her eyes trained on the passing landscape and clamped her jaw together, trying to keep the tears at bay.

The graveside service passed in another wave of readings from scripture, punctuated with a rifle salute in honor of Dani's service and concluded with a lone bugler and the doleful twenty-six notes of Taps that echoed over the hallowed ground.

Twice during the short ride back to the church, Nate tried to draw her into conversation, but both times, Maggie held up her hand and shook her head. She wasn't ready to discuss anything except how much she regretted her sister's death. He reached for her arm when he helped her from the car, but she moved out of his grasp, knowing any act of kindness would unleash the tide of tears she was trying so hard to contain.

The well-wishers seemed sincere at the reception where food lined a huge table not far from where she stood. A mix of civilians and military in uniform formed an impromptu receiving line to offer their condolences. After they expressed words of sympathy, they filled their plates with food and chatted amicably with others who gathered in small clusters around the fellowship hall.

The heartfelt sympathy of the people at Fort Rickman warmed Maggie's heart. Their comments reflected their honest admiration for Dani. The positive impact she had had on so many lives was in direct contrast to the dark mood that had been so present at their father's funeral.

Encouraged by the support for her sister, Maggie realized she had been too hard on Nate. If he were like the other military officers and noncommissioned officers she had met today, he only wanted to serve his country and do the best job possible.

Nate brought her a glass of water, which he placed on a side table near where she stood. She appreciated the gesture and recalled their first encounter, when the same small token of his concern had struck a warm chord in her grief-stricken heart. Could it only have been less than seventy-two hours since they'd met?

As the line of mourners dwindled at last, she looked around the hall, searching for Nate. He was standing by his commander, Chief Warrant Officer and Agent-in-Charge Wilson, a tall African-American who Maggie had met immediately after the service. As much as she had wanted to talk to the chief, she refused to discuss the sensitive subject of her sister's death with so many people standing nearby.

Better to approach Chief Wilson now. Nate knew the way she felt and had heard her arguments before. Maybe he would even lend support. Relieved to finally have an opportunity to state her case to the CID commander, and with the funeral behind her, Maggie felt her spirits lift. As she neared the two men, the words she overheard Chief Wilson utter made her euphoria plummet into despair.

"I signed your request for transfer to the 105th Airborne." Chief Wilson patted Nate's shoulder. "Hate to see you leave us here at Fort Rickman to head back to Afghanistan, but I understand your desire to rejoin the fight as soon as possible. The unit's due to deploy in three weeks. If I place a rush on the request, you should be able to join them within a fortnight. I just need to know if you can be ready to leave post that soon."

Maggie tried to breathe. Nate was leaving Fort Rickman and returning to Afghanistan?

"I'll get back to you on that, sir." Nate turned from his commander and caught sight of her. His face opened into a smile. Did he realize she'd overheard his plans to leave Rickman and, in so doing, leave her, as well?

"Corporal Mills drove your car over from the BOQ and parked it in the church lot," Nate said, oblivious to the effect the information was having on Maggie. He dug in his pocket for the keys to her car and handed them to her. "I won't be able to give you a ride back since one of the Postal Inspectors called me a few minutes ago."

She tried to focus on the words he was saying, but she couldn't get around the fact that in just a few weeks, he was scheduled to deploy—a deployment Nate had requested.

"A package mailed from an APO in Afghanistan arrived at the Garrett post office," he continued. "The inspector hopes they'll be able to detain the point of contact when he moves in to claim the box. I need to be on-site. Things should move along quickly, and I plan to be back on post by late-afternoon."

Nate was sidestepping the issue of his deployment and letting her believe he was still determined to find what Dani had uncovered in Afghanistan.

"Maybe we can go out for dinner tonight?" His eyes held no hint of guile as he stared at her.

"Maybe. Give me a call when you get back." Hopefully, he couldn't see the pain she tried to mask. "Excuse me for a minute."

Turning her back to him, she headed toward the ladies' room. Her head pounded, and the tears that had threatened to spill returned once again. Nate had known all along he was leaving post.

Don't rock the boat. Was that it?

He didn't want to do anything to counter his boss or infringe on Chief Wilson's agreement to accept Nate's request for transfer. No wonder he hadn't investigated Dani's death further.

"Maggie?"

She turned at the sound of Chaplain Grant's voice. He followed her into the hallway. "I would be happy to drive you back to your lodging. I know this is a difficult day."

She scrubbed her hand over her face, attempting to wipe away her seemingly perpetual trail of tears. "My car is parked outside, Chaplain, so I'll be able to drive myself back to Agent McQueen's BOQ, but thank you for the kind words you said about my sister today."

"All true." He looked at her with compassion, causing her determination to hold her tears at bay to falter and nearly crumble into oblivion. She tried to smile, but didn't succeed, and knew her dam of self-control would soon break if she didn't get away.

"If you'll excuse me," she said in parting. "I need to freshen my makeup." Instead of the ladies' restroom, she headed for the side door and quickly made her way outside.

Packing the few things she had at Kelly's BOQ wouldn't take long and then she would head back to Alabama, much as she regretted the way she was leaving post. Her sister's murder hadn't been resolved, but Maggie couldn't remain at Fort Rickman any longer.

At some point in the last seventy-two hours, she had started to believe everything would end differently. In fact, she'd even thought that something ongoing could continue with Nate. Now she knew he wasn't interested in making their relationship more lasting.

"Good riddance," she grumbled. Then she thought about his warm gaze and the way her heart fluttered whenever he was near. The realization of her true feelings shook her to the core. Despite everything that had happened and even though he was leaving her behind, Maggie had to admit the truth. She had fallen in love with Nate Patterson.

Nate watched Maggie head to the ladies' room. All morning, she had been quiet and withdrawn as he had expected she would be during her sister's funeral. Silly to think Maggie would have been affected by the magnetism that had drawn him to her right from the start. She had closed all doors to her inner world and hung a "Do Not Disturb" sign on her heart. Would this evening be different or would she still be hiding behind the permanent divider she refused to tear down?

Someone tapped his shoulder. Nate turned to see an older gentleman, probably early seventies, who held out his hand. "Mr. Patterson, my name is Glen Rogers."

The provost marshal at Fort Rickman when Maggie's father had died. Nate shook his hand. "Nice to meet you, sir."

"I've been out of town, visiting my daughter and grandchildren and drove back in time for the service today. I found your voice mail on my phone but didn't have an opportunity to call you prior to the funeral. You wanted information?"

"That's correct." Classrooms surrounded the main fellowship hall, and Nate motioned the retired colonel into the closest empty space and shut the door behind them. "We should be able to talk privately in here, sir."

"Your message mentioned Dan Bennett's death."

"Yes, sir. The case file was rather sketchy. I'm investigating his daughter Major Bennett's death, and the circumstances are similar."

"From what I've heard, she copied her father in many ways." The retired colonel shook his head. "Such a shame."

"Do you recall any information about the circumstances of the lieutenant colonel's suicide? Anything that might have bearing on the daughter's death."

"How could I forget? Dan's wife had cancer and needed a costly treatment the army refused to cover. He was the head of comptroller's shop on post at that time, which, as you know, handles funding. Dan uncovered two noncommissioned officers who were altering the books for their own gain."

"Embezzling money from Uncle Sam?"

"Regrettably, yes. Dan was worried about his wife, so he took a bribe to remain quiet and to help pay for the treatment she needed. At least that's what he confessed when one of the NCO's pilfering came to light. In deference to Dan's long career and because of the situation, the commanding general accepted his resignation in return for exposing the second man in the operation. Dan planned to retire quietly. Major General Able, the post CG, ordered me to wipe the record clean of Dan's involvement."

"But he took his own life before he could retire?"

"Dan feared he'd have to testify in court. He didn't want his daughters to find out about his wrongdoing. He was a reserved man who took his job seriously. Unfortunately, he had made a bad decision that he couldn't live with. Of course, his daughters had gotten into trouble just a few days earlier. Dani had been picked up for shoplifting by the Freemont police."

"You were notified?"

"That's right. Major Bennett gave her parents fits. She'd started to run with a rather wild group of local town kids."

"Do you know anything about a pet being killed?"

The retired colonel nodded, his eyes solemn. "The second NCO, whose name hadn't been revealed at that time, killed the dog to warn Dan to keep his mouth shut."

"So none of the kids from high school were involved in the dog's death?"

"That's right, but losing the pet made Dan realize he

needed to come clean. In return, we attempted to keep his involvement closely held. Only a handful of people on post knew what had really happened. The commanding general and his aide, as well as a few people in the JAG office who were working on the embezzlement case."

"Were there suspicions the Lieutenant Colonel's death was anything except a suicide?"

"None whatsoever. He hung himself late one night from a rafter in his home."

"Do you recall if the light was left on in the attic?"

"I may be getting old, Mr. Patterson, but my memory's sharp. The attic light alerted one of my men on patrol. The CG was big on energy conservation and had ordered all unnecessary lights to be turned off at night. An MP on duty stopped by the house, despite the late hour. Mrs. Bennett went to the attic and found her husband."

Nate could only imagine her shock.

"Fact is," the colonel continued, "I ran into that soldier not long ago in the Post Exchange. He's back at Fort Rickman and ready to retire. You probably know Sergeant Thorndike."

A thread of concern tangled up Nate's spine. Thorndike had never mentioned knowing about Lieutenant Colonel Bennett's death. "Sir, you said the *daughters* had been in trouble, but you only mentioned the shoplifting incident. Had the younger sister been involved, as well?"

The colonel rubbed his hand over his jaw and thought for a moment. "A party down by the river as I recall. The Freemont police busted up the gathering and drove everyone home. Dan's younger daughter was part of the group so I was notified."

"Both girls had run-ins with the law shortly before their father's death?"

"That's why I told Mrs. Bennett they needed to know the truth about their father. Teens are totally absorbed in their own worlds. I feared the girls would think their father had taken his life because of what they had done. That's a lot of guilt for any young person to carry."

"Yes, sir. Regrettably, that guilt could follow them into adulthood." After thanking the colonel for his help, Nate returned to the fellowship hall.

The crowd had dispersed and only a few people remained. The women who had prepared the luncheon were cleaning up the serving table. Chaplain Grant stood nearby, fork in hand.

"Glad you finally had time to eat, sir." Nate noticed as assortment of desserts piled high on his plate.

"Not what the doctor ordered since I should be cutting calories, but I couldn't resist."

Glancing around the hall, Nate asked, "Have you seen Maggie?"

The chaplain pointed toward the hallway. "She was headed for the ladies' room about thirty minutes ago. I haven't seen her since."

With a hasty word of thanks, Nate hurried outside. The parking lot had emptied. Not a silver Saturn in sight.

His phone rang. He checked the caller ID as he pulled the cell to his ear. "Hey, Jamison. What's up?"

"A guy has been hanging around outside the post office in Garrett. The inspectors think it may be Lance Davis, who was the contact name for this P.O. on the list we found in Major Bennett's quarters. They're ready to close in. You need to get here ASAP."

"Is Sergeant Thorndike with you?"

"I expect him in the next ten minutes or so."

"Don't let him leave the area."

Nate double-timed to his car. He had some important questions to ask Thorndike about why he hadn't been forthright about the late Lieutenant Colonel Bennett's death. With any luck, the sergeant might provide more details about the initial suicide, which could have bearing on Major Bennett's death.

Pulling onto the main road that headed off post, Nate thought about calling Maggie, but the new information he had learned about her father needed to be revealed in person.

He and Maggie had more in common than he had ever realized. They both felt responsible for the loss of a loved one. Maggie had tried to help him move beyond the guilt he still carried because of Michael. Even if Nate couldn't clear his own conscience, he wanted to help Maggie get over her father's death. Bottom line, she wasn't to blame. But after sixteen years of feeling responsible, Maggie would need time to accept the truth about what had happened so long ago.

Chapter Fifteen

After changing into the orange sweater and jeans she had worn on the drive to Fort Rickman, Maggie packed her bag and threw it into the back of her Saturn. She wrote a note of thanks to Kelly and then headed out of the BOQ complex. Thoughts of her father rumbled through her mind. She needed something of his to hold on to, something that would remind her of the man she loved whether he had loved her or not.

The front entrance into the Hunter Housing Area was blocked by a utility truck parked in the middle of the road while a man worked on the streetlight. A detour sign routed her into the alley that ran behind the quarters. Maggie entered her sister's house through the back door and headed straight to the coffee table in the living room.

Just as Dani had done, Maggie would display the flag, which had draped their father's casket, and the shadow-box that contained his medals in her own home. If Graham would part with her sister's medals, Maggie would sit them alongside their father's awards. When people asked, she'd say Dani had followed in his footsteps and both had died while serving their country.

Maggie found a plastic bag in the kitchen pantry. After wrapping the chosen items in newsprint, she carefully placed them in the bag then stopped short when the garage door rumbled open.

Her heart pattered in her chest. "Nate?"

An MP stepped into the kitchen. She recognized him as Corporal Mills—the soldier who had no doubt searched her bag the night of Dani's death. "I saw your car and wondered what you were doing here, ma'am."

Before she could answer, the doorbell rang. "I'll get it." Maggie scurried into the foyer, wishing Nate would be waiting on the doorstep. Instead she saw a teenage boy, heavily tattooed with a silver stud in his left nostril.

"My stepmom said the mailman delivered this to the wrong address." The teen shoved a package into Maggie's hands before he ran back across the street. The address label had been written in Dani's hand.

A sense of relief and elation swept over Maggie. At long last, she had evidence that, hopefully, would prove her sister had been murdered.

Closing the door, Maggie turned, surprised to discover the MP blocking her way.

"I'll take that." He reached for the package.

"No, you won't." She clutched the box to her chest, knowing it contained the evidence her sister had mailed home. "Agent Nate Patterson has been waiting for this package. I'll take it to him before I leave post."

"That won't be necessary. From the looks of your car out back and the suitcase in the rear seat, you must be headed home to Alabama."

"But I've got time to stop by Nate's office." She attempted to step around the soldier, but he stopped her forward progression.

She squared her shoulders and glared up at him, hoping to mask her fear. "Is there a problem?" Her voice was firm and laced with more bravado than she felt.

"Now, ma'am, you wouldn't want to delay your trip." He grabbed the box and her hand at the same time.

She tried to jerk free of his hold. "What are you doing?"

"Making sure this box doesn't end up in the wrong place." She tried to scream, but he wrapped his arm around her neck, constricting her airway.

"You…can't…get…away with this," Maggie gasped, fighting to free herself.

"I can and I will."

"Agent Patterson…knows…I'm here."

"Sorry to inform you, ma'am, but the last time I saw him, he was headed off post." Easing up on her throat, he twisted her arm behind her back. "Which is exactly where we're going."

She sucked in a ragged breath. "The neighbors will see you."

He jerked harder on her arm. "In case you didn't notice, the quarters to the right are currently unoccupied, and the major who lives on the left is en route home from Afghanistan. If you think someone will see my car, it's parked in the garage so no one knows I'm even here."

The MP had an answer for everything.

"As soon as I get you taken care of, I'll move your Saturn into the garage and dispose of it later where no one will find it for days. Maybe weeks."

"Dani told me the military police couldn't be trusted."

"Yet it seems you trusted Mr. Patterson."

Maggie jerked at the mention of Nate's name. "Are you saying he's involved?"

Mills laughed. "Patterson's a straight arrow. He plays everything by the book."

"And you're the exact opposite. Whatever you're involved in is despicable. Dani knew something was going on. That's why you killed her."

He shoved Maggie through the kitchen and into the garage. She stumbled, nearly falling. Nearing the military sedan, he opened the trunk. "Climb in."

The thought of being locked in the confined space sent her heart crashing against her chest. "I...I can't."

He raised his hand. "You can and you will, lady." The MP struck her on the side of her skull. She staggered, trying to remain upright.

"Do you know what happens to people who disobey my orders? They end up dead, like the soldier in North Georgia who tried to keep a shipment meant for someone else." A second blow took her breath away. Darkness overshadowed her, and she tumbled forward. The trunk slammed shut, enclosing her like a coffin.

"Nate?" she called out before she floated into oblivion.

Nate's mood was at rock bottom when he drove back to post. Thorndike had been a no-show, and the guy hanging around the Garrett post office left the area before the Postal Inspectors could pick him up for questioning. Nate had hoped the point of contact would shed light on all those involved in the mail scheme and reveal exactly what the packages contained.

In Nate's opinion, drugs ranked at the top of the list of possibilities. Dogs randomly sniffed for illegal substances mailed back to the U.S, but the number of troops in Afghanistan and the high volume of shipments made the odds in favor of the smugglers.

If information had come to light that had bearing on Major Bennett's death being a homicide, Nate would have been able to go to Wilson and make the case for further investigation he now believed it warranted.

In spite of the lack of evidence, Nate needed to contact his boss and ask Wilson to disregard the request for transfer. Now that Maggie had come into his life, Nate wanted more time at Fort Rickman. Independence, Alabama, where she lived, wasn't that far away. He could make the trip in a couple hours.

Needing to hear her voice, he called Maggie's cell. When it went to voice mail, he disconnected and tried Kelly's BOQ landline, surprised when the special agent answered.

"What are you doing back on post?" he asked. "I thought you'd be in North Georgia for a few more days."

"My mother's in the hospital. Wilson told me to take as much time as I need so I'm packing some things before I leave for home."

"I'm sorry about your mom, Kelly."

"Thanks, Nate. She's had medical problems for a long time so it wasn't completely unexpected."

"Did you learn anything new concerning the soldier who died?"

"Only that he gave his girlfriend expensive jewelry. His latest gift had been a large emerald pendant."

"On an E-4's paycheck?"

"Exactly."

"Is Maggie around? I need to talk to her."

"She's gone, Nate, and so is her suitcase. She left a note thanking me for my hospitality."

Nate hung up and tried Maggie's cell once again. Unable to connect, he speed dialed Jamison. "Any word on Thorndike?"

"Negative."

"I'm headed to Hunter Housing Area. I want to talk to Kyle Foglio. Mills questioned the family after Major Bennett's death and learned nothing, yet I wonder if the young man may be holding something back."

"Let me know if you learn anything, Nate. I'll call you as soon as Thorndike contacts us."

"Haul him in for questioning. He was the first on the scene at Major Bennett's murder and at the BOQ after someone had broken in through the back door. He had glass in his boots, although Corporal Mills did, as well. But Thorndike made a point of making excuses for the shards that had dug into his soles. Plus he hovered close when Maggie had picked up a box delivered to Quarters 1448. If Thorndike planned to intercept the shipment, he may have thought Maggie's photo was whatever evidence Major Bennett mailed into the U.S."

"What photo?"

"It's a long story. Just find Thorndike."

Maggie's first indication she was still alive was the roar of raging water, followed by pain. Her head ached as if her skull had shattered into a thousand pieces. Moaning under her breath, she tried to remember what had happened, but her mind refused to focus on anything except the flashes of white lightning that zigzagged through her brain.

She moved slightly, causing her stomach to roil. Clamping down on her jaw, she tried to calm the internal storm that was assaulting her body, yet her head pounded even more.

A muffled voice filtered through her broken world. She blinked an eye open. A burst of light sent a volley of electric jolts across her temples, forcing her to retreat back into the darkness.

The voice grew louder, and the static of background noise subsided long enough for Maggie to make out bits and pieces of the one-sided conversation. Once again, she forced her eyes open. The MP stood with his back to Maggie, a cell phone at his ear.

"Roger that, sir." She blinked the digital patterned uniform into focus. "She's alive, but out cold. I'll return to post and get rid of her car before I get rid of her."

Maggie's stomach roiled once again. Another wave of vertigo pitched her into blackness, and she heard nothing except distant thunder and rushing water.

Nate parked in front of Quarters 1448 and crossed the street. He held up his identification when Mrs. Foglio opened the door to her quarters. "Mr. Patterson, CID, ma'am. I need to talk to your stepson."

Frustration flashed from her eyes. "Can't you leave him alone?"

"I'm sorry, ma'am, but this is important."

"That's what you people keep saying." She stepped back from the door, allowing Nate to enter the foyer. A television played in the rear of the house.

"Kyle, someone wants to talk to you."

The kid frowned as he lumbered down the hallway. "Yeah?"

Despite the boy's attitude, Nate noticed that he had removed two of the three studs in his nose, and when he spoke, his tongue was free of metal, as well. Maybe Lieutenant Colonel Foglio and his wife were having a positive influence after all.

"The night Major Bennett committed suicide, did you see anything outside?" Nate asked. "Anything that looked unusual?"

"He was sound asleep," Mrs. Foglio interjected before her stepson could answer. "I was out of town, visiting my sister that night, but my husband talked to the MP who questioned everyone on the block."

Nate held up his hand. "Please, ma'am, I need Kyle to answer."

"My husband said Kyle went to bed early and slept late, Mr. Patterson."

"Ma'am, please." Nate turned his attention to the boy. "Your bedroom is in the front of the house and looks onto the street. What did you see that night?"

Kyle glanced down at the floor then shrugged. "A cop car kept cruising the neighborhood. He probably wanted to make sure I wasn't getting into trouble."

"Were any cars parked near the house, either on the main road or in the alley behind the quarters?"

Kyle wiped the palms of his hands on his jeans. "I snuck out that night to meet a friend."

"Oh, no," the stepmother groaned.

"Go on." Nate held the young man's gaze. "Tell me what happened."

"I cut through the open field behind 1448 on the way home. That's when I saw the MP car parked in the alley."

Nate raised his brow. "The same car that had patrolled the neighborhood earlier?"

"I'm not sure, but the MP came out of Major Bennett's house and drove away."

"What time was that?"

"My girlfriend texted me right afterward." The teen pulled his cell from his pocket and punched a few buttons. "Twelve-forty."

"Did you see anyone else?"

"Yeah. A guy dressed in regular clothes left a little later and walked to a red Mustang. The streetlights were out, and it was pretty dark so I couldn't see his face. All I know is that he was a big guy, like my dad."

"Built?"

Kyle nodded. "Totally."

Nate's gut clenched. Graham Hughes.

"Have you seen either of those two men since then?"

"I think the MP was back today. I saw him after I gave the package to the lady."

Nate's gut tightened. "Which lady?"

"The postman delivered a box that was addressed to 1448," Mrs. Foglio volunteered. "I had Kyle take it across the street. He said Dani's sister answered the door."

"Did you see her leave the house, ma'am?"

"No. But Kyle saw an MP car pull out of the garage about ten minutes later."

Nate's heart exploded in his chest. "Do you still have the key to the quarters?"

Mrs. Foglio must have recognized the urgency in his voice. Without delay, she hurried into the kitchen and returned with the key.

Nate raced across the street and pulled his weapon as he entered the house. A rapid search of the downstairs revealed no changes from the last time he was there, except for the plastic bag, containing the wrapped flag and medals. Taking the stairs two at a time, he checked the bedrooms then threw open the attic door. Fear iced his veins, imagining what he might discover.

Slowly, he climbed the stairs, his eyes searching the rafters. Finding nothing, he let out a ragged breath and retraced his steps. Once in his car, he called Jamison and quickly filled him in on what the Foglio boy had said.

"Send in a team to sweep the quarters for prints. Send a *Be On the Lookout* notice to the Georgia and Alabama Highway Patrols for a silver Saturn and a red Mustang. The MPs should have both license plate numbers in their database."

"Roger that."

"Maggie was right. Graham Hughes came back to the house and parked his Mustang in the alley the night Major Bennett was killed. Thorndike may be involved. Haul both of them in. Search their homes. Search their offices. Go into their computers. Find any information you can that might determine what they've done with Maggie."

Chapter Sixteen

Jamison met Nate at the door to the CID Headquarters. "No one's seen Graham Hughes. We located the gal from the bar and grill. She said Graham planned to go down to the Gulf Coast for a few days."

"Can she call him on his cell?"

"He's not answering."

"Contact Florida law enforcement. Tell them to locate Graham and bring him back to Fort Rickman."

"Roger that, Nate. What about Wanda?"

"Pull her in. I want to talk to her, as well. Maybe she knows something about Maggie."

A jackhammer pounded in Maggie's head. She grimaced and shifted on the thin mattress where she lay. Glancing around the cabin, she spied a sink, stove and refrigerator in the far corner. Dani's package from Afghanistan sat on a small table nearby.

Licking her dry lips, she longed for a drink of water and an aspirin. Preferably two. She sniffed the damp air that smelled like a musty basement and wondered about the perpetual hum of running water. Attempting to roll to her side, she realized too late that her hands and legs were tied to the bedposts. She yanked at the restraints, but the plastic ties cut into her wrists and held her bound.

"God, please help me."

The rumble of a car engine sent a shiver of apprehension up her spine. She stared at the door, praying it would remain shut while thoughts of Dani and Kendra played through her mind. Had they been killed by the same MP who planned to "get rid of her" as soon as he returned from disposing of her car?

Fear clasped down on her gut and made her want to lash out at anything and anyone. She'd fight to the death, of that she was sure. Then she tried to raise her head and was overcome with a combination of vertigo and nausea.

No matter how strong she wanted to be, she'd been knocked unconscious and had probably suffered a concussion. Her body couldn't regroup to fight off anyone at this point, but at least she could put up a struggle.

Footsteps approached. The doorknob turned. Her pulse went into overdrive, and adrenaline pulsed through her veins, adding more pressure to her head that already threatened to explode.

Maggie closed her eyes, hoping to appear unconscious.

Footsteps scurried across the wooden floor and stopped at the bedside. A hand grabbed her shoulder. "Maggie?"

She recognized the voice.

Opening her eyes, she didn't know whether to scream or rejoice.

"Graham?"

* * *

Nate looked up as Jamison stuck his head through the door to his office. "Thorndike walked in on his own accord. We've got him in interrogation room one."

"Thank God." Nate raced out of his office.

Jamison caught up with him in the hallway. Placing his hand on Nate's arm, the agent cautioned, "Don't lose your cool."

As much as he wanted to pound information out of Thorndike, Jamison was right. Nate needed to stay in control. Rage would only compound the situation.

When he entered the interrogation room, Sergeant Thorndike jumped to his feet. "Sir, what's going on? I had car trouble on the way to Garrett. My cell was out of range so I had to hoof it to Pine City to get help."

"Sit down, Sergeant."

"Not until you tell me why you hauled me in today."

Nate put his knuckles on the table and leaned forward. "I said sit down."

Thorndike fisted his hands. Fire smoldered in his eyes, but he lowered his weighty body into the chair and continued to glare at Nate.

"You were the first on scene for Major Bennett's suicide, is that correct, Sergeant?"

"Yes, sir."

"What about sixteen years ago when Lieutenant Colonel Bennett took his own life? Do you remember being the first on scene that night, as well?"

Thorndike's face clouded. "You think I killed the major?"

"You tell me."

"I didn't do it, sir."

"You knew about her father's death, yet you didn't reveal that information?"

Thorndike hung his head. "Sir, I'll tell you the truth. I didn't make the connection between the two cases until a couple days ago when I was going through some of the awards I've received over the years. Found a picture of me with Colonel Rogers, the provost marshal at that time. I got to thinking about all the cases I'd been involved in and realized Daniel Bennett was the major's father. I was embarrassed about not telling anyone and figured I'd look like a fool coming forth with the information this late in the investigation. Plus I didn't see any reason it would have a bearing on the case. It's been sixteen years, sir."

"You were first on scene when Agent McQueen's BOQ was broken into, isn't that right, Sergeant?"

"Ah, yes, sir."

"The soles of your shoes were crusted with glass."

"Which I brought to your attention."

Thorndike had pulled a number of tours in Iraq but had never served in Afghanistan where the mail ring originated. Still, AmeriWorks, the company Graham Hughes worked for, had contracts in that country. Thorndike could be working with Graham, which would explain how the sergeant's "little woman" afforded to shop in all the high-end boutiques on her frequent trips to Atlanta.

After a volley of rapid-fire questions from Nate, Thorndike shrugged and averted his gaze. "Fact is, sir, my memory's been slipping this past year. Time for me to retire and head south. Get that house the little woman and I have been dreaming about."

Nate needed information, not some excuse about

old age. Before he could ask another question, a knock sounded and the door opened. Jamison motioned to Nate. "I need to see you." Letting out a pent-up lungful of air, Nate joined him in the hallway.

"According to Wanda, someone borrowed Graham Hughes's Mustang the night Major Bennett was killed. Wanda received a large sum of money in return for keeping Graham occupied inside the bar until she got an all clear. By that time, she had decided to take Graham home for the night."

"Did she provide a name?

"Her contact was Wally Turner."

"As in Wally's Pawn?"

"You got that right."

"Notify the FBI. They'll want to talk to Wally as well as a guy named LeShawn and one named Ronald Jones, who goes by Bubba. I mentioned them earlier." Nate hesitated before he asked, "What about Maggie?"

"Wanda doesn't know anything about her, but we'll keep pressing."

In Nate's opinion, that wasn't good enough.

Graham stared down at the restraints holding Maggie bound. His face wore a mix of anger and frustration. The same emotions she was feeling.

She tugged on the ties, trying once again to free herself. "I was right all along, wasn't I, Graham? You killed Dani, but no one believed me."

"No one believed you because it isn't true."

"Maybe you didn't hang her from the rafter, but you planned her death even if you had that military guy do the job."

Graham stepped into the kitchen area and opened one drawer after another. "What military guy?"

"The brute who knocked me out and shoved me into the trunk of his car."

Removing something from the last drawer, Graham returned to her bedside and leaned over Maggie. She could feel his breath on her cheek. Her pulse raced with fear.

"Do you still remember the night we were together down by the river?" he asked.

Her cheeks burned. As if she could forget what happened. When he raised his hand, she saw the butcher knife he held. She had to keep talking to distract him. "You were using me to get back at Dani."

"The truth was I was using Dani to get to you. I told you how I felt, but you never answered my letters. I wrote every week until I finally realized you didn't want anything to do with me." He touched his finger to the blade, checking its sharpness.

She shrunk back. "I…I never received any letters, Graham."

He lowered the knife.

Maggie's heart catapulted against her chest and she tried to backpedal in the bed, knowing in half a heartbeat the razor-sharp blade would cut through her flesh.

Nate needed information no one could provide. If only he could think clearly, but all that came to mind was that Maggie was in danger. When he closed his eyes, he saw her sister's lifeless body hanging from the rafters and Kendra's child, who no longer had a mother to love her. *Come on, Nate. Why can't you pull this case together?*

He opened his eyes to Wanda, who sat across the table from him, crying like a baby.

"Do you have any idea who Wally was working for or who was setting up Graham to be the fall guy by using his Mustang?" Nate asked.

Wanda shook her head. Her face was splotched, her eyes red and swollen. "I thought it was some type of a joke they were playing on him."

Yeah, right. "Is Wally a regular at the bar and grill?"

She blew her nose into a tissue. "He comes in about once a week."

"Who does he talk to?"

"No one. He's a loner." She paused and then held up her hand. "But there's another guy who stops by every so often. Funny last name. Seems to me I saw him with Wally about a month ago."

Nate needed an ID. "What's the guy look like?"

"Kind of nondescript. He's a big guy but not too smart."

"But his last name's unusual?"

"Starts with a *Z*."

An alert siren went off in Nate's head. "Zart?"

"That's it."

Jamison dashed into the room followed by Corporal Raynard Otis. "One of the choppers from the 5th Aviation Detachment just landed. On the way back to post, they spied something from the air."

Nate followed the two agents into the hallway and listened as Jamison filled him in. "Otis got word they spotted a red Mustang heading south along the River Road."

"Where's that road lead?"

The corporal held up a map. "Eventually to Florida. The river narrows around the bend. There's a rise on the other side where a few fishermen have cabins. The only way across are two somewhat makeshift bridges. The closest is an old, rickety wooden structure. The distant bridge is a bit more stable."

Nate put his hand on Jamison's shoulder. "Contact the Freemont police and State Highway Patrol for help. Tell them that we're looking for Arnold Zart. Call Florida and have them stand by in case he heads that far south."

"What about Graham?" Jamison asked.

"I'm not sure. Zart's got to be involved. He flies in and out of Afghanistan on a regular basis. Easy enough to set up a mail ring while he's in that country, but in my opinion, he's not smart enough to coordinate the whole operation. His desk sits next to Graham's in the contracting office on post so he had access to Graham's keys and could have made a spare for both his quarters on post and his car."

Jamison pulled out his phone. "I'll start contacting the civilian law enforcement agencies."

Nate motioned to the corporal. "Come with me."

With Otis in pursuit, Nate raced to interrogation room one and threw open the door, startling Thorndike. "You fish with a few guys on post. Did Arnold Zart ever join you?"

The sergeant nodded. "A couple of times."

"Didn't you tell me about a cabin south of post on the opposite side of the river? I need to know how to get there."

Thorndike gave him directions. On his way out the door, Nate yelled at Otis over his shoulder. "Tell Jamison to dispatch a unit to the cabin. Then contact 5th Aviation and tell them to scout out the area from the air."

"Sir, a storm's coming in. All aircraft are grounded."

Nate needed help. "Come on, God. Give me a break."

"Sir?"

"Tell Jamison to use the southern route to the cabin. I'll cross the river at the more northern access."

"But, sir, we got word the water's cresting the bridge. You'll be washed downstream."

"Then pray I can swim, Corporal."

"Yes, sir."

Chapter Seventeen

"Someone kept my letters from you, Maggie. Either your mother or Dani."

Confused by what Graham had just said, Maggie watched him cut the ties and free her hands and feet. Grabbing her shoulder, he pulled her up to a sitting position. The room swirled around her. She moaned, overcome with another swell of nausea.

"Are you okay?"

She rubbed her wrists. "Give me a second." The room stabilized, but her thoughts remained jumbled.

Graham had written her?

"You thought I was using you because I'd used other girls. But you were different, Maggie."

"I was just another conquest for you, Graham." She shook her head at her own naïveté. "And to think what almost happened that night."

He let out a ragged breath. "If you hadn't stopped me, we would have had even more to regret."

She looked up, startled. "I...I stopped you? I always thought it was the other way around."

"You said you couldn't do that to Dani. Plus you were a nice girl. That's why I fell for you."

Bile soured Maggie's stomach at the memory of what she had done. "Nice girls don't go into the woods with their sister's boyfriend. You may have used me, Graham, but I used you to get back at Dani."

Maggie thought of the hateful words Dani had hurled at her, words that cut her to the quick about how their father didn't love her, how Maggie was ugly and timid and she would never have anyone who really cared about her.

If only she had endured Dani's outrage in silence, like she had the other times. Instead she had gone to the party by the river and flaunted herself at Graham. Then she'd followed him into the nearby woods when the other kids weren't watching. The cops eventually closed down the party and took the teens home to their parents. Late that night, Maggie told Dani everything—except that the "other" girl had been Maggie.

Dani hadn't known how to react to Graham's rejection. Their father had been tied up with his own problems and was even more distant than usual. Looking back, Maggie realized Dani had shoplifted in hopes of getting their father's attention. The commanding general called their dad into his office, and the next thing they knew, he'd been relieved of his duties. The following night, their mother found him in the attic.

"My…my mother kept saying over and over again that all the problems had started with me." The shame of what Maggie had done swept over her, filling her with anguish. "When Dani and I met for lunch in Alabama I wanted to tell her the truth and ask her forgiveness."

"She knew."

Tears stung Maggie's eyes. "But she never said anything."

"Dani forgave you long ago, but she didn't know how to ask you to forgive her."

A lump filled Maggie's throat. Graham wrapped his arm around her shoulders and pulled Maggie to her feet. "We need to get out of here. My car's outside."

Steeling herself, she swiped her hand over her cheek and sniffed. "The box." She pointed to where it sat on the table. "Nate needs the evidence."

Grabbing the package with one hand, Graham held her up with the other. With his help, she stumbled forward. He pushed the door open, and she followed him outside, chilled by the wind that gusted through the trees and the light mist that had continued to fall.

"Just a little farther, Maggie."

"How…how did you find me?"

"I knew Dani wouldn't have taken her own life. Someone made her death mirror your father's. There was only one person I had ever confided in about his suicide. Shortly before Dani redeployed home, he came over one night with a bottle of red wine in hand. The alcohol and his leading questions loosened my tongue. We had been together socially a number of times. He seemed like a nice guy, or so I thought. But before long, I had revealed everything. Today when I stopped by the house to pick up some things, I saw your dad's medals and flag in the plastic bag. I knew you wouldn't leave them behind. Then it was just a matter of putting together some of the things I had overheard at work and determining where he had taken you."

"He?"

"The person who masterminded this entire operation that Dani must have stumbled onto in Afghanistan. I realized he had to have been the one who killed her. I just didn't know why. When I went back to the office and checked the AmeriWorks records, everything made sense."

Tires screeched in the distance, causing them both to look toward the road. Graham nudged her forward. "Hurry."

Reaching his Mustang, Maggie leaned against the rear door. Graham dug for the keys in his pocket.

Before he could open the door, a silver Saturn— Maggie's silver Saturn—pulled into the clearing and braked to a stop. The MP who had been on the cell earlier crawled from the passenger side. A second man sat behind the wheel, but his face was hidden by the tinted windows.

Mills pulled his weapon.

Graham pushed Maggie to the ground and gunfire exploded around them. Something warm and wet spread across her back as Graham's full weight fell momentarily upon her shoulders. The package from Afghanistan had taken a hit and shattered into scraps of shredded cardboard and broken earthenware.

Struggling to rise, Maggie put one hand on the car door and reached for Graham with the other. As if in slow motion, his hand slipped out of her grasp. When she looked down, all she could see was the gaping hole in his chest and the precious gems scattered around his body from the broken package.

Another burst of gunfire caused her to turn. The MP fell across the hood of her car, and the driver lay slumped over the wheel.

Whimpering, she watched the shooter step into the

clearing. He aimed a gun straight at her heart. "You and I need to take a little walk down to the river."

Nate headed south out of post along the narrow, two-lane road that wound through the countryside. Usually the trip was relaxing, but today, with the steady stream of rain and the strong wind adding to his worry over Maggie, conditions were less than ideal. As far as Nate knew only a handful of folks lived on this side of post, and many of them had evacuated the area due to the rising water.

Common sense told him to bypass the first bridge and head for the more stable southern access, but he went with his gut instinct that kept screaming Maggie was in danger and he needed to find her fast. Besides, if Zart had made it to the other side, Nate would, as well.

An isolated fishing cabin would be the ideal spot to hold her hostage. Nate shook his head and groaned. He should have listened to Maggie. She'd been convinced her sister had been murdered, but Nate had been too focused on evidence that never materialized.

Eight months ago, he had made a mistake by allowing his brother to sway his opinion, which had cost Michael his life. Nate had become too cautious so he'd closed his mind to what Maggie offered as a logical explanation.

The rain intensified, making it difficult to see the road. Nate clamped his hands around the steering wheel—white-knuckled, struggling against the powerful wind that threatened to push the car off the narrow roadway.

The bridge appeared in the distance. Corporal Otis had been right about the rickety structure. The crossing had been constructed years ago without side guardrails. If only the aged wood could withstand the pressure from the driving water long enough for Nate to make it to the other side.

A momentary lull in the storm cleared his view. He spied the cabin huddled close to the water's edge. A blur of metallic red was visible through the underbrush.

Graham's Mustang.

Nate picked up his cell phone and pushed the speed dial for Jamison. "I'm approaching the bridge. Water's spilling over the sides, but it looks navigable. I've got a visual on the red Mustang parked in the underbrush near the cabin. I'm moving in."

"The bridge from the south is washed out, Nate. We won't be able to get to you."

"What about from the air?"

"Not in this storm."

"Then I'll have to handle this one on my own."

When Jamison failed to respond, Nate glanced at his cell. *Call Disconnected.* No bars. No reception. He threw his phone on the passenger seat, knowing he couldn't rely on anyone else for help.

Anyone except the Lord.

Pulling in a ragged breath, he gripped the steering wheel even harder. "I don't deserve Your help, God, but Maggie does. Let's work together to save her."

The bridge lay ahead. Water washed over the wooden planks. Nate shifted into low gear and eased the car onto the bridge, keeping an even pressure on the accelerator. If the engine died, he'd have to risk hoofing it to the other side. Feeling the pull of the water, Nate knew he'd be sucked into the river and washed downstream.

"Stay with me, Lord," he muttered. Without railings, he could be headed off the bridge and straight into the swirling mass of water. Once the wheels gripped pavement on the far side, he let out a sigh of relief. Maybe God was listening after all.

Increasing his speed, Nate approached the cabin and parked in the underbrush, knowing surprise would be an advantage. He pulled his weapon from his holster, grateful for the sound of the rushing water and the rumble of thunder that muffled his footsteps. Two cars sat in the clearing. Rounding the Mustang, his heart leaped to his throat.

Graham lay on the ground, the broken shards of earthenware and the remains of a shipment box still in his hand. His gut hung open, and blood, mixed with rainwater, pooled around his ashen body. The mail ring hadn't been about drugs, but precious gems like the stones scattered in the debris.

Maggie's Saturn was parked nearby. A second victim lay slumped over the hood. Blood oozed from the back of his head. Nate turned the body over and groaned. Corporal Mills stared back at him with a bullet hole between his eyes.

Flicking his gaze around the clearing, Nate stepped to the driver's side, keeping his gun raised and his senses on high alert. He opened the door and, using his free hand, lifted the third victim's shoulder until he could make an ID. Arnold Zart.

Nate's neck prickled. A noise made him turn. Footsteps broke through the underbrush along a path that led to the water's edge.

Knowing Kendra's body had been pulled from the river, Nate's gut constricted. *Oh, dear, God, no. Not Maggie.*

Chapter Eighteen

Lieutenant Colonel Foglio stepped into the clearing. Nate saw a flash of steel and heard the bullet fire immediately after he got off the first round.

Hot, searing pain cut through his left upper arm. Nate gasped, firing another round that caught Foglio in the chest. He crumbled onto one knee.

Racing forward, Nate grabbed Foglio's lapels and raised him off the ground. "What have you done with her?"

The officer shook his head. "She's gone."

Nate shook him again. "Tell me."

"The water. The last I saw she was headed downstream." He tried to laugh, but choked on the blood that gurgled in his throat.

Nate threw him down on the ground and kicked his gun into the underbrush. Foglio might survive, but he wouldn't leave the area on his own accord.

Determined to find Maggie, Nate ran along the path. The bushes pulled at his clothes. He shrugged out of his jacket and dropped his gun on the ground near the water's edge. Toeing out of his shoes, he scanned the wide expanse of river. A sea of dark, churning water raced south. Running in the direction of the flow, Nate searched for any sign of her.

"Maggie," he screamed, knowing she'd never hear him over the river's fury.

A huge pine tree, uprooted by the rain, lay half submerged in the water. Its branches had formed a makeshift dam.

A splash of orange caught his eye.

Maggie!

Nate dove into the river. The cold took his breath away. He came up gasping for air, unable to orient himself. Finally he saw her hung up in the downed foliage.

The current propelled him forward. He neared the pine and grabbed one of the branches that broke before he could establish a firm hold. Kicking with all his might, Nate steered his body closer to where the current had entwined her among the boughs. Her eyes were closed, but her head was above water.

"Maggie," he screamed again.

Her eyes opened. She flailed. The motion caused the pine to shift. Nate caught her just as the tree groaned and released her from its hold. He pulled her close and encircled her with his good arm.

"Feetfirst," he screamed, turning her so her face would be protected from any obstacle floating in the water.

His fingers tightened on her shoulder. *God, don't let me lose her now.*

Lightning illuminated the darkening sky, and thunder cracked overhead. If the river didn't kill them, the storm could.

"Keep your legs up, Maggie. Watch out for rocks and floating debris."

The water sped them along like a kayak on rapids. Waves broke over them, spewing brown water, thick with mud, into their eyes and mouth. Maggie coughed, once again flailing. The motion turned them about-face and prevented Nate from seeing what lay ahead. He kicked his legs, grateful when they reversed position.

Growing intensely fatigued, Nate lifted his left arm out of the water. His raw flesh oozed red. He hadn't realized how much blood he was losing. Continuing at the present rate would be his undoing.

Please, God.

Up ahead, a portion of a boat dock had broken free and was jammed between two boulders, forming an oasis in the middle of the swirling river.

"Aim for the platform." Nate kicked and forced Maggie forward. She grabbed the edge of the wooden barrier and held on tight. Her face was too pale, and she shivered in the frigid water. She wouldn't last much longer. Land was too far away, and the current too strong for them to swim to shore.

Nate encircled Maggie with his arms, hoping his body heat would warm her. If only she could crawl onto the dock. "Honey, try to shimmy up onto the wood."

Maggie struggled to raise herself, and with Nate's help, she eventually collapsed onto the platform, gasping for air.

"Now you, Nate." She reached for his hand.

"I...I'm okay in the water." He could barely hold on to the side of the dock. His feet were being yanked under by the current, and he no longer had the energy to withstand the strong pull.

So many things swirled through his head that he wanted to tell her about her dad and how she wasn't to blame for his death. Hopefully, Colonel Rogers would reveal all that if she ever made it to safety.

Then he mentally corrected himself. *When* she made it to safety. *Please, Lord, make it happen.*

Nate's face was white as death and blood seeped from the wound on his shoulder. Maggie tried to pull him onto the platform, but she lacked the strength to do so, and he was too exhausted to help.

"You…you were right, Maggie, about your sister's death. I should have listened to you from the beginning."

"Shh, Nate." She put her finger to his lips. "Don't waste your energy. It doesn't matter now. At least I know Dani didn't take her own life."

"You're…you're not to blame for your father's death, either." Nate's eyes closed.

She grabbed his good shoulder. "Help will be here soon. Don't leave me, Nate."

The frigid temperature and loss of blood were sapping the life from him. She lowered herself into the water and cradled him in her arms.

"God brought us together for a reason. I'm not going to let you go." But as the sun began to set over the horizon and the temperature dipped even lower, Maggie began to fear that neither she nor Nate would live to see the dawn of a new day.

Chapter Nineteen

Maggie had to remain strong. Nate was depending on her. The rain subsided, and the clouds parted bringing the last rays of the evening sun to shine down on them as if the Lord were touching them with His light.

Maggie turned her face toward the sky, hoping to feel warmth from the setting sun. She didn't feel anything except the cold wind, but she heard a sound that stirred her heart.

Searching the sky, she saw a tiny pinpoint of black in the distance. The spot grew closer and brought with it the *whomp, whomp, whomp* of a helicopter flying overhead.

"Nate!" She shook him and pointed to the heavens. "Look. They found us."

Despite the hypothermia that had settled over him, he smiled. Maggie waved her arm in the air. She felt a surge of elation when the chopper hovered above the water and dropped a harness down to them.

Nate grabbed for the straps. "Fasten…these…around you," he said through tight lips.

Once the harness was securely around her chest,

Maggie reached out for him. "Hold on to me, Nate. We'll go up together."

"You'll...you'll never make it with me hanging on." He raised his hand, signaling the crew in the craft. The harness started to rise, taking her from him.

"No," she screamed. Nate wouldn't survive long enough for the crew to lower the harness again. "Grab my hand. We'll do this together."

"I...I can't."

"You saved me, Nate. Now let me save you."

She opened her arms.

He reached for Maggie, and she pulled him close. He straddled the harness with her in it, and together they were lifted into the air.

The crew pulled them into the chopper. Maggie collapsed onto the floor of the craft next to Nate. She reached for his cold hand and entwined her fingers through his.

"We made it, Nate." Looking into his lifeless eyes, Maggie realized the truth. They may have made it to safety, but it might not be in time for Nate.

Maggie left her hospital room, in spite of the doctor's orders to remain in bed. She had to see for herself.

A team of specialists had been waiting when the chopper landed at the military hospital on post. Nate's condition had been touch and go throughout the night. While in the O.R., he had received four units of blood, and although the wound on his shoulder had been stitched up, infection was the biggest concern. Round-the-clock IV antibiotics were working to stave off the virulent organisms that had spiked his temperature and threatened to shut down his major organs. Although Nate still wasn't in the clear, the last report had been more favorable.

Maggie was taking oral antibiotics and had been watched closely after a CAT scan revealed a severe concussion. Her vital signs were good, but not good enough to be walking around the hospital.

Finding Nate's room, she pushed through the door and stepped to his bedside. A wave of anxiety passed through her when she gazed down at his ashen face. Unable to keep her hands to herself, she reached out and touched his cheek, surprised to see his eyes flutter open.

"Maggie."

She smiled, feeling her heart swell with emotion.

"How...are...you?" he asked through cracked lips.

"Fine, now that I'm with you." Her eyes clouded as she thought of what could have happened. "For a moment there, I didn't think you wanted to go with me into the chopper."

His lips curled into a weak smile. "That was hypothermia talking."

A knock sounded at the door. Maggie turned in time to see Jamison and Chief Wilson step into the room. "The nurse told us you were both doing better," the chief said as the two men moved to the bed and smiled down at Nate. "Proves a good CID agent can withstand just about anything, even a raging river."

"The doctors weren't very optimistic when they brought him in last night," Maggie reminded them. Both men had been there when the helicopter had touched down and had stayed until morning.

The chief's upbeat expression sobered. "We were all worried about you, Nate. You went above and beyond on this one."

"Thank you, sir."

"I'm sure you're interested in what happened," the chief continued. "Foglio confessed to murdering Major Bennett."

"With Corporal Mills's help," Jamison added.

"Did you find out what happened in Afghanistan?" Maggie asked.

"Seems the driver killed in the IED explosion suspected his roommate was involved in a mail ring," Jamison said. "He took one of the earthenware figurines to your sister, Maggie, and asked her what he should do. She convinced him to go to Captain York, the company commander, with the information, and since she wasn't sure who was involved on that end, she mailed the evidence back to the U.S."

The chief nodded. "The roommate must have realized they were on to him. CID in Afghanistan called and told us he confessed to setting the IED that killed the company commander and the soldier."

"And the guys from the pawnshop?" Nate asked, his voice somewhat stronger.

"They've been arrested," Jamison said. "Evidently Graham pawned a gun some time ago that Foglio planned to use on Major Bennett if the copycat suicide didn't work. He borrowed Graham's Mustang, knowing if murder was suspected and if anyone saw the car the night of Major Bennett's death, they'd pin the crime on Graham."

"Then he used the gun on Corporal Mills and Arnold Zart," Nate added.

"Exactly." Jamison nodded. "In his twisted mind, Lieutenant Colonel Foglio thought Graham would be charged with their deaths while he walked away without anyone suspecting his involvement."

Maggie sighed. "I'm just relieved it's over."

The chief glanced at his watch. "We need to get back to the office, but I'll pass on the good news that you're doing better." The men headed for the door and then the chief stopped short. "Oh, I almost forgot. I tore up your paperwork for transfer, Nate."

With a broad smile and a final wave, the chief left the room. Jamison gave his friend a thumbs-up before he followed Wilson out the door.

Maggie turned back to Nate, almost afraid to ask. "Paperwork?"

He squeezed her hand. "I had wanted to go back to Afghanistan before I met you, Maggie. But all that has changed."

"So you're not going to be deployed?"

"I'm staying at Fort Rickman." A smile pulled at the corners of his cracked lips. "Although I plan on spending a lot of time in Alabama."

Her heart skipped a beat. "Sounds like a great idea to me."

He lowered his gaze for a moment. When he looked up at her, his face was serious. "I heard the family counseling office on post has a vacancy."

She didn't need to think about her answer. "Now that's an opportunity I wouldn't want to pass up."

Nate's eyes twinkled. "I was hoping you'd say that."

Knowing there was more information he needed to hear, Maggie said, "Colonel Rogers paid me a visit this morning and told me the truth about my dad. Now I know what you were trying to explain while we were in the water. Dani wasn't to blame for our father's death. Neither was I."

She paused before adding, "For a long time as a kid, I was jealous of my sister. She seemed to have everything I wanted—a group of friends and a guy who liked her and, on rare occasions, even attention from my dad. I told myself none of that was important to me, but of course, it was. I made a number of mistakes, trying to have what was hers, never realizing love comes to different people in different ways and at different times."

Nate rubbed his fingers over Maggie's hand. "When I was in the recovery room, I asked the Lord to forgive any mistake of mine that had bearing on Michael's death."

"I'm so glad, Nate."

"This morning, I called my parents. My mom started crying when she heard I was in the hospital. She said she knew I wasn't to blame. I didn't know if my father would be as forgiving."

Nate licked his lips before he continued. "My dad…" He hesitated a long moment. "My dad said he was proud of me."

"What's that tell you?" Maggie asked.

"That I don't have to run away from the past."

She leaned over him and took pleasure in seeing the spark of interest light up his eyes. "Not only are you an excellent CID agent, Nate Patterson, but you're also a fast learner." She smiled playfully. "Guess what?"

His lips twitched into a smile. "I don't know, what?"

"I'm proud of you, too." Then Maggie did what she had wanted to do for a very long time. She lowered her lips to his. Despite the IV, he wrapped his good arm around her waist and drew her close. Her last thought as she sank into his embrace was that she would have waited a lifetime to find Nate.

Epilogue

Nate pulled his car to the curb. Rounding to the passenger side, he opened the door for Maggie. She stepped to the sidewalk and looked at the one-story brick quarters. A bed of flowers edged the porch—bright red geraniums and white begonias interspersed with bushes of blue hydrangeas.

Maggie nodded her approval. "Nice curb appeal."

"It's not Hunter Housing Area, but we can move in as soon as we get back from our honeymoon."

She squeezed his hand. "It's a wonderful house, Nate, and it's ours."

He wrapped his arm around her waist. "Until Uncle Sam moves me to a new assignment."

"The counseling service on post said they'd transfer me to your next duty station when you get orders."

"They don't want to lose someone as empathetic as you."

"You're biased."

He nuzzled her cheek, making her laugh. "You bet I am."

Wrapping his arm around her, they walked toward their new quarters. "How's Kyle Foglio doing?"

"He still refuses counseling, but he and his stepmom are talking and that's important. I told Kyle he wasn't to blame for his father's actions."

"Did he believe you?"

"I don't think so. He's leaving in a few days to spend the rest of the summer with his mom."

"And Mrs. Foglio?"

"She's adjusting to civilian life, although she doesn't talk about her husband. Maybe with time, she'll be more forthcoming."

"Must be hard to live for years with someone and not really know them."

Maggie nodded. "I'm beginning to believe all families have secrets. Some are more painful than others."

Nate slipped the key into the lock and pushed the door open. "This time we walk in together." He winked. "Next time, I carry you."

Stepping into the cool interior, he closed the door and took her in his arms. Without a doubt, Maggie was the best thing that had ever happened to him. "Every night before I go to sleep I thank God for bringing you into my life."

Her eyes filled with tears of joy, and laughter bubbled from her throat. "Then He's getting two thank-yous, because I do the same thing."

"Two peas in a pod, eh? Maybe we need to make this permanent."

She gently slapped his shoulder. Although his wound had healed, he still had residual pain. "In exactly two weeks and three days, it will be permanent."

"Hard to believe, isn't it?" He felt his gut tighten, this

time not with fear or anxiety, but with overwhelming love for Maggie. Pure, wondrous love that was warm as the summer sunshine and better than anything he'd ever known.

"I love you, Maggie."

"Oh, Nate, I love you so much."

"Promise…" He hesitated, soaking in the feel of her in his arms. "Promise you'll love me forever?"

"Longer than forever." As he lowered his lips to hers, he thought of the journey they had traveled. Both of them had carried heavy burdens from the past that, at the time, had seemed insurmountable. Now, holding the woman he loved more than anything, Nate vowed to enjoy this moment and every moment God gave them, knowing the Lord had a wonderful future planned for their lifetime together.

* * * * *

THE SOLDIER'S SISTER

Glorify the Lord with me;
let us exalt his name together.
I sought the Lord, and he answered me;
he delivered me from all my fears.
—*Psalm* 34:3–4

Heartfelt thanks to
Ann Yingling,
AW2 Advocate,
Atlanta Metropolitan Area and North Georgia,
and
Nancy Carlisle,
AW2 Advocate,
Fort Benning, Georgia,
for providing invaluable information about the
Army Wounded Warrior Program.

With gratitude to
LTC Stony Lohr, US Army Retired,
for his help with the
Military Investigations series.

Chapter One

The gathering dark clouds had mirrored Stephanie Upton's mood since she'd returned home to Freemont, Georgia, two days earlier. Grateful as she was to get the job as the Army Wounded Warrior advocate at nearby Fort Rickman where her brother Ted was convalescing from his war injuries, she was frustrated that he had refused to see her or answer her phone calls.

So much for a happy homecoming.

The August storm hit just as she left town, heading back to post. She leaned forward in the driver's seat, wishing she'd replaced the old windshield wipers that failed to clear the heavy downpour. Squinting, she could barely make out the yellow dividing line on the road.

A small strip mall appeared in the distance. She turned her Corolla into the parking lot to wait out the deluge and reached for her cell phone. Glancing at her client file on the passenger seat, she tapped in the number for Private First Class Joshua Webb and smiled, remembering her younger brother's high school friend.

"Joshua, this is Stephanie Upton, Ted's sister," she said when the call went to voice mail. "I'm back in town

and took the position at Fort Rickman as the AW2—
Army Wounded Warrior—advocate. I know this is short
notice, but you're on my caseload. Since we need to
schedule an appointment, I thought I'd stop by now while
I'm the neighborhood and see how you're doing."

She glanced at her watch. "I'm about ten minutes
from your house. As soon as the rain lets up, I'll head
your way. Looking forward to seeing you soon."

Joshua and Ted had served in the same unit in Afghanistan and both had been injured by an IED. Josh
had lost his legs, while her brother had sustained burns
on his stomach and lower extremities. The two friends
had been medically evacuated to hospitals in the United
States and finally sent back to Fort Rickman.

Eventually, Josh would learn to walk with prosthetic
legs, but for now he was wheelchair bound, which was
probably the reason he hadn't answered her call. Hopefully, he would retrieve the message before she arrived
on his doorstep.

Three years ago and just a few weeks after both
guys had graduated from high school, Stephanie had
left Freemont, never expecting to return. At least not so
soon. Over time her feelings had mellowed and eventually taken a backseat to helping her brother through his
current recuperation.

Ted had been headstrong and difficult to handle in
his teen years. She had hoped his stint in the military
would be a positive influence. Although she didn't need
an abundance of brotherly love, she had expected civility
and a glimmer of hope that with time they could eventually heal the past.

The one bright note was the warm and enthusiastic welcome from the folks with whom she would be

working at Fort Rickman. Stephanie had held a similar position as the advocate for wounded soldiers at Fort Stewart, a three-hour drive east, and was well aware of the importance of making initial contact with the military personnel on her caseload.

She had visited two soldiers in Freemont this morning and had planned to stop by Josh's house on her way back to Fort Rickman. Seeing Ted's old friend would be an opportunity to catch up on Josh's plans for the future. As a teen, he had always been optimistic and upbeat. In spite of his recent injury, she hoped he retained the zest for life that had endeared him to her as a kid.

As soon as the rain eased, she pulled back onto Freemont Road and headed south. Ten minutes later, she saw the sign for Josh's subdivision.

She put on her signal, and just before she made the turn, a pickup truck perched on oversize tires screeched around the corner, its rear end fishtailing on the slick pavement.

The truck flew past—narrowly missing her car—in a blur of red paint and steel chrome. Muddy water, kicked up from the big, knobby tires, shot through the air, streaking Georgia clay across her windshield.

She laid on the horn and glanced in the rearview mirror as the truck crested a rise in the road and then disappeared from sight.

Her heart pounded like a reverberating snare drum, its cadence keeping time with the tension that throbbed across her forehead as she realized how close she'd come to a collision. Pulling in a number of cleansing breaths, she turned into the Cypress Springs subdivision, determined to focus on her visit with Joshua instead of the runaway truck.

Although the rain had stopped, the sky remained dismal and gray. She swerved around a scattering of leaves and twigs that littered the roadway and parked in front of the last house on the end of one of the side streets, a modest ranch Joshua was renovating to be wheelchair accessible.

Curb appeal and a low price tag made the neighborhood of new homes a great buy for a returning soldier starting over. As Josh's advocate, she should have felt a surge of elation that he was focusing on his transition to civilian life, but all Stephanie could think about was her own close call and her rapid pulse that failed to calm.

Grabbing her purse, she stepped onto the sidewalk, closing the car door behind her. A gust of humid air tugged at her skirt as she headed toward the house, her heels clipping along the sidewalk. She pulled her damp hair back from her face and climbed the ramp to the tiny front stoop.

The enthusiastic voice of a sports announcer sounded from inside the house. The full-blast volume of the radio drowned out her knocks on the door.

When Joshua failed to answer, she tried the knob. Locked. Surely he hadn't left the house with the radio blaring.

"Josh?"

Determined to be heard, she pounded on the door again and again, to no avail. Finally, letting out a frustrated breath, she headed around the corner to the kitchen entrance, where a second sheet of plywood served as a wheelchair ramp.

The sound of the ball game spewed through the back door that hung open, sending another round of concern tangling along her spine. Flicking her gaze over the backyard, she searched for some sign of the injured soldier.

"It's Stephanie Upton," she called, aware of the nervous tremble in her voice as she stepped inside. "Can you hear me, Josh?"

The smell of fresh paint and new carpet greeted her, along with the announcer's voice echoing through the empty rooms.

She paused in the middle of the kitchen, straining to hear something, anything other than the backdrop of cheering baseball fans.

Running water?

She raised her brow. "Joshua?"

A flutter of new fear flowed over her. The hair on her arms prickled as she peered into the living-dining combination straight ahead.

"Braves six, Astros two."

"Josh?"

Turning left, she entered the hallway that led to the rear of the house.

"It's the top of the fifth with Atlanta in the lead."

Her neck tingled. A double amputee bound to a wheelchair brought to mind all sorts of scenarios.

Hopefully, he wasn't hurt.

The announcer's voice sounded over the rush of water. Glancing into the bathroom on the right, she gasped. Her hand flew to her throat.

Joshua lay on the floor fully clothed, his body crumpled next to an overturned wheelchair and surrounded by sharp shards of a broken vanity mirror. Blood pooled under his left arm. The cloying smell filled the tiny room.

Water gushed from the spigot into the rapidly filling

tub. Aware that someone else could be in the house, yet terrified for Joshua's well-being, she turned off the faucet and dropped to her knees beside the soldier. His face was pale as death, his eyes glassed over. She searched for the artery in his neck and groaned with relief when she found a faint but steady pulse.

"Josh, can you hear me?" Stephanie raised the sleeve of his blood-soaked shirt and almost heaved. Rich, red blood pulsed from the deep gash on his upper arm.

Frantic, she dug in her purse for her cell phone and hit the programmed nine-one-one.

"State your emergency." The operator's monotone drawl was barely audible over the sports announcer's booming voice.

Balancing the phone between her shoulder and ear, Stephanie groped her hand along the bathroom vanity, found the docked iPod and turned off the game.

"There's been an accident." Stretching, she grabbed a towel from the overhead rack and jammed the thick terry against the open wound. "A man's been cut by glass. He's bleeding and needs medical attention. Tell the EMTs to hurry."

"What's your address?"

"One-forty-something Cedar Springs Drive. Third house on the right."

"I need the house number, ma'am. Could you check outside?"

Josh's breathing was shallow. His partially opened eyes appeared dull and lifeless. She wanted to scream at the woman on the other end of the line who failed to recognize the severity of the situation.

"Operator, I'm trying to keep this man from bleeding to death. I can't leave him. Get an ambulance and get it here fast."

She clicked off and speed dialed Joshua's unit at Fort Rickman. A deep male voice answered on the second ring.

"WTB."

"Major Jenkins?"

"No, ma'am. This is Special Agent Brody Goodman with the Criminal Investigation Division on post."

Her eyes widened. "I dialed the CID?"

"You dialed one of the units on post, namely the Warrior Transitional Battalion. Major Jenkins is out of the office at the moment and asked me to catch the phone. May I take a message or have the major call you back?"

"Tell him Stephanie Upton phoned. I'm the new AW2 advocate." Her breath hitched. "One of the men on my caseload—Private First Class Joshua Webb—fell from his wheelchair and cut his arm. He's lost a significant amount of blood. An ambulance is on the way."

"Give me the address."

Once again, she relayed directions to the small house.

"Major Jenkins just stepped back into the office. I'll fill him in on the emergency. Hold tight, ma'am. We're heading your way and should be there shortly."

Stephanie didn't know Brody Goodman with the calm voice and take-charge attitude. Nor had she previously dealt with anyone in the CID. Usually they handled serious crimes on post. Perhaps Special Agent Goodman and Major Jenkins were friends or working together on a special project. She had only yesterday met the executive officer for the Warrior Transitional Battalion, but she felt a sense of relief that the two men would soon be en route.

"Josh." Her brother's voice sounded from the front of the house.

Glad for help, she called, "He's in the bathroom, Ted."

"Someone's there with you?" the CID agent asked.

"Another soldier. I can't talk, Agent Goodman. Get here as soon as you can." Unable to stem the flow of blood, she dropped the cell to the tile floor and, using both hands, pushed even harder on the towel.

Footsteps sounded in the hallway.

Ted appeared in the open doorway, his slender face pulled tight. Confusion, then anger, flashed from his eyes. "What did you do to him, Stephanie?"

Hurt by his accusation, she pursed her lips. "I didn't do anything. He fell. An ambulance should be here soon. Go outside and flag down the EMTs when they turn onto the street."

"I'm not leaving Josh." Her brother knelt beside her. "Let me hold the towel."

"I've got it."

"Just like you had Hayden? You let him die. I won't let you kill Josh, too."

"Ted, please." Why did he have to bring up their painful past in the middle of this crisis?

"Please what, Stephanie? Forget about what happened? I told you never to come back to Freemont."

Her stomach roiled. No matter what she did, her relationship with her brother would never change.

"Ms. Upton, answer me. Are you all right?"

Hearing the agent's urgent voice, she raised the cell to her ear again. "I'm sorry. I...I thought I had disconnected." She glanced down at the stained towel. "I'm okay."

But she really wasn't. She'd nearly had a fatal collision with a psycho driver just a short while earlier. Now Joshua's life was slipping away as she watched.

"Hurry," she finally warned. "Before things get any worse."

"What do you know about the new AW2 advocate?" Brody asked as he drove out the Fort Rickman main gate and headed north along Freemont Road. Recalling the urgency in Stephanie Upton's voice, he pushed down on the accelerator.

Major Jenkins sat next to him, equally worried about the situation. "She held the same position at Fort Stewart. Our former advocate had some unexpected medical problems and had to retire. Stephanie transferred here to fill the vacancy."

"And PFC Webb?"

"Lost both his legs in an IED explosion in Afghanistan."

Brody shook his head, feeling the frustration of too many young men and women being injured in the line of duty. Casualties were a horrific by-product of war. Not what he or anyone associated with the military wanted.

"Joshua Webb was initially treated at Walter Reed," the major said, "and was recently assigned to Fort Rickman."

"Do you have anyone named Ted in your battalion?"

Jenkins nodded. "Ted Upton."

"Related to the advocate?"

"Ted's her brother. He was in the same convoy that hit the IED. Upton was burned and treated at the Army Burn Center at Fort Sam Houston."

"Now they're home, getting ready to transition out of the military?"

"Private Webb will probably get a medical discharge. He's waiting for his new prostheses. Upton has the option of returning to active duty. The burns have healed, but he's still in counseling."

Brody raised his brow. "Over the phone, he sounded antagonistic toward his sister."

"I don't know anything about their relationship. I met her yesterday so it's just a first impression, but she seemed levelheaded and competent. PFC Upton's like a lot of other soldiers. He's young and wondering what the future will hold."

"What about Webb?"

Jenkins smiled. "PFC Webb's got a strong faith and a desire to make a difference in life. He'll do okay."

Your faith will sustain you, folks had told Brody nine years ago. *Lean on the Lord,* a statement he never understood. Why would he lean on a God who had let him down so tragically?

Brody shoved the thought aside. "What's your take on Upton? Is he stable?"

"His squad leader and first sergeant say he's guarded and doesn't readily share his feelings. The counselors encourage the soldiers to talk about their problems."

"Just as you and I had discussed earlier in conjunction with post-traumatic stress disorder."

The major nodded. "Exactly."

"What does the doc say about Upton?"

"That he needs more counseling."

The entrance to the Cedar Springs area appeared on the left. Brody turned into the subdivision littered with debris from the storm and made a right at the third street. At the end of the road, two Freemont black-and-whites sat curbside, their lights flashing. An ambulance had backed into the driveway. Its rear door hung open. A gray Chevy and an older-model Corolla were parked nearby.

Brody led the way into the house, glancing first at the police officer and then at the tall, slender woman standing near the fireplace. Arms wrapped defensively around her waist, she turned as he stepped forward, her eyes as blue as the sky and strangely haunting. The furrow of her brow and the downward tug on her full lips provided a glimpse of the concern she felt for the injured soldier.

Her pastel skirt was smeared with blood, her blouse, as well. A crusty streak lined her pale cheek. If the victim's injury hadn't been accidental, the blood-spattered advocate might be a likely suspect, but her reason for visiting the soldier seemed legit.

Confusion covered her face, probably due to the shock of finding the injured victim. Images of the scene he had walked into nine years ago replayed through his memory. His breath caught in his chest. Sweat broke out on his upper lip. He clamped down his jaw and forced the image to flee, just as he'd done a thousand times before. Today he needed to focus on the woman with the questioning eyes that bored into his soul.

She looked at him the way Lisa had. After all these years, he still needed to guard himself against the pain. More than anything, he never wanted to be vulnerable again. Especially to someone who reminded him of the woman he had loved and lost.

A young man leaned against the counter in the kitchen. The guy wore cargo pants and flip-flops with an army T-shirt. From the high, tight haircut and the splotch of angry, red skin on his left arm, he was more than likely the advocate's younger brother.

His right hand was bandaged. Blood spotted his shirt. The wail of accusation Brody had heard over the phone replayed in his mind.

Seeing his commanding officer, the kid pulled himself upright. "Afternoon, Major Jenkins." He raised his injured hand to his forehead. "Thanks for coming, sir."

"How are you doing, Ted?"

The kid nodded a bit too enthusiastically. "Fine, sir."

While Jenkins talked to Private Upton, Brody continued into the hallway, where a transport stretcher filled the narrow space. Moving past the obstruction, he looked into the bathroom. Two EMTs, one male, one female, knelt over the victim.

Brody flashed his badge at the cop standing at the side of the doorway. "CID, Fort Rickman."

The Freemont policeman nodded. "Didn't take you long to get here from post."

"What do you have?" Brody pressed, uninterested in small talk.

"Joshua Webb was renovating his house along with his friend, Ted Upton. The guy's in the kitchen. He's pretty shook-up."

"You questioned him?"

"Briefly. Seems they were trying to install a new vanity mirror that dropped and shattered. Ted Upton cut his hand. Joshua insisted he have it checked out at the hospital. When Ted returned, the woman was on the floor next to Joshua, using a towel to stop his bleeding. She called nine-one-one."

Josh Webb appeared to be physically fit other than his missing limbs. Short hair, youthful face, strong upper body. His wheelchair lay on its side.

"Looks like he was trying to clean up the broken

glass, maybe extended his reach too far, and fell while his friend was gone." The cop pointed to a blood mark on the side of the faux-marble sink. "Must have hit his head as he went down. A piece of the mirror sliced a deep gash in his upper right arm."

The female EMT glanced up at Brody. "The glass cut his artery. He almost bled out. Vitals aren't good. We're transporting him to the military hospital on post."

Brody eyed the head wound. Blunt-force trauma as well as a laceration. Taking out his smart phone, he photographed the pattern of broken glass on the floor, blood spatters on the wall and the injuries to the victim's head and arm.

He also snapped a shot of the bathtub. "Why the filled tub?"

The cop shook his head. "No clue at this point."

The female EMT started to stand. "We need some space."

Brody backed out of the hallway and headed for the kitchen, where Jenkins introduced him to Ted Upton. Ted shrugged off a handshake by holding up his bandaged fingers and explained how he'd been cut.

"How long were you at the hospital?"

"A couple hours." The kid rolled his eyes. "You know how slow emergency rooms can be."

"You went to the hospital on post?"

"That's right."

"How was PFC Webb when you left him?" Brody asked.

"The same as always, laughing and talking about the future. He planned to do some small jobs in the kitchen and then grab some chow from the fridge."

Brody opened the refrigerator. Two store-wrapped

sub sandwiches sat untouched. "What time did you get here this morning?"

"Shortly after ten."

"Anyone else stop by?"

The PFC shook his head. "No, sir."

"What did you see when you returned to the house?"

"My sister was on the floor in the bathroom, holding a towel to Josh's arm."

"Did you notice her car parked outside?"

"I thought it belonged to one of the neighbors."

"Do you know the neighbors?"

"Only Nikki Dunn."

Brody raised his eyebrow, waiting for more information.

"She works at the exchange on post." Ted glanced into the living room and watched the EMTs roll the stretcher carrying Josh's unresponsive body out the front door. The policemen hastened behind them.

"Do you recall anything bothering Josh recently?" Brody asked. "Had he argued with anyone?"

Ted shook his head. "Josh does his own thing. We're friends, and we go back a long way, but he keeps his business to himself."

Stephanie entered the kitchen.

Ted glanced at Major Jenkins. "If you don't mind, sir, I'd like to follow the ambulance to the hospital."

The major patted the soldier's back. "I'll go with you. Give me a minute. I want to speak to your sister."

"Roger that, sir."

Jenkins talked quietly to Stephanie while Brody moved even closer to Ted. "It's a shock to see your friend injured."

The soldier licked his lips. "Yeah, but I've seen worse."

"Your convoy was hit in Afghanistan."

Ted nodded. "That's how Josh lost his legs."

"You were injured, as well."

"Goes with the job, if you know what I mean."

Brody doubted the PFC had worked through the trauma of the IED explosion. More than likely, he was covering up the way he really felt.

Ted dug in his pocket for his keys. "I borrowed my squad leader's car today to help Josh. Tell Major Jenkins I'll be outside in Sergeant McCoy's gray Chevy."

Brody nodded. "Take care of that hand."

"Will do, sir."

He watched the PFC leave the house. Major Jenkins concluded his conversation with Ted's sister and exited through the kitchen.

"Ma'am." Brody approached where she stood. "I'd like to ask you a few questions."

"You're the CID agent."

He nodded. "Brody Goodman. We talked on the phone."

"Thanks for getting here so quickly."

"Can you tell me what you saw when you came into the house?"

She nodded. "The front door was locked. Josh had his iPod tuned to the Braves game. The volume was high. I didn't think he heard me knock."

"How'd you get in?"

"The kitchen door was hanging open. He's on my caseload so I stepped inside and called his name."

"Did he answer you?"

"No." She let out a tiny breath. "The radio was so loud I doubt anyone could have heard me."

"So it was easy for you to enter the house without him knowing?"

Her brow rose. "I don't see what you're getting at."

"The door was open, ma'am, and you came inside unannounced."

"I wasn't trying to do him harm."

Brody raised his hand and smiled apologetically. "I wasn't implying you were, but if someone had wanted to sneak up on Private Webb, they could have."

"They would have found him on the floor. His wheelchair had overturned. He must have hit his head when he fell. Glass cut his arm."

"He was bleeding?"

She nodded. "I grabbed a towel and tried to stop the flow."

"You mentioned calling nine-one-one."

"That's right. Then I phoned his battalion."

"Your brother was in the house at the time?"

"Ted arrived when I was on the phone with you." She glanced out the window at the ambulance before turning her gaze back to Brody.

"Did your brother know you had accepted the AW2 position?" he asked.

"I've only been in Freemont for a couple days, Agent Goodman. My brother and I have been playing phone tag."

"For that long?"

"I really don't see how any of this has bearing on Josh's fall."

"Force of habit for a CID guy, I guess." He smiled. "You found lodging rather quickly."

"My father has a house in town. He's away on business. I'm staying at home until I can find an apartment."

Brody eyed her for a long moment and then asked, "Was the water running in the tub when you arrived?"

She nodded, her eyes somber. "I turned it off before it overflowed."

"What about outside? Did you see anything suspicious when you pulled into the housing area?"

"Not really."

He raised a brow. "Meaning?"

"Meaning a pickup raced out of the subdivision and nearly ran into me just before I turned into the housing area."

"Can you ID the vehicle or the make and model?"

"A red truck. Souped-up. Big knobby mud tires. Lots of chrome."

"Did you see the driver or the license plate?"

"Everything happened too quickly. It was raining. My windshield wipers couldn't keep up with the downpour."

"Which direction were you coming from?"

"I'd visited two of my clients in Freemont and was heading south to meet with Joshua."

The pickup could be some kid's ego ride, but it could also be the vehicle the perpetrator used to race away from the scene of the crime. Either way, Brody would encourage the Freemont police to track down the red truck with big tires.

He glanced outside. The door to the ambulance was closed, and the vehicle pulled out of the driveway escorted by one of the squad cars. The remaining officer reentered the house. Brody excused himself and met the cop in the living room.

"You might want to take a second look at the blood

spatters on the bathroom wall." He pointed toward the hallway. "The pattern indicates the PFC's arm was cut when he was still in his wheelchair."

The cop narrowed his gaze. "You're saying he cut himself?"

"Or someone else inflicted the wound. Ms. Upton said the back door was open when she arrived on the scene. Earlier someone raced out of the subdivision. A red pickup with oversize tires. Might be prudent to knock on a few doors in the neighborhood and see if anyone saw the truck or anything suspect this morning. A lot of people have had access to the house, but you could still check for prints."

The officer nodded, and when Stephanie stepped back into the living room, he took out his notebook and pen. "Ma'am, I need to ask you a few more questions."

"What kind of questions, Officer?"

"About the truck and the back door and how you entered PFC Webb's house."

Stephanie bristled.

"He's just trying to determine what happened," Brody volunteered.

"What happened is that Joshua Webb fell from his wheelchair and cut his arm, and if I hadn't arrived when I did, he might have died."

"Your brother was here earlier," Brody said.

Her face clouded. "You think Ted had something to do with Josh's injury?" She shook her head, her eyes wide and eyebrows arched. "That's preposterous."

"Is it? Then you shouldn't object to the questions."

Brody often relied on his gut feelings when investigating a crime, and nothing about the pretty advocate seemed suspect. He was more prone to consider Ted Upton as someone of interest.

Bottom line, no matter what she told the cop or how convinced Brody was that she wasn't involved, he planned to keep his eyes on both Stephanie Upton and her brother.

The police officer's questions were similar to the ones the CID agent had asked Stephanie earlier, except they lacked the accusation she had heard in Brody's voice. The local policeman was thorough, while attempting to make her feel as comfortable as possible, which she appreciated.

Throughout the questioning, Brody stood to the side and watched her with dark eyes that revealed nothing about his own feelings concerning the case. At least six inches taller than her five foot seven, he had deep-set eyes and full lips that failed to smile.

She mentioned phoning Joshua and having her call go to voice mail, which sent Brody on a hunt through the house to uncover the missing cell. He returned to the living area with a smug look on his angular face. "Looks like he retrieved your message."

At the conclusion of the questioning, Stephanie gave both the officer and the CID agent her business card. "You know where to find me if you have any more questions."

She hurried from the house without as much as a backward glance at the special agent. Checking her watch, she let out a frustrated breath at being held up so long. She needed to join her brother and Major Jenkins at the hospital. As the AW2 advocate, her job was to be a liaison between the military and the injured soldier and to help with all his needs, including medical. She was also concerned about Ted and wanted to ensure he was coping with Joshua's accident.

Before she reached her car, a small, two-door sedan pulled to the curb. The driver hustled toward her.

"Ms. Upton?"

She didn't know the man, but she saw the high-tech digital camera in his hand.

"I'm a reporter with the Freemont paper." Without asking her permission, he raised the camera and clicked a series of pictures. "I'd like to interview you for a story about the rescue."

"Rescue?"

"You saved Josh's life. Just like you did three years ago."

Her stomach soured. Surely he didn't plan to resurrect the past.

"I'm not interested in an interview or having my picture in the paper," she insisted, her voice firm.

The shutter clicked again.

Stephanie raised her hand to hide her face. "Please!"

"You heard the lady."

She turned to find the special agent charging along the sidewalk to where the reporter stood.

"No interviews. No pictures. Is that understood?"

The newsman hesitated.

Brody stepped closer. His eyes narrowed and his lips clamped together in a downward frown.

"Got it." The reporter took a step back. "Not a problem. I'm outta here." He scurried to his car and raced from the subdivision.

Brody touched her arm. "Are you okay?"

She nodded. "I'm fine, but thanks for the help."

"The reporter mentioned a previous rescue. You mind telling me what he was referencing?"

"It has nothing to do with today."

Brody stared down at her with questioning eyes.

She sighed, knowing he wouldn't give up until she told him what had happened in the past. "If you must know, a storm came up on a nearby lake and caught Josh and my brother and a few of their friends unprepared. I arrived in time to pull some of the kids from the water."

"Some?"

"One of the boys—my cousin, Hayden—drowned."

"I'm sorry."

"So am I."

He continued to stare at her. "Are you sure you're okay?"

She nodded decisively. "I'm positive. Now, if you'll excuse me, I have a soldier on my caseload that may need help at the hospital."

Frustrated with the mix of emotion bubbling up within her, Stephanie climbed into her car. She hadn't wanted to talk about the accident on the lake, but Brody seemed to have pulled the information from her.

She regretted her defensiveness, which he must have recognized. In truth, she wanted to know what had happened to Josh as much as Brody did. Just so he realized she and Ted weren't at fault.

Maybe her brother had been right.

Maybe she shouldn't have come back to Freemont.

Chapter Two

Stephanie parked her Corolla next to the Fort Rickman Hospital's emergency room and hurried inside. The clerk at the desk directed her to the intensive-care unit. She rode the elevator to the third floor and followed the signs to the ICU, where she checked to ensure Josh's hospital-entrance forms had been properly filled out.

Satisfied his paperwork was complete, she continued on to the ICU waiting room, where she found Ted sitting on a vinyl couch with his elbows on his knees. He looked younger than his twenty-one years and so very vulnerable.

He glanced up when she entered the room.

"Any news yet?" she asked, wanting to put her arms around him and draw him close.

He shook his head. The glare in his eyes warned her against any display of affection.

Major Jenkins stood nearby. "The doctor ordered three units of blood. The nurse said they won't know anything for a number of hours. His parents are with him now."

With a deep sigh, Ted stood and walked toward the

large window. He stared down at the parking lot below, as if trying to hide the worry that was plastered over his pale face. "The...the nurse said everything was being done to save his life."

"I'm sure he's getting the best of care." Stephanie knew the struggle her brother was waging to remain in control. "Joshua is a fighter, Ted. He'll pull through."

"Dad said Mom was a fighter, and you know what happened to her."

"That was different."

He turned, his face tight with emotion. "Different because she had cancer or different because you weren't around to watch her life waste away?"

Stephanie's breath hitched. She hadn't expected the bitterness she heard in his voice.

Working to keep her own voice calm, she said, "Mom wanted me to finish the semester at college, but I came home every weekend."

"Which wasn't enough."

How many times would he need to hear the truth before he could accept what happened? Her mother regretted not having the opportunity to get a degree and had insisted Stephanie continue her studies.

A freshman in high school, Ted had needed someone in his life. That someone should have been their dad, but he'd buried his own pain in his job. Stephanie had tried to fill the void on the weekends when she came home, never realizing it wasn't enough for Ted. Worried though she was about Joshua's condition, she was even more worried about her brother.

Footsteps sounded in the hallway. She turned, expecting to see Joshua's physician. Instead, she saw Brody Goodman.

He hesitated in the doorway, glancing first at her and then at Ted, who stared out the window. "Did something happen?"

"The doctor's with Josh now," she said, hugging herself. "He's critical and receiving blood."

Ted's cell trilled. He pulled the phone to his ear and nodded. "You heard right. Josh was admitted to ICU. Third floor. The waiting room is at the end of the hallway."

He disconnected. "Paul Massey's downstairs. He's home on leave with orders for Fort Hood and heard about the accident." Ted glanced at the major. "Paul stopped by Josh's house, sir. One of the neighbors mentioned seeing an ambulance."

Stephanie was surprised by the change in Paul when he joined them in the waiting room. Previously a gawky kid with big eyes and long hair, the soldier who greeted Ted was tall and tan and sure of himself.

"Hey, man, what's going on?" Paul asked as he and Ted gripped hands.

"The doc said they'll know more after he's transfused. They won't let anyone back there except his parents."

As the soldiers talked, Brody and the major stepped into the hallway. Stephanie couldn't hear what they were saying, but she was convinced it had something to do with the CID agent's suspicions about Josh's injury.

The major nodded and glanced at her ever so briefly, his expression difficult to decipher. Brody waved a hand in the air and then paused. His eyes locked on hers for a long moment.

Her cheeks burned.

Averting her gaze, Stephanie smiled at Paul, who gave her a warm hug.

"Glad you're back in town, Steph."

"She took over as the AW2 advocate." Ted's tone was anything but enthusiastic.

Paul nodded with approval. "You'll be good at that job."

If only. Seemed her brother would be her biggest challenge. Right now, she didn't feel up to the task.

She glanced at her watch. "I need to get back to work, Ted. I'll call you later."

He fiddled with his phone. "Whatever."

"Sorry to interrupt." Stepping into the hallway, she looked first at the CID agent and then at Major Jenkins. "I need to change clothes before I make another house call."

"Why don't you take the rest of the afternoon off?" the major suggested. "You still have to get settled, and the Hail and Farewell starts at four o'clock."

Jenkins turned to Brody. "I saw your name on the list of folks being welcomed to post."

"Glad you reminded me. After three weeks, I feel like an old-timer." Brody tilted his head and smiled at Stephanie. "So I'll see you there?"

"Probably."

She didn't want to go to the social event, but it was a command performance. After the new people on post were welcomed, she planned to hurry back to her father's house.

Not that she wanted to be there, either. Too many memories remained of her mother and the way life had been before cancer took her life. The change in Ted after her death, coupled with their father's detachment, had added to Stephanie's grief.

The problems had culminated that night on the lake.

A night that had changed her life forever.

A night she never wanted to think about, yet coming back to Freemont threatened to put it front and center once again.

After talking to Major Jenkins, Brody returned to CID headquarters and headed for the chief's office.

He knocked and then pushed the door open. "Sir, do you have a minute?"

"What do you need, Brody?"

Wilson was big in stature, with a short buzz of black hair and equally dark eyes set in a round mocha face. He glanced up from the open manila folder as Brody approached his desk.

"An incident involving one of our injured soldiers." Brody relayed the information about Josh's accident.

"You think it was intentional?" the commander asked.

"Yes, sir. Due to the blood spatter. The woman who found the victim is the new AW2 advocate. Her brother was with the victim earlier in the day. He injured his hand and went to the hospital for stitches. While he was gone, Webb was attacked."

"Seems a bit coincidental."

"Yes, sir. He and Webb are both assigned to the Warrior Transitional Battalion. PFC Upton seems to have a short fuse, especially when it comes to his sister."

Wilson nodded. "Sounds like a problem waiting to explode. The Freemont police are handling the investigation?"

"Currently they're in charge, although their first assessment missed the mark."

Wilson's full lips twitched. A spark of amusement

glimmered in his brown eyes. "I presume you set them straight."

"I pointed out the obvious, sir. All with deference to their position as lead investigators on the case."

"How'd you learn of Webb's injuries?"

Brody explained about the call to Joshua's battalion. "I was in Major Jenkins's office at the time. He was called away from his desk for a few minutes and asked me to man his phone."

"That was fortunate. You were discussing your interest in PTSD?"

"Yes, sir. Major Jenkins agreed to let me speak to the battalion. They've received support from other on-post agencies, but I want to make sure they're aware the CID could provide additional resources."

Wilson leaned back in his chair. His right hand tapped a mechanical pencil against a tablet on his desk. "What you experienced was regrettable, Brody. I applaud you for turning tragedy into something positive for other military personnel."

"That's my hope, sir."

"Seems you've arrived at Rickman at the right time. The post commanding general is concerned about the growing number of violent shootings around the country. A handful of veterans have been involved. The media seems to focus on their tie-in with the military, which paints all of us in a bad light. General Cameron is insistent that we remain proactive at Fort Rickman and defuse any problems before they get out of hand, especially when redeployed soldiers are involved. I realize the local police are investigating, but I want you involved, too. Keep your eye on the advocate, as well as her brother. Family troubles can escalate in a heartbeat."

"Yes, sir, but isn't the CID short staffed at this time?"

"As is the entire army." Wilson pointed to a folder on the corner of his desk. "We have two new special agents transferring here within the next few months, which will resolve our manpower problems. Until you hear otherwise from me, follow up on this current case. Take as much time as you need. I'll know where to find you."

"Yes, sir."

"Keep me posted on Webb's condition. Be sure to let the Freemont police know of our interest in their investigation."

"Yes, sir."

"Tact is important when working with local law enforcement. We've had a fairly good relationship in the past. I wouldn't want that to change."

"I agree, sir."

"They've got a new chief of police. Name's Don Palmer. I'll call him and mention your interest in the case."

"Thank you, sir."

Wilson shifted forward, a visible sign the discussion was over. "I'll see you at the club this afternoon."

"Four o'clock. I'll be there, sir."

Returning to his desk, Brody logged on to the internet and pulled up the local newspaper's home page. He wanted to learn as much as he could about the Upton family, and the local rag would, no doubt, provide information.

Tapping into the archives, he searched for stories on Stephanie Upton. A number of articles popped up.

Brody shook his head in amazement.

Stephanie's accomplishments ranged from swim team

to prom queen. The pictures showed a teen with sparkling eyes, shoulder-length hair and an inviting smile.

His own high school in California had four times as many students as Freemont High. He'd played sports and had his own fair share of news mentions, but nothing compared to the hometown darling who was also dubbed Girl Most Likely to Succeed.

On a more solemn note, he uncovered an obituary for a Jane Upton. "Survived by husband, Davis, daughter Stephanie and son Theodore." Brody did the math. Ted had been a freshman in high school. Stephanie must have been in college. "Memorial donations can be made to the American Cancer Society." All too well, Brody knew the toll malignancy took on families. His maternal grandfather had died of colon cancer, a disease that with proper screening could have been prevented.

Stephanie had mentioned her father was out of town on business. He entered the dad's name in the search box and clicked on an article that recapped the elder Upton's success growing his company into a large enterprise that provided jobs for many folks in the local area.

Mr. Upton's picture showed a tall man with a receding hairline and twenty extra pounds tucked around his middle. Davis Upton appeared to be an older and heavier version of his son.

Returning to the archives, Brody found a story on the drowning incident at the nearby lake—Lake Claims Local Teen.

He opened the file and quickly read about the group of teens who had partied on Big Island Lake shortly after their graduation. As Stephanie had mentioned, the frivolity turned deadly when a storm hit unannounced. The teens were caught in the rapid currents on the straits that ran between Big Island and Small Island to the south. Stephanie had boated to the island and pulled the teens to safety. All except Hayden Allen, a cousin on her mother's side.

Brody leaned in closer and read Keith Allen's comment on Stephanie's attempt to save his brother.

"My mother and I appreciate Stephanie's heroic efforts to find Hayden. Without regard for her own safety, she searched tirelessly for my brother, for which we are grateful."

A team of divers eventually found the missing teen's body tangled in debris.

Brody saved the article to his hard drive as well as his smart phone and then inserted a printed copy into a manila folder labeled Investigation: PFC Joshua Webb.

On a hunch, he dialed Major Jenkins.

"It's Brody, sir. I've got a question for you."

"Shoot."

"You said Joshua Webb and Ted Upton enlisted at the same time. Do you have the date they entered the military?"

"Not at my fingertips, but I'll call you back."

According to the article, the two PFCs, along with Paul Massey, had been part of the group of teens at the island. The tragedy happened three years ago on June 10, just twelve days after the group had graduated high school.

Brody wrote the names on a clean sheet of paper and added Stephanie's at the bottom. Next to hers, he drew a large question mark.

His phone rang. "Special Agent Goodman."

"I found the information, Brody." Jenkins's voice.

"Yes, sir."

"Both Webb and Upton enlisted three years ago, on the thirtieth of June."

Twenty days after Hayden's death. Fast-forward to a deployment in Afghanistan and an IED explosion that injured both soldiers.

Brody picked up the printout of the article. On the bottom of the page was a photo of Stephanie Upton. The girl named Most Likely to Succeed had failed to save her cousin.

The expression she wore revealed deep emotional pain and a tragic sense of loss. Hayden's brother had offered praise for her attempts, but the slant of her eyes and heavy pull on her shoulders told a different story.

All too often what happened in the past had bearing on the present. Stephanie could have suffered as much trauma as her brother had in Afghanistan and still be fighting her own internal battles. If so, she might not be the best person to help Fort Rickman's wounded warriors.

No law enforcement officer worth his badge believed in coincidence. Nor did Brody. The Upton siblings had some history with a dead relative and a group of friends who had joined the military, perhaps to distance themselves from the lake tragedy.

Call it a long shot, but Brody wondered if that history played into what had happened to Joshua Webb. If so, he needed to uncover the truth about the struggle between Stephanie Upton and her brother. At this point, neither person was a suspect, yet Brody had to be open to any possibility. In the days ahead, he planned to keep his eyes and his attention focused on both of them.

He would talk to Major Jenkins about Ted, but he'd keep his concern about the AW2 advocate to himself. He was more intrigued than suspicious about her involvement, but either way, she needed to be watched. Wilson had given Brody an assignment, one he was determined to fulfill.

Chapter Three

On her way to the Fort Rickman Club later that afternoon, Stephanie drove past the large brick quarters that surrounded the main parade field. So many families had lived in the homes since they had been built in the 1930s. Growing up, she'd known a few "Post Toastees," as the locals called the army brats, but she'd always associated with kids from Freemont. Now she regretted her own attempt to isolate herself from the military. She'd been young and too focused on herself.

Her mother's illness and Ted's troubles during high school had changed her outlook on life. Not that her family hadn't had their share of problems before her mom had gotten sick. After her death, everything had been exacerbated by a workaholic father who preferred to stay at the office rather than deal with the situation at home.

Evidently, her father still hadn't changed. Case in point, his current trip to Europe, supposedly to oversee the start-up of a satellite company. To his credit, he had visited Ted often at Fort Sam and had provided for additional specialists to consult with the military docs, yet he handled Ted as if he was a business venture instead of his needy son.

Over the past few years, Ted had rejected Stephanie's outreach so many times that she had finally decided their relationship could never be reconciled. Then the job had opened at Fort Rickman, and she'd transferred home.

If she believed in God's intervention, she would be convinced He had stepped in. As it was, she had severed her relationship with the Lord three years ago.

Refusing to spend any more time focused on the past, she turned into the lot for the Fort Rickman Club and found one of the few remaining parking spots in the last row, farthest from the brick facility. Hot air wrapped around her as she climbed from the car. Beads of sweat had dampened her brow by the time she entered the club, causing her to shiver in the cool, air-conditioned interior.

She rubbed her arms in an attempt to stave off the chill, as well as her own nervousness at having to make small talk with people she didn't know. Hopefully, as soon as the introductions were over, she could slip out unnoticed.

First thing tomorrow morning, she planned to see Joshua, if he was allowed visitors by then. The last word from the hospital was that his condition remained critical.

A swarm of military and civilian personnel filled the club's main ballroom. Threading her way into their midst, she stretched on tiptoe and searched for Major Jenkins and any of the other people with whom she now worked.

"Stephanie?"

She turned to find Special Agent Goodman standing

behind her. His dark eyes, which had been elusive earlier, now flashed with warmth.

"I didn't think I'd ever find you in this crowd."

He'd been looking for her?

To cover her surprise, she glanced quickly around the
ballroom. "Everyone on post must be here."

He pointed to a table set up in the corner and raised
his voice to be heard over a group of young officers clus-
tered nearby. "I was on my way to grab a cold drink.
May I get you something?"

"A bottle of water would be great."

Brody leaned closer to be heard over the surrounding
chatter. A subtle hint of aftershave wafted past her—a
masculine scent that caused a tingle of interest to play
along her neck.

"Do you mind coming with me? I don't want to lose
you in the crowd."

She hesitated for a fraction of a second before his
hand touched the small of her back. He guided her across
the room. A number of folks smiled. Others nodded in
passing.

At one point, Brody halted her forward progression
in order for a distinguished couple to pass. The man was
dressed in the army's digital-camouflage uniform. Two
stars were attached to the center front tab.

"That's General Cameron, the post commanding general, and his wife." Brody's lips hovered close to her
ear. "They're nice folks. He's a by-the-book type of guy
who puts his soldiers first. Mrs. Cameron is a charm-
ing Southern belle who treats everyone with sincerity
and warmth."

A younger couple waved and then headed toward
them. The guy—dressed in a sport coat and tie, just

as Brody was—slapped Brody's shoulder in greeting and turned to Stephanie, his eyes twinkling with mirth. "Don't believe anything this guy tells you."

The attractive woman at his side smiled. "I'm Michele Steele, and the CID agent giving Brody a hard time is my husband, Jamison."

"Nice to meet you both."

"Stephanie's the new AW2 advocate," Brody told them.

"An important position." Jamison's smile was encouraging. "It's good to have you on board."

"Jamison and I work together," Brody told her. "Michele is Colonel and Mrs. Logan's daughter." He pointed to the older couple talking with the commanding general and his wife. "Her parents are as nice as she is."

"You and Stephanie need to come over for dinner." Michele looked at her husband, who nodded in agreement. "Jamison could throw some steaks on the grill."

Grateful though Stephanie was for the invitation, she wasn't sure socializing with the special agent was a good idea, especially after the pointed questions he had voiced earlier.

After chatting for a few more minutes, she excused herself to look for Major Jenkins and spotted him standing near the stage.

"The general will call your name shortly," he said as she approached. "I provided him with information he'll mention when he introduces you. All you'll have to do is shake his hand and smile."

Stephanie adjusted her skirt and tucked her hair behind her ear, a bit on edge at the thought of being introduced, especially knowing Brody was in the crowd.

When her name was called, she joined the general on

the raised platform and smiled at the sea of faces and military uniforms. In the distance, she spied Brody. His eyes held her gaze for a long moment, causing a flush of heat to work along her neck.

The general recounted the previous job she had held at Fort Stewart and praised her background in social services. She appreciated the information Major Jenkins had provided.

"I know our injured soldiers will find the support they need with Ms. Upton filling the AW2 advocate position."

"Thank you, sir." After shaking the general's hand, she hurried offstage.

Relieved to have the introduction behind her, Stephanie said goodbye to the major and headed for the door. Before reaching the exit, she heard Brody's name announced. Turning back, she watched the ease with which he climbed the platform and stood next to the general.

The post commander praised his accomplishments and valor during four deployments to the Middle East. A number of men and women in uniform cheered when his time in combat was mentioned. As the next name was called, Stephanie left the club and hurried across the parking lot.

Nearing her car, she groaned. The left rear tire was flat as a pancake. What else could go wrong today?

Her brother's hateful comments at Josh's house came to mind. What better way to prove his point than to put obstacles in her path?

He wouldn't have hurt Josh, but deflating her tire wasn't outside the realm of possibilities. As a teen, Ted had gotten into trouble for doing exactly the same thing.

Tears of frustration and aggravation burned her eyes. In addition, she felt betrayed.

Retrieving her cell from her purse, she called his number. More than anything, she wanted to stop the downward spiral of their relationship before things got completely out of hand. When he failed to answer, she disconnected instead of leaving a message. What she had to say should probably be done in person.

Plus, she needed to focus on the current problem. Namely her flat tire. How hard could it be to put on the spare?

Her moment of optimism plummeted when she opened the trunk and stared down at the numerous parts of a jack she didn't know how to assemble.

Brody Goodman had come to her aid with the newspaper reporter, but recalling the effect his aftershave had had on her earlier, she didn't want to get too close to him again. Even if she had to call a cab, she was better off having nothing to do with the CID agent. As far as she was concerned, Brody was the last person she should ask for help.

Chief Wilson motioned to Brody after he left the stage. "The provost marshal is here, along with some of his people who have been on a temporary assignment in D.C. He wants you to meet them."

The commander of the Military Police Department on post was personable and talkative. He introduced Brody to the returning members of his staff. By the time Brody edged out of the group, Stephanie was nowhere to be found.

Frustrated, he left the club and headed to his car, surprised to see her in the distance, staring into her open trunk.

As he neared, she glanced up. "I seem to have a problem." Which was evident by her clutched hands and wrinkled brow.

Bending down, he examined her tire. "I don't see any big gashes in the rubber. Smaller holes are often difficult to find."

"I ran over some gravel on the way to the club."

"That shouldn't have been a problem, unless a nail or some other sharp object became embedded in the rubber. A mechanic would be able to tell."

He unscrewed the cap on the air valve and whistled. "I found the problem. The valve core's been removed. It regulates the flow of air in and out of the tire. No wonder it's flat."

Standing, he brushed off his hands. "I'll put on your spare, but that's a short-term fix. You'll need to stop by a tire dealer in the morning."

"Could the valve have jostled loose when I was driving?"

"Hardly. The core was intentionally removed." He pulled out his phone. "We'd better notify the military police."

She shook her head. "I don't want the MPs involved."

"Because—"

"Because I'm new on post. A solider on my caseload was injured this afternoon. I've stirred up enough problems for one day."

He didn't understand her logic. "Someone vandalized your property, Stephanie."

"But—"

They both turned at the sound of a car. Paul Massey was at the wheel of a metallic-blue Dodge Dart with Ted next to him in the passenger seat. A woman sat in the rear, a small blonde who waved when the car braked to a stop.

"Need some help?" Paul asked as he stepped to the pavement.

Brody shook his head. "Thanks, but I can handle it."

Stephanie frowned as her brother rounded the car. "Haven't you done enough for one day, Ted?"

His neutral expression soured. "What's that supposed to mean?"

"My tire's flat. Someone tampered with the air valve. Does that bring anything to mind?"

Before he could reply, the backseat blonde exited the car and scooted next to Ted. "Hey, Stephanie."

"How are you, Nikki?"

"Bummed about Joshua. Ted said you saved his life."

"I merely called nine-one-one. Luckily the paramedics arrived in time."

Nikki Dunn. Brody recalled the girl's name. "Don't you live in Joshua's housing area?"

"That's right. Just down the street."

"I'm Special Agent Brody Goodman with the Criminal Investigation Division. Ted mentioned you today. Were you at home this morning?"

"Until eight-thirty when I left for work."

"Did you see anyone hanging around the area?"

"A couple of neighbors heading into town."

"Any strange cars?"

She shook her head.

"What about a red pickup with jumbo tires?" Brody's gaze flicked between the three twenty-somethings. "Know anyone with that kind of ride?"

Ted's eyes narrowed. He glared at his sister.

"No one in my area." Nikki seemed oblivious to the tension between the two siblings.

Paul glanced at his watch. "If you're okay with the tire, I'll take Ted back to his barracks."

"Any chance you guys drove by here earlier today?" Brody asked rubbing his jaw.

"We've been at the PX since three." Ted tapped his foot against the pavement.

"Playing with the iPads in the entertainment section," Nikki added. "They were waiting until I got off work. We went for pizza after that."

"At the Italian Parlor? How many of the free peanuts did you eat?" Stephanie stared at her brother.

Nikki patted Ted's arm and smiled. "I told him he had to be careful, especially since you and your mom were both allergic."

"Yeah, but as Stephanie knows, I take after my dad on that count." He turned and motioned to Paul. "We better get going."

"I heard Ted's angry comments earlier today over the phone." Brody stepped closer to Stephanie as Paul's car left the lot. "Seems he doesn't know how to deal with the IED explosion and his injuries so he's taking it out on you."

"That's not true."

"Isn't it? You're protecting your brother because you love him, but that's not helping him heal."

"Having the MPs question Ted won't help, either."

"Did he vandalize tires as a kid?"

When she didn't respond, he took a step closer and looked into her troubled eyes. "I can call the local police to find out, or you can tell me and make it easier on both of us."

She pulled in a fragile breath. "My mother died of cancer when Ted was in high school. He had a hard time dealing with her death and got into trouble."

"Tampering with air valves," Brody filled in. "You think he did this today?"

"I don't know what to think." She wrapped her arms around her waist and looked both vulnerable and needy.

Brody wanted to put his arm around her shoulder to offer support, but he doubted Stephanie would approve of the gesture. Instead, he reached for the jack. "After I change your tire, I'll follow you home. In the morning, I can arrange to drive you to work while your tire is being repaired."

"That's not necessary."

"Maybe not, but it's the least I can do under the circumstances. Besides, how do you plan to get to work tomorrow?"

She tried to smile. "Okay. I'll accept your offer, but you don't have to worry about my relationship with my brother. We'll get through this one way or another."

Brody's heart went out to Stephanie. More than anything, he wanted to tell her everything would be okay, but if Ted had tampered with her tire, his aggression could escalate to something worse. Add Joshua's attack to the mix and Ted became a serious threat.

Stephanie thought her family's problem could be resolved—and maybe things between them would eventually straighten out with professional help for her brother. In the interim, Brody wanted her to be safe instead of sorry. He'd keep investigating the case, but he would also ensure nothing happened to Stephanie.

Chapter Four

Brody kept Stephanie's car in sight as she drove through town and then eased onto a narrow two-lane street that wove through the countryside. The road eventually led to a large brick entryway with a stucco sign that read Country Club Estates.

She turned into the upscale community with Brody close behind. They drove past a number of homes ablaze with floodlights that illuminated the massive structures and sleek construction. Huge picture windows offered views into the expansive interiors and multilevel living spaces.

Brody had grown up in a modest ranch smaller than the pool houses showcased in floodlights at the rear of a number of the vast properties. Hopefully, the wealthy provided loving environments for their own families amongst the lavish trappings of their success. Supposedly God loved the poor, but the poor often didn't love their own. Case in point, his father.

Stephanie pulled into the driveway of a brick house with a wide front porch, white trim and wrought-iron gaslights that should have been turned on. Instead, the house sat dark and shadowed and made Brody thankful he had accompanied her home.

He glanced around the well-manicured front yard as he stepped from the car. "Nice digs."

Flicking his gaze to the rear of the property, he looked for anything that might cause problems. Brody noted the fairway and green, edged by dense woods that sat about fifty yards from the rear of the structure. "I didn't know Freemont had a golf course."

"It's off the beaten path, which is what the developer wanted when he proposed the area. My parents were some of the first folks who built here. The newer homes are more elaborate. My dad opted for comfortable and easy to maintain."

Comfortable was an understatement. Brody walked Stephanie up the stairs to the porch and reached for the keys she held in her hand.

"Allow me."

Although he couldn't see her expression in the darkness, he heard the slight intake of air. Maybe she wasn't used to men who opened doors for her. The thought brought a smile to his lips that quickly vanished when the door swung open.

"Didn't you lock your door?"

"I…I thought I did." She raked her hand through her hair. "I came home to change and was in a hurry to get back to post for the Hail and Farewell."

She started to enter the house.

With his hand on her arm, he held her back. "Let me check everything first."

He stepped into the darkened interior and pulled back the edge of his jacket. His fingers touched the leather holster that held his service revolver, just in case.

The croak of tree frogs and buzz of cicadas filtered through the open door. His eyes adjusted to the darkness, revealing plush furniture and large palladium windows. A patio and swimming pool were visible beyond the deck in the backyard.

Moonlight filtered through the windows and provided enough light to guide his steps as he moved from the dining room past the butler's pantry to the huge kitchen with eat-in breakfast nook and keeping room. At the far end of the house, he found a master bedroom and bath with walk-in closets that were larger than the living room in his bachelor officer's quarters on post. Another hallway led to a pair of smaller bedrooms and adjoining baths.

With meticulous thoroughness, Brody checked the many nooks and crannies in the home where someone could be lying in wait. Once he was assured that the first floor was empty, he flicked on the lights and circled back through the rooms.

A stone fireplace graced one side of the expansive main room, flanked by two full-size couches and a collection of maritime memorabilia. The nautical theme continued into the hallway where a collection of watercolors of naval vessels decorated the walls.

Opening the door to the three-car garage, he saw a late-model Cadillac and a BMW convertible and let out a long whistle in appreciation of her father's good taste in cars.

Satisfied that at least the first floor was secure, Brody returned to the front door and held it open. "Everything looks okay on this floor, but I still need to check the upper floor and basement."

Stephanie tilted her head and tapped her foot. "Does that mean I can come inside now?"

He smiled at her impatience. "Sure, but wait at the door while I check the other floors. It shouldn't take long."

True to his word, Brody returned a few minutes later. He found Stephanie in the kitchen. Her demeanor had changed. She appeared shaken and totally focused on a photograph lying on the counter.

His neck prickled when he gazed down at the five-by-seven glossy of a group of four teenage boys. A red bull's-eye had been drawn with some type of marker around the head of one of the guys and superimposed with a large X.

"It's Josh." Stephanie's voice was shaky as she focused on the face behind the markings. She pointed to a sheet of typing paper lying nearby—"Why did you come back to Freemont?"

Brody read the typed message and then glanced back at the photo. "I recognize Paul and your brother. Who's the other kid?"

"Hayden Allen. My cousin who drowned. This was the last picture taken of the four guys together." Her voice caught. "Ted kept the photograph on the bulletin board in his room."

"He must have come home today and typed the note and marked the photo."

"It wasn't Ted." She shook her head. "He never would have done this."

"Surely he has a key to the house."

"I presume he does, but—"

"If Ted didn't do it, then someone else entered your house and desecrated the photograph. He, or she, left a threatening note. Either way, I need to inform the local police."

"No, Brody." She grabbed his arm as he pulled his cell phone from his pocket. "I don't want them involved."

Because of Ted.

Once again, Stephanie was protecting her brother, yet Ted was the most likely suspect. He undoubtedly had a key to the house and, from what Brody had overheard today, was upset with his sister.

Either in anger or distress, the PFC had marked the photo and typed the message. Was he warning Stephanie someone else would be hurt if she didn't leave town? Or was he telling her the next person in the bull's-eye might be her?

Stephanie pulled in an anxious breath. The bull's-eye didn't make sense. Ted and Josh had been friends since elementary school. Surely what had happened in Afghanistan hadn't altered their relationship, yet someone wanted to scare her into leaving Freemont.

The nerve endings on her arm tingled and confirmed the effectiveness of the warning. The front door hadn't been locked when Brody tried the key, although she had engaged the dead bolt when she left for post. At least she thought she had.

Just as Brody implied, her brother was the only other person with access to the house.

"Stephanie?"

Brody was staring at her with his dark eyes. She heard the question in his voice that said more than just her name. He, too, realized the significance of the picture and typed message.

Stepping toward the sliding glass door that opened onto the deck, she flipped the wall switch that turned on the recessed lights in and around the pool.

An antique maritime bell hung at the edge of the landscaped area. One of her father's treasures from the past and a reminder of the night her mother had died. Stephanie could still see Ted, a skinny and gaunt high school freshman, standing in the dark night, ringing the bell over and over again. Probably to get their father's attention, but their dad had been too involved with his own grief to worry about his children.

Brody moved beside her. Even without looking, she knew he was searching the yard and golf course beyond. No doubt searching for some sign of Ted.

"Your brother comes home often?" His question sounded more like a statement.

"I'm not sure." Turning away from Brody, she reached for the photo.

He grabbed her hand. "Not so fast. I need to check the picture for prints."

"You'll find Ted's. I told you the photo belongs to him."

Brody continued to grip her hand as if he feared she'd ignore his request. Drawn to the controlled strength of his hold, she glanced up once again, finding his gaze intense. There was something under the surface that Brody wasn't willing to share, something more than his concern for an injured soldier. In that fleeting moment, she glimpsed an unspoken need. For what, she wasn't sure.

A flash of awareness passed between them. He pulled in a breath and released her hand.

The separation jarred her. Surely she hadn't wanted him to continue touching her. Or had she?

Surprised and angered when tears pooled in her eyes, she blinked them back. What was it about this man that caused such a mix of emotion to well up within her?

She didn't need someone to protect her. She needed someone to tell her how to heal the deep, destructive rift with her brother.

Not that Brody could help. He made everything worse. Or so it seemed. In fact, he was the least likely person to help her heal the past—both her own and her brother's.

Ignoring the connection that had passed between them, Brody pointed to the typed text on the note. "Look at the words *you* and *come* and *to Freemont.*"

She leaned closer. "The *o* is smeared in each case."

"That's right. It's not crisp like the other letters. I saw a computer and printer in your father's office."

Stephanie followed Brody to the downstairs level and into the home office. Her father's nautical collectibles lined the bookshelves. A ship's wheel hung on the wall next to a brass porthole cover and a large print of a battle on the high seas.

The only nonmaritime item was a picture of her with Ted and their mother. The perfect family. At least that's what most people thought.

Brody turned on the computer and the printer. "Do you know your father's password?"

She typed in the code. When the screen opened, she stepped back to give Brody room. His strong hands played over the keyboard.

He typed, "Why did you come back to Freemont?" The words appeared on the monitor. He hit Print. A mechanical hum filled the silence. A sheet of paper rolled onto the printer tray.

They both gazed down at the typed message. Each letter was crisp and clear without a hint of a smudge, including the *o*.

Relief swept over her. "I told you it wasn't Ted."

"The only thing we can rule out is that he didn't use this printer. I'll check the ones at the Warrior Transitional Battalion tomorrow and the adjoining barracks where your brother lives. The library on post probably has computers, as well."

"Are you going to tell Ted what happened?" she asked.

"I'll ask him if he came home recently and whether he has a key to the house."

"This is his home, Brody. He has every right to come and go as he pleases."

He let out a frustrated breath. "A man was injured today, Stephanie. I need to find out who did it and why. Your brother's actions could play into that investigation. I'm especially interested in learning why he doesn't want you around. Is there anything you haven't told me?"

"You're making more of this than it warrants. Brothers and sisters don't always get along. Our relationship has nothing to do with Josh's accident."

From the determination she saw on Brody's face, she knew he wasn't accepting what she had to say.

"Change your locks, Stephanie. You've got a security alarm system. Be sure to use it, and don't let your brother into the house."

He dug in his pocket and handed her his business card. "Program my phone number into your cell. Call me if you feel threatened in any way."

Brody's nearness caused heat to warm her neck. She raised her hand to cover her flushed skin. She didn't want the CID agent to realize the way she reacted to his closeness and his questions. As appealing as he was in one way, the accusation she read in his penetrating gaze brought a very different type of reaction—one she didn't like—to tingle along her spine.

"I'll keep your phone number close by, Brody, but I'm sure I won't need to call you."

"Then I'll see you in the morning. Any idea what time the mechanic will be on duty?"

"Walt prides himself on opening by seven o'clock. He even includes it in his advertisements."

"I'll be outside your house at six forty-five. You can leave your car at the garage and I'll give you a ride to work. Unless you want to drive the Caddy or BMW."

In spite of what he thought about Ted, she appreciated Brody's thoughtfulness. She didn't want to be beholden to her father, and driving his cars would do exactly that. "I'll take you up on the ride."

Returning to the kitchen, Brody placed the picture and printed note in a plastic bag she provided and tucked it carefully in his jacket pocket.

Together, they walked into the foyer. At the door, he turned too quickly, leaving her a breath away from his broad shoulders.

"Remember, lock your doors and turn on the alarm. If your brother shows up, call me. No matter what time." Brody leaned closer, his gaze intense. "Do you understand me, Stephanie? Call anytime. My phone will be on."

She squared her shoulders, willing herself to be unaffected by his nearness. "I'll be fine, Brody."

Before she could say anything else, he was out the door. She hesitated, evidently a moment too long, because it opened once again.

"Turn on the alarm and lock the door." His voice was firm. "I'm not leaving until you do both things."

She made a shooing motion with her hand. Once he stepped back onto the porch, she closed the door and turned the lock, feeling somewhat satisfied as she twisted the dead bolt and heard the resounding click when it slipped into place.

Stepping toward the security-alarm panel, she tapped in the code. The warning lights flashed, and a beep confirmed the system was engaged.

Brody's footfalls sounded down the porch steps.

She pulled back the curtain in the living room window and watched him climb into his car. The engine engaged.

Even in the darkness, she saw him turn and stare at the house. His eyes flashed in the night. Or was her mind playing tricks on her again?

The headlights came on, illuminating the road as he pulled away from the curb.

With a heavy sigh, she turned from the window and gazed into the massive entryway and living area beyond.

Why did you come back to Freemont? The words of warning flashed through her mind.

Pulling her cell phone from her purse, she tapped in Ted's number and sighed with frustration when it went to voice mail. "It's Stephanie. Call me. I'm at home."

Hanging up, she headed to her childhood bedroom, overcome with a sense of déjà vu. If only her mother hadn't died, everything would still be good, the way she wanted her life to be.

Despite the warning, she wouldn't run away from Freemont. She'd done that once. So had Ted. Now they were both back, and this time she wouldn't let him down.

She flipped on her bedroom light. As keyed up as she was, she'd need to read to calm her frayed nerves before she tried to sleep. She hadn't eaten, but food was the last thing on her mind. Maybe she'd make a sandwich later.

In the bathroom, she scrubbed her face and changed into her nightgown, feeling a bit more refreshed. Glancing at the books on the shelf near her bed, she reached for an anthology of short stories her mother had given her. Finding comfort from the well-worn volume, she grabbed the corner of the plush comforter and pulled back the covers, eager to crawl into bed and lose herself in one of the stories she loved to read.

Glancing down, she moaned.

Tears clouded her eyes. Her heart skittered in her chest and her shoulders tightened.

As much as she wanted to run away, she couldn't pull her gaze from the bull's-eye that marked her bottom sheet. Superimposed over it was a large red X, just like the one that had covered Joshua's face in the photo.

A typed note was pinned to the pillowcase. "Leave Freemont or you'll be in the bull's-eye."

Her brother would never do something so hateful.

Yet, if Ted wasn't playing a terrible joke on her, then who had been in her house and what was the real meaning of the bloodred markings?

Chapter Five

A sense of foreboding settled over Brody when he drove away from Stephanie's home. Glancing back, he had seen her at the window, staring into the night. He hadn't made any points with her this evening, but then his job wasn't to impress her. He needed to convince her to be cautious and to realize her brother's struggle could lead to more problems.

Tomorrow he would talk to her about changing the locks as well as the code on the security alarm, even if she didn't think either precaution was necessary. More often than not, folks outside law enforcement failed to realize the need to be proactive when it came to their own safety. Couldn't she see these threats were personal?

Turning left at the next intersection, Brody drove through the upscale community, focusing on the thick patches of underbrush as well as the shadows behind cars and around fences, searching for anything suspect.

He passed two other vehicles on the road as he canvassed the area, getting to know the layout of the terrain. Although everything seemed in order, someone could be hiding in the darkness. A man on foot could easily pass from house to house and never be seen under the cover of night.

Was Ted Upton in the local area, or had he returned to the barracks? Brody reached for his cell and tapped in the executive officer's number. Major Jenkins answered on the fifth ring.

"Hey, sir. It's Special Agent Brody Goodman. Sorry to bother you after duty hours."

"Not a problem."

"I wanted to determine PFC Upton's whereabouts. Could you notify the duty sergeant and ask him to check Upton's room?"

"Do you mind telling me why you're concerned? Has there been a problem?"

"His sister had an unwanted visitor earlier this evening, which could have been Upton."

"Was she harmed?"

"Negative, but I want to ensure her brother remains on post tonight, and I'd appreciate your help."

"You've got it, of course. I'll have one of the sergeants stop by Upton's room and keep an eye on him."

"I appreciate it, sir."

"Anything else I should know?"

"Only that Ms. Upton may be late for work tomorrow. She had a flat tire and needs to see a mechanic in the morning."

"Why am I thinking it's strange you're the one providing that information?"

"Just trying to help. She'll probably call you in the morning. I'm giving you a heads-up."

"Good enough. I'll contact the WTB."

Wanting to check the Upton property one more time, Brody retraced his route. The night seemed as placid as the water in Stephanie's backyard pool, until he turned onto her street and saw the lights blazing from every room in her house.

His neck tingled a warning. He reached for his cell and tapped in her number. Each ring seemed to last an eternity. His gut tightened. He pulled to the curb, ready to throw the phone on the console, leap from his car and race toward her house with his weapon drawn.

She answered with a cautious "Hello?"

"It's Brody."

He jerked the car door open and stepped onto the pavement. "I'm standing outside, Stephanie. You've got every light on. Are you all right?"

"Yes, of course. I'm fine."

She sounded mildly vexed at him for calling. Whether she liked it or not, he wouldn't leave until she provided a logical answer to the light issue.

"Do you have a problem with the dark?" He couldn't hide the concern in his voice.

"Meaning what, Brody?"

Meaning why didn't she give him a satisfactory answer?

"Electricity costs money, Stephanie. I'm just wondering why every light is on."

He could hear her sigh over the phone. "I was checking the house, just as you did earlier."

His heart softened. He'd scared her, which he hadn't wanted to do. She needed to be cautious, but not fearful.

"You want me to hang around for a while?"

She laughed. The sound lightened the moment. "Thanks for the offer, but I'm feeling better now."

"Why don't you reassure me by opening the front door?"

"Once again, you're being overly protective."

"Humor me, okay?"

She let out another sigh. "I've already changed for bed."

"Then wave from the window."

"If you insist." Her tone had warmed.

The curtain in the dining room moved and Stephanie appeared, backlit. She raised her hand and waved.

"You're okay?" He pulled the cell closer to his lips and stepped toward the window where she stood.

She turned ever so slightly. The light played over her face, allowing him to see her upturned mouth and nodding head.

"I'm okay, Brody. Besides, it's time for me to call it a night. You should go home now."

"Your door's still locked?"

"Of course."

"And the alarm's on?"

"Exactly as it has been ever since you left thirty minutes ago."

"I checked your house, Stephanie. You're locked in. I drove through the neighborhood, as well. Everything seems secure, but if you hear anything outside, call me."

"I'll be fine tonight."

"Then I'll see you in the morning."

He disconnected and headed back to his car. As he climbed behind the wheel, he shook his head. Stephanie probably thought he was crazy for hanging around, but he felt better knowing she was okay.

Glancing back, he watched the lights flick off one by one. The backyard was dark, but the floodlights on the front porch and upper deck remained lit, which would be a deterrent if anyone were wandering around in the night.

Plus, Stephanie had the alarm.

Slowly, he turned onto the main road and drove back to Fort Rickman. Once on post, he headed to his office and checked the photo for prints, finding none, which meant the glossy finish had been wiped clean. He'd have someone go over the note in the morning.

Returning to his car, he drove to the local fast-food restaurant on post and picked up a burger with fries, supersized, and a cold drink.

Usually he would have been anxious to get home, but with the questions that circulated through his head about Stephanie Upton and her estrangement with her brother, Brody doubted he would get a good night's sleep. Instead, he would probably stay up late, pretending to watch the sports channel, while he tried to put together the pieces of this investigation.

What was it about Stephanie Upton that bothered him? He sighed. *Bothered* wasn't the right word. She'd gotten under his skin. He didn't know how or why.

He hadn't been attracted to anyone since Lisa and had never thought those types of feelings would surface again. Yet here he was thinking about a woman who was totally focused on repairing her relationship with her brother, a man Brody considered a threat.

Once inside his quarters, he shoved the burger and fries into his mouth and gulped down the cola. His mixed emotions might have been brought on by hunger, but even after eating, he couldn't get Stephanie off his mind.

Talk about a conflict of interests. Maybe he should turn over the investigation to someone else at headquarters and move on. He shook his head, knowing that wasn't an option, especially as short staffed as they were. Besides, something had happened to him today. Whether appropriate or not, he was already involved.

Stephanie exhaled, deeply confused by Brody. Why had he been hanging around her house? Surely it had nothing to do with her and everything to do with Ted. She never should have allowed the special agent to follow her home or to come inside.

She hadn't told him about the markings on the bedsheets, fearing he would instantly suspect Ted. If his attitude toward her brother changed, she would show him the note that had been pinned to her pillowcase. Taking care not to touch her hand to the paper, she had used tweezers to enclose the message in a Ziploc bag, just as Brody had done with the note in the kitchen. He could run a fingerprint check later, when and if she told him about the incident. For now, she would keep the information to herself.

After turning off the lights, she headed for the guest room, knowing she'd never be able to get any rest in her own room with the marked bedding. Once again, she tried unsuccessfully to call Ted.

Tomorrow, she would track him down and have a heart-to-heart talk.

Would he listen?

More than likely, he'd fiddle with his smart phone and check his email, maybe send a text message or two to indicate that he wasn't interested in healing their relationship or in anything she had to say. She'd already gotten that message with her unreturned phone calls and his hateful comments at Joshua's house earlier today.

Regrettably, Brody had heard those comments, too. If only she could erase what had happened and start fresh.

But it was too late for that.

Brody would be back bright and early the next morning. She needed to get some sleep, but when she turned off the light, she saw Joshua's face and the blood on the bathroom floor.

She tossed and turned for what seemed like hours until she finally drifted into a fitful slumber, studded with horrific dreams. She was in the water, swimming through murky blackness. The wind howled around her, hurling large whitecaps that crashed over her head. A deadly cold soaked into her bones along with a heavy lethargy, yet she had to go on.

Diving down into the turbid water, she reached for Hayden. His hand slipped from hers, replaced with a flash of memory. Something she'd buried from her youth in the deep recesses of her psyche.

The flash disappeared.

She was on *The Upton Queen,* her father's boat. Ted stood at the stern, his hand gripping the rope attached to the ship's bell. Over and over again, he yanked on the cord, causing the bell to peal into the night.

She could see it play out with dreamlike clarity.

Nikki leaned against the railing, a large beach towel around her shoulders, staring with big eyes into the lake. Paul and Josh sat on the deck, impaired by the alcohol they had consumed. Another teen, Cindy Ferrol, appeared too pasty white, her shoulder injured from jumping off the rope swing into the rapid current. Tears streamed down her blotched cheeks.

The bell continued to peal.

Stephanie tried to drown out the death knell that sounded too loud, too real, too—

She sat up in bed, a cold sweat dampening her neck. The bell hadn't been a dream.

As she listened, it tolled again. Once, twice, three times.

The chilling sound filled the night and sent her scurrying down the hallway and into the great room. She stepped to the window and peered out at the dark pool and the yard beyond, expecting to see Ted.

Instead, she saw the water and the trees and the now-silent bell.

Was her mind playing tricks on her?

Or was someone out there? She thought of the photo of the old gang and the bull's-eye covering Joshua's face. Nikki, Cindy, Paul? They had heard Ted ring the bell. Were they trying to scare her tonight? Or were they all in danger?

Stephanie had made a mistake three years ago. She couldn't make another mistake. The stakes were too high.

Today Josh had been injured and could have died.

Next time, would it be Ted? Or Paul?

If only she could remember what she had seen that night as she searched for Hayden. A flash from her past that eluded her even now.

A sound on the front steps caused her to turn from the window and stare through the foyer at the oak door. Had it been a creaking porch floorboard or footsteps?

She held her breath, listening. All she heard was her pounding heart mixed with the drone of the air-conditioning system and the hum of cool air coming through the vents.

Glancing down, she realized her cell phone was in her hand. She had programmed Brody Goodman's cell number into her contacts file. As much as she wanted to call him, she couldn't feed his growing antagonism toward her brother.

The security alarm was on. The doors and windows were locked. Earlier, Brody had assured her she was safe. Nothing had changed, except now she didn't feel safe or secure. Was she in danger?

Chapter Six

The front door opened the next morning before Brody had climbed the stairs to the Uptons' porch. Stephanie stood in the threshold, wearing a flowered top and flowing skirt and a smile that sent a warm glow to his midsection. An unexpected breeze picked at her skirt and swirled the thin, gauzy cotton around her legs. The motion of the material drew his eyes to her strappy sandals and pink toenail polish.

The collar of his white shirt felt tight. He adjusted his tie and pulled his gaze away from her toes and back to her eyes, which were regarding him with a hint of mischief, as if she realized the effect the pink polish had on him.

Attractive though she was, and as cute as her toes were with the flashy polish, Brody had to admit he was even more taken by her attempt to be upbeat after everything that had happened yesterday.

"Give me a second to set the alarm and then I'll be ready," she said. The system beeped as she tapped in the activation code. A longer buzz indicated the program was set.

Grabbing her purse and briefcase off a small table in the foyer, she stepped outside. "Something tells me you didn't grow up in a small town." She pulled the door shut behind her.

"Only if you call L.A. small."

She laughed, a throaty sound that caused a curl of interest to tighten his chest. "Here's how it works in Freemont. We may have home security alarms, but we rarely use them."

He gave her a mock salute. "Then thank you, ma'am, for humoring me today by arming and activating your system."

"I wouldn't want you to worry." She laughed again, but as close as they were standing, Brody could see the tiny lines of fatigue that pulled at the corners of her smile. Evidently, she had slept as little as he had.

"Ferrol's Garage is on one of the side streets downtown," she said as they walked toward her car.

Brody pointed to the rear tire. "That spare doesn't look very dependable, Stephanie. I'll be right behind you if there's a problem."

He held the door and inhaled the sweet floral scent of her perfume as she slipped past him into the driver's seat. Once she buckled up, Brody climbed into his own car. Stephanie drove at a modest speed, and they reached Ferrol's Garage's parking lot without incident.

The door to the mechanic's bay hung open. A man in jeans and a gray short-sleeved shirt peered out from under the hood of a car.

"Long time, no see, Stephanie." He walked outside to greet them, wiping his hands on a small towel that was shoved in his back pocket. "I heard you were staying at your dad's place."

"Until I can find an apartment." She introduced Brody, who shook the mechanic's strong, work-worn hand.

Walt Ferrol was about five-eleven and stocky, with a thick neck and beady eyes that narrowed even more when he glanced at Brody's gray slacks and lightweight sport coat.

"You must be a civilian."

"Actually, I'm a warrant officer and special agent with the Criminal Investigation Division. We wear civilian clothes when investigating a case."

The mechanic's face tightened. "Don't tell me you're here because of what happened to Joshua?"

"Are you aware of anyone who would want to harm Private Webb?"

"Not Josh. He was always a good kid. Shame what happened to him in Afghanistan."

"What about a red pickup with oversize tires? Anyone you know own that type of vehicle?"

Walt whistled, long and low. "Sounds like that juiced-up Ford Hayden Allen used to drive."

Stephanie shook her head. "It was raining, and the visibility wasn't good, but I never thought it was Hayden's truck."

"What happened to the Ford?" Brody asked.

"You'd have to talk to Keith," Walt said.

Brody remembered the name from the newspaper story. "Hayden's brother?"

Stephanie nodded. "That's right."

"Keith has an office at Freemont Real Estate," the mechanic volunteered. "He started working for them right before the influx of new military folks came to town. Made a killing, or so folks said."

Brody raised his eyebrow ever so slightly at the mechanic's choice of words.

Walt tugged at his chin. "How does Hayden's Ford tie in with what happened to Joshua?"

"It wasn't Hayden's truck," she insisted.

"Stephanie saw a red pickup with mud tires leaving Josh's subdivision right before she discovered his injuries," Brody said, watching how Walt processed the information.

The mechanic hesitated a moment, and then leaned toward her. "Did you recognize the driver?"

She shook her head. "Everything happened too fast."

Walt sniffed. "Probably just a coincidence, then."

Brody pulled a business card from his coat pocket and handed it to the mechanic. "Call me if you hear anything that might have bearing on this case. I want to know who's responsible."

Walt nodded enthusiastically. "I feel the same way. Especially since Josh and Cindy were such good friends."

"Who's Cindy?" Another name from the newspaper article, but he would let Walt tell him what he already suspected.

"My baby sister. She and Josh went to school together." He pointed to Stephanie. "Along with her brother, Ted, and Hayden and Paul Massey and Nikki Dunn. They were inseparable, but after Hayden's death, the whole gang fell apart."

Shaking his head at Stephanie, he added, "My sister rarely sees Nikki, yet the two girls were so close in high school."

"People grow up and grow apart, Walt."

He pursed his full lips. "I suppose you're right. Cindy works for me in the office now. Helps out in the shop if we're busy. She's got herself a little place east of town. A few acres."

"Good for her."

Walt pointed to Stephanie's Corolla. "Looks like you could use a new tire on that back wheel."

"That's why I'm here." She opened the trunk and stepped back so Walt could inspect the flat tire. "There's a problem with the valve stem."

The mechanic chuckled. "What happened? Ted playing tricks again?"

She bristled. "Of course not."

He rubbed his fingers over the worn rubber tread. "Don't like being the bearer of bad news, but the tread's about gone on this baby. Doubt it would last to the end of the week, even with a new valve stem."

Brody agreed. "Is there a tire dealer in town?"

Walt jammed a thumb back at his own chest. Pride flashed from his eyes. "You're looking at him. If you want, I'll order you a new tire, Stephanie. Should take a couple days. Although if you want my advice, I'd replace all four tires. To be safe."

She groaned internally. Her monthly budget was already stretched too thin. "I'll have to think it over. Get a quote. Then call me."

She pulled a business card from her purse and scribbled another number on the back before handing it to Walt. "My cell number's listed under my name. The landline to my office is on the other side."

A late-model sports car pulled into the lot. The driver, a woman, early twenties with brown hair, waved. She wore tight jeans and a gray polo that matched Walt's shirt.

Big silver loops dangled from her ears, and a number

of bracelets clinked as she walked toward them. "Hey there, Stephanie. I heard you were back in town. Ted must be glad to see you."

Ignoring the comment about her brother, Stephanie introduced Brody to Walt's sister, Cindy.

"How are you, ma'am?"

"A few minutes late this morning. Is there anything you need, Walt?"

"Check the price on new tires for Stephanie's car."

"Will do."

Walt gave Stephanie's card to his sister and pointed to Brody. "Special Agent Goodman asked about Hayden's truck. Someone driving a similar vehicle may have been involved in Joshua's accident."

Cindy shook her head. "I haven't seen his truck around these parts for at least two years. Keith would know for sure." She glanced at her watch. "He opens his office at eight, but he usually eats breakfast at the diner. You might find him there."

Once back in his car, Brody turned to Stephanie and smiled. "I'll buy breakfast."

"You don't need to talk to Keith. The truck wasn't Hayden's."

"You're sure?"

She sighed. "I told you, everything happened rather quickly. All I saw was a red pickup with oversize wheels that screeched out of the subdivision. I was more concerned about not getting hit rather than the make and model, yet it didn't seem as big and bulky as Hayden's truck."

Brody glanced at his watch. "No pressure, but we've got some time before work and I'm hungry. If we see Keith, so much the better."

With a look of resignation, she pointed to the next intersection. "Turn right on Third Street. The diner's not far from the courthouse on the square."

Brody headed toward the center of town. "From what Walt said, I gather Cindy and Ted were friends in high school."

Stephanie nodded. "All the kids hung around together. Ted and Nikki dated most of their senior year. They broke up, and she ended up going to the prom with Hayden."

"In his spruced-up red Ford?"

Stephanie smiled. "Which all the girls loved. Hayden was a ladies' man as well as a good kid."

"Walt said the group fell apart after his death."

"The guys enlisted. Cindy used to help her mom with a home-cleaning business. I'm not sure when she started working for Walt. At some point Nikki got a job at the PX on post."

"How did she take Hayden's death?"

"Nikki was devastated. All the kids were. Folks in town mourned his death, as well. Hayden had been accepted to Georgia Tech and planned to be an engineer like his dad. People thought he'd come back to Freemont and help to put the town on the map."

"So his death was tough on everyone."

Stephanie nodded. "Especially his mother. Hayden was Aunt Hazel's pride and joy. Her marriage wasn't the best, and my uncle died when Hayden was in middle school, which is probably why she clung so tightly to him. He was definitely her favorite."

"She's your mother's sister?"

"That's right."

"Tell me about Keith. Growing up, were you two close?"

She tilted her head. "Keith was two years older than me and had his own friends."

"What about his relationship with Hayden?"

"There was a bit of sibling rivalry, which happens in a lot of families. Hayden excelled in just about everything he did. Folks thought he would go far."

"And Keith wasn't the shining star?"

"He didn't have the spark that made Hayden stand out. Everyone liked Hayden, and my aunt made no attempt to hide which son had her heart."

"Was Keith jealous of his brother?"

"Not that I could tell."

"How's his relationship with his mother now?"

"I'm not sure. Aunt Hazel suffered a stroke not long after Hayden's death. Keith couldn't care for her at home and placed her in the local nursing home."

A sad situation all around.

The diner appeared in the distance. Brody parked in the lot behind the small restaurant. Stephanie nodded to a number of the early-morning patrons, who smiled as they entered. A waitress pointed them toward a booth and brought two cups of steaming coffee along with menus.

"How's the food here?" Brody asked once they were seated and the waitress had retreated to the counter.

Stephanie glanced at him over the menu. "Home cooking and very Southern."

"Which means grits and biscuits and gravy are a must." Brody's mouth watered.

Before he could motion the waitress back to the table to place their order, a man stepped inside. Early thirties with slicked-back hair. He was wearing a light blue, button-down collared shirt and khaki slacks and stopped to talk to a number of the diners before he spied Stephanie and waved.

Her shoulders tightened and the tendons stood out on her slender neck as he approached their table.

"How are you, Steph?"

"Fine, Keith."

He shoved a hand in Brody's face. "Keith Allen. Walt said you're from the fort."

Brody stood and accepted Keith's outstretched hand. "Special Agent Goodman, with the CID."

"Investigating what happened yesterday." Keith shook his head with regret. "I hated to hear that Josh was hurt."

"Walt phoned you?" Brody asked.

"He wanted to make sure I met up with my favorite cousin." Keith smiled down at Stephanie, still sitting in the booth. "Mother asked about you. She heard you came home."

"How is Aunt Hazel?"

"The same. No better. No worse." He turned to the waitress and held up his hand. "Coffee, Charlotte."

She poured a cup and headed his way. "You want a menu, Keith?"

"Not today. Bring me the usual."

"You joining these folks?" the waitress asked.

Stephanie glanced at her watch. "I wish we could stay, but I've got to be at work soon."

So much for Southern cooking and a hot breakfast. Brody followed Stephanie's lead and dropped a handful of bills on the table. "Coffee's all we have time for this morning, Charlotte."

Stephanie slid from the booth. "Brody's looking for a

red pickup with big tires. Walt told him it sounded like Hayden's Ford, but you got rid of the truck some time ago, right?"

Keith nodded. "I sold it at Old Man Lear's car auction a few months after Hayden's funeral."

"Who made the purchase?" Brody asked.

"A farmer from Alabama, but I can't remember his name. I've probably got it at home someplace. Does it have bearing on what happened to Josh?"

"Not necessarily. Do you know anyone who would want to do Josh harm?"

Keith shook his head. "Not in this town. Folks are interested in giving him a hand up. I've got a group of business folks who want to cover his home-remodeling expenses." He glanced at Stephanie. "We can talk about those plans once Josh's condition improves."

"I know he could use the help," she said.

Brody handed his card to the real-estate agent. "If you find the farmer's name, call me."

"Good seeing you, Keith." Stephanie turned to leave.

"Wait, Steph." He grabbed her arm. "I heard you were the new AW2 advocate on post. I was working with the guy who held the position before you. We planned a picnic for some of the soldiers in the WTB a week from Saturday. Did you happen to see the file in his office?" Keith shrugged and smiled sheepishly. "I guess it's your office now."

"I looked it over briefly. I…I didn't realize you were coordinating the event."

He held up his hand. "I'm just one of many folks interested in supporting our military. We've got lots of corporate sponsors. It should be a great day. I rounded up the old gang and asked them to get involved."

"The old gang?"

He nodded. "That's right. Paul took leave so he could help. Nikki's volunteered, and Cindy, too. I wanted everything to be special for Ted and Joshua. Of course, after what happened yesterday, I don't know if Joshua will be able to attend."

"Did you get Major Jenkins's approval?" Stephanie asked.

Keith nodded. "He's behind it one hundred percent."

"A week from Saturday doesn't leave much planning time."

"Not to worry." Keith smiled. "Everything's on schedule—in fact, a few of us are meeting today to check out the facilities. Why don't you join us? Two o'clock at the marina, or we can meet up on the island if you want to take your dad's boat. The city recently renovated the picnic facilities and they're top-of-the-line."

"I'll check my schedule and get back to you." Once again she glanced at her watch and then at Brody as if needing his help. "I've got to go or I'll be late for work."

Brody followed her outside. Something was going on between Keith and Stephanie, an undercurrent Brody couldn't explain. Every family had its own secrets, although in small towns secrets were often hard to keep.

He thought of the note left on Stephanie's kitchen counter. Had someone other than Ted warned her away from Freemont?

"You mind explaining what the problem is with you and Keith?" he asked once they were in his car.

"There's no problem."

"Come on, Stephanie. I could feel the tension between you two."

"It's nothing that's relevant to your investigation, Brody."

He glanced at her for a long moment before he pulled onto the road. "We're going back to your house."

"Why?"

"So you can get a change of clothes and some better shoes if we're going to the island later today."

"We?"

"I'll drive you. Besides, I told Major Jenkins I wanted to help the WTB."

She glanced at her watch. "I don't want to be late for work."

"You won't be. I promise."

But when he drove into the Country Club Estates and turned onto Stephanie's street, Brody's gut tightened, knowing he wouldn't be able to keep his word.

"What happened?" Stephanie's eyes were wide as she stared at her house.

A police car was parked on the curb. Two officers stood on her front porch, staring into her windows, their guns drawn.

Stephanie opened the passenger door before Brody had put the car in Park. He grabbed her arm. "Stay in the car."

"It could be Ted. I need to know what happened."

"Let me check it out first." Before she could object, he had rounded the car and closed the passenger door.

The air-conditioning was running, and the cool air from the vent brushed against her hair but did nothing to calm the anxiety that rolled through her stomach.

She opened her door again and stepped onto the sidewalk, determined to hear what Brody was saying as he approached the officers and held up his CID identification.

The car engine muffled their voices so she caught only snippets of conversation.

"…the alarm…"

"…locked…checked the rear…"

Brody nodded and walked back to where she stood.

"Did something happen to my brother?" she asked, half-afraid to hear his response.

"The security alarm went off. The police responded, but the doors are locked. Give me your keys and we'll check the house."

"Did they say how it happened?"

"Only that sometimes the motion sensors can be activated if there's a pet inside. Even dust in the system can be a problem."

She shook her head. "No pets."

"Wait here."

The three men disappeared into the house. She caught glimpses of them through the windows as they fanned out to various areas of the two-floor structure.

In a shorter time than she had expected, Brody appeared in the doorway, his face somber. He motioned her forward.

Anxiety tingled along her spine. She knew full well what he had found. Something she hadn't mentioned either last night or this morning.

"We found a bull's-eye on your bedsheets." His voice was tense but controlled as she climbed the steps.

"I know, Brody. The marks and the note were there yesterday. That's the reason I had the lights on last night."

"But you didn't tell me?"

"I didn't want to alarm you."

He clenched his hands for a moment and then relaxed them as he gently took her arm and ushered her inside.

The two police officers were in her bedroom. "They're getting prints," Brody explained. "The sheets will be taken in as evidence."

"Nothing happened to me last night."

"Someone marked your bedding, Stephanie. He, she or they left a warning. That's not something to laugh about."

"I'm not laughing."

"But you failed to tell me."

She straightened her spine. "Because you would have suspected Ted."

"Do you think he's responsible?"

"Absolutely not."

"Who else would come into your home and desecrate your bedding? Is there something from your past? Maybe something that happened after Hayden's death? Someone that wants you out of town?"

She shook her head, suddenly seeing everything through Brody's eyes. "I should have told you."

"What about your job at Fort Stewart? Is there anyone who might follow you here and try to do you harm?"

"Not that I'm aware of."

"Anyone who was confrontational?"

"Never."

"Where did you find the typed note?"

"Pinned to the pillowcase. I used tweezers to put it in the plastic bag."

"Then you did plan to give it to me?"

She sighed. "I don't know what I planned to do."

"Is there anything else I don't know, Stephanie?"

"The bell." She glanced through the large windows and pointed to the backyard. "I awoke in the night and thought I heard it ringing, but when I went to the window no one was there."

"What time was that?"

"After midnight."

"Anything else?"

"A sound on the front porch. It was probably the wind."

"You said probably. If it wasn't the wind, what else could it have been?"

"It sounded like footsteps."

His eyes widened ever so slightly. "But you didn't call me."

She shook her head. "The alarm was on. The doors were locked. You told me I was safe."

His voice softened. "I told you to call me."

She turned away, unwilling to see the disappointment in his gaze. In hindsight, she had made a mistake by not calling him. Last night, her only thought had been to protect Ted. This morning she realized how vulnerable she had been.

Someone had entered the house.

To scare her?

Or to do her harm?

Chapter Seven

The Freemont police gathered evidence and checked the front door for prints before they left. Stephanie packed a small tote with an outfit and shoes appropriate for the trip to Big Island and met Brody back in the living room.

"I really am sorry," she said. "A lot happened yesterday. I've been worried about my brother. The shock of finding Joshua. All the blood." She tried to smile, knowing she wasn't successful. Surely he recognized her struggle.

"I wasn't thinking straight," she continued to explain. "Plus, we had only just met yesterday, and calling in the middle of the night didn't seem right. If I had felt threatened, I would have dialed nine-one-one. You can see from the officer's response today, help would have arrived."

He nodded. "I don't want you to be unduly afraid, but the bull's-eye on your sheets was significant. You've got to be cautious and aware of your surroundings at all times."

"I understand."

"You also need to change your locks and your alarm."

"It's my father's house. I don't have that authority."

"You could call him."

"I could, but I don't think it's necessary at this time."

Brody shook his head as if exasperated by her response. "At least promise that if anything else happens, you'll call me. That's why I gave you my number."

"I will."

"Now, let's get you to work."

She walked with him to his car, relieved they had reached an agreement of sorts. He seemed less certain that Ted was involved and more concerned that someone else could have entered the house. Why had she left the door unlocked yesterday? Or had it been locked, as she'd originally thought?

Sitting next to him in the passenger seat, she turned to look out the window as he headed for Freemont Road, which led to post.

At least everything was out in the open now, and she would call Brody if there was a next time, which hopefully there wouldn't be. Surely what had happened yesterday was a once-in-a-lifetime occurrence. If only she knew what had triggered the anger someone must harbor against her or her family.

Her dad had made enemies in his years running a large company. Some folks had been laid off. Others were upset about his expansion in Europe and questioned why he didn't grow his United States assets. With the downturn in the economy, she was sure he had a number of disgruntled employees. Perhaps the attack had been aimed at him.

She sighed inwardly, knowing the warning had been for her. Her sheets had been marked, and the note had been pinned to her pillowcase.

Paul and Hayden had been close prior to their senior year. After Hayden's death, Paul had turned to Ted for support and had followed both Josh and her brother into the army. She'd heard talk that he had wanted to be deployed along with his buddies and regretted his stateside assignments.

Ted blamed her for what had happened to Hayden. Did Paul, as well?

She turned toward Brody, his steady gaze on the road, his lips downturned. Lips she didn't want to look at now.

He was probably mentally going over what had happened, just as she had been. His left hand gripped the steering wheel. The other one rested on the console, so very close to hers.

Too close.

She wiggled toward the door. Everything about Brody had become a huge distraction.

She swallowed hard. The air-conditioning blew on her face. She adjusted the vent.

"Are you too cold?" he asked.

"A little." She rubbed her hands over her arms.

Brody adjusted the thermostat. "Better?"

"Yes, thanks." She needed something to focus on instead of Brody's penetrating eyes, which seemed to look into her soul.

"I'm surprised Keith is involved with the Wounded Warriors," she finally said. "He didn't have much good to say about the army when he was younger."

Brody nodded. "Some kids are drawn to the military. Others aren't."

"The old Keith wouldn't have thought about Josh or Ted. Nor would he have called the gang together and gotten them involved."

When Brody failed to comment, she pursed her lips and shrugged. "Maybe he's changed for the better." She fiddled with her hair and added, "I worried about Keith after the drowning. He was in denial, pretending to be fine, but he had to hurt as much, if not more than anyone else." She dropped her hand to her lap. "You can't lose someone in your family and not be overwhelmed with pain."

Brody nodded.

"Families are important," she continued. "They provide affirmation and support and love."

"Did Keith feel loved by his mom?"

"I'm sure he did, even if she doted on Hayden. Maybe that's why Keith was reserved as a kid. He didn't want to compete with his brother."

"Everyone needs love and affirmation, but people grow up and become stable adults in spite of dysfunctional families and the mistakes they made in their youth." Brody smiled. "I made some poor decisions when I was a kid."

"I'm sure you never messed with someone else's life."

"Mistakes happen, Stephanie."

"Some mistakes are worse than others."

He glanced at her. "Who are we talking about?"

She let out a frustration sigh. "Why, Keith, of course."

"What mistake did he make?"

"Not being there for Hayden."

"Maybe he had to work so hard to protect himself that he didn't realize Hayden needed help, too."

Stephanie thought back to that day on the lake. Keith had been delayed in Atlanta and had failed to pick the teens up from the island. Surely that memory haunted him still, yet he'd never told her why he'd been held up.

"Did you know about the picnic for the Warriors?" Brody asked.

"I saw something on the appointment calendar and glanced at some notes the former advocate had made. The only sponsor mentioned was Freemont Real Estate. I didn't tie it to Keith."

"Sounds like it could be a nice day. Especially if Keith has the WTB commander's approval."

"Maybe, but Big Island isn't the best place for a picnic. It's in the middle of a large lake, and storms come up quickly. We'll have to check that the weather is going to be clear that day."

"I'd be happy to stop by city hall and find out about the facilities before I pick you up this afternoon."

"That would help reassure me. Thank you, Brody."

She sat back in the seat and tried to relax. "You're probably right. The day should be lovely, and I'm sure everyone will be safe."

She wouldn't tell Brody the main problem was that she never wanted to go back to Big Island. Too many memories still haunted her.

If she felt that way, Ted would, as well. He didn't need anything else to upset him. Especially memories neither of them had been able to forget.

After dropping Stephanie off at her office, Brody talked to her brother's squad leader. Ted had been in his barracks last night, according to the sergeant. Brody didn't know whether to feel relieved or even more concerned.

He called Fort Stewart CID and asked them to question the WTB there, and also the folks who had worked with Stephanie, in case she hadn't realized a danger that someone else may have suspected.

Stopping by his office, he called the Freemont Police Department and set up an appointment to talk to the new chief. Don Palmer, a big guy—midforties—with broad shoulders and a thick neck, greeted him a short while later with a firm handshake.

"My men told me you pointed out a few flaws in their investigation at PFC Webb's house yesterday." He motioned Brody to sit while he poured two cups of coffee. "Appreciate the help."

"Not a problem, sir." Brody accepted one of the cups. The two men discussed Josh's injury and Brody's suspicions. The chief said his men had gone door-to-door in the neighborhood, but no one had seen anything or anyone. In addition, they'd checked for prints but hadn't found anything conclusive.

Brody shared the photos of the bathroom he'd taken on his phone and discussed the angle of the blood spatter and Josh's head trauma.

"I agree with your assessment," the chief said. "Looks like someone attacked him from behind. Any idea about the bathwater?"

"Not at this point. Although I'll question the other soldiers in the Warrior Transitional Battalion where Josh is assigned and let you know if I hear anything."

Chief Palmer nodded. "I'd appreciate any help you can give us. If you work the on-post angle, we'll investigate in Freemont. Two more set of eyes and ears would be a win-win in my opinion."

"I'll be happy to help."

Brody mentioned the bull's-eyes and notes left at

Stephanie's home, hoping the chief might be able to shed light on the vandalism.

"If her door wasn't locked, anyone could have entered the house," the chief said, pointing out the obvious.

"She thought she had engaged the lock, but admitted being in a hurry." Brody shrugged. "New job, rushing to get to post for a social event."

"I'll increase patrols in the Estates."

"Have there been any break-ins?"

"Not recently, but things can change in a heartbeat."

Which Brody knew too well. "I met Keith Allen this morning. He works for Freemont Real Estate."

Palmer nodded. "Keith's a nice guy who does a lot of good in town."

"What about his past?"

"Past as in his youth?"

"If you've got information."

"I grew up in Freemont. The Allen family has always been prominent, although we came from different sides of town. My family was from a less affluent area."

"The Allens were well-to-do."

"*Wealthy* would be a better choice of words. They lived in the Country Club Estates. His father started the development, and his home was the first one constructed in the area."

"So Daddy was in real estate."

"A contractor, who died of a heart attack much too young. His marriage was rocky, and most folks said he worked himself to death. He built many of the buildings in town, as well. Plus, he won a number of bids at Fort Rickman."

"What about Davis Upton? Isn't he a manufacturer?"

"Who also received a number of federal contracts."

"Did the two men work together?"

Palmer shrugged. "I'm not sure, but they both had dealings with new construction on post."

"And both benefited from those jobs."

"That's right." The chief straightened in his chair. "I'm in favor of a man making a living, Agent Goodman, so I don't understand your point."

"Just trying to see the dynamic between the two families. Mrs. Upton and Mrs. Allen were sisters."

"That's right, but the families weren't particularly close." Palmer took a long swig from his cup. "Jane Upton was about six months' pregnant with Ted when Hazel Allen became pregnant. Up until then, the two families had mingled socially. After the boys were born, some type of split developed, and the two women were rarely seen together after that. About the same time, the Allens' marriage went south."

Brody raised his brow.

The chief shrugged nonchalantly. "A lot of folks are related in a small town like Freemont. Sometimes we like our kin. Sometimes we don't, but they're still kin."

"Tell me about Keith growing up."

"He was a quiet kid. Didn't apply himself to his studies. The same could be said for a lot of high school boys."

"And his brother, Hayden?"

Palmer nodded. "Now I see where you're headed. Hayden was the golden boy who could do no wrong. Everyone in town liked the kid, even though he started running with a wild crowd in his senior year."

"Ted Upton?"

"That's right. They were in the same grade at school, although Hayden was a bit younger. Paul Massey was part of the group. Joshua Webb, as well. The guys were determined to push the envelope in most things they attempted. Two girls hung around with them, Nikki Dunn and Cindy Ferrol. Not that the girls were bad, but they made poor choices in the guys they dated."

"Nikki dated Hayden?"

"She was sweet on Ted at first. They broke up their senior year. Not long after that, she started dating Hayden and went with him to the prom, which seemed to surprise everyone."

"How'd Ted take it?"

"He got stopped for drag racing later that same night."

Brody sat back in the chair. "All this happened three years ago, yet you seem to be pretty sure about your details, Chief. I don't want to be disrespectful, but you mind telling me how you can recall everything with such clarity?"

"My daughter was in Ted's class. For whatever reason, girls like bad boys. I wanted to know everything there was to learn about Ted Upton, and you can bet I kept my eyes on him. Last thing I wanted was to find him with my daughter."

"Did anything develop between them?"

"I didn't let it. In fact, I insisted she head to college for summer semester right after high school graduation. Getting her out of town was the best decision I've ever made. Didn't take her long to realize there were a lot more eligible guys at the University of Georgia, in Athens, rather than back in Freemont, Georgia."

"What about Ted's drag-racing charge?"

"His father got it dropped. Ted enlisted. Josh and Paul followed suit, and life became a whole lot easier once the boys left town."

"They were a constant problem?"

"More like a bigger-than-normal nuisance. Ted came from an okay family, although his daddy was more interested in growing his business than forming a relationship with his teenage son. The mother was a nice lady, liked by all. Shame was, she got cancer and died when Ted was a freshman in high school. The kid went downhill from then on."

"What about his sister?"

"Stephanie tried to keep him on the straight and narrow, but the job was more than she could handle. Ted had a surly mouth and a bad attitude and didn't listen to her. Most folks thought Stephanie did more than she should have to help the kid. With her dad gone most of the time, she reconnected with her aunt Hazel, but that relationship eventually ended."

Brody leaned forward ever so slightly, waiting for more information.

The cop pursed his lips. "You've probably heard about the drowning at Big Island Lake?"

"Bits and pieces."

"Ted, Hayden, Josh and Paul had spent the day on the island. They were drinking. Nikki and Cindy joined them at some point. There used to be a rope swing that swung out over the rocky channel between Big Island and Little Island to the south. Currents can be strong in that area. The water's deep, and storms make the situation even worse, which is what happened."

"Keith Allen was supposed to pick the kids up?"

Palmer nodded. "But he had driven to Atlanta and didn't return until later that night."

"So the teens were stranded."

"And in the water when the storm hit. After all the booze they'd consumed, getting to shore became a prob-

lem. Hayden and Cindy jumped from the rope swing.
She hurt her arm. Supposedly Hayden hit the water hard.
He may have been knocked unconscious or got caught
in the current."

"And was never seen again?"

"Until the underwater crew pulled his body to the
surface."

"How'd Stephanie Upton get involved?"

"Ted had called her earlier, when Keith didn't show,
and said they needed a ride back to the mainland. By
the time she arrived, the storm was in full fury, and the
kids were struggling in the water. To her credit, Stephanie rescued everyone except Hayden."

Brody's heart ached for her. No wonder Stephanie
didn't want to face her aunt or didn't have a more forthright relationship with her surviving cousin.

"Did you talk to Keith after the incident?"

"He was pretty shaken. Blamed himself for being
held up in Atlanta."

"What about Mrs. Allen?"

Palmer shook his head. "She was never the same after
her son's death. It was as if the life had been taken from
her, as well. Not long thereafter, she had a stroke. Probably the stress and grief."

"Hayden had a red Ford pickup truck, mud tires. Supposedly, it was sold at auction. You know anything about
it?"

"Easy enough to find out. Earl Lear runs the only
auction in this area. I'll call him." The chief reached for
his phone and tapped in a series of digits.

He rubbed his chin. "Hey, Earl, this is Chief Palmer.
I need some information about that red, jacked-up truck

Hayden Allen used to drive." He nodded. "Can you tell me who bought it?"

Palmer eyed Brody and pulled his mouth away from the receiver. "Earl's checking his records. Shouldn't be too hard to track down the buyer."

Palmer reached for a pen and positioned a small tablet on his desk. "I'm ready to copy."

He jotted a name and phone number on the paper. "Thanks, Earl."

The cop rewrote the message, tore the page from the spiral notebook and handed it to Brody. "The truck sold to a Sam Franken. The guy lives on a rural route not far from Montgomery over in Alabama. You think it might be the same truck that Stephanie Upton mentioned yesterday?"

"I have no idea, but both vehicles fit the same relative description."

"We'll pull Department of Motor Vehicle records and check on any trucks, red in color, belonging to folks in this area. Could be a lengthy list, but I'll let you know what we find."

"Sounds good, Chief." Brody gave his card to Palmer and then dropped the disposable cup in the trash. "Appreciate the coffee and your time. I'll be in touch."

Brody left the station with more information than he had expected. Just as he had feared, Ted had been on a downward spiral in high school. The military may have helped to straighten him out, but he still had a problem when it came to his sister. A bigger problem than anyone, except Brody, seemed to realize.

Chapter Eight

After glancing at her watch for the fourth time, Stephanie pushed away from her desk and shoved the papers she was working on into her bottom drawer. Grabbing her purse and tote, she changed clothes and shoes in the restroom and left the office to wait for Brody outside. As a rule, military guys were punctual, and his car turned into the lot before she reached the sidewalk.

"I hate pulling you away from your CID work, Brody." He bounded around the front of the car and stood holding the passenger door for her, which made her smile. He, too, had changed and was dressed in a polo and khaki slacks and Top-Siders. His phone was strapped to his waist. Knowing how conscientious Brody was, he'd probably used an ankle holster for his service weapon.

His smile was warm and welcoming as he climbed behind the wheel. "I stopped by city hall. The clerk said Keith reserved the entire picnic area some months ago, and since then, Freemont Real Estate matched the municipal funds so the facilities would be ready to use."

"Did you find out what's available?"

"There's a large kitchen, an outdoor dining pavilion and restrooms. They've installed a playground for kids and have wheelchair ramps, which will be perfect for any of the military who aren't mobile. Evidently they're still working to shore up some of the trails. Signs are posted on areas under construction that need to be avoided."

"Keith emailed me a couple hours ago. His message included an itinerary for the day, including volleyball and a fun run."

"Sounds as if your cousin has turned into a staunch military supporter."

"Which makes me glad."

The sunshine coming through the window cheered Stephanie's spirits, and the change of scenery helped improve her outlook. Taking a drive on this lovely summer day was just what she needed.

She and Brody talked about everything except her brother or Josh or bedsheets painted with a bull's-eye. By the time they arrived at the marina, she was feeling refreshed, but once she glanced at her father's cabin cruiser moored to the dock, her stomach soured.

She walked to where Keith stood looking out at the lake. Brody was a step behind. He quickly caught up with her and smiled as if offering support.

Keith greeted them warmly and then said, "I expect the others should be here soon. You can wait with me or go on ahead."

Brody glanced at the boats, staring long and hard at her father's sleek cabin cruiser. The Upton Queen was painted in fancy script along the side of the sturdy craft.

"My father's pride and joy," she said, then pointed to a small motorboat tied nearby. "I prefer *The Princess.*"

"Is it yours?"

"By default. Dad got the boat for my mother, but she never shared his affinity for the water."

"Stephanie takes after her father on that count," Keith volunteered. "He loves boats and anything nautical."

A Dodge Dart pulled into the lot. Nikki and Cindy climbed out from the backseat. Ted and Paul slammed the front doors and headed toward the docks with the girls close behind.

"Looks like you'll have a lot of folks to transport," Stephanie said to Keith. "Brody and I'll ride over on *The Princess*."

She waved to Ted. "Do you want to go with me?"

He shook his head. "I'll stay with Paul."

Stephanie sighed. Why had she even asked?

"Walt said we could use his boat," Cindy volunteered.

Stephanie appreciated her willingness to help. "That's not necessary. Keith has room for all of you. Brody and I will meet you on the island."

Brody helped Stephanie untie the mooring lines and then sat next to her as she maneuvered *The Princess* out of the marina. Overhead, a gull cawed.

She glanced back to where Nikki leaned against the dock and pulled at a lock of her hair over and over again. Keith stood on the deck of his craft. Cindy motioned for everyone to follow him onboard.

Brody sighed with satisfaction once they headed into open water. "It's like another world."

"I used to come here often as a kid." She increased the throttle and raised her voice over the motor. "When I got older I did competitive swimming and spent most of my time training at an indoor pool with my team. Life got busy, and I forgot how much I loved the lake."

She turned and smiled at him. "Growing up in L.A., you must have spent time at the beach."

He shook his head. "My mom never took me. I learned to swim at summer camp."

"Summer camp? Sounds like you were a privileged kid," she teased.

"Hardly. Dad left when I was twelve and my mother worked two jobs to make ends meet. Luckily, a church in the suburbs ran a two-week camp for needy kids."

"Any siblings?"

He shook his head. "Spoiled only child."

If money was tight, Stephanie doubted Brody had anything extra growing up. In contrast, she had taken so many things for granted in her youth, yet what she wanted most had always eluded her.

"Do you miss your dad?" she asked.

"At times. Although even when he was there he wasn't interested in being a parent."

Stephanie could relate. "My mother always called my father a good provider."

"Meaning he worked long hours and was never home?"

She nodded. "That was pretty much the case. Mom tried to make it up to us. Ted didn't seem to mind, but I remembered when I was younger and Dad was around more." She laughed ruefully. "You know kids. They blame themselves. I always thought if I worked harder, he'd be proud of me, and life would return to the way it had been."

"So you swam on teams and loved the water to get his attention."

"Silly, huh?"

"Not at all. I joined the military to become what my father wasn't."

"What made you decide to go into the CID?"

His gaze narrowed. "A friend of mine died in a violent crime on post. I wanted to right that wrong."

Stephanie heard the pain in his voice. "I'm sorry, Brody." She expected him to share more about what had happened, but he stared at the water and remained silent.

Once *The Princess* was secured at the small dock on the island, they headed to the picnic area. Keith and the others soon joined them there.

Ted and Nikki had paired up. Paul stood next to Cindy and listened while Keith gave an overview of the itinerary.

"Nikki, you're supervising the kitchen. Some local folks will be helping. Make sure the place is clean and tidy by the time we pack up and head back to the marina. Probably about five o'clock."

He turned to Cindy. "You volunteered for the zip line and adventure climb. A couple of the sergeants from the WTB will help you."

She nodded. "I'll be happy for their help."

"If the weather cooperates, swimming will be an option. The city's providing paddleboats and a pontoon."

Stephanie raised her hand to get Keith's attention. "I'll need to get medical approval for some of the soldiers to take part in the more strenuous activities."

"That works for me." Keith glanced at his watch. "Check out the area and let's meet back here in about half an hour."

Brody followed Cindy up the hill to inspect the zip line while Stephanie headed into the kitchen. She was impressed by the cleanliness of the entire facility, including the latrines and first-aid station.

Once back at the meeting area, she gazed upward at the tall tower and the steel-cord zip line that ran across the narrow channel, from Big Island to neighboring Small Island.

Concerned about the dangerous currents that swept between the two bodies of land, Stephanie turned to Keith. "Can you call the city to be sure the zip line meets all safety regulations?"

"I've already done that. It's up to code." He pointed to a narrow path visible in the distance. "There's even a rope footbridge the soldiers can walk over that connects the islands. Supposedly there's a park on the other side. We've got time if you want to check it out."

"It shouldn't take me long."

Inhaling the sweet smell of the honeysuckle, Stephanie made her way along the path that led to the rocky gorge separating the two islands. Looking down, she saw the churning current that crashed against the cement slabs brought in to shore up the sides of the island from erosion.

Up close, the hanging bridge didn't appear as sturdy as she would have hoped. Two ropes anchored the wooden decking into metal eyehooks embedded in cement. Additional ropes served as handrails and protective side webbing. Glancing across to the opposite island, she saw a garden of wildflowers and a number of park benches. Surely the bridge was more than adequate for foot traffic.

Grabbing hold of the thick hemp railings, she stepped onto the wooden deck. The platform swayed. She looked down. Tiny eddies swirled below as the water surged through the narrow passageway.

Her weight shifted ever so slightly. She took a step forward and then another, trying to steady herself.

The sound of footsteps on the path caused her to turn.

Too quickly.

The bridge responded to the movement, throwing her off balance. She grabbed the rope railing and tugged on the hemp to steady herself.

Out of the corner of her eye, she spotted a rush of motion. Someone lunged from the underbrush and hunkered down on the path as if to tie his shoe.

In a flash, he was gone.

She took another step forward.

Crack.

One of the supporting anchors gave way. The deck collapsed underfoot, leaving her dangling above the water. With her heart lodged in her throat, she frantically clawed to get a toehold. White-knuckled, her fingers clutched the railing. The thick hemp cut into her flesh.

"Help!"

She screamed again and again, but the effort went unnoticed. A wave of vertigo swept over her. She clenched her jaw, refusing to give in to the roll of nausea or the fear that had turned her blood to ice. If she let go of the rope, she'd fall into the raging waters below.

High above her, she saw the zip line platform. Brody and Cindy were probably at the park, waiting for her to meet them there. They didn't realize she was in trouble.

Deadly trouble.

"Where's Stephanie?" Brody asked when he rejoined Keith at the picnic area.

"The last I saw of her, she was heading to the footbridge." Keith glanced at the sky. "Dark clouds are rolling in. We'd better start back to the mainland."

"Don't leave until I find Stephanie," Brody said as he hurried along the path.

Worried, he called her name. His eyes flicked right and then left, hoping to catch sight of her.

Rounding a curve in the path, he saw the broken bridge in the distance and screamed to the others for help as he raced forward. His stomach lurched with fear, seeing her dangling above the water.

"B-Brody?"

"I'm right here." Quickly, he realized the danger of adding more weight to the already-compromised suspension bridge. "I need you to inch toward me. One hand at a time."

"I…I can't."

"Yes, you can." Holding on to a nearby sapling for support, he reached forward, stretching his hand to meet hers. "Take it slow."

"My arms—"

"I'll have you in a minute. Work your way to me."

Ever so slowly, she moved her fingers along the rope, until—in one swift motion—he grabbed her and pulled her to safety.

She collapsed into his embrace, trembling. "Oh, Brody."

"It's okay. You're safe now."

"I…I heard someone on the path. He came from nowhere. All I saw was a gray sweatshirt. The hood covered his head. He…he knelt down for a moment. I thought he was tying his shoe."

Brody examined the rope that supported the wooden

deck. Somehow, it had frayed loose from the anchoring rod. "Did you recognize the guy?"

She shook her head.

"Was it Ted?"

She pulled back. "No."

"But it was a man?" Brody asked.

"That's right. He was wearing a gray sweatshirt."

"Like the army PT uniform?"

She threw up her hands and shrugged as if annoyed with his questions. "I don't know whether it was military. I didn't see a logo."

Letting out a frustrated sigh, Brody glanced at the darkening sky. "Let's head to the boat. It looks like we're in for rain."

Before they returned to the path, he looked down at the gorge, thinking of what could have been. His gut tightened when he spotted something shiny wedged in the rocks below. A metal sign attached to a chain.

Danger. Do Not Cross. Bridge Closed for Repair.

The sign at some point had hung across the entrance to the bridge, warning pedestrians. Had it blown free in the wind? Or had someone removed the sign and then tampered with the already-frayed support rope?

What about the man in the gray sweatshirt? Did he stop to tie his shoe or was he doing something else— something to cause the bridge to collapse?

Chapter Nine

Stephanie leaned against Brody as they hurried along the path. Her legs were weak and her arms felt like jelly. The palms of her hands were scraped and raw, but those were minor problems considering what the outcome would have been if Brody hadn't found her.

Approaching the picnic area, he ushered her to a bench. "Can I get you some water?"

She shook her head. "I'm okay."

"What happened?" Keith asked as he neared.

Brody explained about the collapsed bridge and Stephanie's near catastrophe. "Who told her about the footbridge?"

"I did." Keith pointed to himself. "But I didn't know there was a problem."

"Have you seen anyone else, except our group, on the island?"

"No, but I've been in this area the entire time."

"What's going on?" Cindy asked as she and Nikki hurried toward them.

"Did either of you notice any other visitors on the island?"

Nikki shook her head. "I thought we were the only ones here."

Cindy pointed to the zip line. "I saw a jon boat leaving the small dock on the far side of the island when I was on the tower."

"What color?" Brody asked.

She blew out a breath and shook her head. "Ah, dark. Maybe navy. Maybe black. No name on the hull. Outboard motor. One guy, but I can't tell you what he looked like at that distance."

"What was he wearing?"

Cindy shrugged. "Hard to tell. A beige shirt. Or maybe it was gray."

"Heavy? Thin? Old? Young?"

She threw up her hands. "It was too far to tell. Plus, I didn't realize he was important. Just a guy out fishing."

Brody called the Freemont police and had them contact the manager of the marina in case he saw anyone in a jon boat heading back from Big Island. He also requested law enforcement search the island as soon as possible and keep their eyes open for a man in a gray sweatshirt.

Disconnecting, he glanced around. "Where are Paul and Ted?"

"Probably still on the ridge," Keith said. "They were checking the trail for the fun run."

"Were they hanging around the footbridge?" Brody glanced at Cindy.

She shook her head. "Not that I saw."

Brody nodded and then eyed the sky. "We need to head back to the marina soon. I'll check the ridge." He double-timed up the trail.

Cindy noticed Stephanie's scraped hands. "I saw some antiseptic ointment in the first-aid station."

"Thanks, but I'm okay. Just give me a minute to get my heartbeat back to normal."

"Oh, Stephanie." Nikki gave her a quick hug. "I'm so glad you're okay."

The three women talked for a few minutes until Stephanie glanced over her shoulder and saw Paul and Ted some distance away, standing in front of a three-foot stone monument she hadn't noticed earlier. Ted doubled over and dropped his head into his hands.

She turned to Keith. "Go after Brody. Tell him the guys are back."

"Will do."

Stephanie hurried to join her brother and Paul, but stopped short when she neared the monument. Her heart lodged in her throat.

Hayden Allen City Park.

A lovely tribute that had upset Ted.

She caught up to her brother at the dock and grabbed his sleeve. He jerked out of her hold.

"It's been three years, Ted. You've got to let go of the painful memories."

He pointed an accusatory finger back at her. "What about you? How have you dealt with the past?"

"Not very well," she admitted with a low voice.

"Then don't tell me how I should behave." He turned and stared at Paul, then Nikki, who had moved closer. "Hayden was the best of us. Only he's gone, and we have to pretend that it's okay, but it's not."

He flicked his gaze back to Stephanie. "Life isn't fair, which is what you used to tell me when Mom was sick.

I didn't want to listen to anything you had to say back then. I don't want your advice now, either."

"Ted, please."

"Don't worry. I'll attend the picnic and help the guys and gals who are worse off than I am. After all, I'm not hurt on the outside. My only scars are from the burns on my legs and those have healed, but there are bigger scars on the inside, and they're still festering. Or maybe you haven't noticed."

"I want to help you."

"Then stay out of my life. You've done enough to remind me of the past. Don't butt in where you're not wanted."

Ted stomped aboard Keith's boat.

Stephanie turned to see Brody standing near the monument. A frown covered his square face. If he had been waiting for some sign of dysfunction from her brother, surely he had heard enough today to fill a computer file. Ted kept digging a bigger hole for himself.

Brody followed the guys onto Keith's boat and talked to each of them privately. No doubt he was trying to determine if they'd removed the sign from the bridge or tampered with one of the supporting ropes. He also searched the boat and the girls' handbags.

"Your brother will come around, Steph," Keith said as he approached and patted her shoulder.

She sighed. "Did you ever wonder why everything turned out the way it did, Keith? Is it something about our families that causes so much pain?"

He shook his head. "My mom said it was inevitable when Hayden drowned. I never understood what she meant. I often thought there was something she didn't want me to know."

"Like what?"

"I'm not sure. Hayden and I were so different, as if we weren't even brothers. My parents used to argue. Mom always took Hayden's side. After he died, I could never compete with his memory. That's a tough place to be, the underdog. You never had to deal with that. You were the favored child."

"Only because I worked to earn my father's approval." She turned and looked back over the water. "What I really wanted was his love."

Once they were back onboard *The Princess,* Brody applied ointment to Stephanie's hands and wrapped them in gauze. He watched the darkening sky while she navigated the craft into deep water.

Neither of them spoke about Stephanie's close call or whether the guy in the gray sweatshirt had done something to cause the bridge to collapse. Ted had always been a logical suspect in Brody's mind, but this time Keith had encouraged her to explore the park on the smaller island, an excursion that could have claimed her life.

In addition, Ted and Paul's stories had matched when Brody questioned them. They had explored the route for the fun run and never ventured near the footbridge.

The entire island had been visible from the ridge. Brody hadn't seen anyone else on the island, and the jon boat had long disappeared from view.

When he got back to post, he would contact the police in case the marina manager had identified the boat owner. Another long shot; there seemed to be too many, especially when it came to Stephanie's well-being.

So far, she'd escaped injury, other than her scraped palms, but if Brody hadn't found her today—

He couldn't think about what ifs. He had to think about what he knew to be fact. Right now, he had no evidence and lots of suspicions.

Stephanie was visibly relieved when they reached the marina. So was Brody. He wanted to get her back to post safe and sound. Keith had already docked. Ted and Paul were in the parking lot.

"Come on." Nikki motioned to Cindy, who stood at the end of the pier. The wind whipped at her blouse. Her hair flew around her face. She pushed it back with one hand and clutched the railing with the other.

Brody hopped onto the dock and approached the distraught woman. "Cindy, you need to get in the car before it starts to rain."

She turned, tears in her eyes. "I...I didn't think it would affect me like this. I try to be strong, but coming back made everything worse."

Keith took her arm. "It's okay, Cindy. I'll drive you home." He helped her into his car and followed Paul and the others out of the parking lot.

"I wonder if this was the first time Cindy has been at the lake since Hayden's death?" Brody said, once he and Stephanie were inside his car, just as the rain started to fall.

"You go through a tragedy like that and you never want to go back to where it happened."

"Should you cancel the picnic?" he asked.

"That would only hurt the soldiers who are looking forward to the day. I'll encourage Ted to stay at the barracks. Maybe he and Paul can do something together."

"He never should have come today."

She nodded. "Keith probably invited him. Or maybe Paul insisted he come."

"How are your hands?"

"Better. Thanks for taking care of them."

He turned the windshield wipers to high and pulled onto the road to Fort Rickman.

"What was Keith doing in Atlanta the day his brother died?"

She hesitated before saying, "I think he used Atlanta as an excuse. He and his friends often partied at a campsite north of town. Alcohol was usually involved."

"Did he know about Hayden's drinking?"

"I'm sure he did."

"Because?"

She stared out the window and failed to answer.

"Stephanie—"

She shrugged and glanced back at him, her expression pained. "Keith took the boys to the island that day and said he would pick them up by three o'clock."

"Not much time to drive to Atlanta and back. Is that why you think he was in the local area?"

"That's my opinion only."

"How did the boys get the alcohol?"

"Supposedly they found the bottles on the island. They all told the same story. Folks were upset about Hayden's death. No one gave much thought to the alcohol with a dead teen to mourn." She shook her head. "Especially since it was Hayden."

"I'm sure the townspeople would have been upset no matter who had died."

"It's just—" She sighed. "It was as if the whole town was counting on Hayden to succeed. Everyone expected so much from him."

"What about Paul? How did he play into the group?"

"His parents have a house in the Country Club subdivision, not far from ours, so he and Ted were friends growing up."

"Didn't Hayden and Keith live in the Estates, as well?"

"That's right. Josh was the only one who wasn't close by. All the boys were in the same grade, but Hayden was six months younger. He started hanging out with the guys his senior year."

Brody reached for her hand and gently wove his fingers through hers, taking care not to hurt her scraped skin. "I read the newspaper archives of the rescue. You were able to save the other kids. That's got to give you some sense of satisfaction."

"The papers didn't print the whole story."

"So you tell me what happened."

"I was exhausted and couldn't dive deep enough or stay down long enough to save Hayden. That's what no one talks about."

"The article said you had to be pulled from the water."

"I...I wanted to keep searching," she admitted. "I tried to save him. I just don't know if I tried hard enough."

"Stephanie, you gave it your all."

"You weren't there, Brody."

"No, but I know how determined you are to take care of your brother. You don't give up."

She glanced down at their hands, then pulled hers away and looked out the window.

Brody knew about looking back. Nothing good came from replaying what couldn't be changed. When he met

Stephanie, something had sparked to life within him, a part he thought had died long ago.

If he determined Ted was to blame for Joshua's injury, there would be no hope for a relationship with Stephanie. The situation would be even more impossible if Ted had marked her bedding or damaged the bridge today. Although he doubted Stephanie realized that he wanted to help Ted, his first priority was to keep her safe.

After arriving on post, Stephanie and Brody stopped at the hospital to check on Joshua. They rode the elevator to the third floor and walked together into the ICU.

"We're here to see Private Joshua Webb." Brody showed his CID identification to the clerk on duty.

"He won't be able to answer questions at this time."

"I understand. But I still need to see him."

The clerk pointed down the hallway. "Room six. On the left."

Stephanie inhaled a quick breath as she neared Joshua's bedside. His eyes were closed and his face was ashen. He was hooked up to a number of machines that pumped meds and took vital signs at regular intervals.

Brody touched his shoulder. "It's CID Special Agent Goodman. Can you hear me, Joshua?"

He nodded ever so slightly.

"Do you remember who did this to you?"

Stephanie glanced at the heart monitor. Josh's rate increased slightly. "This isn't a good time, Brody."

"I need information, Stephanie. The investigation is stagnant. If Josh can identify who attacked him, we'll be able to put that person behind bars before someone else is hurt."

"The nurse said no questions," she insisted.

"Actually, she said he wouldn't be able to answer questions, but he can blink." Brody glanced back at the patient. "I know you can hear me, Josh. If you saw the person who attacked you, blink twice. If you didn't see anyone, blink once."

The response was immediate. Joshua blinked twice.

"Was it someone you knew?" Brody pressed.

Once again, Josh blinked twice.

"I'm going to mention a few people. Blink if I say the name of the person who attacked you."

Stephanie didn't like the direction of the questioning. "Brody, you're pushing him too hard. If he's medicated, the blinking could be an involuntary response."

Brody glanced at her. "What are you worried about, Stephanie?"

She couldn't give voice to her concern that Brody's bedside interrogation could lead to incorrect information. Information that might incriminate Ted.

"Was it Paul Massey?" Brody asked.

Joshua's eyes remained closed.

"Brody, please."

"Listen carefully, Joshua. Was it—"

A noise sounded behind them.

Stephanie turned to see her brother, standing in the doorway, red faced and angered. Paul stood next to him.

"You shouldn't be here, Ted. You were upset at the marina. Don't upset yourself more."

Ted pushed past her to the bed and grabbed Josh's hand. "Hey, buddy, you hold on. Keep fighting. This is just another battle like we saw in Afghanistan. You can do it."

A nurse in scrubs entered the room. "All of you need to leave."

"Joshua, was it—" Brody pressed.

"Sir, please." The nurse's voice was firm.

"Come on, Ted." Stephanie took her brother's arm. He jerked out of her hold and left the room, with Paul trailing close behind.

Stephanie glanced back at Brody, who followed her into the hallway. As much as he thought he was trying to help, Brody was making everything worse, for Joshua, for Ted and even for herself.

Chapter Ten

❧

Frustrated to learn the new tires hadn't yet arrived, Stephanie accepted a ride from Brody to work the following morning.

"I hate to put you out," she said when he picked her up. His starched white shirt and paisley tie complemented his ruddy skin and brought out the flecks of gold in his eyes. As he held the door for her, she realized his gentlemanly manners and thoughtfulness were having an effect on her in a good way.

How easily she took to the little things he did that showed the respect he had for women. Her own father hadn't been one to fawn over her mother, and growing up, many of the boys in town took a more chauvinistic outlook toward the fairer sex. Stephanie had to admit she enjoyed the pampered way Brody made her feel.

"Major Jenkins said you're coming to the Warrior Transitional Battalion this afternoon to talk to some of the soldiers."

Brody nodded. "We were firming up the details the day you called the WTB. Keeping the groups small is best, so we worked out a schedule that allows me to talk to each company individually."

"That's perfect. They'll feel more comfortable in a smaller environment. Major Jenkins said you wanted to start with Ted's company."

"I thought the session might pull down some of the barriers he's put up," Brody said. "You saw how he broke down at the marina. Plus, I want the other soldiers in his unit to be aware of the signs of PTSD and know the CID is a source of help if they feel in danger or threatened in any way."

"Just don't single Ted out from the bunch."

Brody's brow furrowed. "You think I'd do that?"

She noticed a hint of disappointment in his voice. "I'm not saying you'd do anything wrong, Brody, but I want this to be a healing situation for my brother, not one that would do more harm."

"I've given this class a number of times on other posts, Stephanie. You can trust me to be sensitive to everyone's needs."

She pulled in a deep breath and turned her gaze to the overcast sky. Brody was a strong man who stood for truth and justice. That stance could seem intimidating to some, including her brother, who had always struggled with his own self-worth.

Just so Brody, with his prying questions, didn't seem like a threat. More than anything, she wanted him to reach out to Ted.

Brody could be such a good role model for her brother and someone Ted could look up to and try to emulate. He could use a mentor, especially since their own dad had never been a positive influence in her brother's life.

As much as she wanted Ted and Brody to connect,

she feared the session later today would give Ted more fuel to light the fire of indignation that seemed to consume him these days.

Her brother was walking a fine line between health and breakdown. His buddy Josh's injury only compounded the situation.

Stephanie would attend the class to ensure the information Brody presented to the company didn't hamper Ted's progress, although she wasn't sure getting between her brother and the CID agent would be a positive experience, either for Ted or for herself.

Brody arrived at the Warrior Transitional Battalion ahead of schedule. He had hoped to see Stephanie and spend time with her before the soldiers arrived, but she was nowhere to be found. Trying to mask his disappointment, he arranged the chairs in the conference room and checked the thermostat on the air conditioner. He wanted the soldiers to be comfortable and receptive to the information he would provide.

Once the room was ready, the soldiers filtered in and claimed their chairs. A number of them had suffered significant injuries, including loss of limbs and scars that were hard to ignore. Brody was humbled by the sacrifice of so many who put country before self.

Some of the military personnel, both male and female, had less noticeable injuries. Theirs were the hidden wounds of trauma and the stress of living in a war zone.

Ted shuffled into the room and took a seat close to the door. Brody nodded in his direction, but the PFC averted his gaze and toyed with his smart phone.

Brody checked his watch, hoping Stephanie would be able to attend the program. A hint of concern made the hairs on his neck raise. He tried to shake off his worry and focus instead on the men and women gathered for the talk.

Major Jenkins approached, holding out his hand, which Brody accepted. "Thanks again for being with us today."

"My pleasure, sir." Brody looked around the room. "Do you have any idea where Stephanie Upton might be?"

"She was in her office earlier. I'm sure she'll show up soon."

"I'll leave a seat for her." Brody positioned a chair close to the door. Hearing the clip of heels, he peered into the hallway and saw her racing toward the classroom. A sense of relief swept over him.

"Sorry." A sincere smile tugged at her lips as she hurried into the room. "I was talking to the medical case manager about one of my soldiers."

"No problem. You're here in plenty of time." Brody was taken by the way her hair danced on her shoulders. The sun coming through the window accentuated the golden highlights.

The room quieted as the major walked to the microphone. He quickly provided background information about Brody, including his tours in combat and the list of his medals and awards. "We're fortunate to have him with us today and welcome the information he will provide."

"Thank you, Major Jenkins." Using a PowerPoint program, Brody worked through a series of slides that provided statistics about the prevalence of PTSD, as well as warning signs and interventions.

"In addition to the symptoms we've talked about, any

traumatic injury or experience, whether war related or not, can also lead to memory problems, such as short-term amnesia."

He pointed around the room. "Any of you could fall victim to this disease because of your time in combat. Whether you were injured because of an IED, bullets or mortars, you've been wounded physically, but you've had a psychological trauma, too. Be alert to changes in temperament and behavior. If you know the warning signs and watch out for one another, a more serious situation could be stopped before it gets out of hand."

Stephanie's gaze was warm and encouraging, and the men and women in uniform seemed interested. Many of them leaned forward in their chairs and all of them listened attentively to what Brody was sharing.

"Remember, PTSD can affect anyone, whether military or civilian. Any trauma can cause PTSD and often the symptoms don't appear until well after the event occurred. If you have PTSD, you're not alone. More than fifty percent of our wounded warriors experience PTSD in one form or another. So don't keep any struggle bottled up inside you. Your medical-care team is ready to help. Counselors are always available, and the CID is eager to support you, as well."

When he finished the talk, he opened the floor for questions.

One of the men raised his hand. "What about someone who can't sleep and wanders the barracks at night?"

"I'd say the advocate or medical-care team should be made aware of the situation so the soldier can receive the help he or she needs."

The guy who had posed the question turned to look at Ted, who squirmed in his seat.

"Talk to him, Ted," another soldier prompted. "Tell the special agent about the dreams you've been having."

Ted's eyes narrowed. "Hey, guys, what are you talking about?"

"You don't have to hide it," one of the men called out.

Ted glanced at Brody and then turned to look at Stephanie.

She started to stand. "Maybe we should—"

"Did you plan to gang up on me?" Ted demanded.

"Of course not." Stephanie approached her brother.

He stood and pointed his finger at Brody. "You set me up for this."

Brody moved forward. "I came here to talk about PTSD, Ted. If you've got some of the symptoms, you need help."

"Help?" He flicked his gaze between Stephanie and Brody. "I don't appreciate being the center of a witch hunt."

"That's not what this is," Stephanie objected.

"Isn't it?" He pushed past her and rushed from the room.

She turned and stared at Brody for a brief moment as if he were to blame.

He wanted to reach for her and hold her until the accusation that flashed from her eyes calmed into acceptance. Hard though it was for Stephanie to realize, she wasn't at fault and neither was he.

Ted was struggling with issues that were too difficult for him to handle alone. His reactions today, yesterday and the day before proved how fragile he was at this time.

Stephanie's face clouded. She blinked rapidly and then turned and hurried out of the room.

Brody had wanted to see what type of a reaction Ted would have to the information about PTSD, but he hadn't expected everything to explode. Nor had he thought that Ted would strike out so forcefully at Stephanie.

The last thing Brody wanted was to cause her more pain. She'd had enough already.

As he watched her flee the room, memories from Brody's past surfaced again. So painful, so raw, even after all these years. He remembered his own struggle and the counselor who had been his rock when all he could see was darkness.

Brody knew too well about PTSD and the insidious hold it had on its victims. Just like a flesh-and-blood enemy, the disease had to be combated aggressively. If only Ted would realize he needed help.

The soldiers continued to field questions, and the session concluded on a high note, for which Brody was glad. Had Ted stayed, he might have realized that the WTB, the cadre and medical-care team—and even the other soldiers—were working together for the betterment of all.

Once the military personnel had gone back to their unit, Brody gathered his notes and hurried from the classroom, determined to find Stephanie. He wanted to talk to her about Ted's condition and what he could do to offer support and encouragement.

But recalling the way Stephanie had looked at him, Brody feared she wouldn't want to see him now. He wasn't sure she would ever want to see him again.

Stephanie ran after Ted, but he had disappeared by the time she got outside. Hearing the rev of an engine, she turned and saw Paul's blue Dodge Dart leaving the WTB parking area.

Letting out a long sigh, she raked her hand through her hair. At least Ted wasn't alone. Hopefully, Paul would be a listening ear, which Ted needed.

If only he would open up and share his pain, not only the pain from the IED explosion and war injuries, but also the pain from their mother's death and the tragedy that had claimed Hayden's life. The combined toll on Ted was all too evident today.

She made a mental note to notify his counselor and the other members of his care team about the hard time her brother was having. Shaking her head, she almost laughed at the understatement. Ted's condition was far worse than she had previously thought. Why had she refused to see the truth? Perhaps because she always felt responsible for her younger brother.

The other soldiers in his unit were aware of the situation. She should have been, as well.

Shame on her.

If she had ignored the signals from Ted, no telling what she had missed from the other men.

Discouraged and wondering if she could ever be effective in her job, Stephanie headed back to her office.

Brody was waiting for her.

The warmth she saw in his gaze told her more than words. He didn't blame her for her brother's outburst. Nor did Brody think she had let Ted down, which was what she wanted to believe but couldn't.

Ever since their mother had died, Stephanie had tried to fill the gaps in Ted's life. If he failed, she considered herself at fault. Everything changed that day on the lake when she'd finally realized her brother had to take responsibility for his own actions.

Tough love, some called it. At the time, she thought she was making the best decision for Ted.

Yet nothing good had come from it. Only more pain.

Hayden had died, and she would carry the guilt of that burden for the rest of her life.

"Ted didn't mean what he said, Stephanie." Brody stepped closer, his voice filled with concern.

She tried to smile. "He's so confused right now and struggling with so many issues. I thought I could help him, but I can't seem to do anything right."

"You love him, and that's what he needs most."

Brody rubbed his hand over her shoulder, his touch soothing away her frustration.

"All I want is for Ted to heal," she finally whispered.

"Let me help you."

Stephanie had been alone for so long. She needed someone to lean on, at least for a while. Someone who cared about her and accepted her, despite her failings.

Brody opened his arms and she stepped into his embrace. Feeling secure at long last, she rested her head on his chest and took comfort in hearing the steady beat of his heart. Her own struggle eased as if being in Brody's arms had the power to transform the pain she carried into something whole and healed.

"I'm so sorry," he said, his voice husky with emotion.

His breath warmed her cheek. She nestled closer, knowing the moment would pass too soon and she'd return to being an advocate for soldiers who had faced horrific traumas. She needed to be strong in order to help them. She needed to be even stronger to help Ted.

Right now, she was grateful for Brody, who wanted

to help her, and more than anything, she wanted to remain wrapped in his arms.

After Brody left her office, Stephanie received a phone call from Ted's counselor. Her brother had kept his appointment and seemed eager for the next session. Although he didn't share specifically what had been discussed, the counselor was enthusiastic about the progress that had been made.

Ted was taking positive steps forward. With medication for his anxiety and depression, and additional counseling sessions, the counselor felt fairly confident that Ted could turn everything around.

Stephanie's spirits soared with the news, but her optimism plummeted when Major Jenkins called soon thereafter and shared that Ted had asked to be taken off her caseload.

"I won't act on his request at this point," the major said. "See what you can do to change Ted's mind. Besides, I know you have your brother's best interest at heart."

She hung up feeling conflicted. How could she reach her brother when he remained closed to any attempt on her part to help?

After what had happened today, she wasn't sure their relationship would ever improve. No matter what she did, the divide between them just kept getting bigger.

Chapter Eleven

Brody checked with the WTB first sergeant to ensure Ted headed back to the barracks after his counseling appointment. The sergeant promised to keep him busy around the battalion. He also promised to call Brody if Ted showed any signs of depression or aggravation.

Once he returned to his office, Brody kept thinking of Stephanie and realized his distraction would continue until he called her.

Hearing her voice when she answered made him smile and ask if she wanted to join him for dinner that evening.

"There's a restaurant in Alabama about an hour's drive from Freemont that has an outdoor patio and lots of atmosphere. Plus, the cooking is the best in the area that I've found."

"The Tadwell Inn?" she asked.

"You know the place."

"And love going there. But I have a meeting this afternoon that will probably run until five or five-thirty."

"Five-thirty works for me," Brody said. "I've got a number of loose ends to tie up around here."

His next phone call was to the farmer in Alabama. The man that answered sounded like a no-nonsense, salt-of-the-earth type of guy.

Brody identified himself and then said, "Sir, I'm calling about the Ford truck you bought three years ago at an auction in Freemont, Georgia."

"The Ford's long gone, Agent Goodman."

"How's that?"

"Totaled."

"Did you have the truck repaired?"

"What don't you understand about totaled? The Lord saved me, but He destroyed the Ford." The farmer sighed. "Only good thing was that I was driving instead of my son. I ended up with a few cuts and bruises. Nothing serious. Doubt my boy would have been as lucky. He's got a lead foot like his late mother."

"I'm sorry about your wife, sir."

"Appreciate the condolences. Sandra was a fine woman. The Lord took her too early."

Brody empathized with the man's loss.

"I had to accept the Lord's will for my life, in spite of my grief and loneliness," Mr. Franken continued, seeming eager to talk.

"Yes, sir."

"He's given me a fine son, even though he has a heavy foot on the gas pedal." The farmer chuckled. "Plus a daughter-in-law and a grandbaby on the way. I miss my wife, but I've got folks to love. God made me look to the future, which helped me overcome my grief."

"I'm glad things are better, sir."

"Made me realize when tough times come, I need to lean on the Lord."

Brody had been told the same thing after Lisa's death.

Although he didn't believe in coincidences, the repeated message seemed exactly that. Or was the Almighty sending a reminder Brody had ignored years earlier?

"Thank you, sir, for the information about the Ford. Best wishes to the new parents."

He scratched Sam Franken's name off his to-do list and called Don Palmer at the Freemont Police Department. "Hayden Allen's truck was a dead end." Brody explained about the vehicle having been totaled. "Did you get those DMV records on red pickups in the Freemont area?"

"We're checking for any of them that might have off-road tires. Nothing to report yet."

"What about the bedding and note from the Upton home?"

"The bull's-eye and X were made with a standard washable marker sold at every store that carries school or business supplies. No prints. No identifiable markings. No evidence."

"And the island search?"

"Again, nothing turned up. The city claims the danger sign blocked access to the footbridge. They have no idea who would have removed it. The rope supporting the wooden deck appeared frayed, but the integrity of the structure could have also been compromised by some external force, for whatever that's worth. No one at the marina could provide information about a fisherman in a jon boat. We're batting zero, the way I see it."

"Something will turn up," Brody said before he disconnected, although he felt anything but encouraged.

For the rest of the afternoon, he busied himself at work, but eyed the clock and counted down the minutes until he could pick up Stephanie. Once they were together, he was thankful to see some of the worry she had worn earlier had eased. Knowing Ted had gone to counseling and was now occupied at the battalion had to be a relief.

The evening drive bolstered both their spirits. Brody took a back road that wound by the river and eventually crossed into Alabama at a scenic spot that led to the heart of a small town with a picturesque square.

He turned to glance at her. A warm swirl of attraction bubbled up within him. She titled her head as if questioning why he was focused on her.

He smiled and, at that moment, the world suddenly looked brighter.

"Mind if I turn on some music?" Brody asked. "Are you a country gal?"

She laughed. "Sure. It's appropriate for the surroundings."

He selected a CD. "How about *The Best of Nashville?*"

"Perfect."

The mellow mix of guitars and banjos played softly in the background as a popular country-and-western voice opened his heart to the woman he had never expected to love.

Stephanie tapped her left hand against the console in time with the music. Brody couldn't help but notice her long, slender fingers.

Without thinking, he wrapped his hand over hers, taking care to not touch the place where the rope had rubbed her palm. He enjoyed the softness of her skin and the warmth of her hold.

She turned to smile at him, a look of genuine happiness covering her oval face. As pretty as she was, surely

Stephanie had captured a number of guys' hearts. Maybe there was a special guy at her old base, Fort Stewart.

As much as Brody wanted to know, he wouldn't ask. Right now, he needed to believe he had a chance—a second chance at love.

Then he realized the truth. After everything that had happened, it was doubtful Stephanie would want anything to do with him long-term. Their paths had crossed because of the investigation. After it was over, they'd go their separate ways.

The sun had set by the time Stephanie and Brody finished dinner. She laughed as they headed back to his car. He held the door for her and touched her arm as she slipped past him onto the seat. The gesture seemed natural and filled her with a sense of peace as if some of the struggle she had felt earlier had dissipated, for which she was grateful.

During dinner, they had talked about the Wounded Warrior Program and the opportunities available to the injured. Her responsibility was to ensure the soldiers took advantage of the benefits provided for them and were able to navigate the paperwork and bureaucracy that went along with government programs.

Brody seemed genuinely concerned about the injured soldiers on her caseload, and he mentioned his own hope that Ted would be able to heal with counseling.

The trip back to Freemont passed quickly. They had turned to lighter topics, including Stephanie's high school swim team and her love of the water. Brody mentioned that he often swam laps at the indoor pool on post. Having that shared common interest made their time together even more enjoyable. Once they arrived at her house, inviting him for a swim seemed appropriate.

"I usually take a dip after dinner," she said. "Why don't you go back to your BOQ and pick up your suit?"

Brody's eyes twinkled. "Sounds great. My trunks are in my car."

Once he unlocked the door, she flipped on the entryway chandelier before disarming the security alarm. After he retrieved his gym bag, she pointed him toward a spare bedroom.

"You can change in there."

She quickly donned a one-piece suit and a cover-up and was in the kitchen when he joined her.

"Care for a cola or coffee?" she asked.

"I'll take some coffee after the swim."

She handed him a colorful beach towel. "The stairs on the deck lead down to the pool."

Brody followed her to the patio, where a wrought-iron table and chairs were positioned next to the kidney-shaped pool. Recessed lights in the landscaped area reflected across the water like tiny diamonds. A plastic raft floated in the deep end.

"I'm glad you asked me out for dinner," Stephanie said as she dropped her towel on the table.

He followed suit and placed his gym bag next to both their towels before he stepped closer. "And I'm glad you said yes."

The intensity of his gaze made her turn and point to the water. "Last one in the water makes the coffee tonight."

He grabbed her arm. "Not so fast."

She playfully tried to free herself from his hold.

His grip was strong but gentle. He pulled her closer

until she was standing a breath away from him. They stopped laughing at almost the same moment. Stephanie looked into his dark eyes and saw far more than she expected.

Brody slipped his hand around her waist. She could see a pulse beating in his temple and could smell the heady scent of his aftershave. The masculine fragrance swirled around her and added to the intensity of the moment.

Gazing at his angled jaw and full lips, she felt a portion of her inner core melting, the part that worried about the past. She stared into his dark eyes and leaned closer.

"You were saying?" He smiled.

"Weren't we talking about making coffee?"

His finger twirled a strand of her hair, sending a delicious warmth pulsating along her neck.

"Are you thinking about coffee, Stephanie?" His voice was deep and dangerous.

"I'm not thinking of anything, except—"

"Except what?" His upper lip twitched ever so slightly.

Every nerve ending tingled within her.

"About whether you plan to kiss me." She closed her eyes and waited half a heartbeat until his mouth covered hers.

The night stood still. The sound of the cicadas and crickets faded into the distance. All Stephanie could focus on was the tenderness of his kiss. Gently, he drew her deeper into his embrace.

Just when she thought he would kiss her forever, Brody pulled back.

His look of need turned lighthearted. "We were heading into the water."

"We were?"

He pointed to the pool. "Last one in, remember?"

She remembered his kiss and how comfortable she had been—far too comfortable—in his arms.

Needing to reel in her emotions, she turned, took off her cover-up and dove into the pool. Before she entered the water, she heard a loud crack. Brody screamed her name.

Confused by the sharpness of his tone, she touched bottom and pushed back to the surface.

"Stay in the water." He had pulled his weapon from his gym bag and was hunkered down behind the wrought-iron table, his eyes trained on the fairway and the woods beyond. "Keep your head below the rim of the pool."

Treading water, she saw the shattered flowerpot that had sat on the table next to where they had stood only a moment ago.

He raised his cell to his ear. "This is Special Agent Goodman, Fort Rickman CID. There's been a shooting." He gave Stephanie's address. "I need police backup. Now. Notify Freemont Chief of Police Don Palmer immediately."

She followed his gaze to the dense forest. "I...I don't understand. I thought a car backfired."

"It was a gunshot, Stephanie."

Her mouth went dry. A roar filled her ears. She wanted to dive underwater and swim until her lungs burned. Surely, Brody had it all wrong.

"But—" She stared into the darkness, unable to pick out anything except the tall trees and the sounds of the night.

"Stay where you are. I'll check the area."

Bile rose in her throat. Crossing the fairway would make him an open target. In spite of the warm night, she shivered, knowing Brody could be in the line of fire.

He left the patio, but instead of heading toward the clearing, he picked his way around the neighboring houses and circled through the underbrush. She could barely make out his shadow in the darkness.

More than anything, Stephanie wanted to run inside and hide, but she knew her own safety depended on staying put. She prayed Brody would remain safe, as well.

Tears stung her eyes. She blinked them back, angry at her mixed-up emotions and inability to comprehend what was happening to her life. She and Brody had had such a nice evening, but now he was running headlong into danger.

Why hadn't he waited for backup? Because he had to be the macho cop and catch the bad guys and make sure she didn't get hurt. Much as she appreciated his protection, she couldn't take someone else getting hurt because of her. Especially not Brody.

She bit her lip, hoping to control the fear that clamped down on her chest. Listening for any sound, half expecting to hear gunfire, she counted off the minutes, not knowing who or what Brody would have to confront.

Huddled at the far edge of the pool, she inched her head up to stare into the distance, seeing nothing except the darkness.

Just when she was convinced something had happened to him, Brody stepped from the shadows. Grabbing a towel for her, he stood guard as she climbed from the pool. "Stay low and head for the back door. Someone could still be out there."

"What did you find?" she asked when they were safely inside.

"Nothing."

"Which means what?"

"Someone wanted to frighten you, or they were a bad shot." Brody's face was tight with emotion. "Does Ted know you swim at night?"

"It's something I've always done. I...I guess so."

"He thought you'd be alone."

She shook her head and took a step back. "It wasn't Ted," she insisted.

Yet Ted and his friends had often played paintball at night with toy guns in this very same fairway in their youth.

"How can you be sure it wasn't your brother?"

"Because I know Ted."

"You know the way he was when you were growing up. He's a different person now. You've got to believe me."

The only thing she knew for sure was that she had been fooled by Brody's sweet words and even sweeter kisses.

Sirens sounded in the distance. The police would soon arrive and canvass the neighborhood. What would they find? Nothing to prove any of Brody's suspicions about Ted. In his mind, her brother was the shooter, but Brody was wrong.

So very, very wrong.

Brody appreciated Don Palmer's efforts. The Freemont police chief had pulled in a number of his men to search the Country Club Estates and the surrounding wooded area.

Both Stephanie and Brody had changed back into their street clothes. For the past two hours, she had sat huddled on the couch in the keeping room while the police milled around outside. Fatigue pulled at her drawn face and made him aware of how vulnerable she really was, especially all alone in the big house.

"There's a lodge on post, Stephanie. Why don't you stay there for the next few nights until we find out who fired the shots?"

"What if you don't find the person who's responsible? How long will I have to stay holed up in some motel room?"

"You'll be safer there."

"Chief Palmer said he'd increase patrol cars in the Estates and stationed an officer outside to watch my house."

"For tonight. But what about tomorrow?"

"I'm taking it one day at a time."

He sighed, knowing she wouldn't change her mind.

She picked at a thread on the couch. "I overheard some of the officers talking. One mentioned a hunting area not far from my house, but—"

He waited for her to continue.

"Another one said they found a bullet embedded in one of the posts outside that support the upper deck. It appeared to be the same caliber as used in military rifles."

Was she worried Ted might be involved?

"All military weapons are locked and accounted for in each unit's arms rooms, Stephanie. They're drawn only in certain instances and only with the authorization of the commander."

"So the soldiers don't have access to the rifles?"

"That's right."

"Have you..." She hesitated. "Have you heard back from Major Jenkins?"

He nodded, realizing he should have mentioned the call. "He phoned about thirty minutes ago."

She looked surprised. "Why didn't you tell me?"

"I was outside, talking to the chief at the time. Your brother has been in the barracks all night."

"So he didn't fire the shot."

"Evidently not."

Just because Ted Upton had nothing to do with tonight didn't mean he hadn't caused some of the other problems that had befallen Stephanie over the past few days.

"It's getting late." She stood and rubbed her hands over her arms. "How long before the police leave?"

"They're finishing up now, but I can stay for a while."

"No, Brody. I'll be fine."

He stared long and hard into her eyes. She didn't blink. With a resigned sigh, he grabbed his gym bag and followed her to the door.

"Keep away from the windows," he cautioned. "Don't spend time on your deck or patio. I'll pick you up at seven tomorrow morning for work. Unless that's too early."

"I'll see you then."

Brody hated to leave her, but she needed sleep and he wanted to follow the chief back to police headquarters. Someone had been found about three miles from the Estates, inebriated and talking about his marksmanship. He seemed an unlikely shooter, but he needed to be questioned, and Brody wanted to hear what the guy had to say.

Once outside, he checked that a squad car was in place to watch the Upton house throughout the night. Brody planned to be back after the interrogation, but he needed to know Stephanie would be safe until then.

Before climbing into his car, he turned to look back at the house, wishing he could catch a last glimpse of her. The curtains were drawn. He'd cautioned her to stay away from the windows. This time, Stephanie had taken his advice.

Chapter Twelve

Unable to face Brody, Stephanie called a cab early the next morning. She had slept fitfully, her slumber punctuated with dreams of his strong hands and dark eyes and a horde of police officers that wandered through her yard. She'd awakened with a headache and puffy face from the tears she'd cried before she'd fallen asleep. All the emotion she'd kept bottled up for so long had spilled out as she'd sobbed into her pillow.

The ride to post made her head hurt even more. She blew her nose and applied lipstick before the cab pulled into the WTB area. After paying the driver, she hurried into her office.

By the time the other workers arrived, Stephanie had completed a stack of paperwork that had piled up in her in-box.

A civilian clerk who worked in the records section knocked twice on the door to her office and then entered. With a wide smile, she placed a box of oatmeal-raisin cookies on Stephanie's desk.

"These arrived for you. They're from the Cookie Palace on Fourth Street. They deliver in town and on post."

Stephanie was touched by the thoughtful gesture. "The WTB must have sent them as a welcome gift. I bet Ted told them oatmeal raisin is my favorite type of cookie."

Noticing the clerk's eagerness for her to open the box, Stephanie quickly added, "Are the cookies from you?"

The woman shook her head and pointed to an attached envelope. "The card should tell you who sent them."

Stephanie read the note silently. "Sorry about last night. Brody."

She smiled. "They're from a friend." Evidently he had asked Ted about her preference. Or maybe Nikki.

After removing the outer wrapper, Stephanie handed the box to the other woman. "Would you like to pass them around the office?"

"Don't you want one?" she asked.

"Maybe later."

The clerk returned after a few minutes. "Everyone said to thank you." She placed the remaining cookies on Stephanie's desk and headed back to work.

Unable to resist any longer, Stephanie reached for a particularly large cookie packed with plump raisins. Smiling at Brody's thoughtfulness, she bit into the soft sweetness. Maybe she had reacted too quickly last night.

There was so much she liked about the special agent.

Her office phone rang. She pulled the receiver to her ear, expecting to hear Brody's voice. Instead, the call was from her regional director.

"Ms. Upton, we've had a complaint from one of the soldiers on your caseload."

Her stomach tightened.

"Private Upton has lodged a formal grievance against

you. I'll fax over a list of forms you'll need to fill out. Please return them to me promptly. We take something like this very seriously."

"Yes, sir. I'm not happy about it, either."

When the director hung up, Stephanie dropped her head into her hands. Her cheeks were hot and a bitter taste filled her mouth.

She glanced again at the box of cookies. Surely, they didn't contain peanuts. She was very careful to never eat ones that did, yet the way her throat was feeling, she wondered if she could be having an allergic reaction.

Her skin itched. Looking down, she saw the red rash and patches of hives. Reaching for her cell, she turned on the phone and then hit the saved number for the medical unit attached to the WTB.

"It's Stephanie Upton. I'm sorry to bother you, but…" She struggled to catch her breath. "I'm allergic to peanuts and seem to be having a reaction."

Frustration!

That's what Brody had been feeling since he'd spent the night at police headquarters questioning a number of displaced persons who were wandering the streets of Freemont. One of the police officers had suggested the shooter was some novice outdoorsman who didn't know gun safety or the hunting laws in Georgia. Which Brody didn't buy. Hopefully the chief of police didn't, either.

By the time Brody left P.D. headquarters and arrived at Stephanie's house, she was long gone. Either she had called a cab or driven one of her dad's cars to work. Mad at himself, he had phoned to apologize, but her cell went to voice mail.

Surely, she wasn't rejecting his calls.

He groused the entire drive back to post and was equally frustrated when he was tied up in a meeting that lasted all morning. At lunchtime, he hurried to his car and called her as he neared the WTB.

"I'm sorry I didn't get to your house early enough this morning," he said when she finally answered.

"Don't worry. I took a cab to post, Brody."

"I tried calling you."

"My phone was off. I only realized it a few minutes ago when I phoned my doctor."

Brody spied the ambulance when he turned into the WTB area. He pulled into a parking space, jumped out of his car and ran toward her office.

"What happened?" he said, the phone close to his ear.

She hesitated. "I…I must have had a reaction to the cookies."

A chill settled over him. "What cookies?"

"The note said you were sorry about last night."

He pushed through the door and raced toward her office. Barging into the room, his heart constricted. She was sitting in a chair with the doctor from the WTB hovering over her, two EMTs at his side.

"Tell me she's okay," he demanded when the doc looked up.

"She's okay. An allergic reaction, but she called us in time."

"In time?"

"She's allergic to peanuts. Evidently, the cookie she ate contained nut particles."

"You didn't know, Brody," she said. Her smile was reassuring, except he was anything but reassured.

"I didn't send you cookies. Someone else must have, but it wasn't me."

Worry flashed from her eyes. "If it wasn't you, then who sent them?"

Someone who knew about Stephanie's allergy. Who would have that type of information?

One person came to mind. Brody fisted his hands.

Ted Upton.

"You've had an allergic reaction." Dr. Carter confirmed what the military physician had told Stephanie earlier. Rejecting the EMTs offer to transport her to the Freemont Hospital, she had instead insisted on seeing her family allergist, which the WTB doctor had agreed would be a good idea.

Dr. Carter had treated her mother for years before her death and Stephanie trusted his diagnosis, which was why she had asked Brody to drive her to his office.

"I've only had minor incidents prior to this," Stephanie assured him. "This time I ate an oatmeal-raisin cookie, which shouldn't have peanuts in it, and I had an almost immediate reaction."

"There could have been cross contamination." He glanced at Brody. "You might want to check with the bakery. Sometimes two types of cookies are prepared in the same area. Even a small amount of antigen could cause a reaction."

The doctor turned his gaze back to Stephanie. "As you probably realize by now, allergic reactions are unpredictable. The next one could be minor, but it could also be much more severe. The response might be immediately after you come in contact with the allergen. Then again, you could have a delayed response. I'm telling you this so you don't discount any reaction you might have in the future."

He handed her a prescription. "Get this filled at your pharmacy on the way home. It's for two EpiPen Auto-Injectors, which each contain a single dose of epinephrine. Keep at least one of them with you at all times. You'll find directions printed in the insert."

The doctor glanced at Brody. "If you notice any allergic symptoms, have her use the EpiPen and then be sure to seek medical help. I don't want to scare you, but things can happen quickly once a reaction starts."

The doctor made a note in her file and then patted her arm. "You take after your mother with her big heart. She was a good woman. So are you."

Stephanie's cheeks burned under the doctor's gaze, and knowing Brody was staring at her caused her even more embarrassment.

"I've known your family for years," the doctor added. "Don't let your concern for Ted keep you from living your own life. He'll find his way. You don't want to miss your own opportunities because you're caring for him."

Stephanie had little to say as Brody drove her to the pharmacy. As much as she appreciated Dr. Carter's advice, she and Ted were a family and needed to stick together. Even if Ted didn't seem to understand what being a family meant.

"That was nice of the doctor to mention your mother," Brody said after they parked and were walking toward the pharmacy. "She must have been a special woman."

Hearing Brody confirm what she already knew made her appreciate him even more. Despite the gun on his hip and his job handling military crime, he had a compassionate side that she had noticed. This was one of those times.

As if he realized her own internal struggle, he circled her with his arm. She leaned into him, supported by his strength.

She shouldn't allow herself to indulge in the moment, but she didn't want to pull back from his closeness. They would separate once they entered the store. Until then, she wanted to pretend they were together and that what they shared was special.

Too soon, she'd have to go back to being the Wounded Warrior advocate and the sister of a soldier who was struggling to find his way. Brody would once again be the CID agent who didn't trust Ted and weighed everything Stephanie said in light of her brother's supposed involvement.

The doctor's words circled through her mind. *You need to live your own life, Stephanie.*

What did she want her own life to entail? At this moment, she wished it included Brody.

Once the prescription was filled and Stephanie had the EpiPens safely tucked in her purse, Brody let out a sigh of relief.

"I'll take you home now," he said.

"I need to go back to work," she insisted. "Keith emailed the report for the island picnic. I have to review his plans and then pass them on to Major Jenkins."

"The major told you to take the afternoon off," Brody reminded her.

"He's been more than kind."

"You've done a great job. Major Jenkins said he can see the strong bonds of trust that you've developed already with the soldiers on your caseload. He also said the class on PTSD had a positive influence, which was good to hear. Since then, a number of the guys have opened up and shared more readily about their own inner struggles."

"Did he mention Ted?"

"Only that he wanted to be removed from your caseload. Jenkins assured him the request would be reviewed, although he hopes to delay the final decision and give you both more time."

"I have a feeling you had something to do with that."

Brody smiled. "I told him you were working to overcome some history that probably played into Ted's current problems. Jenkins suggested I talk to your brother's counselor. I told him you would probably have more information to offer."

She nodded. "I met with his care team and counselor. Ted has been quite reticent about his life before the military. Of course, many soldiers have more than one problem. Often they're dealing with outside issues in addition to their injuries, no matter how traumatic those may be."

"Talking about those other situations helps in the healing process, which I hope Ted realizes." Brody glanced at his watch. "I'm going to have the cookies you received analyzed, but I also want to talk to the folks at the bakery who made them. Do you feel like joining me? If not, I can take you home first."

She smiled. "I told you I need to go back to work, but the bakery isn't far. Nikki Dunn's sister works there. I'm sure Diane can answer any questions you might have. We can stop in and talk to her before we drive back to Fort Rickman."

Brody parked in the small lot behind the bakery. A few people milled about the store when they entered. The smell of freshly baked cookies made his mouth water.

He noticed a sign hanging near the checkout register. "Products containing nuts are made in this facility."

A woman waved to Stephanie. She was in her midthirties and wore a white apron, a hairnet and a warm smile. She bore a striking resemblance to Nikki and was, undoubtedly, the sister Stephanie had mentioned.

The two women embraced before Stephanie introduced him. "Pleasure to meet you, ma'am," he said as they shook hands.

"I placed an order for you this morning."

"Actually, that's why we're here," Brody said. "Could you find the order form?"

Diane rifled through a stack of papers behind the counter. A look of success passed over her face as she pulled one free. "Here it is. Two dozen oatmeal-raisin cookies. The order came in sometime yesterday. Pat was working the counter."

"Is she here today? I'd like to talk to her."

Pat was an older woman with gray hair. Yesterday had been a busy day. She didn't remember anything about the order or the person who had requested the cookies. She apologized for not being able to provide more information before she returned to the kitchen.

Brody briefly mentioned Stephanie's allergic reaction, and then asked Diane, "When was the last time you baked anything containing nuts?"

"Our schedule never varies. We bake sugar and oatmeal in the morning. Chocolate chip, peanut butter and macadamia nut follow. We wipe down the equipment between batches, but a contamination could easily occur. That's why we post the warning." She pointed to the sign Brody had seen upon entering.

"What about your sister, Nikki?" Brody asked. "Does she know the baking schedule?"

"Probably, we haven't changed the routine in years. She used to help out when she was in high school. In fact, Nikki stopped by yesterday with Paul. He bought a dozen macadamia-nut cookies for his mom and dad. They left on a three-day trip this morning."

Diane glanced at Stephanie and lowered her voice. "Truth be told, I'm worried about him. Nikki said he feels guilty. I think it eats at him that his friends were injured."

"Maybe I should encourage Paul to get some help," Stephanie suggested.

As the women talked, Brody peered into the kitchen where Pat was using a large metallic scoop to add an ingredient to the batter she was preparing.

Maybe the problem hadn't been cross contamination.

When he explained his concern to Diane, she ushered him into the kitchen and pointed to the flour and oatmeal bins, and where they kept the other ingredients. Nothing seemed suspect until Brody opened the lid on the raisins. Using a scoop, he sprinkled some on the metal worktable.

Diane gasped.

Brody stared at the tiny particles that appeared to be nuts mixed in with the dried fruit. "I'll need to have this container analyzed. Contact the distributor and see if they've had other complaints."

"Of course. It was probably an error on their part."

"Unless it was done locally by someone who wanted to contaminate your products."

Diane's face paled as she undoubtedly realized the significance of Brody's statement.

"Why?" she asked. "Why would anyone sabotage our bakery?"

Which was exactly the question Brody needed to have answered.

Chapter Thirteen

To prevent Stephanie from having a second reaction, Brody made her stand back until he placed the container of raisins in his trunk. No doubt, the ground particles were some type of nut. Who had mixed them with the raisins and for what reason was yet to be determined.

Had it been done so that Stephanie would have an allergic reaction? Or was she simply the unsuspecting bystander who happened to get involved? Again the question of coincidence came into play. Too many coincidences didn't add up, especially when they all involved Stephanie.

"I can't understand how nuts could get in with the raisins," Stephanie said as she settled into the passenger seat of Brody's car. "Surely no one would do that on purpose."

"There are sick people in this world with a skewed sense of right and wrong."

"I guess you're right."

Brody rounded the car and climbed behind the wheel.

"Diane mentioned being worried about Paul. Did he and Josh get along?"

"They were always close. I doubt things have changed."

"Unless Paul saw Joshua's injury as too tragic," Brody said. "Some people have flawed ideas about quality of life."

"Josh is the type of guy who makes good things come from whatever life throws his way."

"Yet Paul may not have seen it that way. Did Ted ever give Paul a key to your house?" Brody asked.

"Of course not."

"What about Ted and Nikki? Anything going on between them?"

"They're friends. That's all."

"You said they dated in high school, but Nikki went to prom with Hayden. What about Paul? Did he have a girlfriend?"

"He and Cindy dated."

"Were they serious?"

"About as serious as any seventeen-year-olds can be. They both had a lot of growing up to do."

"Cindy seems to have her feet on the ground now."

Stephanie nodded. "She always knew what she wanted. Money was tight. She didn't go to college. Instead, she helped out with her mom's cleaning service. I'm not sure when she started working for Walt."

Glancing at her watch, Stephanie added, "Since we're not far from the garage, would you mind if we stopped by to see if my car is ready? You've been so kind to chauffer me back and forth to work, but I'm sure you'll be relieved when I get my own car back."

Giving Stephanie rides provided a way to see her and keep her close, which Brody needed to do for the investigation. He also liked being with her.

"We'll check on your car, but you haven't been a burden or a problem. In fact, I've enjoyed our time together."

She hesitated for a moment and looked at him, the sun shining on her hair. "You're very thoughtful, Brody."

Thoughtful? That wasn't what he wanted her to think. He was hoping for a word that was more in keeping with his own feelings, although he'd be hard-pressed to express the way he really felt.

Somehow he got his feelings for Stephanie mixed up with his memory of Lisa. Yet Stephanie was different. She was here, and Lisa was gone.

Instead of dreaming about Lisa as he'd done for so long, he had started to dream about Stephanie and that had him wondering about this investigation.

He was reacting like someone who was too involved, too committed. Not to the case, but to Stephanie.

"The tires came in yesterday," Walt told Stephanie once she and Brody arrived at the garage. "I meant to call you."

The cost of the four tires would put a significant hole in her bank account, which was one of the reasons Stephanie was glad she could live at home, at least until she received her first paycheck.

"Where's the car?" Brody asked after she paid the bill.

Walt handed her the keys and pointed behind the garage. "It's parked out back."

"My radar for danger is picking up bad vibes," Brody said as he and Stephanie rounded the garage. Her Corolla was parked next to a wooded area well away from the street. "I'm glad you didn't come here at night alone."

She shook her head, somewhat amused. "Do you CID guys always imagine the worst-case scenario?"

He raised his brow and held up four fingers. "Joshua Webb was attacked. Your house was broken into and a warning left. A bridge collapsed with you on it. You were almost shot." He raised his thumb. "Should we add the mysterious cookie delivery?"

She held up her hand to stop him. "It's daytime. You're with me, and the car looks fine."

"I'll follow you back to post."

"I usually take the two lane through town that runs along the river."

"Got it. The scenic route. But I'm still following you."

He helped her into her car and waited until she started the engine before he climbed behind the wheel of his own car. Stephanie hummed a tune as she pulled out of the parking space and headed along the winding River Road.

The sun was shining and warmed the day. Stephanie turned up the air conditioner and appreciated the coolness that soon circulated through the car. Glancing repeatedly at her rearview mirror, she watched for Brody's car to appear.

As much as she liked having her Corolla back, she had enjoyed having a reason to see Brody. Hopefully, they'd continue to get together. Maybe he could schedule another class for the WTB. She'd call him once she was back at her desk and see what they could arrange.

A sharp curve appeared ahead. A sign on the side of the road warned trucks to apply their brakes. She glanced at her speedometer and, realizing she was going faster than the limit, tapped the brakes.

Instead of slowing down, the car gained momentum. She pressed down harder on the brake pedal and swallowed a ball of anxiety that climbed into her throat.

Gripping the steering wheel with one hand, she downshifted with the other. The vehicle shuddered and the speed dropped ever so slightly, but once she entered the curve, she struggled to keep the wheels on the road.

The steep downward slope of the roadway ahead made her stomach roil. A huge semi tractor-trailer chugged up the hill in the opposite lane. She flashed her lights to signal her distress.

The trucker flashed back, no doubt oblivious to her need.

She glanced again at the speedometer. Seventy miles per hour. Too fast.

Bile soured her stomach.

If Brody were behind the wheel, he'd know what to do. *Think. Think.*

The semi neared. She held her breath. The trucker blew his horn as she whizzed past him.

A straight stretch of roadway lay ahead, flanked by thick woods to the left and a five-foot drop-off to the river on the right.

She tramped on the emergency-brake pedal. The car slowed ever so slightly before accelerating once again.

A sports utility vehicle approached.

A woman sat at the wheel with three little heads perched in car seats behind her.

Stephanie's car shimmied out of control and swerved into the left lane. She tugged on the steering wheel, nearly sideswiping the SUV before she lost control. The Corolla crossed the right-hand lane, jumped the curb and slid down the hill.

Her heart lodged in her throat.

The last thing she heard was the name she screamed. "Brody!"

* * *

Brody increased his speed, needing to catch up with Stephanie. A series of red lights had delayed him in town. Now on the open roadway, he hoped to make up time.

He spied her car rounding a curve up ahead.

His heart lurched. She was going fast. Too fast.

He raced forward.

God, help her. The internal prayer came without forethought.

He pushed down on the accelerator and took the curve at a fast rate. His own heart beat wildly as a huge semi rolled past him, followed by an SUV.

Searching the distance, Brody saw only the empty road.

Where was she?

A swirl of dust caught his eye.

His gut tightened.

"Stephanie," he screamed.

Screeching to a stop, he punched nine-one-one on his cell and sprang from his car, relaying information to the operator.

"Send an ambulance and medical responders now."

He stumbled down the hill toward where her car had landed on its side. The engine still purred. Peering through the front windshield, he saw Stephanie suspended by her seat belt, the airbag limp around her. Her eyes were closed, her cheek bloodied. Her tousled hair dangled in the air.

He climbed the hood and yanked on the door.

The latch held. Pounding on the driver's window, he screamed her name.

Another fear rose up within him, more deadly than the crash.

Smoke.

If he didn't get Stephanie out, she would be trapped inside the car as it went up in flames.

A voice penetrated the darkness.

Stephanie moaned.

Her body ached. A jackhammer pounded through her brain.

She wanted to slip back into the darkness.

"Stephanie."

Insistent. Pleading.

She recognized the voice.

"Br...Brody?"

More pounding.

"Open your eyes, Stephanie. The door's locked. Release the latch."

She blinked against the light, feeling a swell of nausea. The world hung topsy-turvy around her.

She tried to make sense of the disorder. The only constant was Brody's voice.

Turning her head ever so slightly, she saw his face pressed against the window, his palm pounding against the glass.

"Unlock the door," he screamed.

Lifting her left hand, she flipped the small knob on the door handle.

Smoke swirled around her.

Instinctively, she cowered.

The door opened. With a snap, Brody released the seat belt, grabbed her purse and lifted her into his arms.

Holding her close, he jumped to the ground below.

"Brody," she whispered, wanting to drift away from the chaos.

"Don't leave me, honey."

The acrid smell of smoke and fuel filled her nostrils. Blinking open her eyes, she turned her head ever so slightly, seeing flames shoot skyward.

Sirens sounded in the distance.

Everything seemed surreal except the pounding of Brody's heart and his pull of air as he carried her away from the carnage, away from the fire, away from danger.

Brody hovered next to the EMTs as they worked on Stephanie. A bandage covered the cut on her forehead. The blood had been cleaned from her face, but she still looked pale, which worried him.

One of the EMTs stood. "Can you give us a little room, sir?"

Stephanie glanced up at Brody and smiled, not quite a full grin but enough to reassure him.

"How's the injury to her head?" he asked.

"Looks like she's going to be okay, sir. We're taking her to the local hospital. You can follow us there."

"I'll ride with her in the ambulance."

"Brody, I'm all right." Stephanie tried to reassure him. "Drive your own car. We'll both need a ride home from the hospital."

She was thinking more soundly than he was at this point.

Brody turned to the EMT. "Are you sure she can make the trip?"

"She seems in good shape," the EMT said. "But we want the E.R. doc to check her out first. You understand?"

Brody understood the EMT, but not what had happened.

He glanced at the smoldering pile of twisted metal that had been Stephanie's car.

The Freemont chief of police stood near the wreckage. Brody approached Palmer.

"Any idea what happened?" Brody asked.

"She was going too fast, for sure. She said the brakes didn't work. We'll check out what's left of the vehicle, but it's doubtful we'll ever pinpoint what malfunctioned. If there was evidence, it probably burned up in the fire."

"Did you send someone to talk to Walt at the garage?"

"He wasn't there, but his sister was more than helpful. They've had some problem with vandalism over the past few weeks. We picked up a couple of teenagers last week. They denied everything, but we're pretty sure they're involved. I'm sending someone to bring them back in for questioning."

"Why would they tamper with Stephanie's brakes?"

"Beats me." Palmer scratched his chin. "A lot has happened to Ms. Upton. Are you sure she wouldn't do something like this to attract attention to herself?"

"That's ridiculous. She came back to this area to help her brother. He's the one with the problem. I need to find out if anyone saw him around the garage."

"I talked to Major Jenkins. Private Upton's been in his barracks." He flicked his gaze to Stephanie. "You know very well that some folks make up stories to be the center of attention. Stephanie's mama died young. Her daddy is a workaholic who never gave the kids enough of his time. Now her brother's a war hero." The cop continued. "It's a possibility she needed to feel wanted or protected or important. Maybe all three. Wasn't that long ago when Stephanie Upton was one of the young women to watch in this area. Folks thought she'd do well in life."

Success wasn't important. Staying alive was.

"She *has* done well," Brody countered. "She's got a good job on post and is an effective and compassionate advocate for wounded soldiers. That's something to admire, in my opinion."

"I agree." Palmer patted Brody's shoulder. "Just keep an open mind. Sometimes there's more than one way to look at a situation."

"What about Joshua? She saved his life."

"Ms. Upton was the first on the scene. Does that tell you anything?"

It meant she could have staged the attack to look like an accident, which Brody had first considered but soon discarded after talking to Stephanie at Josh's house.

"The shot last night wasn't her imagination."

Palmer nodded. "I agree, but other things have happened."

Brody thought of the bull's-eye on the photograph in her kitchen and on her bedsheets, as well as the collapsed bridge. So far he hadn't discussed the allergic reaction with the chief. He'd save that for later, once he knew for sure what was mixed with the raisins. No reason at the present moment to add more fuel to the fire.

Glancing at the burning embers of what had been Stephanie's car, Brody knew the chief had enough suspicions of his own.

Brody didn't want to hear anything negative about Stephanie. She wouldn't have attacked Joshua or purposefully crashed her car.

Looking at where Stephanie lay brought back memories of Lisa.

The pain of loss twisted his gut. Lisa had been murdered by a killer no one suspected, least of all Brody.

If only he had put the warning signs together that were so evident in hindsight.

What sign was he missing now?

He thought of everything that had happened as he followed the ambulance to the hospital. The paramedics wheeled Stephanie into the E.R., where a competent team of medical personnel rushed her into the treatment room. He paced the hallway until the doctor opened the door and announced she could go home.

Relief swept over Brody, replacing the oppressive heaviness that had surrounded him since the accident.

He couldn't help but smile as he stepped into the trauma room.

She sat on the edge of the stretcher. Without saying a word, she reached for him.

He wrapped his arms around her. A surge of joy coursed through him. He buried his head in her hair. Despite what she'd been through, he could smell the scent of her shampoo mixed with the smoke that lingered on both of them.

"Thank you," she whispered. "If you hadn't followed me…"

"I should have gotten there sooner."

"You saved me, Brody. You saved my life."

He knew what could have happened. The thought made him hold her even more closely.

"No matter how hard I stepped on the brake, the car didn't respond." She shook her head. "There was a truck and then an SUV with kids in the back."

"It's okay, hon. You don't need to think about it now."

"But if something else had happened—"

She didn't finish the thought.

Brody told her about the teen vandals and the chief of police's concern that they could have been the perpetrators.

"I'm surprised you don't suspect Ted," she said at last.

"He's been in the barracks, Stephanie. Ted wasn't involved."

She nodded, appreciation evident in her gaze. "At least, we agree on that."

"Let's go." He grabbed her hand and hurried her out of the E.R. "I'm taking you someplace safe."

Chapter Fourteen

Brody held the door open to his bachelor officer's quarters on post.

"Your apartment's lovely," Stephanie said as she walked through the doorway. Brody watched as she glanced around the room, taking in the overstuffed couch and chair, the plasma-screen television and speakers and the bistro table with four chairs and serving sideboard.

He had decorated the living area in earth tones, pulled together with an Oriental rug, which her surprised expression said she hadn't expected.

Her eyes widened with appreciation as she stepped toward a group of framed charcoal sketches that decorated the walls, all desert scenes of stark hills and big boulders piled next to a two-lane road that cut through the wilderness.

"They're beautiful, Brody."

Her gaze dropped to the artist's name. Goodman.

She turned. "Someone in your family?"

He smiled. "I'm glad you like them."

"Your mother? Father? Grandfather?" She glanced at

the next sketch, again pointing to the Goodman name. "Who's the artist?"

"They're mine. I started drawing to pass the time in Afghanistan. The sketches you see here are from Fort Irwin, in the Mojave Desert, where I was stationed following my first deployment."

One sketch was of a noble mountain outlined against the desert terrain, the sun setting behind the peak. In the distance, the vast arid terrain stretched barren and lonely.

"The stark surroundings are haunting," she said. "Barren. Lonely. They remind me of a time in my life shortly after I left Freemont. I missed my home and my brother."

Brody moved toward her and wrapped his arm around her shoulder as they both stared at the drawings. "I sketched those pictures when I was a young soldier. The army had provided a way for me to make something better than the path I was on back in L.A. My family had problems." He shrugged. "I guess a lot of families do."

Stephanie nodded as if she understood. "What are you working on now?"

He shook his head. "I haven't sketched anything in years."

"Because—"

He let out a deep breath, knowing he needed to share the past with Stephanie. Maybe then she would understand his concern about Ted.

"A girl from home came to visit me about the time I sketched these drawings. She had written me during my first deployment, and I wanted a nice place for her to stay. I didn't have a car. Barstow was the closest town, and it was more than a thirty-mile drive from post through the desert."

Stephanie pointed to the picture of the two-lane road, cutting across the stark terrain. "What you've sketched here."

He nodded. "My first sergeant's wife was a jewel. She had a heart as big as Texas, where she and the Sarge were from originally. She invited Lisa to stay with her."

Stephanie tilted her head, no doubt hearing the pain in his voice.

"Sarge seemed like a good guy. No one realized he was having problems. Trouble sleeping. Bouts of rage. That night…"

Brody turned, not wanting to continue.

"You told the soldiers that it helps to talk about situations in the past." Stephanie touched his shoulder and hesitated a moment before asking, "What happened, Brody?"

He rubbed his hand over his jaw. "They pieced it together. Sarge must have had an episode that night. He killed his wife. He killed Lisa, too, and then he killed himself."

Stephanie wrapped her arms around him.

"I was the first one at the scene the next morning."

"Oh, Brody, I'm so sorry."

"That's why I worry about Ted. No one knew about Sarge's outrages. Looking back, it's easy to see he was probably suffering from PTSD."

He turned to stare into her crystal-clear eyes. "I can't protect you all the time, and that's what scares me. You've got to protect yourself when it comes to your brother."

"But I can't turn my back on Ted."

He had to show her how he felt. Staring down at her parted lips, he sensed the swell of emotion that coursed between them. He didn't want to think about the past—not his or hers. He just wanted to think about the present moment and how much he cared about her.

She looked at him expectantly, and then rose on tiptoe. He lowered his mouth, tasting the sweetness of his lips.

He raked his hands through her hair and pulled her even closer. The swell of his own heart seemed to explode within him; suddenly he wasn't alone anymore, and everything that mattered was in his arms.

At that moment, her phone chirped.

She pulled back ever so slightly. Regret wrapped around her pretty face. Her cheeks flushed, and she pushed her hands against his chest, needing space, which he gave her, feeling an instant sense of loss.

She searched in her purse and raised the cell to her ear.

"Ted? You heard about the accident." She looked relieved. "I'm okay. My car was totaled, but I wasn't hurt."

Brody stared at the painting of the lonely desert landscape. Stephanie would always put Ted first. Selfish as it may seem, he didn't want to be second-best, not when it came to a lifetime commitment.

But then he was getting ahead of himself and his relationship with Stephanie. If there even was a relationship.

He'd been alone for so long. Now that Stephanie was in his life, he didn't want to let her go.

Brody fixed Stephanie a sandwich with chips and insisted she relax on the couch while he headed to his home office in the spare bedroom.

The first call he made was to his boss at CID headquarters. He filled Chief Wilson in on what had happened.

"Do you think her brake problem is random?" Wilson asked.

"I don't know what to think, sir. The Freemont chief of police mentioned vandalism in that area of town. I'm going to call the garage and see what the owner has to say."

"Walt's worked on my car a number of times. He runs a good business, but looks can be deceiving."

Which brought to mind the police chief's concern about Stephanie wanting to be the center of attention. Brody saw no reason to relay Palmer's suspicions.

"A lot has happened to Ms. Upton," the chief mused.

"Yes, sir."

"Make sure nothing else does, will you, Brody?"

"That's my goal, sir."

"See what you can find out today and brief me in the morning."

"Will do, sir."

He disconnected and dialed Ferrol's Garage. Walt answered with a curt greeting and quickly answered Brody's questions about the vandalism problem the local area had been having.

"As I told the police, the kids have done some pranks, but nothing as significant as this. Although Stephanie's car was an older model, I had it humming like a baby when I signed off on the work order."

"Someone could have tampered with the brakes either in your garage or when it was parked out back."

"Whoa there, Mr. Special Agent. You're jumping to the wrong conclusion and getting me riled up, to boot.

I stand by my work. I wouldn't do anything to cause a problem."

"Then who did?"

"Exactly what I've been trying to find out. I just checked online for any recalls on that make and model. A couple years back, there had been a number of cases of brake failure. Stands to reason that could have been Stephanie's problem."

"Wouldn't she have been notified?" Brody asked.

"If she bought the car used, the recall notice may have been sent to the original owner or lost in the mail. Everything looked good when I was under the hood. No telling what malfunctioned."

"Do me a favor and call the chief of police and let him know what you told me."

"Will do."

Brody's next call was to the hospital for an update on Joshua's condition. The news wasn't good.

He disconnected and headed to the living room, where he found Stephanie asleep on the couch. He stood for a long moment, staring down at her, wishing things could be different. If only she trusted him. Together they'd be able to help Ted, Brody felt sure.

But she didn't want him involved.

He touched her shoulder. "Stephanie?"

She opened her eyes, then smiled. Her lips were puffy with sleep and so inviting. His chest tightened as he realized how strong his feelings were for her.

"Joshua's taken a turn for the worse," Brody said. "I'm gong to the hospital."

Stephanie sat up and glanced around his BOQ. "Point me to your restroom so I can comb my hair and freshen my lipstick. I want to go with you."

She returned quickly, all hint of her sleepiness gone. He grabbed her hand and together they hurried to his car.

"I'll call Major Jenkins and alert him," Stephanie said. "Joshua's parents need to be notified, as well as the WTB chaplain."

She'd completed the calls by the time Brody parked at the hospital. He placed his hand protectively on her back as they rode the elevators to the ICU.

"We're here to see PFC Joshua Webb," Brody said as they approached the nurse's station and flashed his CID identification.

Stephanie's grip on Brody's hand tightened when they stepped into the small room. Joshua's face was pale as death. An IV bag dripped medication ever so slowly into his vein. If only it would combat the infection that was running rampant through his body.

"Josh, it's Stephanie." She touched his feverish arm. "Special Agent Goodman is here with me. Remember he visited you in the hospital earlier?"

"Good to see you, Joshua."

Stephanie smiled at Joshua, but her eyes were filled with concern. She patted his arm. "Don't worry about anything, except getting better. When you're stronger, we'll take you to your house. A local group of businessmen want to help with the renovations."

The soldier's lips moved ever so slightly.

The WTB chaplain, a tall lieutenant colonel with a long face and compassionate eyes, entered the room. He nodded to Stephanie and Brody before he approached the head of the bed and bent down to talk with Josh.

Brody and Stephanie stepped back to give them privacy.

After a few minutes, the chaplain motioned them forward. "Would you join me in prayer?"

Stephanie folded her hands and bowed her head. Standing next to her, Brody did the same.

"Dear Lord," the chaplain began, his voice strong and determined. "We call upon You in this time of need, and ask Your help to bring Joshua through this illness. He is Your child, and we know Your love for him surpasses any human love. You want the very best for Josh, and we're confident that, at this moment, You are surrounding him with Your love and mercy. Fill his heart with love for You, Lord. Help the doctors and nurses who care for him, and allow the medication to be effective to combat the infection. We ask for renewed strength for Joshua as he places his trust in You. For this we pray, amen."

Before the minister had opened his eyes, a scuffle sounded in the hallway. Stephanie turned to see Ted standing in the doorway. His face was filled with pain.

He glanced at Stephanie. "You…you didn't tell me he was in such bad shape."

"I didn't know until just a short while ago."

Tears swam in Ted's eyes. "You called the chaplain, but you didn't call me. My squad leader told me the news."

Ted's world was caving in around him once again. Another person in his life was being taken for him. The look on his face showed too clearly the knife that had lodged in his heart.

He took a step back to where Paul stood, his face pale, his eyes wide as if he, too, was struggling with a wave of emotions he couldn't handle.

"It's just like it was when Mom died, isn't it, Stephanie?" Ted said. "You didn't let me know. You and Dad kept it from me. Yet I was the one who had been with her through it all while you stayed at college."

"Which is what Mom wanted, Ted." Her voice was low and filled with compassion. Why did he fail to remember her repeated requests to stay home that semester? "I did what Mom wanted."

"You keep telling me that, but it's not true. You did what you wanted, and then at the end, you were the one standing at her bedside. You let her die without calling me."

"I called the school and told them you needed to come home. Aunt Hazel picked you up."

"Too late. I was too late."

"Mom was still alive when you got home, Ted. But you refused to see her."

He shook his head. "You're lying."

He turned and ran from the ICU.

"Ted!" Stephanie ran after him.

He opened the door to the stairwell and raced down the steps.

She followed, calling his name. "Ted, stop."

The outside door on the first floor opened. She ran even faster, her feet tripping down the stairs. She had to reach him, but when she stepped into the hot afternoon, he was nowhere to be seen.

She had called the high school that day to notify the school that Aunt Hazel was coming to pick up her brother. The secretary had trouble locating him, and when Ted arrived home, their mother's breathing was labored. Knowing she didn't have much time, Stephanie had encouraged Ted to go to her bedside. He had balked. The pain of seeing their mother moving from this life to the next was too hard for him.

Ted remembered what he thought had happened, but it was far from the truth. If only he could see the past with clarity. She needed to, as well. Maybe then, she'd stop blaming herself for everything that had gone wrong.

Chapter Fifteen

"Direct me," Brody said to Stephanie once they were in his car again. "Where would Ted go when he's upset?"

"Maybe the cemetery where my mother's buried. He might go to her grave site."

On the way off post, she called Paul, but his phone went immediately to voice mail. She called Nikki next, who didn't know about Joshua's decline. Nor did she know anything about Ted.

"Phone me if he contacts you," Stephanie said before she disconnected.

Brody saw the worry weighing down her shoulders. "What about Cindy? Would your brother contact her?"

"I'll try her cell." Stephanie pulled the number from her contacts file and paused before she looked at Brody. "It's going to voice mail."

She left a message while Brody called the garage. Walt answered.

"Stephanie needs to talk to your sister," Brody told him. "Could you put her on?"

"She's helping our mom with her cleaning business this afternoon. Anything I can pass along?"

Brody explained about the decline in Joshua's condition and Ted's reaction. "If Cindy runs into Ted, have her call Stephanie."

"That boy's had a lot of loss in his short life. 'Spect seeing his buddy in such bad shape is eating at him. What about Paul? He might know something."

"They're together. Stephanie's trying to reach Paul now."

Eventually, Paul answered his cell, but he refused to let Stephanie talk to Ted. From the one-sided conversation Brody heard, Paul was struggling as much as her brother.

Stephanie filled Brody in on their conversation once she disconnected. "He talked about Joshua not wanting to live since the amputation, but Paul's wrong. Josh has always been optimistic about the future, and from what everyone at the WTB has told me, his outlook never changed, even after he lost his legs. Paul's transferring his own feelings onto Josh, which concerns me. I offered to schedule an appointment for Paul with one of the social workers. I told him talking about his feelings would help."

"Did he agree to see someone?"

"Yes, although he didn't seem too enthused."

She called the mental-health office on post and gave the receptionist Paul's name. "They'll squeeze him in tomorrow afternoon," she told Brody.

When she called Paul back, he failed to answer once again. She left the information about his appointment in a voice mail before she disconnected.

Once they turned into the cemetery, her outward demeanor changed. Brody could see the pain in her gaze as he parked by a small knoll near a number of grave sites. Without speaking, she exited the car and walked slowly to a granite marker. Brody stood back, giving her space and privacy.

He studied the surrounding hills and manicured grounds, looking for any sign of Ted or Paul. The sun beat down overhead, causing sweat to dampen his neck.

Stephanie retraced her steps, her gaze sweeping the area. "I had hoped Ted would be here."

"Where else would he go?"

She shook her head. "Maybe back to our house."

They drove in silence, the heaviness of seeing her mother's grave evident in the slump of her shoulders and the way she toyed with her watch.

Brody longed to pull to the side of the road and wrap her in his arms, but she was focused on Ted and the past and the pain that she and her brother still carried.

Arriving at her house, he walked her to the porch where he waited until she had unlocked the door and disengaged the security alarm.

"I know you won't change the locks, Stephanie, but you could change the alarm on your own. The owner's manual will explain what you need to do. It just means plugging in another code. I'll help you."

When she hesitated, he added, "You didn't think Ted was in the house the other night, and if he wasn't, then someone else was here. Let me walk you through the steps."

"What if Ted comes back?"

"You'll hear him at the door. That shouldn't be a problem."

She let out a long sigh. "Maybe you're right. I'd probably sleep better."

She looked tired and worried.

He helped her reprogram the alarm and turned his back when she entered the new four-digit code.

"You can watch, Brody. I trust you."

He shook his head. "I want you to be the only one who knows this code."

Once the alarm was reprogrammed, they headed into the kitchen. "Grab some water from the bottom shelf in the refrigerator," Stephanie said. "I'll check the phone for messages."

A sound on the front porch caused them both to pause.

A key turned in the lock.

"It's Ted." Stephanie hurried into the foyer.

The front door opened just as Brody caught up to her.

Ted's eyes widened as he looked from Stephanie to Brody. "What's he doing here?"

The security system beeped. Ted tapped in the code. The old code.

Brody anticipated the scream of the alarm seconds before the system activated.

The deafening screech filled the house.

Ted stepped back, his face awash with disbelief and pain. "You changed the code, didn't you?" He pointed to Brody. "It's because of him. He convinced you I'm dangerous. That I'm crazy. That I could hurt you."

"Ted, please," she pleaded.

"You had a decision to make, didn't you, Stephanie? You could trust me or him. You chose him." Ted ran from the house and into the night.

Brody chased after him, but lost sight of Ted in the woods at the rear of the property. He returned to the house just as Stephanie backed her father's Cadillac out of the garage.

"What are you doing?"

"I'm going after him, Brody. You're still living in the past. I'm not Lisa, and my brother isn't the sergeant that killed her. You made me change the alarm, but I can't do things your way anymore. I transferred to Fort Rickman to help Ted. He's my responsibility."

"Stephanie, please."

"I've got to do this on my own. Don't follow me, Brody."

"I want to help you."

"You've done too much already. Stay away from me, and stay away from my brother."

Stephanie raced out of the driveway and through the Estates until she arrived at Paul's house. She pulled to the curb in front of the three-story structure that was far larger than the Upton home. The grounds were perfectly manicured and decorated with flower gardens and clusters of ornamental trees. In the daylight, the home was a showplace, but tonight it sat dark and foreboding.

She ran up the walk and climbed the steps to the porch. Not wanting to waste time with the bell, she pounded on the door.

"I'm coming," Paul's voice sounded from inside the house. Hopefully, she'd find Ted inside and be able to explain what had happened.

Paul's surprise at seeing her was evident when he opened the door. "I dropped Ted off at your house, Stephanie, not more than ten minutes ago."

"He ran away from me, Paul. Where would go?"

"The Italian Parlor isn't far, especially if he takes the shortcut across the golf course. You might try there."

She hurried back to her car. Paul was right. The pizza parlor was a favorite spot for many of the local kids and an easy hike using the golf-cart paths and nature trails. By road, the trip took longer, but she eventually pulled into the parking lot and raced inside, hit by the pungent aroma of freshly baked pizza. Bowls of peanuts sat on each table, the discarded shells scattered on the floor.

Careful to stay clear of the debris lest she have an allergic reaction, Stephanie scanned the tables and quickly spied Nikki. A guy sat across from her in the booth, his back to the door. They turned as she neared.

"Keith?"

He smiled sheepishly while Nikki held up an open folder. "We're going over the plans for the Wounded Warrior picnic," she said.

Keith nodded a bit too quickly. "I wanted Nikki to review everything before I gave you the final copy."

"You already submitted the plans," Stephanie said.

"Those were tentative." He placed a second folder, containing about ten pages of typed notes, on the table in front of her and tapped it twice with his hand. "You'll find everything in here. Let me know if you want me to change anything."

She appreciated the work he had done on the project. He seemed to be genuinely concerned about the military and eager that the picnic be a special day for the soldiers. Maybe she had underestimated her cousin.

"Have either of you seen Ted?"

Nikki nodded. "He was here a few minutes ago, out of breath and saying he needed wheels."

"I volunteered to drive Nikki home," Keith said. "Which solved his transportation problem. He left in Nikki's car not more than three minutes ago."

"Do you know where he was headed?"

Keith shrugged. "He didn't say."

"But he did tell us Josh wasn't doing well and asked me to pray for him," Nikki shared.

"Really?"

The younger woman nodded. "His squad leader's been talking to him about God and how much He loves us. Ted's never been much of a believer, but he's been listening. I guess some of it rubbed off."

Stephanie remembered going to church regularly with her mother when she was young. They would sit with Aunt Hazel and Keith. All that changed after Ted was born.

"He also mentioned wanting to visit Keith's mom," Nikki continued. "Ted said he hadn't seen her since he left for Afghanistan."

After bidding them a hasty farewell, Stephanie returned to her dad's car and drove toward Magnolia Gardens Nursing Home. The facility sat along a narrow two-lane road on the outskirts of town.

Pulling into the parking lot, she rubbed her free hand over her stomach in an attempt to calm her agitation. She wasn't ready to face Aunt Hazel, but she needed to find Ted.

Hurrying inside, she approached the receptionist, who pointed her down the hall. "Hazel Allen's room is 110, the sixth door on the left."

Stephanie's footfalls clipped over the tile floor and kept time with the thumping of her heart. She hadn't seen Nikki's car in the front lot, but additional spaces were available in the rear, where Ted could have parked.

Stopping outside room 110, she gazed at the sleeping woman who reminded her so much of her own mother. Hazel had the same high cheekbones and warm smile, and even from this distance, Stephanie was struck by the resemblance.

As much as she wanted to draw closer, she didn't have time. If Ted wasn't with Aunt Hazel, where could he be?

Driving back to town, Stephanie felt an added weight pulling her down. Her brother had to feel rejected and pushed aside, unwelcome even in his own home, which wasn't the case, of course.

Brody's rationale for changing the security code had seemed logical at the time. She never thought how it would affect Ted until the alarm sounded. The sense of betrayal that played across his face revealed the depth of his pain.

Stephanie would give anything to change what had happened, just as she wanted to change that afternoon on the lake. If only mistakes could be corrected with a wave of the hand. Instead, they often festered, causing long-term pain and deep divides that tore families apart.

Arriving back in town, Stephanie headed toward the town square. On the way, she passed the brick church on the corner of Freemont Road and Third Street. Surrounding the church were a number of alleyways where the congregation parked on Sunday mornings. Stephanie didn't want to lose precious time circling the neighborhood in hopes of spotting Nikki's car. Instead, she pulled to the curb and hurried toward the church.

Pulling open the massive door, she stared into the dimly lit sanctuary and empty pews. An overwhelming need to talk to the Lord drew her forward. She walked down the center aisle and slipped into the front pew.

Brass candelabra graced the oak altar, which was draped with a linen cloth. Although the candles weren't lit, the smell of beeswax hung in the church like a sacred scent, bringing back memories of services in her youth.

In the stillness, she remembered her mother's laughter, the sound like music that made tears stream from her eyes.

"I tried to love him like you did, Mama." Stephanie dropped her head into her hands. "I wanted to fill the hole in my own heart, but even more so, I wanted to knit together his brokenness. I…I tried to be you." She swiped her hand across her cheeks. "Ted didn't want me. He needed you and Dad, but you know how that went. I thought Dad might change after…after your death. But he'll never change, I finally realized."

Her own voice broke as she thought back to her mother's funeral and then Hayden's.

"I'm…I'm sorry for what I did. For my anger at Ted. For waiting too long and for not getting there in time."

Stephanie shook her head. She couldn't let her brother down again. His well-being depended on her just as it had three years ago. Regretting the mistake she had made then, she had to find Ted. Not knowing where to turn, she turned to the Lord.

Dear God, I feel so hopelessly lost. Help me find my brother.

Chapter Sixteen

Driving back to town, Brody called the Warrior Transitional Battalion, hoping Ted had returned to his barracks. The squad leader had questioned Ted's roommate and others on his floor, but no one had heard from him.

The second call was to the chief of police. Brody filled him in on what had happened. "If anything develops, call me."

"Anything meaning what?" Palmer asked.

"A vehicular accident, a soldier walking alone along the river or getting drunk at some hole-in-the-wall bar. Ted Upton shows symptoms of PTSD. He's balanced on a tightrope that could be dangerous to himself or someone else. Just tell your officers on patrol to keep their eyes open."

Brody also informed CID headquarters and the military police on post. He wanted to be proactive and ensure Ted's situation didn't become more severe. And he didn't want anyone else hurt.

Stephanie's bitter words played over in his head. She didn't want him interfering with her brother, but she failed to realize the terrible consequences of what could happen.

Once again, he recalled the carnage, and Lisa's body lying in a pool of blood. Tonight that memory seemed so raw.

Then, instead of Lisa, he saw Stephanie with her blue eyes, the color of a clear sky on a summer's day, and her hair like stands of silk that caressed his cheek when he held her close, which is what he wanted to do now.

His cell rang. He grabbed it from the console. "Special Agent Goodman."

"Sir, this is Sergeant McCoy from the WTB."

Ted's squad leader. Brody felt a surge of euphoria. "Did PFC Upton return to the barracks?"

"Negative, sir, but the guys said he likes the Italian Parlor in town. This time of night, he often stops in for pizza and a couple of beers."

"Bowls of roasted peanuts on the tables?"

"That's the place." The squad leader gave Brody directions.

Pulling into the parking lot, Brody spied Keith and Nikki leaving the restaurant.

Rolling down his window, he quickly asked about Ted.

"Stephanie stopped by right after Ted left," Keith said. "She may have gone to the nursing home. It's located north along the Freemont Road."

He handed Brody a manila folder. "She left in a hurry and forgot to take this file on the Wounded Warrior picnic. You'll see her before I will."

With a quick thank-you and a sigh of relief, Brody tossed the folder on the passenger's seat and then increased his speed as he headed toward the nursing home.

Halfway through town, he spotted the Uptons' Cadillac parked in front of a small, brick church on Third Street and pulled into the parking lot.

Taking the steps two at a time, he raced inside, overcome with relief when he saw Stephanie sitting in the front. Unwilling to interrupt her conversation with the Lord, he stood shadowed in the rear and watched as she heaved herself up from the pew and turned toward the door.

If only she would accept his help. Almost afraid of what she would say, Brody pulled in a deep breath and stepped into the light.

She gasped. Her hand clutched her throat. "Were you watching me?"

"I was waiting until you stopped praying. I want to help you find Ted."

He could see the tears that filled her eyes and the puffy redness to her cheeks even in the half light.

She shook her head. "I told you, I have to do this alone."

"I'll follow you, just to keep you safe."

"Didn't you hear me earlier? I'm not Lisa."

Of course, she wasn't Lisa. Lisa had been gone for so long that he hardly remembered what she looked like. Stephanie was real and warm and sweet and soft every place she should be, and being with her made Brody feel whole again for the first time in so very long.

"I'm worried about your brother and his safety, but I'm also worried about you." He hoped she heard the sincerity in his voice. "I can't separate the way I feel about you from the job I do in the military, a job that is at the heart of who I am, Stephanie. I won't get in your way unless you're in danger."

The look on her face told him she was softening. He remembered what he and his friends had said when they were kids.

"I won't get in your way," he repeated. "Cross my heart." He raised his right hand and made a small cross over his heart. The childlike promise took on a new meaning in the church with the larger cross hanging behind the altar.

His heart had opened somewhat to the Lord, but he wasn't willing to put Stephanie's safety solely in God's hands. He needed to be with her to ensure she wasn't in harm's way.

She didn't have a choice. Neither did he.

Brody would die himself rather than let anything happen to Stephanie. He'd made a horrific mistake with Lisa. She was in the past, but he wouldn't make a second mistake that would cause another woman to lose her life.

Especially when that woman was Stephanie.

A woman he now realized he loved.

Stephanie glanced into her rearview mirror and spied Brody's headlights. True to his word, he'd followed her as she had driven through town looking for her brother. He had also alerted the military police who were searching for Ted on post.

Brody assured her law enforcement wouldn't do anything to threaten Ted or cause his fragile mental health harm. She'd already done enough by changing the security code.

She shouldn't have listened to Brody. Not long ago, she had hoped something might develop between them, especially in the weeks to come, when Ted's condition improved.

How silly to think anything good could come from knowing Brody.

He saw everyone—especially her brother—as a threat. Stephanie wanted to heal Ted's pain and help him move forward. Her brother and Brody were polar opposites that would never be reconciled. No matter how much she was attracted to Brody, Ted would always stand between them.

A lump filled her throat, but she refused to cry. She'd cried too many tears already. Now she needed to be practical and think of where her brother could be holed up.

Flipping on the radio, she turned the knob until the static cleared and the weather report came on. The sky looked clear, but this time of year storms blew in without warning.

Her thoughts turned again to that stormy night so long ago. She saw the angry waves pounding the side of her father's cabin cruiser. The rain, the wind…

The marina.

Why hadn't she thought of it earlier?

Pushing down on the accelerator, she headed south and then west, toward Big Island Lake where her father kept his boats.

She shivered. Surely Ted wouldn't take *The Upton Queen* or *The Princess* out onto the water. Not when he was so mixed-up with the turmoil bubbling around him.

"Oh, please, God, keep him safe."

Surprised by calling on the Lord again this evening, she turned on her high beams and raced along the back roads. Brody followed behind her.

Her phone rang, but before she could answer, it went to voice mail. The call was probably from Brody, wondering where they were headed.

A second call came in.

She raised the cell to her ear. "Brody?"

"Ah, no, Steph. It's Paul."

The soldier's voice sounded thick with alcohol.

"I called a minute ago and left a voice mail. Then I thought I'd try you a second time. I just got your message about the appointment with the shrink tomorrow."

"It's at two in the afternoon, Paul. Actually, she's a social worker, not a psychiatrist. But she's good at what she does and she wants to help."

"I don't want help, Steph. You've got it all wrong. I'm not having any problems."

"Paul, you've been drinking. Where are you?"

"I'm home."

"Go to bed and get some rest. We'll talk in the morning. You haven't seen Ted, have you?"

"He wants to be alone. Ted told me he doesn't need you."

"Maybe not, but I need him."

Hopefully, in the morning, once Paul had slept off the effects of his night of drinking, he'd realize counseling would be helpful.

Her mother always said things happened for a reason. Maybe it was good that Ted had run away this evening; otherwise, he might have been drinking with Paul.

As she neared the marina, a bell tolled in the night, the bell on her father's boat. She parked and stepped to the pavement as Brody pulled to a stop beside her.

"Stay here. Ted's by the water. I don't want him any more upset than he already is."

"He could have a gun, Stephanie."

She shook her head, tired of Brody's incessant attempts to make Ted into a killer. "He's my brother. Let me talk to him alone."

"I'll be waiting at the entrance to the dock."

"I don't need your help, Brody."

"I'm not leaving you."

"That's your choice, but don't interfere."

She stomped off, angry that he was so intent on staying put and yet grateful he was there. Her father had scoffed any time she had been afraid. Having someone who put her safety first was a good thing. Just as long as Ted didn't see Brody as a threat.

She hurried along the wooden ramp. Ted stood beside the cabin cruiser and stared into the water. His right hand was wrapped around the rope attached to the bell. Every few seconds, he yanked on the cord.

"Ted."

Hearing her voice, he turned. "How'd you find me?"

She eased forward. "I went everyplace else first. The marina was the only place left to look. I should have known you'd be here. That day on the lake, I…I was mad at you."

"You forbade me to go out on the water. I told you I was spending the day at Paul's house. Only that was a lie."

She took a step closer. "I was proud of you for not going with the other kids. I baked a cake for you so we could celebrate your good decision."

He glanced back at the water. "I didn't think you'd find out, and I didn't care if you did."

"You were angry about our mother's death. It wasn't your fault, Ted."

"I wanted you home with me."

"Mom asked me to continue my studies."

"She always thought of your needs instead of her own."

"College was important to her, Ted. She had to drop out of school when her own mother died. She didn't want the same thing to happen to me." Holding out her hand, she beckoned him forward. "Let's go home."

He shook his head. "You don't want me there."

"That's not true. I changed the alarm because someone came into the house a few nights ago. They left a note that said I never should have come back to Freemont. I wanted to ensure that person wouldn't get inside again."

"Did you think I left the note?"

She shook her head. "I knew it wasn't you."

He glanced up at the top of the marina where Brody stood watching them.

Ted pointed. "He thought I hurt Joshua. He probably thought I'd left the note."

"I told him you didn't, Ted." She glanced at Brody. "He believed me."

Ted sighed. "Can I stay at the house tonight?"

"Of course." Once again, she held out her hand.

He dropped the cord on the bell and shuffled toward her, his head hung and shoulders slumped.

Her heart broke for him and for the struggle he was undergoing internally, a struggle that needed to be healed. He had opened up tonight. Hopefully, it was a good start that would continue in the days ahead. If only he trusted her enough to know that she wouldn't let him down again.

Together they walked to where Brody stood.

"We're going home," she told him.

"Major Jenkins expects Ted back at the WTB."

"Call Jenkins, Brody." Her voice was firm. "Tell him he'll be there in the morning."

She helped Ted into the car and turned to find Brody staring at her, the frustration in his eyes making it clear he didn't approve of her decision.

"I won't leave him, Brody. A door has opened just a crack. Maybe it can open even more tonight."

"It's not safe for you to be alone with him, Stephanie."

"You're thinking of the past and not the present. I told you before. I'm not Lisa."

He clamped down on his jaw. "I'm well aware of who you are. Stubborn and headstrong." He shook his head and sighed. "But you're also determined to help your brother, and I admire you for that. Let me stay at the house. If anything happens, I'll be there."

She shook her head. "I need to do this alone."

Stephanie slipped into the driver's seat, not knowing what would happen during the night. She had this one chance with Ted, and she wouldn't do anything to ruin that fragile beginning to a new relationship.

As she pulled onto the main road, she looked into her rearview mirror. Brody was standing under one of the lights in the marina parking lot. He didn't understand, because he was still trying to make up for what had happened to his girlfriend. That was his personal struggle.

Just as she had hers.

Life wasn't easy. No one said it would be, and sometimes she felt totally alone. But tonight she had Ted beside her.

Coming back to Freemont may have been the right decision after all, if she and Ted could heal their relationship.

And Brody? Would he ever be able to forget what

had happened? If he could move beyond the past, there might be hope for them. But right now, he was too focused on being a special agent instead of a man who cared about the future.

Heavyhearted, Brody stood at the entrance to the marina. Stephanie had made her choice and refused to listen to his concerns about her safety.

Once her taillights disappeared from sight, he let out a deep sigh and turned to look at the Upton cabin cruiser. It was state-of-the-art and a boater's dream, yet Stephanie wanted nothing to do with the luxury craft.

He pulled out his phone, clicked on the photo he had saved from the Freemont paper and watched it unfold across his screen.

A water-drenched Stephanie stood on the deck of the cabin cruiser, a blanket hung around her shoulders. Her eyes were wide, and a look of shock and disbelief wrapped around her face.

Her brother was also onboard. Nikki huddled next to him. Paul and Joshua were sitting, shoulders slumped, while EMTs worked on a woman who appeared to be Cindy.

Stephanie had taken her father's larger craft to the island that day. The painful memories probably kept her from boarding the cabin cruiser again.

Brody could relate. He hadn't sketched since Lisa's death.

His phone rang.

"Goodman."

"It's Nikki. I'm worried about Ted. He's not answering his cell. Stephanie's phone goes to voice mail, too."

"They're together and heading back to their house."

"I'm so glad."

Brody wished he shared her enthusiasm. "Your car's parked at the marina, Nikki. Can someone give you a ride in the morning?"

"I'll call Paul."

On his way back to post, Brody phoned Major Jenkins. "Private Upton's with his sister. He plans to stay at home tonight. Stephanie will drive him back to the WTB in the morning."

"You sound worried."

"I told Stephanie she was putting herself in danger. She refuses to see beyond the fact that he's her brother."

"Being with his sister might do Ted good."

Brody wasn't as optimistic as the major. When he disconnected, he contacted Don Palmer at home. "Sorry to bother you, Chief, but I need a favor. Any chance you could increase surveillance again tonight in the Country Club Estates, specifically the Upton home?"

"Did something else happen?"

"Only that Stephanie and her brother are together, trying to reconcile."

"But you're worried?"

"I just want her to be safe."

The chief sighed. "Okay, I'll increase the patrols and instruct my officers to keep their eyes and ears open."

"I owe you, sir."

"Help me wrap up this investigation, and we'll call it even."

Once back on post, Brody headed to the hospital and the ICU, relieved that Joshua was still holding on.

Brody approached the soldier's bedside.

Joshua had sacrificed his own well-being for his country and had come home as a double amputee. Adversity hadn't dampened his enthusiasm for life, from what Major Jenkins had said. But to have the attack happen when he was trying to make a future for himself…

"Why, Lord?" Brody couldn't understand how a loving God decided who would live and who would die.

Lisa. Hayden.

Those two deaths had changed Brody and Stephanie's lives. Both of them were still too caught up in the past.

Would he ever be able to get over what had happened? What about Stephanie? Would she ever be able to move beyond Hayden's death?

No matter how much Brody wished things would be different, he and Stephanie didn't have a chance. Their paths would soon part and stay apart no matter how much he wished things would be different.

Chapter Seventeen

Stephanie and Ted talked until his eyes grew heavy, and she knew he needed sleep. After he headed to his room, she retrieved the messages from her cell phone. Nikki had called a number of times to check on Ted.

The concern she heard in the girl's voice warmed her heart. Nikki seemed to genuinely care about Ted's well-being. A refreshing change from the way Brody regarded her brother.

The last voice mail from Nikki was more ominous.

"I've been trying to get Paul on his cell and home landline, but he fails to answer. I know he was upset about Josh and wanted to be alone tonight. It's not like Paul to ignore my calls. I'm worried, Stephanie. Could you check on him?"

Glancing at her watch, Stephanie groaned. Almost eleven-thirty. Too late to be traipsing around the neighborhood. Surely by now, he'd be sleeping off the effects of the alcohol and probably wouldn't respond, even if she pounded on his front door.

Still, he was a good kid and Ted's friend. If anything

happened, she'd feel responsible, and she didn't need more guilt piled on her already-overloaded shoulders.

Quickly, she wrote a note for Ted and left it on the kitchen counter, not far from where she'd found the typed message and marked photograph of the old high school gang.

No need to think of the past, she reminded herself. She and Ted were in a better place. Grabbing her purse, she quietly left the house and climbed into the Cadillac parked at the curb.

Within a few minutes, she pulled in front of the Massey home. Just as earlier this evening, the front porch was dark, but a light in the rear cast the backyard in shadows. Perhaps Paul was on the deck. Hopefully, he wasn't still drowning his sorrows.

She shivered, realizing the significance of the expression, especially since the Masseys had a pool and hot tub. Cross one bridge at a time, her mother used to say.

Determined to find Paul, hopefully groggy with sleep, and then hurry back to her own house, Stephanie climbed the steps to the front porch. She rang the bell three times and then pounded her hand against the heavy oak.

When he failed to respond, she rounded the house and called Paul's name as she approached the backyard. Light from the overhead deck played over the pool. Her stomach tightened thinking of what she could find. If only she had brought her phone. Knowing she could call for help would have bolstered her courage. Instead, she had inadvertently left it on the counter at home. As much as she didn't want to be prowling around Paul's house, she needed to be certain he was okay.

Working to ignore the nervous tingle that played

along her spine, she neared the wrought-iron fence surrounding the pool and peered into the water, seeing nothing except dark shadows.

Flicking her gaze over the patio area, she spied the hot tub in the far corner. The plastic top sat askew. Strange to have it half on, half off, especially in the middle of the summer.

A beach towel sat neatly folded on a nearby lounge chair. Her pulse kicked up a notch. She swallowed, her throat dry, her palms suddenly moist. She wiped them over her skirt, knowing she had no recourse except to enter the fenced enclosure.

The gate creaked as it swung open. A gust of hot, humid air rustled through the trees and caught her hair. She tugged the loose strands out of her face and blinked, willing her eyes to adjust to the darkened area under the deck where the plastic lid held her focus.

Her heart thumped a warning as she neared.

"Paul?"

She glanced again at the beach towel, then lowered her gaze to where something lay under the corner of the chaise.

An empty vodka bottle.

Her breath hitched and a roar filled her ears.

Bending down, she grabbed the plastic lip of the hot-tub cover, raised the lid and peered into the shallow pool.

Her heart stopped. The patio swirled around her as her knees buckled.

She screamed at seeing Paul Massey's eyes staring at her from under the water.

"Thanks for notifying me," Brody said to the Freemont police chief. Three patrols cars sat in front of the Massey home, their lights flickering through the night. Officers milled about on the front lawn while the crime-scene team worked in the patio area.

"I need to thank you for requesting extra surveillance," the chief said. "One of my men happened by just as Ms. Upton ran screaming from the backyard."

Brody glanced at the patrol car where Stephanie sat hunched over in the backseat.

"At this point everything appears fairly cut-and-dried," Palmer continued. "Paul left a suicide note and mentioned wanting to ease Joshua Webb's misery." The chief shook his head. "Luckily, he wasn't successful on that count."

The chief filled Brody in on what had happened and then pointed to the squad car. "If you want to talk to Ms. Upton, I'm ready to send her home. She's been very cooperative."

Stephanie glanced up as Brody approached. Her face was noticeably pale and drawn. Fatigue added to the worry he saw on her furrowed brow and tight lips.

"You doing okay?" he asked, hoping she heard concern and understanding in his voice.

"Not really."

"I'm sorry you had to find him."

Tears filled her eyes. "Nikki called me. She was worried something might be wrong. I never..." She swallowed. "I never thought..."

"I'll drive you home."

She handed Brody the keys to her father's car. He wrapped his arm around her shoulders and ushered her forward, out of the glare of the police lights.

She was silent on the way to the house.

"May I come in?" he asked as they climbed the stairs to her front porch. "We need to talk."

She shook her head. "Not tonight. I...I have to get some sleep."

"You shouldn't be alone, Stephanie."

"Ted's still here. I'll be okay."

He unlocked the door, and she hesitated before stepping inside. "It's over, isn't it?"

"You mean about Josh?"

"And Ted. Chief Palmer said Paul left a note. You can't blame my brother anymore."

Brody wished he could assure Stephanie, but while Ted was no longer a suspect in Joshua's attack, he had showed too much antagonism for Brody to give him a total pass now. Only time would tell.

Which Stephanie wouldn't want to hear.

She must have suspected the reason for his hesitation because, with a heavy sigh, she hurried into the house and closed the door behind her. The dead bolt clicked into place.

"Good night, Stephanie."

He double-timed back to the Massey home. He wanted to see the crime scene for himself. Too many questions needed to be answered, but his thoughts continued to revolve around Stephanie and how he wished things could be different.

As much as Brody didn't want to look back, he also didn't want to think about tomorrow and the day after that and the day following if it meant he wouldn't have Stephanie.

Stephanie woke the next morning to someone pounding on her door. She glanced at the clock. Six a.m.

Wrapping her robe around her waist, she hurried along the front hallway, hoping the knocking wouldn't awaken her brother.

She peered out the front window, somewhat relieved when she recognized the car in the driveway.

Pulling open the door, she squared her shoulders.

"Brody, why in the world are you pounding on my door at this hour?"

"I need to talk to Ted."

She groaned. "Haven't we been down this path before?"

"He's still here, isn't he, Stephanie?"

"Yes, but he's sleeping."

"The note Paul supposedly left had the same flawed *o*. Just like the note in your kitchen."

"Paul wrote the warning?"

"I checked the printers in his house. The letters weren't smeared."

"Which means what?"

"Which means the suicide note may have been written by someone else. Someone who planned to do Paul harm. That's why I need to bring Ted in for questioning."

The air sucked from her lungs. She took a step back. Surely Brody didn't suspect Ted. "Did the medical examiner determine when Paul died?"

"The M.E. provided an estimate. Sometime between nine and midnight."

"That rules out Ted," she said.

"How can you be so certain?"

"My brother and I were together from ten o'clock on. You were at the marina with us."

"He could have killed him earlier."

"Impossible. Paul called me at nine-fifty. He'd been

drinking. I pulled into the marina and saw Ted minutes later."

"Show me your phone."

Hurt that he didn't believe her, she steeled her jaw. Brody was determined to find Ted at fault no matter what evidence she provided.

Retrieving her cell, she showed Brody the call log. "Do you see the time the call came in? Nine-fifty, which was when I was approaching the marina. No other cars passed me en route, and Ted was at the marina by the time I arrived. I told the chief last night."

She pointed to the phone. "Access voice mail and you'll hear the message Paul left initially. He sounded drunk and said he was going to bed. I thought he needed to sleep off his binge. In hindsight, I should have notified someone. When Nikki phoned and told me he hadn't responded to her calls, I decided to check on him."

"You could have phoned me." Brody worked the prompts and lifted her cell to his ear. Once Paul's message had completed playing, he lowered the phone.

"The Freemont police will need to listen to the message and check time frame. They also need to talk to Ted."

She stared at Brody, unable to comprehend how he could continue to think Ted was at fault.

Her brother's bedroom door opened. "Is something wrong?"

Brody stepped inside. "You need to come with me to police headquarters, Private Upton."

"You called him?" Ted looked from Brody to Stephanie. "All of this was so you could set me up."

The advances they had made last night collapsed in

that one moment. Her relationship with her brother had hit rock bottom.

Would she ever be able to explain the truth about what had happened?

Would Ted believe her?

Only if Brody was out of her life.

Chapter Eighteen

The next three days were rainy and overcast, which fit Brody's mood. Paul's voice mail to Stephanie and her assurance to the Freemont police that she had found her brother at the marina shortly after the message had been sent confirmed Ted's innocence.

Paul had told a number of people in town that Joshua didn't want to live as an amputee. The chief of police was convinced Paul had planned a mercy killing, which Stephanie had prevented by finding Joshua in the nick of time. When Paul's plan failed, he had become despondent and had taken his own life.

The case was wrapped up, at least as far as the Freemont police were concerned. Brody had his doubts. Mainly because of the so-called suicide note Paul had left with the blurred print.

Plus, he had died in his parents' hot tub. An empty bottle of vodka had been found nearby. The police believed he'd gotten drunk, lost consciousness and drowned. All of which could indicate an accidental death, if not for the note.

Brody rubbed his temples and ignored the half-filled

cup of coffee on his desk. He'd had too much caffeine over the past three days.

Too much caffeine and not enough sleep.

Every night, thoughts of Stephanie kept him pacing the floor in his BOQ.

He checked his watch and headed to Chief Wilson's office. "Sir, I'll be at the Main Post Chapel for Private Paul Massey's funeral. I've requested two men from the military police to join me there. Jamison said he'd be there, as well."

"You're still not convinced the death was a suicide?"

"It's a gut feeling, sir, but drowning in a hot tub doesn't seem the way a soldier would take his own life. A bullet hole to the head would be more logical in my opinion."

The chief rubbed his chin. "The stats would prove you right. But you need evidence to back up your hunch."

If only Brody could find the printer with the blurred vowel.

"What about Joshua Webb's condition?" the chief asked.

"Still guarded. He's been on antibiotic therapy to counter the infection and was improving. Then the bacteria that caused the infection became resistant to the medication. The doc's trying another combination of antimicrobials, but he's not optimistic."

"Have you talked to the AW2 advocate?"

"Not since her brother was questioned by the Freemont police."

"PFC Upton will attend the funeral?"

"I believe so."

"Watch him."

"Yes, sir."

The heavy chords of the organ filled the sanctuary when Brody entered the Main Post Chapel. A steady flow of mourners streamed into the pews, many in uniform. Even more were civilians, friends of the family, no doubt, from Freemont.

Brody stood in the rear and searched for Stephanie. Hearing the clip of high heels, he turned as she entered the church.

Their eyes locked for half a heartbeat before she glanced away and walked toward the front of the church. Nikki followed her into a pew and scooted over to make room for Cindy.

Brody clamped down on his jaw, steeling himself to her rebuff. Deep down, he had hoped time would temper her feelings toward him.

As much as he wished things could have been different, Brody wouldn't have changed the way he had handled the situation. He still wasn't sure Ted was completely stable.

His phone vibrated. Stepping outside, he raised the cell to his ear.

Instead of a greeting, the Freemont chief of police quickly explained the reason for his call. "The toxicology report came back on Paul Massey."

Brody smiled. "You must have friends in high places."

The chief laughed. "I told them the case involved U.S. Army heroes and needed to be handled stat."

"As quickly as you got the results back, they must have listened. Did they find anything?"

"Clonazepam. It's in the benzodiazepine family of drugs."

"Usually prescribed for panic attacks."

"That's right. As well as seizures. Law enforcement

in Atlanta is keeping a sharp eye on the drug because of its street use."

"As a date-rape drug." Brody was well aware of clonazepam's side effects.

"Exactly. Which may shoot my suicide theory out of the water."

"Unless Paul was having panic attacks. I'll contact the head of the hospital at his last duty station and request a copy of his medical records. You'll question the local docs to find out whether he got a prescription around here?"

"I've already got two officers doing exactly that. They're also contacting the area pharmacies. I'll notify you if I hear anything."

Brody disconnected and watched the hearse pull to a stop in front of the chapel. Six pallbearers spilled from the narthex. Ted Upton walked next to Keith Allen.

Dressed in his military uniform, Ted looked strong and stoic, but the twitch in his cheek and the downward turn to his shoulders spoke volumes about how he really felt.

Paul Massey's parents—an older couple with drawn faces—stood nearby. The woman leaned into the man for support and dabbed a tissue at the corners of her eyes.

As the chaplain greeted the family, Brody slipped past them and reentered the sanctuary. Stephanie glanced back as if sensing his return.

Trying to ignore her gaze, he nodded to the two military policemen standing in the rear. Earlier, he had briefed them about watching the crowd gathered at the funeral and cemetery and to alert him to anything that seemed suspect. Jamison Steele was on-site, as well.

The deep, resonating sounds of the organ filled the

church. The congregation stood and began to sing. The pallbearers proceeded up the middle aisle, carrying the casket. Ted glanced at Brody as he passed. The private's face was pale and drawn.

The family followed and filed into the front pew on the left. The pallbearers entered the pew directly opposite. At the conclusion of the hymn, the chaplain approached the pulpit and opened the service with prayer.

Brody bowed his head, thinking back to Lisa's funeral. The minister that day had preached words of consolation, but all Brody could remember was his own despair.

Fisting his hands, he refused to dwell on the past and instead flicked his gaze around the sanctuary, knowing someone in the congregation could have attacked Joshua and staged Paul's death to look like a suicide.

Was clonazepam the missing link in this twisted chain of events? Or was there something else Brody wasn't seeing?

Once again, he visualized the filled bathtub in Josh's home. Had the attacker planned to drown Joshua? Stephanie's arrival could have forced the perpetrator to flee before he had time to submerge Josh in the water.

Stored on his phone, the newspaper photo of the teens huddled on the Upton boat flashed through his mind. What if one of them was avenging Hayden's death?

His gaze settled on Nikki. She and Hayden had gone to prom together. Had she fallen for the town's shining star and lashed out when the returning soldiers came back to Freemont, angry at those who had lived when the boy she loved had died?

Nikki knew the schedule at the bakery and had even voiced concern that Ted could have inherited his mother's allergy. Easy enough for her to send Stephanie cookies, knowing she was allergic.

But would she have left the note and bull's-eye in the house? She would have needed a key to get inside, which Ted could have provided, along with the code for the security alarm.

Were Nikki and Ted working together? Or was Ted guilty and acting alone, just as Brody had suspected all along?

Was he avenging Hayden's death, or had something happened that day on the lake that Ted, in an emotional state brought on by PTSD, wanted to cover up by killing the other guys involved?

"We know the past always has bearing on our lives." The chaplain's voice filled the church. "Our relationship with the Lord forms who we are and how we react in situations. Paul was a fine son and a good friend to everyone who knew him. He was also a military hero who put his country first."

Brody watched Ted's response. He sat with his arms folded across his chest and appeared to be grieving. As Brody knew too well, looks could be deceiving.

"Although we will never know exactly what happened the night Paul died," the chaplain continued, "we do know death is not the end but the beginning of new life lived with the Lord. The pain of the present world is over for Paul. He has journeyed home, which should bring comfort and peace."

Brody signaled to the military policemen and then Jamison that he was leaving. As he stepped into the humid afternoon, the minister's words replayed in his mind. Would he ever be able to look beyond the horrific circumstances of Lisa's death?

If only he could believe in a loving and compassionate God, then perhaps he would see hope for the future and have some sense of peace about the past.

He'd been given a second chance with Stephanie, but that relationship had failed, and now, just as before, he was on his own.

Stephanie needed someone he could never be.

The realization tore at him and made Brody want to pound his fist into a wall.

To distance himself from the pain, he pulled his cell from his pocket and called Chief Wilson. "Sir, I need to make a stop on post. Then I'll head to Freemont to talk to the chief of police. I feel there's an area of the investigation we haven't explored."

"Take as much time as you need."

The chief's response was what Brody had hoped to hear. He phoned Don Palmer and told him his latest idea. "I'll stop at the Post Exchange and check their computer printers. I suggest you do the same at the bakery in town."

"You think Nikki's involved?"

"Actually, I still think Ted's our most likely suspect. But he and Nikki are friends. I want to ensure she didn't help him out. You might question Nikki's sister. See if anyone in the family takes clonazepam."

"What about Ted?"

"I talked to the medical-care team at the Warrior Transitional Battalion. He's on medication, but not that particular drug."

"What about his sister? Could she be taking it?"

Brody didn't appreciate the inference. "Let's put that on hold for now until we learn about Nikki and Ted's involvement."

By the time he arrived at police headquarters, Brody was less than optimistic. None of the PX printers produced the flawed letters. The chief didn't find anything at the bakery, either, and no one in Nikki's family was under medical care.

According to the sister, Nikki didn't have a computer or printer and relied on her smart phone and the library in town when she needed the internet. The chief sent one of his men to check the library printers, but he soon returned empty-handed.

By evening, Brody felt discouraged. He and the chief continued to hash over the information they had for a few more hours, until finally, at eight o'clock, Brody knew it was time to go home.

He left police headquarters eager to watch Braves baseball and focus on his favorite team instead of the case, but when he slid behind the wheel, he spied Keith's folder with the information about the Wounded Warrior picnic. Information Stephanie needed. Brody smiled. Information that would provide a reason for him to stop by her house this evening.

He shook his head. Stephanie didn't want to see him, he felt sure, and he was too tired to dance around the conflict that stood between them. Especially when he planned to, once again, haul Ted in for questioning in the next day or two.

Go home and stop thinking about Stephanie, his voice of reason cautioned.

The truth was, he couldn't get her out of his thoughts. Even more troubling, he couldn't get her out of his heart.

Chapter Nineteen

"Don't think about him," Stephanie told herself as she puttered around the house, struggling to keep her mind on anything except Brody. She had looked for him after the interment, but he was nowhere to be found.

What would she have said if he had found him? Perhaps they would have chatted about inconsequential topics that skirted the real issue that was lodged between them.

If only Brody would hang up his badge and his gun at times and be a friend instead of a special agent. At one point, she had hoped their friendship would blossom into something more long lasting. Now she doubted there was anything to salvage.

Brody seemed antagonistic, if not confrontational, toward her brother. She couldn't invite into her life someone who harbored ill feelings toward Ted, especially when she and her brother were beginning to find common ground.

Ted had come back to the house briefly with Nikki after the funeral. Keith and Cindy had stopped by, as well. Everyone wanted to reminisce about Paul and old times. Before the day at the lake. Before the boys had enlisted.

Now that they had left, Stephanie needed fresh air to clear her mind. She poured a second glass of iced tea from the pitcher in the refrigerator that she had served earlier and took a long, cool sip before she carried the glass onto the patio. The group had been nice enough to help clean up the kitchen and put away the snacks before they left, which Stephanie appreciated.

She settled into one of the chairs by the pool. A light breeze tugged at her hair and provided a reprieve from the heat.

Her phone chirped. She smiled when she saw Ted's name on her call screen.

"Hey, Steph." He sounded good. "I'm back at the barracks for the night, and my squad leader stopped by to make sure I was doing okay. He said to alert him if I have any problems."

"I'm glad, Ted. Don't hesitate to ask for help if you can't sleep or are troubled by dreams."

"Joshua's condition hasn't improved." Ted hesitated for a long moment. "The sergeant suggested I pray for him."

Which Nikki had mentioned. "That sounds like a good idea."

"Would you pray, too?"

She had closed God out of her life, but maybe it was time to make a change. "Yes, I'll pray."

She disconnected, feeling a warm sense of relief well up inside her. Her troubled relationship with her brother was starting to improve. Reaching once again for the glass of tea, her hand trembled.

Too much caffeine, perhaps, or too little sleep.

She hadn't gotten a good night's rest since she'd found Joshua on his bathroom floor. The sergeant was right. The injured soldier needed prayers. So did Ted.

Lord, help both guys heal.

She should go back inside, but her eyes were heavy. Totally relaxed, she struggled to remain awake. Her chin dropped to her chest.

A sound interrupted her sleep.

Startled, she tried to turn toward the shuffling footsteps and raised voice, but her body wouldn't respond to her promptings. Unable to decipher the words that were blurred with rage, she flicked her gaze over her shoulder but saw only darkness.

A forceful weight slammed into her from behind. With a gasp, she fell onto the patio. Her head hit the concrete. Pain shot through her skull.

She groaned and clawed at the rough surface, trying to escape from the voice that railed through her.

Someone kicked her. Pain ricocheted through her lower back.

"No," she moaned.

Cowering, she huddled in a protective ball and tried to fend off strikes that came one after another.

Rough hands grabbed her arms and half lifted, half dragged her across the patio toward the pool. She thrashed against their hold, unable to break free.

With a forceful heave, she was shoved into the shimmering water. Gulping air, she tried to stay afloat, but her limbs hung heavy, like deadweight.

She swallowed a mouthful of water and coughed. Unable to remain buoyant, she slipped beneath the surface.

Gravity pulled her downward into the deep abyss. She couldn't breathe.

Garbled though it was through the water, she heard laughter, maniacal laughter that intensified her fear.

Her lungs burned. She tried to push off from the bottom and realized too late the horrible reality that she would drown, just like Hayden.

Another sound. The clang of a bell ringing over and over again.

If only someone would save her.

Brody?

She had closed him out of her life. He would never find her. At least, not in time.

Chapter Twenty

Pulling to the curb outside the Upton home, Brody grabbed his phone and the file folder before he stepped to the sidewalk. He had planned to go home to Fort Rickman, but an overwhelming need to see Stephanie forced him to drive instead to the Country Club Estates.

The stillness of the night was shattered by the knell of the maritime bell. His blood chilled. Forgoing the front door, he raced around the house to the patio.

A shadowed form darted into the thick wooded area at the back of the property. Brody turned his gaze to the patio. A wrought-iron chair lay overturned. The pool gate hung open.

His breath hitched. Fear jammed his throat.

He ran to the water's edge and dropped the folder and cell to the concrete. His heart exploded when he glanced into the pool.

"Stephanie."

Diving into the water, he was oblivious to everything except her limp body lying on the bottom of the pool.

He pulled her into his arms and kicked violently, propelling both of them to the surface. With three strong strokes, he carried her to the edge of the pool and lifted her onto the deck. Kneeling next to her, he pushed down on her sternum with rapid thrusts.

How long had she been submerged? If only she would respond.

"God, help me," he pleaded, knowing he didn't deserve a response from the Lord. But Stephanie did. "Please, Lord."

She coughed and sputtered.

"Open your eyes, honey. It's Brody. You're going to be all right."

He swallowed hard, trying to keep his emotions in check. Her eyes fluttered open. "I'm here, honey. You're going to be okay."

"Br...Brody?" Her voice was only a ragged whisper.

He nodded. "You were at the bottom of the pool. Who did it, Stephanie? Was it Ted?"

She grimaced.

"Or Nikki?"

She shook her head and tried to sit up, but she didn't have the strength.

Brody reached for his cell phone, lying nearby, and called the Freemont chief of police. Quickly, Brody filled him in on what had happened.

"Stephanie's responsive, but I want to know for certain she's okay. Send an ambulance and medical personnel."

The chief assured him the EMTs would arrive shortly, and that he, along with two other police officers, were on their way.

A number of sheets of paper had spilled from the file folder and lay scattered on the concrete. Brody lifted one of the pages and stared at the print.

The letter *o* had the same flawed type as the warning message left on Stephanie's counter and the suicide note found near the hot tub at Paul Massey's house.

Brody shook his head in amazement. They finally had the evidence they needed. "We've got our killer," he told the chief. "You'll never believe who it is."

"Keith Allen?"

Stephanie sat in her living room and sipped a cup of tea. She had been in the emergency room for more hours than she wanted to count. A cherry-flavored drink that contained charcoal rid the remaining drugs from her system. Although the doctor had wanted to keep her overnight for observation, she had insisted on going home. The lab had tested the iced-tea pitcher and found a high level of clonazepam in the liquid that Keith must have added before leaving her house.

Brody paced back and forth across the living room, visibly agitated by her close call.

"I should have been with you," he berated himself.

"You saved me, Brody, for which I'm grateful. Now stop pacing and try to relax. Keith has been arrested and the danger has passed."

She shook her head, trying to get a handle on everything that had occurred. "But why would Keith kill Paul and attack Joshua? It doesn't make sense."

"Not to us, but to someone vindictive about his brother's death it might seem logical. Keith was probably angry because Hayden had died while Paul and Joshua survived."

"If that were the case, wouldn't Keith be equally hostile toward Ted?"

Brody shrugged. "Maybe he had listed the guys in

alphabetical order. Joshua. Paul. Ted would have been next."

Stephanie shuddered, thinking of what could have been.

Footsteps sounded on the porch. A key turned the lock. She glanced toward the front door.

Ted and Nikki stepped inside and hurried to the couch where Stephanie sat. Nikki hugged her and Ted squeezed her hand. "Glad you're okay, sis."

At least they were making progress.

She glanced at Nikki. "Are you sure spending the night won't put you out?"

"Of course not. You shouldn't be alone. I don't have to go to work until noon tomorrow."

"And I plan to be at my desk much earlier than that," Stephanie assured her.

"Ted's taking my car back to the barracks tonight," Nikki said. "He'll pick me up tomorrow."

Ted shook his head as if dumbfounded by what had happened. "I still can't believe Keith attacked you and killed Paul."

"He may have felt overwhelmed with guilt for his brother's death. I always thought Keith had provided the alcohol that day on the lake." Stephanie kept her eyes trained on Ted. He refused to hold her gaze.

"Hayden knew where the bottles had been hidden," Nikki said. "I thought he had stolen them from Keith and stashed them on the island. Isn't that what you thought, Ted?"

He shrugged. "Sounds right to me."

"Did you know there would be alcohol that day, Ted?"

"I thought it was a just a picnic."

But he had consumed the whiskey, just as the other kids had. Temptation was often too hard to resist.

She looked at Brody. He hadn't wanted her to be alone, but he'd voiced opposition to Nikki staying overnight. With Keith behind bars, Stephanie had assured him she would be fine.

His first question after he had saved her life was whether she had seen her attacker. His next question had torn her heart in two. *"Was it Ted?"*

The CID agent would always think Ted was at fault. Then he had mentioned Nikki.

As much as she hated to admit the truth, she and Brody didn't have a future together, not when he continued to look for fault in her brother.

Ted had made mistakes in his past, but he was trying to be a better man and find his way in life. Stephanie was confident that with counseling Ted would heal, but he had to be surrounded by people who believed in him.

Brody would cause more harm than good. No matter how much she cared about the handsome CID agent, she couldn't open her heart to someone so opposed to her brother. Especially now, when her relationship with Ted was starting to mend.

Chapter Twenty-One

The sky was overcast on Saturday. The weatherman predicted showers, but not until evening, long after the Wounded Warrior picnic.

Brody called the chief of police as he drove to the marina. "Any chance the judge will set bail in the Allen case?"

"Not until Monday. We've got Keith locked up at least for the weekend, although he insists he's not guilty."

"Did you mention the printer in his office?"

"And the clonazepam we found in his desk drawer. Keith refilled the prescription last week, yet half the pills were gone. He only takes them when he feels a panic attack coming on. Or so he says."

"Evidently he's panicked a lot recently," Brody said.

"Exactly."

"He stopped by Stephanie's house after the funeral. That's when he must have drugged the pitcher of iced tea."

"He claims he's been framed," Palmer said. "He even asked that his arrest be kept from his mother. I talked to the administrator of the nursing home. He passed the message on to the staff. At this point, that's all we can do." The cop sighed. "I feel for his mom. Tough to lose one son to death and another through crime."

"If the jury finds him guilty." Brody thought about Ted. Had he been wrong about the soldier all along? "Keith doesn't strike me as a killer."

"You still suspect Ted Upton?"

Brody let out a pent up breath. "I'm trying to determine how he fits into the picture. There's something he's not telling me."

"And his sister?"

"She believes her brother isn't at fault."

"We all need someone like that on our side," the chief said.

Brody had to agree, but Stephanie had made it perfectly clear she wanted nothing to do with him once the picnic was over. He'd brought it on himself with his constant concern for her safety.

As much as he needed to distance himself from Stephanie, she continued to be part of his life. Last night, he had dreamed of holding her in his arms and kissing her sweet lips.

Maybe he'd put in for temporary duty. Wilson needed someone to fill a slot in D.C. Getting away from Fort Rickman might be a good thing, at least until he could get a handle on where his life was headed—a life without Stephanie.

The marina appeared in the distance. Brody pulled into the parking lot and walked to where a number of military personnel were loading picnic items onto *The Princess*. A larger military craft was already on the lake, heading to the island, no doubt filled with the bulk of the supplies. Cadre from the Warrior Transitional Battalion were helping out and working side by side with volunteers from town.

Despite Keith's arrest, it looked as if the local merchants were determined to make the event a success for the soldiers.

Hefting a box from the dock, Brody placed it on Stephanie's boat. A gust of wind tugged at her hair. She pulled it back and smiled.

"Thanks."

"The cloud cover might keep the temperature down today," he offered as a greeting.

Her smile faded. "I talked to the meteorologist on post. He said the weather should be clear and bright." She glanced skyward. "He failed to mention the overcast sky and stiff breeze."

"What time is the unit scheduled to arrive?"

"Soon. Major Jenkins authorized a bus to transport the soldiers. A number of local folks will boat them over to the island."

"What about Ted?"

Stephanie averted her gaze. "He's arriving with the unit. Nikki is already on the island. She started cooking early this morning. Cindy's helping with the games. From her connections at the garage, she got a lot of the local townsfolk to help."

"Has anyone mentioned Keith?"

"Only that they don't think he's a killer."

"Did they provide the name of a more likely suspect?"

She shook her head. "Not that I heard. Although I know you have your suspicions."

"I don't think Ted harmed Paul or Joshua, Stephanie."

She turned with wide eyes to gaze up at him. "Really?"

"I was wrong, and I'm sorry. But I still worry about his stability and will continue to be concerned until the counselors tell me that he's worked through what happened in Afghanistan."

She shook her head. "You never change, do you, Brody?"

"If you mean I can never stop being a cop, you're probably right. I always imagine worst-case scenarios so I'm not surprised when bad things happen. Plus, I what-if each situation."

"You worst-cased my relationship with my brother because of your own past. I told you we're different, but you're unable to accept anything I say about Ted."

"Maybe Ted isn't the problem."

She inhaled sharply. "What's that mean?"

"You didn't tell me everything about that day on the lake and what happened between you and your brother."

Before she could reply, the bus filled with soldiers pulled into the parking lot. They disembarked with shouts of revelry and laughter and quickly filed onto the various boats waiting to transport them.

"I'll see you on the island," Brody told Stephanie.

He waited until her brother boarded one of the boats and then took a seat near him. If Ted couldn't handle returning to the island, Brody would be close by to keep things from getting out of hand.

Once they docked, Brody helped unload the supplies. He carried the food items to the kitchen where Nikki smiled, an apron around her waist and her hair piled on top of her head.

Cindy explained the plans for the day and pointed the soldiers toward the various activities. Families arrived, and soon the picnic area was bustling with smiling faces.

Later, the guys and gals had fun floating on the calm side of the lake, staying well away from the channel between Big Island and the smaller island to the south. Some of the more mobile soldiers climbed the tower and rode the zip line that hung between the two bodies of land. Beach volleyball games ran throughout the day and a fun run around the island was held with ambulatory soldiers helping those in wheelchairs.

Brody found himself partnered with Ted, and the two men began to have an understanding as they helped some of the handicapped guys with the various events.

Ted's laughter could be heard across the island, and a few times, Stephanie turned to watch her brother. A smile covered her face, something Brody had seen so rarely.

When she saw him staring at her, her smile wavered, and she turned back to whatever chore she was doing at the time.

As the afternoon waned, the men boated back to the marina to catch the bus that would take them to the barracks. Most of the families had returned earlier in the day.

Stephanie stood near a picnic bench, checking off the last of the supplies that were being loaded onto the military crafts.

"Did you get a chance to eat?" Brody asked.

"Nikki fixed something for me." Stephanie pointed to the untouched plate of food on the table.

Seeing an empty peanut oil container in the trash, Brody became concerned. "You can't eat the chicken if it was deep-fried in peanut oil, Stephanie. You need to be careful."

"Nikki grilled my chicken and didn't use oil."

"But you're still not eating it."

Turning away, she avoided his gaze. "I'll eat once I get home."

Although Stephanie sounded confident, she was probably fearful of having another allergic reaction. He stared at Nikki, who appeared in the door to the kitchen, wondering if she could have had something to do with the recent attacks.

Ted helped Cindy load the overflow items onto her boat. They were laughing and seemed to enjoy working together. Nikki walked toward them. The look she flashed Cindy was anything but friendly.

"The kitchen's clean and everything's packed away." She checked her watch. "I need to get back to the mainland. The Post Exchange gave me the afternoon off, but I have to work the evening shift."

Cindy jabbed a playful finger at Ted. "I'm trying to convince this guy to ride the zip line. What's with you, Ted? You've been working all day, and the picnic was for you."

His cheeks flushed. "I wanted to give Stephanie a hand."

"Everyone's left the island." Cindy pointed to the last military craft, heading back to the marina.

"Maybe Ted doesn't want to change into his swimsuit," Nikki said, an angry edge to her voice.

"Oh, come on, Nikki," Cindy mocked. "You never were the adventurous type."

Stephanie glanced at the tall tower and the rather bulky harness that had carried the soldiers along the thin cable. "You don't have to do anything you don't want to do, Ted."

"It's not a problem," he said, smiling back at Cindy. "Give me a minute to change."

By the time the supplies were loaded in Stephanie's boat, Ted had returned, wearing swim trucks and an army T-shirt. The scars on his legs showed the extent of his combat injuries.

Brody could only imagine the pain he had endured and the long months of healing that had bought Ted to this point.

"I'm not sure you should do the zip line, Ted," Stephanie cautioned. "Nikki needs to get back to the marina so she won't be late for work. Why don't you boat back with us?"

"Come on, Stephanie. Don't pull that mother routine on me."

She bristled. Brody hadn't expected the comment and knew she hadn't, either. The look on her face revealed the pain her brother's words had caused.

"I'll stay with Ted if you want to take Nikki back," Brody volunteered. "Cindy can give us a ride to the mainland when he finishes riding the zip line."

Stephanie scanned the sky.

"Don't worry about the weather," Brody said.

"Storms come up quickly out here."

"Now look who's imagining the worst-case scenario."

She smiled, which was a good sign. "Okay, you're in charge. I'll take Nikki back with me."

"We'll be right behind you."

"Goodbye, Brody."

Stephanie's words hung in the air and made his heart heavy, as if she were bidding him a final farewell. The case was resolved. At least that's what everyone thought, so why would Brody continue to feel that the perpetrator was still on the loose?

After untying the moorings, Stephanie steered *The Princess* away from the dock. He watched her craft until it was a small spot on the horizon, then she turned a bend and disappeared from sight.

Brody glanced up at the zip line tower. Cindy had connected Ted into the harness. He glanced down to where Brody stood on the sandy shore. From the look on his face, Ted was having second thoughts about being up so high.

Raising his hands to his mouth, Brody shouted, "You can change your mind, Ted. You don't have to ride—"

Before he could complete his sentence, Cindy shoved Ted forward and activated the slide.

He screamed, which sent a chill down Brody's spine. The kid had been doing so well today. Hopefully, the rapid descent wouldn't set him back. Brody had assured Stephanie her brother would be all right.

With lightning speed, Ted sailed along the line and over the rough water with the strong currents that formed between the two islands. A dark cloud rolled in and hid the sun. For an instant, Brody's attention turned skyward.

He heard the second scream before he realized Ted had fallen into the whirling water below.

Cindy was racing down the hill to where Brody stood. "The harness must have snapped."

"Did you fasten it securely?"

"Of course."

"Let's take your boat." Brody raced toward Cindy's craft. "The current is forcing him out into the deep water."

To her credit, Cindy reacted quickly. Once away from shore, she gunned the engine and made straight for where Ted floundered in the water, still partially attached to the heavy harness.

"He's not the best of swimmers," she called to Brody. "You better go in and help him. I'll pull around and pick you both up."

A life preserver was in the back of the boat. Brody threw it into the water. "Grab hold, Ted. It'll keep you afloat until I get to you."

Ted clutched the white ring, but the look on his face told Brody he needed to get to him fast.

After emptying his pockets, Brody toed off his shoes. He threw his cell phone to Cindy. "Call nine-one-one. Tell them to send an ambulance and rescue personnel."

He dove into the water. Surfacing some feet away from the boat, he kept his eyes on Ted as he used a modified Australian crawl to cover the distance from the boat to Ted.

The sound of the throttle made him glance back. Cindy had turned the craft and was barreling straight toward him.

"Stop," he shouted, raising his arm. Surely she could see him in the water.

The look on her face chilled him.

"I'm going to kill both of you," she shouted over the roar of the engine.

An icy thread of fear wove its way along Brody's spine. The police had arrested the wrong person. Keith Allen wasn't the killer. Cindy was.

Diving deep, Brody saved himself from being run down. Once he surfaced again, he watched her turn the craft around. At least, she wasn't aiming for Ted, who floated on the life preserver about fifty feet away.

"You killed Paul." Brody needed information.

"And I would have killed Joshua, except Stephanie called his house and said she was on the way. I wanted him to drown like Hayden had."

"You drugged Stephanie and tried to drown her."

"She would have died except for you. You won't be able to save her this time because I'll make sure you're dead. Ted won't survive long in the water."

"Why, Cindy?"

"Because Hayden loved me. He told me that day on the lake, just before he jumped into the water after me. Stephanie saved everyone except him. She never liked Hayden because of what his mother had done. He was everything Ted should have been and wasn't. Stephanie was always so protective of her brother. She tried to be his mother and that upset him even more. He didn't want a second mother, he wanted his dad. But his father never had time for him." Brody tried to follow her ramblings.

Before he could ask about Hazel and what she had done, Cindy pushed on the throttle.

"The storm clouds are moving in," she screamed. "I'll make sure you won't survive." Her face twisted with rage, her teeth clenched together, her eyes wide.

Brody glanced at Ted, floating away from the path of the craft. Hopefully, Cindy would keep going to the marina, thinking Ted would perish in the rapidly churning water.

The boat approached. Sucking in a lungful of air, Brody dove deep but not deep enough. The rotor caught his leg, cutting a deep gash into his flesh. Blood swirled from the wound and floated to the surface.

The engine wound down. Hopefully, Cindy saw the blood. His chest burned, but he remained submerged. The longer he stayed below water, the more likely she would think he had perished.

His lungs screamed for air.

Another second and they would surely explode.

The sound of the engine came at the moment he surfaced.

He gulped air.

A crash of thunder sounded overhead.

Cindy glanced back. Once again, Brody dove underwater and surfaced as the craft headed for the mainland. He turned to search for Ted, but in the growing darkness and the rising crest of the waves, he could see only the water and the lightning that zigzagged across the sky.

Chapter Twenty-Two

Noticing the darkening sky, Stephanie hurried to unload the rest of the supplies. She had sent Nikki back to post so she wouldn't be late for work.

Glancing first at her watch and then at the water, she expected to see Cindy's boat bringing Ted and Brody back to the marina. Ready to set out to find them, she let out a pent-up breath when the boat rounded the bend.

Stephanie knew the relief she was feeling was not just for Ted but also for Brody. He'd helped in so many ways today, and she'd taken comfort seeing how he and Ted had worked together, whether hauling supplies or aiding some of the other, more seriously wounded soldiers. They'd even formed a team for the fun run and had pushed two other men in wheelchairs.

Although the foursome hadn't won the timed awards, they'd come first in the wheelchair competition with a bevy of high fives around. Seeing the sense of accomplishment on Ted's face when he and Brody stood together with their handicapped teammates had made her reconsider what she had thought about Brody. Perhaps there was hope for them after all.

Knowing she was getting ahead of herself, Stephanie carried the last box of supplies to her car. When she returned to the dock, she saw Cindy tying up her boat.

A tingle of concern gave her pause as she looked around the empty marina. "Where are Ted and Brody?"

"They stayed behind. One of the other soldiers came by with his boat. Ted wanted another turn on the zip line."

Stephanie glanced at the lightning in the distance. The strikes had to be hitting close to Big Island. "The zip line is the last place he should be in this storm."

Cindy's smile was reassuring. "I'm sure they're headed back by now." She pointed to the water. "They're probably right around the bend. I wouldn't worry, Stephanie."

But she *was* worried and also angry that Cindy had returned to the marina without them.

"Who's the soldier?"

"I can't remember his name. He was there today. I saw you talking to him. Big guy. Brown hair, cut in a military buzz."

Which would fit most of the guys at the picnic. "Sam Taylor?"

"That's him. He should be here in a minute or two."

Cindy stepped closer and stared at Stephanie's face. "You forgot to use sunscreen."

Stephanie touched her cheeks, knowing they were probably pink. "I was too busy."

"I've got some great aloe that takes the sting out of any sunburn and also helps so you won't peel." She dug in her purse and pulled out an unmarked plastic spray bottle. "I buy it in a large size and then keep the smaller atomizer in my purse." She sprayed a hefty dose over Stephanie's face.

Stepping back, she groaned and wiped her hand over her lips. "It got in my mouth, and it tastes terrible, Cindy, and smells even worse. I think I inhaled half the bottle."

"You've got some on your cheeks that needs to be rubbed in. It's grainy but effective."

The spray wasn't cooling or pleasant. Stephanie shook her head. "That's enough. Thanks."

"Here's a tote one of the ladies left on the island." Cindy handed the bag to Stephanie. "The name tag on the outside says it belongs to Maureen Meyers. Could you see she gets it?"

"Maureen's the wife of one of the soldiers. Sure, I'll drop it off at her quarters when I'm back on post."

Cindy glanced at her watch. "I've got to hurry. Walt wanted me to join him for dinner, and I don't want to keep him waiting."

Once again, Stephanie turned her gaze to the choppy water. "Cindy, are you sure Sam was heading back to the marina?"

"Of course. He'll be here in a minute or two."

With a wave of her hand, Cindy raced to her car and soon left the marina.

With a frustrated sigh, Stephanie grabbed her purse and hurried to the end of the walkway where she scanned the lot, hoping to see Sam Taylor's Hummer. Even used, the vehicle was much too expensive and had probably soaked up all Sam's reenlistment bonuses and monthly paychecks, as well as his hazardous duty pay while he was deployed.

The Hummer wasn't in the marina lot.

From the top of the walkway, she could see Big Island

in the distance with no boats in sight. What she did see was the descending darkness, and a sheet of rain heading across the lake toward the marina.

Whatever had happened wasn't good.

She raced toward *The Princess,* but it was too slow and too small to navigate the choppy waters. She had to take *The Upton Queen.*

The boat she hadn't been in since the night Hayden died.

Tonight Ted was in danger as well as Brody. She needed to get to Big Island as quickly as possible.

"Oh, please, God. Help me save both of them, so no one else has to die."

Chapter Twenty-Three

"Mayday, Mayday." Stephanie repeated the distress alert over the cabin cruiser's radio. Once she received a response, she relayed her location and that she needed help on Big Island Lake.

Glancing at the gas gauge, she realized too late the tank was riding on empty. She had to make it to the island. From there, she could wait out the storm as long as she knew Ted and Brody were safe.

The wind howled and rain pummeled the craft. Giant waves splashed against the bow, rocking the vessel and causing her to worry whether the boat would survive the forceful winds and vicious surf.

Once again, she was back three years ago. She'd forbidden Ted to go to the Big Island with the rest of the kids. He'd promised her he would spend the day with Paul at his house.

Stephanie had taken his compliance as a good sign and was relieved that her work with Ted was starting to pay off. She decided to show him how happy she was about his change of heart and had prepared a carrot cake, which was his favorite. He'd called while she was making the cream cheese icing. First he'd told her where he was and then that he and the others needed a ride back to the marina.

Keith had said he would pick them up, but he had gone to Atlanta and was tied up getting out of the city. Stephanie had done so much and was so tired of failing with her brother, she refused to ruin the cake, plus she wanted him to realize how disappointed she was with his decision to go with the kids instead of obeying her.

So she had waited thirty minutes until the cake was done and sitting on the counter before she left the house, angry and ready to give her brother a piece of her mind.

Her delay that day had caused Hayden's death. She could never forgive herself. Now this evening, she couldn't let another mistake cost someone else's life.

Not her brother's. Not Brody's.

God had failed to respond to her pleas for help three years ago. If only He would listen to her now.

"Ted! Brody!" she screamed as she approached the island. She turned on the spotlight and rotated it back and forth, searching for some sign of them. Raising her hands to her lips, she called their names repeatedly as she played the spotlight over the shore, seeing nothing.

Needing something with more volume, she rang the bell, hoping its deep knell would be heard over the thunder and roar of the wind.

Adjusting the angle of the light, she saw something on the swell in the distance and steered forward. There in the light was Ted, desperately hanging on to the life preserver. He raised his hand and shouted back to her.

Tears of relief burned her eyes. She edged near him and stretched out her hand.

Once on board, he pointed to the water. "Brody and I got separated. I thought I heard him call my name."

The wind whipped at her hair. She pushed it back and squinted into the murky water, looking for any sign of Brody as she turned the spotlight into the deep, dark abyss.

"Where is he?" she screamed above the storm.

"There." Ted pointed to where the light cut through the night.

Was that a hand? Without thought, she dove into the water, following the light.

But she couldn't find Brody.

She swam deeper, reaching for anything she saw that could be him, his hand, his arm.

Her lungs burned.

She surfaced, grabbed another breath and dove again, just as she had done so many times in her dreams.

Please, God. Let me find him.

Ted adjusted the light, and she dove again, only this time, as her lungs burned for oxygen, a vision from her past appeared. Something she had seen that night as she labored to save Hayden. Something she had glimpsed too briefly to recognize in her dreams. A memory from her past she had buried as a child when she had walked in on Aunt Hazel in her parents' bedroom. With her youthful innocence, she hadn't realized the significance of finding her father in bed with her mother's sister.

Gasping for air, Stephanie surfaced, upset by the vision as well as her inability to find Brody.

"There he is," Ted screamed.

She saw Brody's shirt. Grabbing him, she pulled him close. Ted threw the life preserver that was attached to the craft by a rope and pulled them toward the boat.

Between them pushing and lifting, they hoisted Brody on deck.

Stephanie placed her hands under his sternum and pressed down, as he had done to her just a few days earlier. One, two, three, the pace was fast, and she used her full weight to keep his blood circulating.

"Radio for help," she called to Ted, "and head for the marina."

The engine throttled forward and the craft moved through the water. Then, like a dying creature, it sputtered and stopped. The rain eased ever so slightly, but fog floated in around them.

"We ran out of gas," Ted called to her through the haze.

"What about the radio?"

"It's not working."

"Ring the bell, Ted. Someone might hear us."

Her brother scrambled to the stern and began to ring the death dirge.

Stephanie had found Brody, but that didn't mean she'd be able to save him.

Brody's chest burned like fire. A weight crashed into his ribs, and he gasped for air.

Turning his head to the side, he gagged. Water spewed from his mouth.

"Oh, Brody, you're alive."

He didn't feel alive—he felt battered and broken, until he blinked his eyes open and saw Stephanie's face just inches from his own.

"Talk to me," she begged. "Tell me you're okay."

"I—I'm o-okay."

A smile covered her mouth, a mouth he wanted to kiss, but he'd have to wait until he could catch his breath and sit up without feeling dizzy and sick.

"Head for the marina," he said.

She shook her head. "We've run out of gas."

"Call for help."

"We have." Yet the call had gone unanswered.

At least the rain had stopped, and although the waves were high, the craft could handle the rough surf. If only her stomach could. She'd never gotten seasick before. She hung her head. The world swirled around her.

Her cheeks were on fire. Not sunburn; something worse. What had been in the aloe spray?

"Are you all right?" Brody sat up and reached for her.

As much as Stephanie wanted to reassure him, all she could do was gasp for air.

"Stephanie!" Brody screamed. Her cheeks were beet red and burning hot.

"She's having a reaction," he called to Ted. "Get the EpiPen out of her purse."

Grabbing the shoulder bag, Ted dumped the contents on the deck. Her wallet and lipstick. A package of tissues and a comb. He shook the purse again. Two plastic EpiPen cases fell onto the deck. "Stay calm, honey. The epinephrine will work in a minute or two."

Her raspy pull for air sent a rush of terror that knotted his stomach. His hands couldn't undo the packaging fast enough.

When he held up the first Auto-Injector, he saw something that made his heart sink. The vial was spent. He opened the second EpiPen and found it empty, too.

"Radio for help again," he told Ted. "This time you've got to get through."

Stephanie's whole body convulsed. She needed more air than her constricted bronchioles would allow.

"Did your mother keep any medication onboard?" Brody asked Ted.

"In the first-aid kit." He raced below deck and returned with the box that he opened and then held out for Brody, who rummaged through the gauze and tape. His fingers dug to the bottom and found nothing.

"Mom kept a small pouch in a cubbyhole under one of the seats. It may still be there."

Brody took Stephanie's hand. Her chest heaved as she tried to draw in the oxygen she so desperately needed.

Ted raced to the stern and returned carrying two plastic containers. "They're out-of-date."

"Then say a prayer that they'll still work."

Uncapping the first applicator, Brody sighed with relief when he saw the medication had not been depleted. In one swift motion, he jabbed the spring-loaded syringe into her thigh.

"Get the next one ready, Ted."

Brody bent over Stephanie, searching for any change in her condition. The wild look in her eyes told him the terrible truth. She still struggled to breathe. The epinephrine must be too old to counter the reaction.

"Please, God." He reached for the second EpiPen.

Once again, he pushed the injector firmly against her thigh. The medication automatically released. If only it would work.

Stephanie continued to gasp for air.

Seeing her distress, Brody feared that he was going to lose her, and without Stephanie, he couldn't go on.

* * *

The sound of the ship's bell rang in the fog of her mind. Stephanie couldn't focus or pull herself out of the haze.

Voices sounded around her.

"Can you hear me? Open your eyes, hon."

She inhaled deeply, enjoying the clean air that filled her lungs. The burning had ended, along with the fear of not being able to breathe.

She lifted her hand toward her face.

"Watch, honey. You're getting oxygen. You're probably feeling the nasal cannula."

Could she be dreaming? Her struggle for air had been so severe.

Someone touched her arm. "Stephanie, open your eyes."

Brody's voice. She wasn't dreaming. Thank God, she was alive.

With another deep inhale, she forced her eyes to blink open. A spotlight caused her to turn her head in order to shield her eyes.

"Move the light," Brody warned. "The glare's too much for her."

She sensed him leaning in closer and felt his warm breath on her cheek. "Now, hon. You can open your eyes."

Once again, she blinked her eyes open and was rewarded with seeing his face close to hers.

"Oh, Stephanie." His voice was husky with emotion. "I thought I'd lost you."

"Br...Brody." She sighed, then inhaled again, comforted by the restorative power of the oxygen-rich air.

She didn't need to look at Brody's drawn face to know how close she'd come to not surviving.

"Ted?" She turned her head, searching for him. A number of boatmen and a few medical personnel huddled close by. A stab of fear made her try to sit up.

"I'm right here, sis." He stuck his head over Brody's shoulder.

Her brother smiled, a wide and heartfelt grin she hadn't seen in so long. He rested his hand on Brody's shoulder, and the two guys exchanged looks that told her a bond had formed between them.

"How...how are you, Ted?"

"Fine, Steph, now that you came back to join us."

"But—" She didn't understand his comment.

"You went to another place. We didn't think you'd come back to life. Mom's old EpiPens kicked in and gave you enough medication to open your airway ever so slightly."

He glanced at the men joining them on the deck. "These guys arrived in time to do the rest of the treatment. They've assured us you're going to be okay."

"Cindy...sprayed my face. I breathed it in. It must have contained..." She couldn't go on. The thought of what Cindy had done brought back memories of that day on the water three years ago.

Brody quickly recounted what Cindy had told him about loving Hayden and wanting to avenge his death.

"She was angry that all of us lived when he didn't," Ted added. "Hayden liked to flirt. He had given her the wrong impression, which cost Paul his life."

"What about Joshua?"

"We'll find out how he's doing as soon as we get

back to the mainland. The chief of police is searching for Cindy."

The fog had lifted somewhat by the time they neared the marina. Two of the men stepped to the front of the boat to talk to Ted. Stephanie sat next to Brody. He wrapped his arm around her shoulder and pulled her close. She continued to think about Cindy's vindictive actions. The aloe spray must have contained ground nuts, just as they'd found in the raisins.

In a flash of clarity, Stephanie remembered the tote. Her heart pounded a warning when she realized they were still in danger.

She grabbed Brody's hand. "Stop the boat. We can't dock."

"An ambulance is ready to transport you to the hospital. You're going to be okay, honey."

"No." She shook her head. "You don't understand. Cindy said one of the wives had left a tote at the picnic. She insisted I take it back to post, but it's still on my boat."

Brody's eyes locked on hers. His smile disappeared and was replaced with the keen gaze of a law-enforcement officer.

"Don't enter the marina, Ted. There could be a bomb on that small craft." Brody pointed to *The Princess,* then looked down at Stephanie. "Where's the tote?"

"In the front. It's a yellow cloth bag decorated with fabric flowers."

The lead cop called headquarters. "Send the bomb crew and make sure the marina is sealed off. If this baby blows, I don't want anyone else injured." He nodded, the phone still at his ear. "We'll head for the small dock south of here. I'll have the ambulance meet us there."

Two patrol cars quickly arrived and secured the marina. The police boat that had come to their rescue remained a distance out from shore. Once the bomb crew was in place, the boat followed *The Upton Queen* to the smaller dock and met up with Brody there.

"Chief Palmer said he wants to talk to you, sir." One of the officers held out his phone to Brody.

The police chief came over the line. "We've got her. Cindy was holed up in the large prefab warehouse she erected on her property. She's got her own makeshift garage out there. Evidently, she learned mechanics from her brother. Plus, you'll never guess what was parked inside."

"A souped-up truck with mud tires, red in color."

"You've got that right. She took an old, used pickup and repainted it, added mud tires and rebuilt the engine. She wanted it to look just like Hayden's Ford. Here's the strange part. She claimed to be able to feel his presence when she drove the truck around her property. The woman's deranged, in my opinion, but we'll let a court of law determine what they want to do with her. She had one area of her warehouse turned into a shrine of sorts to Hayden's memory. High school photos, memorabilia. It gave me the creeps."

"Did she admit to nearly sideswiping Stephanie outside Joshua's subdivision?"

"When she accessed Josh's voice mail and heard that Stephanie was en route to his house, she had to change her plans and nearly ran Ms. Upton off the road while trying to get away."

"It appeared to me that she hit Joshua from behind and planned to drown him in the tub."

"That's what she admitted doing, although not in nice

terms. She kept railing that Ms. Upton shouldn't have come back. Cindy had wanted to take her time with her revenge, but when she saw Ted's sister, she knew she had to act fast."

"She was in love with Hayden Allen and felt Stephanie had left him to perish intentionally."

The chief whistled over the phone. "That explains the additional photos we found. Some shots she probably took when Hayden wasn't looking. If you ask my opinion, Cindy made up a fictional world where the boyfriend still existed and still loved her."

"I'm not sure how he felt about her, Chief. That could have made the problem even worse." Brody shook his head, thinking of all the pain Cindy had caused. If only she had gotten help. Counseling, psychiatric care, medication to aid her in overcoming the trauma of losing the boy she supposedly loved. Unfortunately, she'd kept everything inside.

"Have you talked to Walt Ferrol?" Brody asked.

"He's hiring a lawyer and plans to fight the charges against his sister. From the looks of things, the case is airtight. Plus, she said she wants to write down what happened so folks will realize why she had to hurt Joshua and kill Paul."

"She almost killed Ted and Stephanie, too."

"I heard she ran you down in the water. She thought you and Ted had both perished. When I told her you survived, she broke down and cried. And not for joy."

"The EMTs are ready to transport Stephanie to the hospital. I'm going with her."

"Thank her for what she did. Once again, we owe her a debt of gratitude."

"I don't think she wants a fuss made, Chief."

"Maybe not, but her heroism needs to be recognized. You need recognition, as well."

"Negative. Just call my boss and tell him you appreciate the way the CID helped on this investigation."

"You've got it. Anytime you want to leave the military and settle down, say with a pretty local gal, come see me about a job in law enforcement."

Brody appreciated the offer.

"I mean it. I could use a good man like you."

He smiled as he disconnected and then limped to the ambulance. The EMT raised an eyebrow when he climbed in the rear.

Brody held up his hand. "CID from Fort Rickman. It's incumbent on me to remain with the patient."

The guy smiled and nodded. "Yes, sir. I never mess with the cops. Plus—" He glanced down at Brody's leg. "Looks like that cut should be treated at the E.R. I'll leave you two back here. My partner and I will ride up front. Just call out if you need anything."

The door shut, and Brody took Stephanie's hand. He would explain what the chief of police had said later. Right now, he wanted to reassure her everything was going to be all right.

"Ted's driving my car to the hospital."

Her eyes widened. "You trust him?"

"After what we've been through, I trust him with my life."

"And my life, Brody? Do you trust him with that, as well?"

He nodded. "Maybe I was too hard on Ted at first, but he was in a bad place and had a lot to deal with. Hopefully, what we all faced today made him realize life goes on and the past is behind him."

"Is that something you've learned?"

He nodded, leaning closer to her. "I'm only thinking of the present moment and having the doctor check you out and give you a clean bill of health."

"So…" She rolled her eyes and stuck out her lower lip in a pretend pout. "You're not thinking about the future at all?"

"Okay, you're right." He laughed. "I am thinking about asking you out for dinner and taking you to a nice restaurant, and then maybe we can stroll along the river's edge, especially if it's a moonlit night with the stars twinkling overhead."

She sighed. "That sounds delightful."

"We could stop in a secluded spot, and then I could take you in my arms and pull you close so that all I could see would be your beautiful face bathed in moonlight."

"What would happen then?" she teased.

"Then I'd kiss you. Just like this."

He lowered his lips to hers and felt a rush of emotion fill him as the two of them were joined. He wove his hand through her hair and held her close, never wanting anything to separate them again.

They had been through so much, and he had almost lost her too many times, but all that was behind them. Lisa had died by the hand of a man who was confused and suffering, just as Cindy was suffering in her own way.

Being with Stephanie healed the pain of Brody's past. Hopefully, she realized Hayden's death was in no way her fault. She had her brother back, and Brody, at long last, was able to see the good in him and had hope for his future as well as their own.

As he drew away, he heard her sigh, and his heart

skittered in his chest. "I don't want to leave you, ever, Stephanie."

"Oh, Brody."

Once again, he lowered his lips to hers and continued to kiss her as the ambulance raced toward the hospital and the siren screeched in the night.

Chapter Twenty-Four

Stephanie and Brody attended church on post the next morning. Ted and Nikki joined them there. After the service, they visited Joshua in the hospital. His condition had improved, and he'd been moved from the ICU into a private room.

Ted and Nikki stayed with their friend while Brody drove Stephanie to Magnolia Manor. Earlier, she had arranged to meet Keith at the nursing home.

"Are you sure you feel up to this?" Keith asked her as they approached.

She nodded. "Have you said anything to Aunt Hazel?"

"Only that you've come back to town."

"Does she know you were taken into custody?"

He shook his head. "Luckily, no. The nursing-home staff didn't want to upset her, which I appreciated."

She touched his arm. "I'm sorry about what happened, Keith."

He glanced from Stephanie to Brody. "Everything worked out in the end. No one realized Cindy had access to so many places in town through her mother's cleaning business. The real-estate office, the bakery—"

"And my parent's house," Stephanie added. "My mother started using the cleaning service when she was pregnant with Ted. Her morning sickness for the first three months was severe. She needed help around the house and even went into the hospital for dehydration during that time. I was at home with my father."

Keith nodded. "That's when you walked in on your dad and my mother."

"Only I blanked out the memory. I was six years old and didn't understand what I was seeing. When I was searching for Hayden, the memory returned ever so briefly. Yesterday, as I was looking for Brody, I saw everything in a flash of awareness."

Stephanie hesitated for a moment and then added, "Their affair occurred around the time your mother became pregnant, Keith. Do you know who Hayden's father was?"

He shook his head. "I've never asked and never needed to know. Either way, Hayden was still my brother."

"And a very special guy." Stephanie turned to Brody. "You said Cindy's mom was aware of what was going on?"

"Evidently, at some point, she shared what she knew with her daughter."

"My dad continued using the cleaning service after my mother died," Stephanie said. "Cindy made a duplicate house key. Dad had provided the security code so the cleaning team could get into the house even when he had set the alarm."

"Unfortunately, no one realized the bitterness Cindy harbored." Keith glanced at the nursing home. "Are you ready?"

Stephanie hesitated. "There's one thing I never understood, Keith. Did you go to Atlanta that day?"

He nodded. "I wanted to leave Freemont. A job opened up in the city. I went for the interview and would have had plenty of time to get back, but they asked me to talk to some more people in the company that afternoon. I called Mother and asked her to pick up the kids."

"But...but she didn't?"

"I'm not sure what happened. She may have been having ministrokes at that time and forgot I had even called. Not long after Hayden's death, she had her first major attack. I was offered the job but turned it down so I could take care of her."

Stephanie hadn't realized the depth of compassion in Keith's heart. "You never told anyone about calling her."

He shook his head. "My mother had enough guilt to carry. She didn't need me pointing a finger at her."

"You're a good man," she said with sincerity.

"Thanks, Stephanie. That means a lot to me."

She turned to Brody and squeezed his hand. "We won't be long."

"I'll be waiting."

Together, she and Keith entered the nursing home and headed for Aunt Hazel's room. She was propped up in bed, staring at the door through which they entered.

She tried to smile. Her lips sagged with the effort, but her eyes were bright and full of welcome.

"Mama, look who's come to visit you." Keith motioned Stephanie forward.

She neared the bed and took Aunt Hazel's hand. "I've missed you."

Which was true. After her own mother's death, she and Aunt Hazel had drawn closer. But ever since Hayden had died, Stephanie hadn't been able to face the grieving mother. She'd gone to his funeral but left without talking to her aunt.

Hazel gripped Stephanie's hand and struggled to form her words. "You...you're...home."

"I'm working at Fort Rickman, Aunt Hazel, so I'll be able to visit you often."

The woman smiled.

"Keith is a wonderful son," Stephanie continued. "You have so much to be proud of."

Again Hazel nodded, but her face clouded as if she was remembering her own loss.

"Hayden was a wonderful son, too." Stephanie hesitated before adding, "I always thought of him as a brother."

The woman's eyes widened ever so slightly.

Stephanie nodded with understanding. "For a long time, I shut God out of my life, but I've realized the Lord was waiting with open arms for me to return to Him. We've all made mistakes. If we're truly sorry, we need to ask His forgiveness."

She glanced up at Keith before she continued. "Don't dwell on the past, but be grateful for what you have today."

Hazel's eyes watered and a tear ran down her cheek. She released Stephanie's hand and reached for Keith's. Stepping back, Stephanie watched as he sat on the side of his mother's bed. Hazel's mouth moved as she struggled to talk.

"I know, Mama," Keith soothed. "I love you, too."

Dear God, bless this mother and son with the fullness of Your love and mercy.

Knowing they had much to reconcile, Stephanie left

the nursing home. Outside, the sun was shining, and the sky was bright.

Brody was standing by his car, waiting for her, just as he had promised.

She walked into his arms, feeling that special connection, a sense of coming home that wiped away the burdens she had carried for too long and filled her with an anticipation and expectation of what the future could hold. A future with Brody.

"Are you okay?" he asked.

She nodded. "Now I need to call my father."

"What are you going to say?"

"That Ted and I are waiting for him to come home."

Brody hugged her even more tightly. "I'm proud of you."

She shook her head. "It's not me. It's what the Lord revealed to me during all this. I was thinking only of myself by carrying the guilt for Hayden's death. Looking inward, I didn't realize so many other folks were struggling, as well."

She pulled back ever so slightly. "At the hospital, Ted told me he had talked Hayden into bringing the alcohol that day. All this time, Ted felt he was responsible for what happened. He closed me out of his life, knowing if he had done what I had asked, Hayden might still be alive. Ted asked my forgiveness, and for the first time in three years, we hugged and cried and...and healed."

"I'm so glad."

"He's determined to follow through with counseling. Nikki's been encouraging him. I think she's a good influence on him."

"And you're a good influence on me. There's something in the car I want to show you."

Brody reached into the backseat and pulled out a sketch pad. "I've started drawing again." He flipped the pages and stopped at a charcoal sketch of the lake with a boat—*The Upton Queen*—sailing toward the rising sun.

"You've faced your fears, Stephanie, just as I faced mine. If it wasn't for the past, I never would have gone into the CID, and you never would have taken the job at Fort Rickman. But because of what happened to both of us, we found each other."

She smiled. "The sketch is beautiful, Brody." She pointed to the boat. "You even included the maritime bell."

"I titled it 'New Day Dawning.'"

She nodded, appreciating the significance for both of them. A new day, a fresh start, a lifetime waiting for them to share together.

"Let's take a drive," she suggested.

"Where?"

"Someplace special."

It didn't take Brody long to realize where they were headed. Stephanie directed him through town, where they picked up a picnic lunch, and then to the open road that led to the place she had most dreaded at one time. A place that had been tragic as well as redemptive, providing the healing that she and Ted had needed.

Brody pulled into the marina and held the car door for her. She grabbed her purse and the bag containing their lunch.

"You've got your new EpiPens, don't you?"

She smiled. "Two of them, as well as the keys to *The Upton Queen*."

They untied the moorings and headed out of the marina, where Stephanie turned the controls over to him. Brody steered the craft away from Big Island and then eased back on the throttle. Letting the boat rock gently on the waves, he turned to face Stephanie.

"I know your mother must have been a beautiful woman."

Stephanie tilted her head.

"Because she had such a beautiful daughter."

Smiling, she took his hand. "She must have known about Dad's affair with Hazel, but she stayed with him. She was always so forgiving. I wanted to be more like her, but I seemed to have my father's practicality."

"A mix that's perfect in my eyes."

"You know so little about me," she said.

"I know you're strong and determined, and when you care for someone, you'll do anything to help them. I know you've made me think about the future instead of the past, and that when I'm with you the day seems brighter."

He wrapped his arms around her and drew her closer. "I know we haven't known each other long in terms of time, but—"

She stared at him, her eyes wide.

"But I love you more than anything, and—"

"Oh, Brody."

"I know, I know," he said. "We need to take it one day at a time."

She smiled. "I'd like that."

"Really?"

"Cross my heart."

She laughed and playfully kissed his lips. Pulling back, the laughter in her eyes changed, and he saw the love he had been hoping she would feel for him. He drew her closer and lowered his lips to hers, feeling at home with her in his arms.

At some point, they ate. Brody never wanted to stop being with Stephanie, so the boat lolled on the lake until the sun was starting to set.

Pulling back into the marina, they laughed at the gulls overhead. The breeze caught Stephanie's hair, brushing it across Brody's face. He turned again to capture her lips, never wanting the day to end.

But as they walked together back to his car, he knew they'd have more days, so many more. With the setting sun would come the promise of tomorrow and a new day dawning. A new day filled with love and hope, filled with Stephanie.

Epilogue

"I don't remember November ever being this warm," Stephanie said as she placed a basket of potato chips on the glass-topped patio table.

Nikki opened the ice bucket and dropped three cubes into her insulated plastic glass. "I'm glad you had this get-together." She glanced at Ted, sitting next to Brody in the wrought-iron chairs near the pool. "The two guys have become such good friends. Ted told me Brody's like an older brother."

"He's a good role model, which is what Ted needed. The counselor keeps praising his progress."

"I'm glad you came back to Freemont, Stephanie." The younger woman paused, her expression suddenly serious. "Ted needed you, even if he didn't realize it."

"That goes both ways. I needed him, as well."

"And your dad?"

"He's working on being a father, which is a huge change."

"Ted said he's in Europe again."

"But it's just a short trip this time. He insisted we use his house for the gathering today." Stephanie laughed.

"He knew my apartment was too small for a Veterans Day party."

Nikki poured iced tea into the glass she held. "Anything I can do to help?"

"Everything's done. Enjoy the afternoon."

Nikki walked to where Ted sat by the pool. Brody offered her his chair and then joined Stephanie at the table.

"You're working too hard," he said, reaching for her hand.

She wrapped her fingers through his, appreciating his concern for her well-being. "Thanks for arriving early and getting the patio ready." Glancing at the sunny sky, she added, "Even Mother Nature cooperated so we could be outdoors. The weather is perfect."

"When do you want me to start the grill?"

"After a few more of the guests arrive. I invited Ted's care team and Major Jenkins. They should be here shortly, along with some of the other folks from work."

"What about Josh?"

"He asked if he could bring a friend."

Brody raised his brow. "A girl?"

Stephanie nodded. "She works with Nikki at the Post Exchange. They seem to be hitting it off."

"I'm glad. Josh is a good guy."

"Keith offered him a job managing some of the rental properties in town as soon as his discharge from the army comes through. Josh is telling everyone he's only got a few weeks left on active duty."

Ted's smart phone rang. He pulled it to his ear and nodded. "You can do it, buddy."

Hanging up, he grabbed Nikki's hand. "That was Josh. He's out front and has a surprise for us." The young couple left the patio and rounded the house.

Stephanie started after them, but Brody pulled her back into his arms. "We're alone, at least for a few minutes. I wanted to tell you how beautiful you look today."

"We had to be alone for you to pay me a compliment?" she teased.

His upper lip twitched. "I also wanted a kiss."

She stepped closer and snuggled more deeply into his arms. Looking up, she raised her brow. "What are you waiting for?"

He smiled ever so slightly and then his expression changed. What she saw in his eyes made her breath hitch. She waited for what seemed like an eternity as he slowly—ever so slowly—dropped his lips to hers.

Fireworks.

She saw red, white and blue fireworks even though her eyes were closed. Her heart seemed to explode with joy at the same time her knees went weak.

Luckily, Brody was supporting her.

"You've been kissing me for three months, Special Agent Goodman," she said as their lips parted.

"Yes, ma'am."

"And I still get goose bumps even on a warm day."

"So you like my kisses?" His eyes twinkled.

"I like everything about you."

"Funny, but I feel the same about you." He hesitated, his gaze even more intense. "It's not the right time, is it?"

She tried to calm the excitement bubbling within her. "Sometimes you just have to seize the moment."

"You know what I'm thinking?"

She shrugged innocently. "Are you thinking about kissing me again?"

"I'm thinking about spending the rest of my life with you."

She blinked. "Really?"

"Really? But only if that sounds good to you."

She nodded, unable to put words to the emotion welling up inside her.

"I don't want to rush you. We'll do it the right way, with dinner and candlelight."

"A day on the lake would also work."

He nodded. "We could do both."

"I got Dad's permission to change the name of *The Princess*."

"*New Day Dawning*?"

"It's a perfect fit."

"Just like us."

He kissed her again and time stood still. When she eventually pulled back, she glanced over her shoulder to see Ted and Nikki, standing with Josh, who was wearing his new prosthetic legs. Next to him stood a petite blonde who gripped his hand.

Keith came up behind them. "Did I miss something?"

Ted laughed. "Only if Brody and Stephanie have some good news to share."

"You'll be the first to know," Stephanie said with a wink.

Brody shook Joshua's hand after he had walked across the patio, his gait slow but steady. "Way to go, Josh."

"Thank you, sir." He introduced his girlfriend, who smiled briefly at Brody and then turned her gaze back to Josh.

The military and civilians from the Warrior Transitional Battalion arrived and seemed to enjoy the afternoon. By nightfall, most of them had said their goodbyes.

Josh and his girlfriend had left earlier, along with Keith, who planned to visit his mom at the nursing home.

Ted and Nikki helped with the cleanup and then returned to the patio to watch the sunset.

"We need a new way to celebrate the good times," he told Stephanie when she and Brody joined them there. "In the past, I rang the maritime bell when I was filled with pain, but today, I'm bursting with happiness." He smiled at Nikki and then back at Stephanie.

She understood the way her brother felt. "Like you, I'm ready for a fresh start, Ted."

He and Nikki walked to the bell. Ted grabbed the cord and pulled. The sound was sweet as it filled the night, like a church bell calling worshippers to prayer and a reminder of the healing power of love.

As the sun set on the horizon, the bell continued to ring. Brody wrapped Stephanie in his arms and pulled her close. She could feel the steady beat of his heart and the strength of his embrace.

She had come home to help her brother and had found Brody. She had also found her lost faith. Tomorrow a new day would dawn, filled with the promise of God's many blessings.

A man to love, a formal proposal and a wedding in the future. On post or in the little brick church on Third Street, she wasn't sure, just so she and Brody could be joined together in a covenant of love with the Lord, but she was getting ahead of herself. Right now she had something very important to do.

She rose on tiptoe, her lips so close to his. "I love you, Brody," she whispered.

"Oh, Stephanie, I love you more than my own life. You're my today, my tomorrow, my forever." He hesitated, staring into her eyes. "You're my everything."

Then he kissed her, and once again fireworks illuminated the sky, only this time over the golf course to celebrate Veterans Day. With Brody, every day would be special; every day would be a celebration.

As the bell pealed and the fireworks showered them in light, Stephanie stood wrapped in Brody's arms, breathing in the essence of the man she loved and would love until the end of time.

* * * * *

LOVE INSPIRED

Stories to uplift and inspire

Fall in love with Love Inspired—
inspirational and uplifting stories of faith
and hope. Find strength and comfort in
the bonds of friendship and community.
Revel in the warmth of possibility and the
promise of new beginnings.

Sign up for the Love Inspired newsletter
at **LoveInspired.com** to be the first
to find out about upcoming titles,
special promotions and exclusive content.

CONNECT WITH US AT:

Get 4 FREE REWARDS!

We'll send you 2 FREE Books <u>plus</u> 2 FREE Mystery Gifts.

FREE
Value Over
$20

Both the **Love Inspired®** and **Love Inspired® Suspense** series feature compelling novels filled with inspirational romance, faith, forgiveness, and hope.

YES! Please send me 2 FREE novels from the Love Inspired or Love Inspired Suspense series and my 2 FREE gifts (gifts are worth about $10 retail). After receiving them, if I don't wish to receive any more books, I can return the shipping statement marked "cancel." If I don't cancel, I will receive 6 brand-new Love Inspired Larger-Print books or Love Inspired Suspense Larger-Print books every month and be billed just $5.99 each in the U.S. or $6.24 each in Canada. That is a savings of at least 17% off the cover price. It's quite a bargain! Shipping and handling is just 50¢ per book in the U.S. and $1.25 per book in Canada.* I understand that accepting the 2 free books and gifts places me under no obligation to buy anything. I can always return a shipment and cancel at any time. The free books and gifts are mine to keep no matter what I decide.

Choose one: ☐ **Love Inspired**
Larger-Print
(122/322 IDN GNWC)

☐ **Love Inspired Suspense**
Larger-Print
(107/307 IDN GNWN)

Name (please print)

Address   Apt. #

City   State/Province   Zip/Postal Code

Email: Please check this box ☐ if you would like to receive newsletters and promotional emails from Harlequin Enterprises ULC and its affiliates. You can unsubscribe anytime.

Mail to the Harlequin Reader Service:
IN U.S.A.: P.O. Box 1341, Buffalo, NY 14240-8531
IN CANADA: P.O. Box 603, Fort Erie, Ontario L2A 5X3

Want to try 2 free books from another series? Call 1-800-873-8635 or visit www.ReaderService.com.

*Terms and prices subject to change without notice. Prices do not include sales taxes, which will be charged (if applicable) based on your state or country of residence. Canadian residents will be charged applicable taxes. Offer not valid in Quebec. This offer is limited to one order per household. Books received may not be as shown. Not valid for current subscribers to the Love Inspired or Love Inspired Suspense series. All orders subject to approval. Credit or debit balances in a customer's account(s) may be offset by any other outstanding balance owed by or to the customer. Please allow 4 to 6 weeks for delivery. Offer available while quantities last.

Your Privacy—Your information is being collected by Harlequin Enterprises ULC, operating as Harlequin Reader Service. For a complete summary of the information we collect, how we use this information and to whom it is disclosed, please visit our privacy notice located at corporate.harlequin.com/privacy-notice. From time to time we may also exchange your personal information with reputable third parties. If you wish to opt out of this sharing of your personal information, please visit readerservice.com/consumerschoice or call 1-800-873-8635 **Notice to California Residents**—Under California law, you have specific rights to control and access your data. For more information on these rights and how to exercise them, visit corporate.harlequin.com/california-privacy.

LIRLIS22

SPECIAL EXCERPT FROM

LOVE INSPIRED SUSPENSE
INSPIRATIONAL ROMANCE

Publicly vowing to bring a serial killer to justice, Deputy Cecile Richardson solidifies herself as the criminal's next target. Can Sheriff Josh Avery keep her safe long enough to identify and catch the culprit—or will Cecile become the killer's next victim?

Read on for a sneak peek at
Texas Buried Secrets *by Virginia Vaughan!*

Within ten minutes of her call, Cecile's home and property were surrounded by sheriff's deputies and forensics personnel.

Josh was one of the first to arrive. He found her on the couch. He'd never seen her look so fragile before. It worried him—even though her demeanor changed the moment she saw him. She slipped on her mask of confidence as she stood to face him.

"What happened?" He resisted the urge to pull her into an embrace. Not only would that be unprofessional, but he didn't want to blur the lines between them any more than they already were.

"A man broke into my house." She explained hearing the glass breaking and then finding the broken glass and dirty shoe print. "He grabbed me from behind and knocked my gun out of my hands, but I managed to fight him off."

Josh glanced at the trail of blood. She'd connected with the assailant.

"I elbowed him. Think I broke his nose. He ran after that—didn't even take his stuff with him." She gestured over to the counter.

As proud as he was that she'd successfully defended herself, the pride didn't ease his panic at the sight of the shower curtain and clothesline. She could take care of herself, but that didn't make it any easier to accept that she'd been targeted. He didn't know if this had anything to do with the case—but the shower curtain and line the assailant left behind suggested it did. They might have just caught a break, but at what expense? He wouldn't risk Cecile's life even to catch a serial killer.

She rubbed her arms and he spotted goose bumps on them. "I'd better go clean up before someone sees me like this."

She walked across the hall into the bathroom and shut the door. He checked the rest of the windows and then double-checked the locks. The house was as secure as he could make it for now—but that wasn't nearly as secure as he'd like.

The presence of the shower curtain and clothesline seemed to suggest she'd been deliberately targeted. Josh prayed the blood evidence would provide them with a DNA match, but that would be days, maybe weeks, away. They couldn't wait that long. He'd already lost Haley to a killer.

He couldn't lose Cecile, too.

Don't miss
Texas Buried Secrets *by Virginia Vaughan,*
available August 2022 wherever
Love Inspired Suspense books and ebooks are sold.

LoveInspired.com